# *Undone*

# *Undone*

## Susan Johnson
## Terri Brisbin
## Mary Wine

KENSINGTON PUBLISHING CORP.
www.kensingtonbooks.com

BRAVA BOOKS are published by

Kensington Publishing Corp.
119 West 40th Street
New York, NY 10018

All Kensington titles, imprints, and distributed lines are available at special quantity discounts for bulk purchases for sales promotion, premiums, fund-raising, and educational or institutional use.

Special book excerpts or customized printings can also be created to fit specific needs. For details, write or phone the office of the Kensington Special Sales Manager: Kensington Publishing Corp., 119 West 40th Street, New York, NY 10018; Attn. Special Sales Department. Phone: 1-800-221-2647.

Brava and the B logo are Reg. U.S. Pat. & TM Off.

ISBN-13: 978-0-7582-0943-6
ISBN-10: 0-7582-0943-6

First Kensington Trade Paperback Printing: May 2010

10 9 8 7 6 5 4 3 2 1

Printed in the United States of America

# Contents

# As You Wish

## SUSAN JOHNSON

# Chapter 1

*London, March 1785*

The young Earl of Albion's heavy-lidded gaze came up slowly when the door of the breakfast room opened. "Keep your voice down, Kit. I've a hellish headache."

"And a sore cock I don't doubt," the Duke of Richland's youngest son cheerfully said as he walked toward the breakfast table. "You outdid yourself last night at Sally's."

Albion put down his coffee cup and smiled. "Someone had to destroy that ass Harvey's record."

"You surely did." Kit's sandy brows rose. "By five wenches no less."

"Sally's ladies are damned fine," the earl said, a note of satisfaction in his voice. He met his friend's gaze, his own amused. "As for our swaggering Harvey, let him try and best that tally."

"You know he'll try." Moving Albion's discarded coat and waistcoat from one chair to another, Kit took the seat beside the earl and pointed to the covered dishes on the sideboard before turning back to Albion. "He's hated you ever since Eaton when you took pity on the underclassmen he was bullying and beat him to a bloody pulp. Not to mention various intervening rivalries in which he fared equally poorly."

Albion shrugged. "Some people never learn. He's still a bully and a hypocrite. His poor wife has been embarrassed for years by his fucking everything in sight. Not that other men don't stray from time to time, but"—the earl paused at Kit's snort; aristocratic husbands were not as a rule faithful. "Very well—men *often* stray," he amended. "But unlike Harvey, they don't flaunt their orgies and still pretend to be a pious rector of the church. Believe me, hell is made for people like Harvey."

"You and I might have a place reserved there as well."

"Not, however, for hypocrisy," Albion said flatly. "I live my life openly."

Kit grinned. "Much to your parents' chagrin."

"Not Maman's. She understands my wild ways. And the père's not chagrined so much as annoyed at having to deal with all the sly innuendo apropos his scapegrace son. He only reminds me to take care that some irrate husband, father, or brother doesn't have me horsewhipped."

"Because they don't dare face your pistols."

"So he and I understand. I've promised to be more discreet."

Kit laughed so long that the earl had time to empty his coffee cup and signal for a refill from one of the several footmen attending him.

As one flunkey poured brandy into his cup and another added a dash of coffee, Alexander Maccabe Montrose, heir to the Marquess of Pembroke, known to his friends as Mac, to his acquaintances as Albion, to the ladies in his life as darling Alex, leaned back in his chair and waited for his friend's mirth to fade. "We live to amuse you," he drawled when Kit's laughter finally subsided.

"I'm sorry, Mac, but you and discretion don't even have a nodding acquaintance." He smiled his thanks as a footman served him a plate of food.

"I beg to differ. Did I not accept Amelia Rancourt's blatantly false denial of our friendship when her husband confronted us at Cecily's soiree two nights ago? I was the soul of discretion."

"You were saving your own ass," Kit said, scooping up a spoonful of mushrooms and eggs.

"And Amy's as well. As a matter of fact, I was very convincing." He grinned. "For which she thanked me later quite prettily."

"So that's where you went," Kit said through a mouthful of food. "I thought you'd gone home."

Albion's brows rose. "At midnight? Hardly. Cecily had no end of empty bedchambers. As for my supposed lack of discretion, I think you'll agree no one missed us and we were back downstairs before anyone noticed."

"So you're capable of the occasional discretion," the Honorable Christopher Talmadge noted, spearing a kipper. "I stand corrected."

The earl smiled faintly. "You admit then I'm not a *complete* rake."

"That remains to be seen." Kipper in hand, Kit sent a rare, irksome glance at his friend who looked very much the rake. He was pale, his eyes were tired, his lethargy marked. "You *do* recall the wager you agreed to last night."

Lounging back in his chair, his brandy cup on the armrest, the earl contemplated his friend's displeasure with gentle forbearance. "No doubt you will refresh my memory or why else have you arrived on my doorstep at the crack of dawn."

"Noon for those who lead less hectic lives," Kit said, shoving the kipper into his mouth.

Albion softly sighed. "You're intent on needling me today. Have I offended you somehow?"

Kit quickly swallowed. "I just don't think you should do this, Mac. It's not decent."

"Please clarify *this*." The earl's voice was very soft.

"You don't remember. I thought you wouldn't. You were nine parts drunk."

"I didn't say I didn't remember. I just don't recall the wager being particularly indecent."

"So you *do* remember. Do you remember as well that she's a virgin?"

Surprise at his friend's novel morality registered fleetingly in the earl's eyes. "They're all virgins at one time or another," he mildly said, the twitch of one shoulder visible beneath the fine linen of his shirt. "Not that virgins interest me particularly," he casually noted. "But a wager's a wager as you well know. And even if my reputation weren't at stake, twenty thousand guineas is."

"What about Felicity Belvoir's reputation?" Kit charged, his breakfast forgotten.

"She can refuse me. That's what this wager is all about, isn't it? Whether or not I can successfully storm the citadel and gain the prize."

"As if any woman has ever refused you," Kit muttered.

"She very likely might."

"She'll be ruined and you know it."

"I have no intention of discussing the episode afterward," Albion explained in response to Kit's dogged opposition. "She'll be returned to her boudoir unhurt."

"Unhurt? Ruined you mean. Your wager will be the talk of the ton."

"Good God, Kit," the earl finally exclaimed, "do you hold some tendre for this young lady?"

"No. But she's a friend of my sister Jane. I've met her on several occasions at family dinners—that sort of thing—and I've gone by the Belvoirs to pick up Jane from time to time—all of which makes this enterprise far less abstract. Felicity's a damned fine little charmer if you must know."

"What the hell does that mean? Do you have some personal stake in this venture."

Kit's face flushed.

"I mean other than the five thousand you bet on me," the earl sardonically noted.

"No. As for my bet, I was drunk."

"Everyone was drunk. Everyone's drunk most of the time." Albion pushed himself upright in his chair, drained his cup, set it down, shoved aside his plate, and rested his forearms on the table. "Now that we've cleared up the fact that I'm not poaching on your territory," the earl quietly said, having dispensed with the single factor that could hinder his undertaking, "tell me what this chit looks like."

"I shouldn't."

"I'll find out soon enough anyway. You might as well tell me."

"She's not blond." Mac preferred blonds.

"Not exactly a definitive description," Albion drily said.

"She has red hair." At the earl's grimace, Kit added, "Not the kind you think. It's rather nice. Golden highlights, strawberry pinkish at times. Nor does she have freckles like so many redheads do. And she has the most gorgeous violet eyes."

"You do have a tendre for her," the earl alleged, frowning slightly.

"I might if I wasn't head over heels for Emma who has allowed me unprecedented access to her lovely person," Kit said with obvious gratification.

"Ah—finally. Are the banns about to be posted then?"

"Maybe. Probably. I haven't exactly asked her yet."

"But she'll accept when you do." With a smile, Albion lounged back in his chair, his lean, rangy form once again disposed in a lazy sprawl. "Congratulations. Emma will bring you a damned good stable in her dowry." Her family was one of the best thoroughbred breeders in the country.

Kit grinned. "Not to be discounted."

"Indeed. Ask for one of Endemion's foals. Then we'll see whether your horse or mine wins the Derby in a few years." Albion's stud was celebrated, his record of wins at the track testimony to its excellence. "Back to more relevant matters, however," he said, aware of his time constraints. "Is my illusive prize tall, short, middling? Not that it matters I suppose once she's in bed." The earl's eyes narrowed. "She's not a bluestocking, is she? No, you said she was a little charmer, which eliminates bluestockings," he murmured, answering his own question. "A shame she's a virgin, although I may be surprised." He shot a sportive glance at his friend from under a fall of black hair escaped from the ribbon at the nape of his neck. "Perhaps a latent nymphomaniac lies beneath her maidenly facade."

"If so," Kit acidly returned, "you would have found your perfect match."

"It certainly would add more pleasure to the transaction," the earl negligently allowed, shoving the errant tress behind his ear.

"Damn it all, Mac! It ain't right." Rebuke was writ large in his expression. "Can't I dissuade you from this odious business?"

Having lived under a cloud of scandal his entire young life, Albion was unlikely to succumb to censure or reproach. "You didn't actually think you could, did you?" he asked with a conciliatory smile. "Consider—the wager is already written in the betting book at Brooks. Not to mention, I've twenty thousand at stake, you have five which your père will resent paying if you lose since you don't have five thousand. If it helps, I promise the lady will enjoy herself. Does that assuage your newly emergent conscience?" The dispute logically resolved to his satisfaction, the earl signaled to have his cup refilled. "Hair of the dog, Kit?" he queried, glancing at his scowling friend. "Liquor invariably blurs moral ambiguities."

"You should know," Kit grumbled. But he raised his cup to a hovering footman.

"I do indeed," Albion said sliding lower in his chair and stretching out his boot-clad feet as a flunkey handed him his brandy. "This will all be quickly over and soon forgotten," the earl offered in mollifying accents. "I simply have to find my way into her bedchamber, seduce the sweet thing, kiss her good-bye, and bring back the required confirmation. As for her virginity, it's not necessarily a requirement for a brilliant marriage. Your Emma's a case in point, along with other young ladies we know."

"Felicity's père is a damned stickler though. Honorable, sensible, that sort of thing."

"But then he's not marrying her, is he? If she's half as pretty as you say, she'll do well enough in the marriage mart without her virginity. Who knows, she might learn something useful for her husband."

"Christ, Mac. You almost make it sound as if you're doing her a favor."

His eyes crinkled. "We'll leave that appraisal up to her."

"You're shameless," Kit muttered.

"But good at what I do," Albion pleasantly observed.

Kit exhaled in resignation. "When will you be doing her this favor?"

"Tonight."

"Tonight!"

"The spring meets begin at Newmarket day after tomorrow. My horses are already there. Time is of the essence. Now, tell me what you know about the layout of her house."

# Chapter 2

On their early morning ride in Rotten Row, Henrietta Danville heard about the wager from her brother, Charles, under the strict admonition that she tell no one. Actually of two minds on the issue—the infamous Albion was, after all, the gold standard for female pleasure—she finally decided to divulge the details to Felicity who'd been her dearest friend since childhood.

To whit—immediately after leaving Charles at the stables—she hied herself the short distance to Cavendish Square. Finding the household still abed, she was nevertheless shown up to her friend's bedchamber where she found Felicity propped up against her pillows eating her breakfast of buttered brioche and hot chocolate. "I have to speak to you *alone,*" Henrietta breathlessly declared, pulling off the little shako she wore with her riding habit and tossing it on a table.

Felicity smiled at her maid. "If you don't mind, Molly. And by all means, help yourself to my breakfast," she added as Henrietta plucked two pieces of toast from her tray.

"Charles always insists on riding so early I never have time to eat."

"But it's worth being deprived of nourishment for access to all the latest gossip from the masculine enclaves of society," Felicity cheerfully observed.

"Today . . . it was worth . . . more than usual," Henrietta said between chews and swallows as she dropped into a pink and white upholstered chair adorned with an elaborate ruffled flounce. She smiled widely before taking another bite of toast. "*You* happened to be involved."

"How is that possible with the purdah imposed by my new stepmother? I hardly step foot in society because she must needs first gild and festoon me for the marriage block. She's convinced Papa that she knows best. Bitch," Felicity spat.

"Everyone agrees, darling, except your father of course."

"Poor Papa. He's quite unaware, but then Charlotte's twenty years younger and buxom. And Mama's been gone nearly five years." Felicity sighed. "I really can't blame him."

"Yes, yes, that's all well and good," Henrietta said with a dismissive wave of her toast. Felicity's lamentations over her new stepmother had been persistent since her father's wedding six months ago. And while sympathetic, her own announcement was of considerably more import. "Listen now! I have the most provocative news!"

Felicity's eyes flared wide. "Priscilla's having Wesford's child! I knew it! I told you she was being a stupid cow falling in love with a married man with no money of his own who can't keep his britches buttoned. Wesford's wife will cut him off without a penny!"

"It has nothing to do with stupid Priscilla. Did you not listen to what I said?" Henrietta impatiently inquired. "Charles told me the most scandalous gossip about *you!*"

"Yes, yes, very well, tell me, although I can't imagine how it can possibly be scandalous. Unless some young buck was surmising over the gaming tables whether my stepmother intended to marry me off from my bedchamber like our esteemed Duchess of Devonshire."

"No one mentioned marriage over the gaming tables, believe me," Henrietta sardonically replied. "But your bedchamber does play a role in that it's the site of your purdah—which is why you've become the object of this audacious wager. Apparently Albion won the cut of the cards or the toss of the dice or hazarded the most to play—I forget what Charles said. Anyway, the point is, your seclusion is a challenge, the probability of success formidable and thus attractive to the young bucks who engage in such sport," Henrietta explained. "Charles says it's quite reckless play even for Albion. He has twenty thousand at stake."

"For what? As if I can't guess," Felicity drily said.

Henrietta made a moue. "I thought you'd be appalled or intrigued at least or—"

"Astonished that Albion has bet so much for something of so little value?" Felicity smiled faintly. "Men are strange creatures." She'd had abundant evidence of the fact in the parade of lecherous suitors her stepmother had invited over of late to inspect her. "Why virginity is considered such a prize is beyond me," she remarked. "One would think an experienced woman would be preferable."

Henrietta grinned. "Or an experienced man." The topic of amour was much discussed among their female friends. "Like Albion for instance. Everyone says that the gorgeous rogue is a genius at pleasuring women. In fact, I thought you might not mind if he seduces you."

Her cup of hot chocolate halfway to her mouth, Felicity set it back down on her tray and an unclouded smile slowly lifted the corners of her mouth. A vision of freedom had appeared full blown in her brain. "Mind?" Her smiled widened. "On the contrary," she murmured sweetly, "Albion and I *might* be of great *help* to each other. Don't ask me what I mean," she quickly added, casting a purposeful look at her friend, "because you can't keep a secret for any price. If you're questioned, I want you to be able to say in all honesty that you know *nothing at all.*"

"You're planning something devious, aren't you?" Henrietta cheerfully observed.

"Merely a business matter of, shall we say, mutual cooperation," Felicity replied with equal cheer.

"To thwart your stepmother, of course." Henrietta's eyes were sparkling. Neither young lady was a model of comportment.

"Of course. She's planning to marry me off to one of any number of rich, old men I wouldn't waste so much as a glance on. And she's convinced Papa that I actually wish to marry one of the detestable suitors she's dragged in to meet me. I can't upset Papa in his new happiness and Robbie, who always speaks up for me, is in Constantinople. So you see," Felicity said with a dramatic sweep of her arms, "I must take my future into my own hands."

"A word of warning," Henrietta cautioned. "If you think to finagle Albion into marrying you, he won't. Of that I'm certain."

"God no," Felicity shot back. "Albion's a most unsuitable husband from all I hear. I pity whomever he marries." Leaning back against her pillows she softly exhaled. "Albion's profligacies aside, however, I have a feeling we can deal rather well together. More gratifying yet is the fact that my purdah will—*at last*—come to an end." Her sudden smile was dazzling, a flush of exhilaration pinked her cheeks. "Now—when exactly is this wager to be fulfilled?"

Henrietta shook her head. "I don't know."

"Find out."

"Charles may not know."

"I'm sure he will eventually. All the young bloods thrive on these hotspur adventures," Felicity matter-of-factly said. "Gambling, racing, drinking, whoring, and who's doing what to whom in the boudoirs of the ton are the entire focus of their devil-may-care lives. Thank Charles by the way. He's done me a vastly good turn."

"I may wait to thank him," Henrietta guardedly replied. "Once I know your plans haven't ended in disaster. Albion is not to be trifled with. He's so rich he does exactly as he pleases. Do be careful, Felicity," she said, a touch of unease in her gaze. "Promise me that."

"I promise," Felicity said, of the opinion, however, that God helps those who help themselves. "Now be a dear and find out when Albion's doing the deed," she briskly declared. "I have to make plans."

# Chapter 3

Albion took time that afternoon to make plans of his own. According to Kit, Miss Belvoir's bedchamber was in close proximity to her parents' suite which necessitated a change of locale for the seduction. Virgins, he suspected, required more persuasion than the ladies with whom he was familiar, who, in fact, needed none. A certain amount of wooing was no doubt required so he'd best be well away from her parents' hearing.

Did virgins scream?

Or rather did they scream any differently than non-virgins?

Who the hell knew? He certainly didn't.

Christ, he grudgingly thought, he likely would earn his twenty thousand before the night was over.

He dismissed the notion of taking Miss Belvoir to a hotel. The possibility of meeting someone they knew or being the focus of unwanted scrutiny was very real. Also, one could never depend on the confidence of hotel servants. They were paid for racy gossip by the scandal sheets.

Which negative factors caused him to inform his major domo that he'd be bringing a lady home that evening. One who would remain anonymous.

"Very good, my lord." Sanders understood she was to be invisible. "We will speak only when spoken to, my lord."

"She may be nervous or shy. She may not wish to be seen. I'm not entirely sure of her sensibilities. *Or whether he'd be carrying her in bound and gagged.* Have fresh flowers here and there—in my rooms particularly. I'll need champagne on ice and a collation of some kind prepared in the event . . ."

"It's needed. I understand."

"I realize this is unusual," Albion murmured. His amours were conducted elsewhere. He didn't bring women home.

"Not at all, sir," Sanders blandly replied.

Albion exhaled. "Amenable as ever, Sanders. What would I do without you?"

"I'm sure you'd manage quite well, my lord." No one in the household doubted their master's competence. He was in fact the pride of the entire staff, his accomplishments not confined to those of a prodigal and sexual nature. Of those other talents considered indispensable to a peer of the realm, the earl possessed an abundance. He was outrageously handsome, rich as a king, a horseman of distinction, the best shot in England; he held his liquor like a gentleman and he invariably won at the gaming tables. He was a paragon of the nobility in an era that looked upon youthful excess with only measured disapproval.

And that primarily from those of a prudish nature.

Of which there were few in the haute monde.

The king and queen aside.

The royal couple was an anomaly in both their faithfulness to each other and in their unfashionable practice of adding another child to their family with shocking regularity. Aristocratic women usually confined their matronly duties to providing an heir and a spare and once that was accomplished, they embarked on a life of considerable freedom.

"Will you be needing Perkins?" The earl's valet.

"Not once I go out. I wish no servants in my quarters."

"Yes, my lord. What would you like done should callers appear?" Irate ones he meant. News of the wager had arrived below stairs with the breakfast dishes.

"No one's to be admitted. No one," the earl underscored.

"Very well, sir."

Albion blew out a breath, restless under his time constraints. He would have preferred a longer interval in which to prepare for the lady but the race meets didn't wait. His horses were heavily staked to win, his Newmarket house had been opened last week, and not to be discounted, his passion for the track was only equaled by his passion for women.

He smiled faintly.

Correction.

There were times when he loved his thoroughbreds more.

# Chapter 4

Fortunately for the earl's pressing schedule, the night was over-cast. Not a hint of moonlight broke through to expose his athletic form as he scaled the old, fist-thick wisteria vines wrapped around the pillars of the terrace pergola. The house to which the pergola was attached was quiet, the ground floor dark save for the porter's light in the entrance hall. Either the Belvoirs were out or already in bed. More likely the latter with only a single flambeau outside the door.

He'd best take care.

Kit had described the position of Miss Belvoir's bedchamber—hence Albion's ascent of the wisteria. Once he gained the roof joists of the Chinoiserie pergola, he would have access to the windows of the main floor corridor. From there he could make his way to the second floor bedchambers, the eastern most that of Miss Belvoir, where, according to Kit, she'd been cloistered for the last month, being polished by her stepmother into a state of refined elegance for her bow into society a few weeks hence.

Which refinements, in his estimation, only served to make every young lady into the same boring martinet without an original thought in her head or a jot of conversation worth listening to.

Hopefully, there wouldn't be much conversation tonight. If he had his way there wouldn't be any. He hoped as well that she wouldn't prove stubborn, but should she, he'd stuff his hand-kerchief in her mouth to muffle her screams, tie her up if necessary, and carry her down the back stairs and out the servants' entrance. It was more likely though—with all due modesty—that his much practiced charm would win the day.

Pulling himself over the fretwork balustrade embellishing the pergola, he stood for a moment balanced on a joist contemplating which window would best offer him ingress. His mind made up, he brushed himself off, navigated the vine-draped timbers, and reached the window. Taking a knife from his coat pocket, he snapped open the blade, slipped it under the lower sash, and pried it up enough to gain a finger hold.

Moments later, he stood motionless in the dark corridor. The stairs were to the right if Kit's description was correct. After listening for a few moments and hearing nothing, he quietly made his way down the plush carpet and up the stairs. A single candle on a console table dimly illuminated the hallway onto which the bedrooms opened. Pausing to listen once again and distinguishing no undue sounds, he silently traversed the carpeted passageway to the last door on his right.

It shouldn't be locked. Servants required access if the bell pull by the bed was rung. For a brief moment he stood utterly still, wondering what in blazes he was doing here about to abduct some untried maid in order to seduce her. As if there weren't women enough in London who would welcome him to their beds with open arms. Considerable brandy was to blame he supposed and the rackety company of his friends who had too much idle time on their hands in which to conjure up wild wagers like this.

Bloody hell. He felt the complete absence of any desire to be where he was.

On the other hand, he decided with a short exhalation, he'd bet twenty thousand on this foolishness.

Now it was play or pay.

He reached for the latch, pressed down, and quietly opened the door.

As he stepped over the threshold he was greeted by a ripple of scent and a cheerful female voice. "I thought you'd changed your mind."

The hairs on the back of his neck rose.

He was unarmed was his first thought.

It was a trap was his second.

But when the same genial voice said, "Don't worry, no one's at home but me. Do come in and shut the door." His pulse rate lessened and he scanned the candle-lit interior for the source of the invitation.

"Miss Belvoir, I presume," he murmured, taking note of a young woman with hair more gold than red standing across the room near the foot of the bed. *She was quite beautiful. How nice. And if no one was home, nicer still.* Shutting the door behind him, he offered her a graceful bow.

"A pleasant good evening, Albion. Gossip preceded you." *He was breathtakingly handsome at close range. Now to convince him to take her away.* "I have a proposition for you."

He smiled. "A coincidence. I have one for you." This was going to be easier than he thought. Then he saw her luggage. "You first," he said guardedly.

"I understand you have twenty thousand to lose."

"Or not."

"Such arrogance, Albion. You forget, the decision is mine."

"Not entirely," he softly replied.

"Because you've done this before."

"Not this. But something enough like it to know."

"I see," she murmured. "But then I'm not inclined to be instantly infatuated with your handsome self or your prodigal repute. I have more important matters on my mind."

"More important than twenty thousand?" he asked with a small smile.

"I like to think so."

He recognized the seriousness of her tone. "Then we must come to some agreement. What do you want?"

"To strike a bargain."

"Consider me agreeable to most anything," he smoothly replied.

"My luggage caused you a certain apprehension I noticed," she said, amusement in her gaze. "Let me allay your fears. I have no plans to elope with you. Did you think I did?"

"The thought crossed my mind." He wasn't entirely sure yet that some trap wasn't about to be sprung. She was the picture of innocence in white muslin—all the rage thanks to Marie Antoinette's penchant for the faux rustic life.

"I understand that women stand in line for your amorous

skills, but rest assured—you're not my type. Licentiousness is your raison d'être I hear—a very superficial existence I should think."

His brows rose. He wondered if she'd heard about Sally's when she mentioned women standing in line. She also had the distinction of being the first woman to find him lacking. "You mistake my raison d'être. Perhaps if you knew me better you'd change your mind," he pleasantly suggested.

"I very much doubt it," she replied with equal amiability. "You're quite beautiful, I'll give you that, and I understand you're unrivaled in the boudoir. But my interests, unlike yours, aren't focused on sex. What I do need from you, however, is an escort to my aunt's house in Edinburgh."

"And for that my twenty thousand is won?" His voice was velvet soft.

"Such tact, my lord."

"I can be blunt if you prefer."

"Please do. I've heard so much about your ready charm. I'm wondering how you're going to ask."

"I hadn't planned on asking."

"Because you never have to."

He smiled. "To date at least."

"So I may be the exception."

"If you didn't need an escort to Edinburgh," he mildly observed. "Your move."

"You see this as a game?"

"In a manner of speaking."

"And I'm the trophy or reward or how do young bucks describe a sportive venture like this?"

"How do young ladies describe the snaring of a husband?"

She laughed. "Touché. I have no need of a husband though. Does that calm your fears?"

"I have none in that regard. Nothing could induce me to marry."

"Then we are in complete agreement. Now tell me, how precisely does a libertine persuade a young lady to succumb to his blandishments?"

"Not like this," he drily said. "Come with me and I'll show you."

"We strike our bargain first. Like you, I have much at stake."

"Then, Miss Belvoir," he said with well-bred grace, "if you would be willing to relinquish your virginity tonight, I'd be delighted to escort you to Edinburgh."

"In the morning. Or later tonight if we can deal with this denouement expeditiously."

"At week's end," he countered. "After the Spring Meet in Newmarket."

"I'm sorry. That's not acceptable."

He didn't answer for so long she thought he might be willing to lose twenty thousand. He was rich enough.

"We can talk about it at my place."

"No."

Another protracted silence ensued, only the crackle of the fire on the hearth audible.

"Would you be willing to accompany me to Newmarket," he finally said. "I can assure you anonymity at my race box. Once the Spring Meet is over, I'll take you to Edinburgh." He blew out a small breath. "I've a fortune wagered on my horses. I don't suppose you'd understand."

This time she was the one who didn't immediately respond and when she did, her voice held a hint of melancholy. "I do understand. My mother owned the Langley stud."

"That was your mother's? By God—the Langley stud was legendary. Tattersalls was mobbed when it was sold. You *do* know how I feel about my racers then." He grinned. "They're all going to win at Newmarket. I'll give you a share if you like—to help set you up in Edinburgh."

Her expression brightened and her voice took on a teasing intonation. "Are you trying to buy my acquiescence?"

"Why not? You only need give me a few days of your time. Come with me. You'll enjoy the races."

"I mustn't be seen."

*Ah—capitulation.* "Then we'll see that you aren't. Good Lord—the Langley stud. I'm bloody impressed. Let me get your luggage." He moved toward the valises piled beside the bed.

"I'm going to require assurance in writing."

He turned back. "My word's not enough?"

"I'd prefer a signed document."

He smiled. "You *must* be part Scots. Show me where to sign." He had what he wanted—the lady's virginity which may or may not be worthwhile. More importantly though, he'd not lost his twenty thousand and tomorrow he'd be in Newmarket. Hell, he'd sign a dozen documents for that.

Moments later, he'd put his signature to a promissory note in which a young lady's virginity was exchanged for an escort to Edinburgh. Turning from the secretaire, he handed it over.

Folding the single sheet of paper—signed and sealed, the imprint of Albion's signet ring pressed into wax above his signature—Felicity slipped it in her reticule. Looking up, she smiled. "Thank you very much. Now, let me call for my maid and we're off."

"No maid."

It was an order no matter how softly put. "But Molly's my personal servant," Felicity explained. "I can't do without her."

He couldn't say he didn't trust her. Having eluded any number of women intent on matrimony, he viewed disavowals of marriage with suspicion. A personal maid could be used to send a message or serve as messenger herself. Before he knew it, Miss Belvoir's father might be on his doorstep crying rape and coercion and wanting the title of Countess of Albion for his daughter.

"Allow me to be your personal maid," he offered, his smile disarming. "I know the drill."

"I expect you do although I'm sure you're better at undressing than dressing women."

"I do both well," he affably said.

"How smug."

He shrugged. "One learns by necessity. And I have servants enough at Newmarket. It shouldn't be a problem."

"I suppose I can't insist."

"I suppose not."

She stared at him for a moment, stricture in her gaze. "You can be quite ill-mannered."

"I'm sorry."

The silence lengthened.

Albion understood a bluff was a bluff was a bluff. She had more at stake than he.

"Very well," she finally said, her voice cool. "But Molly can't be left behind to deal with my family's inquisition. Surely you understand that."

"Perhaps she wouldn't mind going on holiday." He pulled out a handful of large denomination notes from his coat pocket and held them out. "Here. This should do."

A pursed-lip pause ensued before she spoke. "I suppose she *could* go to her sister's in Bristol."

"Bristol would be excellent," he said in his most cordial tone. Closing the small distance between them, he placed the bills in her hand. "Call in Molly and tell her."

Felicity looked at him with a considering gaze. "You have your carriage?"

"Behind the mews."

"We'd have to take her to a coaching inn for the night."

"Done." Bristol was in the opposite direction from Newmarket and Edinburgh. How convenient.

"You're most agreeable now that you have your way."

"If you'd prefer," he said, aware of the vexation in her tone, "we could take turns having our way."

"Liar. Your life is entirely one of self-gratification."

"And yours isn't?" From the look of the Belvoir mansion, she'd been raised with all the advantages of wealth.

"Not lately."

"Ah—you refer to your recent seclusion. Allow me to gratify you then—in compensation. Make a list," he added with a grin, lifting her cape from the foot of the bed and holding it out for her.

She couldn't help but smile as he dropped it on her shoulders. "How amenable you can be. All because of the races."

"You can't say you won't enjoy them."

"No. I'll enjoy them immensely."

"There, you see." His mouth twitched. "Gratification is once again on your horizon. So long as you're not recognized."

"Don't worry," she said, deftly clasping the closure on her cape. "I'll deal with that."

Her phrase gave him pause; how often had he approached problems with similar insouciance. Miss Belvoir was a willful young lady. Perhaps a scheming one as well. His gaze turned cool, his jaw hardened for an instant.

"Why are you looking at me like that? Have I sprouted horns?"

A devilishly apt phrase. "No. I was just trying to recall the location of the appropriate coaching inn," he blandly lied.

"Molly knows."

"In that case, why don't you fetch her and we'll be on our way?" This was turning out to be more troublesome than he'd anticipated. Then again, dealing with women was often difficult. Reminding himself that this evening was worth twenty thousand, he swiftly readjusted his schedule.

When Molly entered the room, he smiled and cordially said, "Good evening. Might we drive you to the posting inn for Bristol?"

# Chapter 5

By the time Molly had been settled into a room at the inn and they'd been driven back across town to Mayfair, Albion was feeling entirely too sober. As his carriage pulled up to the curb before his house, he wondered for the second time that night what in hell he was doing. Sex was about lust and desire, passion and pleasure—not a business transaction like this. Haggling over a maidenhead was damnably off-putting. Furthermore, Miss Belvoir's indifference over the loss of her virginity inspired a deal of distrust.

Too many pursuing women had made him wary.

He needed a drink. Or ten.

After a footman opened the carriage door and put down the step, Albion jumped to the pavement and handed Miss Belvoir down. As he escorted her up the shallow bank of stairs to the entrance, the door was thrown open and a moment later they stepped into a large, brightly lit entrance hall heady with the fragrance of flowers.

"Evening, Sanders." The earl nodded at his major domo while a footman relieved Felicity of her cape. "I like the flowers." Several large arrangements perfumed the air. "We'll be leaving for Newmarket later tonight. I'll be needing the travel chaise. Have some brandy brought up, will you?" Taking Felicity's hand, he moved toward a broad, marble staircase. "There's champagne for you," he said with a smile for the newly subdued lady at his side. "You're not obliged to drink brandy."

Felicity's answering smile was shaky. "I have a feeling I might *need* some."

"Don't be frightened." Her show of nerves was comforting. Perhaps she wasn't some bold little piece out to deceive after all. "I won't hurt you," he promised as they began to mount the stairs.

"From all I've heard, I didn't expect you would. I just hope I don't embarrass myself." She grimaced. "I've never understood what men find intriguing about virgins."

"Not all men do." Himself included.

"The ones Charlotte paraded before me surely did. They were visibly lusting after my innocence."

*Oh, Christ. Why hadn't he asked her age before? What if she was bloody fourteen?* "How old *are* you?" he belatedly inquired.

"Nearly twenty. Which means I come into Maman's inheritance in a twelve month and six days. Hurrah!"

The tension in his shoulders melted away. "Why in hell are you just coming out *now?*" In terms of young ladies making their bows into society, she was well behind times. Some would say she was practically on the shelf.

"I know it's unusual, but after Maman died, we retired to the country and only rarely came into town. I had friends aplenty in Hampshire and of course, my horses." She flashed him a grin. "You understand *that* obsession. I was perfectly content. It's my stepmother insisting on my debut. She wants me out of the house."

"Ah, the wicked stepmother."

She wrinkled her pretty nose. "Consider yourself fortunate you don't have one."

"Indeed I do. Mother's a darling and while the père can be stiff-rumped at times, we generally rub along well enough."

"They allow you your escapades you mean."

He smiled. "I doubt they could stop them."

"Like tonight."

"I suppose," he ambiguously replied, preferring not to discuss the callous nature of their business. "This way," he said, as they reached the top of the stairs, intent on changing the subject. "My rooms are at the end of the corridor."

As they traversed the wide, carpeted hallway, Felicity took note of numerous paintings of sleek thoroughbreds. "Your racers?" She indicated the equine portraits with a wave of her hand.

"Mostly. Some are early Stubbs's. Your mother must have had her favorite thoroughbreds painted."

"Naturally. They were sold along with her stud. Even the Stubbs's portrait of my childhood pony," she bitterly said.

"Another of your stepmother's injustices?"

"Who else's?" she corroborated tartly. "Charlotte's intent on erasing all evidence of my father's previous life. Myself included. Papa rather dotes on her at this point so—"

"She wields considerable authority."

"Oh, yes, and Papa's completely unaware of her manipulation. Charlotte's quite a bit younger, you see," Felicity said with a small sigh.

"A common enough situation. Not that it's any consolation. I understand you have a brother though." Kit had apprised him of the family tree. "Is he of no help?"

"He's abroad. Robbie's undersecretary to our ambassador to the Porte and busy with his own concerns. I thought about taking ship for Constantinople but women have little freedom there. It hardly seemed sensible to exchange Charlotte's custody for a society equally confining beyond the walls of the British embassy."

"Hmmm," Albion said, not altogether sure he cared to hear that Miss Belvoir was without champions in the world. Although her lack of family *had* its advantages. "You and your aunt in Edinburgh must be on good terms." He wasn't about to accept responsibility for Miss Belvoir other than as escort to the Scottish capital.

"We get along famously. She's as horse mad as I."

He was relieved, disburdened of even the suggestion of responsibility. "You must ride with me at Newmarket," he offered, shifting the conversation to something less encumbered. "My estate offers privacy. You'll be safe from prying eyes and you're sure to like my horses."

"Heaven's yes," she brightly replied. "I'm sure I'll like them vastly!"

He shot her a guarded look. The little chit was suddenly damned cheerful again.

She smiled. "You needn't take alarm. I adore riding, that's all. I have no ulterior motive although I suspect most women you know do."

"Some," he evasively said, this man who was considered the biggest matrimonial prize in the ton despite his propensity for vice.

"I assure you, you're safe from *my* designs. In truth, your arrival was most opportune for I'd been racking my brain trying to find some way to elude my stepmother's machinations. I'm not averse to marriage," she explained. "Just not yet—and never to any of those gross, old men Charlotte fancies because of their fortunes."

"Why old men? There's rich young men as well." Stopping before an elaborately carved door, Albion pressed down on the latch.

"The old ones pay more for virginity," Felicity scornfully noted as he pushed open the door. "I don't mean the way you're paying for it," she said over her shoulder as he waved her in. "This is altogether different being a bet and all. Charlotte's express purpose in thrusting those old men on me was to eliminate the expense of a dowry. Old men care only for my youth and chastity although after tonight my value on the marriage mart should plummet and I shall be delivered from evil. Heavens, what gorgeous flowers! And so many!" Turning around, Felicity offered him a dazzling smile. "How thoughtful of you."

*Sanders must have stripped the conservatory of every bloom. The sitting room was awash with bouquets.* "My pleasure," he casually replied, shutting the door behind him. He lifted one brow and grinned. "How does it feel to have checkmated your wicked stepmother?"

"Absolutely divine!" Felicity gleefully exclaimed, spinning around in a graceful pirouette before dropping into a deep curtsy. "All thanks to you, my lord," she purred as she gracefully came upright again.

"And to a hotspur gamble," he suavely added. But his hackles had instinctively risen at Miss Belvoir's all-too-familiar seductive tone. Was she engaged in some rum caper after all? Would he shortly be visited by the predictably irate father?

Lodged safely within the confines of his home, however, it didn't matter what her plans might be, he decided. Pushing away from the door, he made for the goodly supply of champagne Sanders had provided. "Please, make yourself comfortable," he said. "Would you like champagne?"

"Yes—a very *large* glass." Felicity dropped into the nearest chair in a flutter of white muslin. "When the brandy arrives, I'll have a large glass of that as well."

"Nerves?"

"I'm afraid so. You must tell me what to do."

He silently groaned, the role of tutor uninviting. "Don't worry. It's easy enough," he blandly dissembled, walking the small distance to a table holding a monteith filled with ice and several bottles of champagne. Lifting one out, he uncorked it and poured them both a glass, while contemplating whether or not he should renege on his bargain. Sex with a gauche amateur was bloody unappealing. His horses were sure to win day after tomorrow; he could make up the twenty thousand at Newmarket.

Unfortunately . . . it was about winning, not about money.

And he always played to win.

Quickly draining his glass, he refilled it before carrying over Felicity's champagne.

She drank her glass as swiftly and held it out. "More please."

"Perhaps I should bring the bottles closer," he drolly said, taking her glass and setting it on a nearby table.

"It would save you from getting up every few minutes," she replied with an impertinent grin.

One dark brow lifted. "Or we could take turns."

"If this is a seduction are you not obliged to woo me, to be solicitous and charming? I'm not sure taking turns comes into play just yet."

He smiled faintly. "I don't have to seduce you to win my twenty thousand, Miss Belvoir. I just have to take your virginity."

"Surely that would run counter to your celebrated prowess at making love," she answered with a faint smile of her own.

"But then this isn't about making love," he bluntly said and turned away.

Disquieted by his brusque reply, Felicity understood she might be dealing with an act of force majeure rather than a wooing. On the other hand, she was under no illusion about her future should

Charlotte prevail; Albion was a distinct improvement over that cruel fate. Best of all, her time with the earl was limited, unlike her future should her stepmother's matrimonial plans succeed.

There.

Her momentary trepidation nicely rationalized away, she said to Albion's back, "Forgive my naivete. Truth be told, no matter what you do to me, it will be more to my liking than the alternative I've left behind."

"You don't fancy a decrepit old man climbing on top of you?" Lifting the monteith from the table, he turned around and shot her a cheeky grin.

"I'd much prefer you, Albion. No matter what."

She looked so damned earnest, his resistance diminished marginally and while he still wasn't inspired to mount her, he could say without perjuring himself, "We'll have to see that *no matter what* affords you some pleasure."

"Thank you."

*Christ, she looked pale as a ghost. This was going to be an ordeal.* A moment later, he set the monteith on the floor between their chairs. After pouring two glasses of champagne, he handed over hers, drank his down, and deciding to save himself the trouble of continually filling his glass, picked up the bottle and braced it on his thigh. "Tell me a little about yourself." Perhaps he could distract her from her fears.

As he emptied the bottle and broached another they conversed in a desultory manner, her description of her life cursory and abridged, her delivery stumbling at times. She was drinking but little and was visibly uncomfortable while he was in no mood himself for small talk. Nor possibly for sex. An aberration for a young man who served as stud to every female of beauty in the ton. He frequently glanced at the clock, wondering why his brandy hadn't yet arrived.

"Should we get started?" She'd noticed his marked vigilance.

He looked up from uncorking a third bottle. "No. I'm just wondering what the hell happened to my brandy. Are you really a virgin?" His abrupt query was curt, his gaze baleful. "Feel free to say no."

"Sorry," she said, half under her breath.

He softly swore and was about to shout for his brandy when a rap on the door indicated salvation was near.

As the door opened to admit two footmen, he held out his hand for the bottle. By the time a small repast had been carried in and suitably disposed on a table near the fireplace and the door had closed on the servants, Albion had drunk down several inches of brandy. Which along with the champagne combined to somewhat temper his aversion to maidenheads. Not that he was reconciled to deflowering the virginal Miss Belvoir. But at least, he was no longer thinking of bolting.

"If you don't slow down"—Felicity directed a skeptical glance his way—"soon you'll be too drunk to perform."

He looked up, the bottle in his hand arrested midway to his mouth. "How would you know?"

She shrugged. "Women talk."

He looked amused. "About men who can't perform?"

"Among other things."

"Let me assure you, Miss Belvoir," he silkily said, "you needn't worry on that score." He put the bottle to his mouth and drank.

"Felicity."

Resting the bottle on his thigh once again, he arched his brows. "What's your middle name?"

"You don't like Felicity?"

"It has an unpleasantly virtuous ring."

"Would you prefer Stella?"

"Is that your middle name?"

"No, but Stella brings to mind a femme fatale." She smiled. "Would that be better?"

He grinned, having know a Stella of that ilk. "Oh, hell," he muttered, well aware he didn't have a femme fatale on his hands regardless what she called herself. "It doesn't matter. Felicity is perfectly fine. My friends call me Mac by the way."

"We're not precisely friends."

"Close enough." He held up the bottle. "Do you want some?"

"I didn't dare ask."

He laughed and came to his feet. "I thought you dared anything."

She smiled. "I thought so too until recently."

"We're both treading unfamiliar ground." He poured her a jot of brandy and handed the glass to her with a bow. "To your escape from injustice and old men."

"I'd rather drink to my escape to Edinburgh."

In the past he would have suavely said, "Allow me to offer you another kind of escape." But unstirred by passion he couldn't so easily revert to custom and refilling his glass, he said instead, "I'll drink to my horses. They're bloody beautiful."

She leaned forward, her attention suddenly engaged now that her favorite subject in all the world had been introduced. "Tell me about your thoroughbred racers. How fast do they run the mile? The mile and a quarter, a half. Are you really going to win at Newmarket? How much have you bet? Do you wager only to win or to place and show as well?"

"Only to win," he said. "What about you?"

In contrast to their previous hampered conversation, they instantly fell into a free and easy discourse about thoroughbreds and jockeys, blood lines and trainers, about the merits of various exercise schedules, and whether one or another of the season's races was superior. They spoke with passion and animation, agreeing more often than not, discovering in each other a common level of experience and expertise.

Felicity proudly informed him of the prominent races her mother's thoroughbreds had won; the earl modestly refrained from enumerating his many wins. They finished the brandy, or rather Albion did, and as he broached another bottle of champagne, Felicity suddenly rose to her feet.

Smoothing her skirts with brisk determination, she contemplated Albion's indolent pose with a steadfast gaze. "Could we get this over with? While you say that drink doesn't affect you, I'd prefer not testing that premise." *Should he fall into a stupor before discharging their bargain, her passage to Edinburgh might be in jeopardy.*

Rather than argue his capacity for drink he murmured, "As you wish," and heaved himself to his feet. After a quick glance at the clock he decided if *getting this over with* was accomplished quickly, they could be on the road before midnight. Holding out his hand to the undefiled virgin on the other side of the monteith, whom he neither relished nor desired, he said with well-bred grace, "Shall we?"

"I promise not to cry."

He looked startled. Then he said, "How very good of you, but I hadn't intended to make you cry."

"Oh," she whispered, blushing furiously.

Considerable liquor seemingly took a hand and what had previously struck him as appallingly gauche in the young lady was now enchanting. Her blushing tremulousness was enticing, damned if it wasn't, and bloody rare in his profligate life. Perhaps there was something to be said for arousing an innocent to fever pitch.

Taking her hand, he reached down and grabbed a bottle of champagne from the monteith. As she made to offer protest, he cut her short. "Rest assured, I can drink for a week and still do what I have to do tonight."

She shut her mouth with such hasty deference he felt compelled to apologize. "Forgive me," he said, moving toward his bedchamber. "I didn't mean to frighten you. Please, say what you like. I won't send you away."

"You can't send me away!" she exclaimed, her eyes flashing. "You signed an agreement!" She was not as a rule compliant and if so, never for long.

He smiled faintly. "You're fortunate you didn't say that ten minutes ago."

"Oh," she breathed in another moment of understanding.

"Oh, indeed," he softly countered as he reached the door to his bedchamber and opened it. "Now, let's see about offering you some gratification."

"And you as well."

He hesitated long enough for her to recognize his demur. She laughed. "How ironic. I thought to replace old lechery for young and find reluctance instead. Must I seduce you, Albion?"

"If only you could," he drawled.

"Hmmm," she said in a tone that struck him very like that one would use to persuade a headstrong horse to obey.

Pulling her to a stop midway to his bed he held her gaze and said with suave and gentle tact, "You're too green to seduce me, Miss Belvoir. So we will do this with dispatch. I'll try not to hurt you, you've promised not to cry, and in short order we'll be on our way to Newmarket." His smile was practiced and full of charm. "I expect you'll find the races more to your liking."

# Chapter 6

A moment later, however, he was taken by surprise. Having quickly unhooked Felicity's gown, lifted it over her head, and cast it aside, he found beneath her deceptively innocent white muslin gown a voluptuous body capable of putting Venus to shame. Her sheer chemise and petticoat left nothing to the imagination.

Miss Belvoir was slender and shapely and truly exquisite.

If he hadn't been in such a damnable hurry to set out for Newmarket, the role of amorous tutor to her glorious charms might have been appealing.

But he *was* in a hurry.

And she could very well turn out to be uninspiring in the end.

So, addressing practicalities: he must set about arousing her passions to a point where she was not simply ready to *get this over with* as she'd previously remarked but eager and frantic for consummation. If she was hot and breathless with desire, he was less likely to cause her distress—and more to the point, himself. Sex with a tearful chit didn't appeal.

He didn't question his ability to prepare her to receive him. Inflaming a lady's passions was a talent he'd honed to perfection.

The only question was, how long would it take?

He'd wager a monkey on twenty minutes if he had someone with whom to wager. No matter. It was still a test of his competence.

His next thought was inevitable for a seasoned gambler. Why

not make it interesting and lay odds on Miss Belvoir coming up to the mark? He'd spot her an extra five minutes; if she climaxed in twenty-five minutes, he'd give *her* the 500 pounds.

"You can't change your mind if that's what you're thinking."

He glanced down and met Felicity's determined gaze. "I wasn't. I was thinking about—"

"Newmarket I suppose. Me too. Do let's hurry."

He laughed. "Have you never heard of dalliance?"

"Under the circumstances, it's rather unnecessary, isn't it," she briskly replied. "Should I finish undressing?" She touched the blue satin bow at the neck of her chemise.

"Let me do it. But first"—he lightly grasped her shoulders and drew her near—"since I'm not inclined to cold-blooded sex, why not get to know each other a little." He smiled and kissed her lightly, a butterfly kiss of introduction. "Unlike your many avid suitors, I haven't had the advantage of previously meeting you. Hello."

"Hello if you like," she rather impatiently replied. "And devil take my suitors. Unlike *your* many admirers," she said, paraphrasing his words, "mine are neither young nor beautiful."

His brows rose.

"My friend Henrietta told me all about you. Her brother Charles knows you."

"Charles?"

"Danville."

He grinned. "Christ yes. Charlie and I have shared an adventure or two."

"Promise you won't talk about *this* adventure."

"Of course not." He kissed her again, a brushing caress, delicate and beguiling.

"Umm . . . how very nice. I haven't been kissed much and never like that. The thing is," she said in the next breath, her major concern more urgent than kisses, "I don't want my family to hear the details of this proceeding."

*He'd not previously heard his lovemaking described as a proceeding; his sexual talents were much in demand.* Suppressing a smile, he gravely said, "No one will mention the wager. I'll see to it."

"Oh, good." She exhaled in relief. "Thank you vastly. I know you must think me shameless for doing what I'm doing, but I can't possibly consider marrying any of those awful men and with

Papa willing to yield to Charlotte's authority, you can see . . . my choices are extremely limited," she finished in a rush.

"I'm your sole choice you mean," Albion said with amusement, wondering if she'd continue talking while they made love.

"No—well, yes, although not in any disparaging sense. I know you're considered quite *every* woman's choice. But I wasn't actually planning on relinquishing my virginity—oh dear, how prudish that sounds. The thing is I hadn't thought about virginity one way or another—in fact I could care less about the notion. Why *does* virginity hold such appeal for men?"

"I have no idea." Rather than continue a profitless conversation, he dipped his head and curtailed any further discussion by kissing her—masterfully, expertly and at some length.

Felicity was no less vulnerable to Albion's expertise than any other female. But then Albion's success with women had been proven countless times—Brooks's betting book rife with wagers brought by foolhardy gamesters hazarding their money against Albion's amorous skills—and always losing.

The object of his latest wager responded no less predictably.

Felicity's body was beginning to tingle in places it had never tingled before, her senses were aglow, every nerve quivered in an undefinable, yet wholly enchanting way. In the vast scheme of things, it was really quite fortunate, she decided, that someone like Albion would introduce her to the physical act of love. According to Henrietta, he eclipsed all others in pleasuring women.

And novice though she was, so it seemed.

His kisses were utter perfection—subtle with promise, deliciously languid as if he had all the time in the world to beguile and bewitch, his easy manner warm and charmingly amicable. Although the taste of brandy when he kissed her was intensely male as was his glorious virility blatantly nudging her stomach. His size and strength overwhelmed and captivated her, reminding her of the darkly dangerous heroes from the gothic novels of the day. And for the first time in her life she was in the grip of the wild, frenzied passions heretofore only found in the pages of a book.

Albion's reading, in contrast, was limited to racing publications and bloodstock catalogs, but his wide and varied sexual experience equipped him to deal more empirically with passion. He was conscious of a subtle change in Miss Belvoir's response; her initial naive and tremulous willingness had been supplanted by a mounting ardor auguring well for the possibility of success. Covertly checking the time from under his lashes, he quickly gauged her heated desires against his twenty-minute window of opportunity.

Perceiving that she wouldn't object to a greater intimacy, he took her hands currently resting against his chest and lifted them to his shoulders. As she rose on tiptoe, twined her arms around his neck, and clung to him, he slid his hands down her spine, cupped her lush bottom in his palms, and gently drew her into his rigid erection.

Whether by instinct or previous experience—a fact he'd discover soon enough—she softly sighed, melted into his muscled frame in a decidedly provocative way, and stirred her hips ever so faintly so his rampant penis and her soft mons were in gratifying proximity. A tantalizing overture he pleasantly decided. Miss Belvoir was proving to be a passionate young lady.

He might win the day in under twenty minutes after all.

A thought abruptly nullified as Felicity eased back slightly, looked up, and said blunt as a hammer blow, "*That*"—she pointed downward—"is not going to fit inside me."

"Ah—a romantic," he drolly noted.

"As if romance would be in the least helpful," she replied with a flashing glance. "You're *enormous.*"

Having recently changed his mind about mounting Miss Belvoir, and now in the grip of considerable lust, he was quick to soothe her. "You needn't worry. I know what I'm doing. Trust me."

She hesitated for a fraction of a second. "I suppose you *do* know more about this than I."

He smiled. "I suppose I do." Virgins aside. But he was a confident young man.

"So I'm to trust to your skill," she dubiously said.

*You and several hundred other women.* "You won't be sorry. And consider, you'll soon be on your way to Edinburgh."

"Via Newmarket," she added with a quick smile, the cloud of doubt lifting from her brow.

"Better yet, wouldn't you say?"

"You needn't look so smug."

But she was smiling widely now which was encouraging. "I

can guarantee you pleasure," he gently affirmed. "Why not relax and enjoy yourself?"

"I don't have to do anything?"

"Not if you don't want to." Her breathing had changed, her skin was flushed, he could see the racing pulse in her neck. She was well on her way; he wouldn't have to do much either. "Let me finish undressing you, then you can wait for me in bed."

"Should I undress you?"

*A fumbling tyro?* "Let me," he pleasantly said. "I'm faster."

"You are," she agreed with a dazzling smile, as he swiftly unbuttoned her chemise. "And as good as rumor has it. I'm tingling everywhere and beginning to throb in the most—" She blushed and said instead, "I expect ladies always like when you undress them."

"It depends."

Her gaze held a question.

"Whether there's time to undress," he explained, sliding her chemise down her arms, his cock swelling higher as her large breasts were exposed.

"Does that happen often?"

He took a small breath of restraint, curbing his impulse to precipitously mount her. "Often enough," he negligently replied, controlling his urges. Dropping her chemise on the floor, he untied the bow at the waistband of her petticoat. As the light fabric slid down her hips, leaving her fully nude, he lifted her into his arms, and with a glance at the clock, moved toward the bed. Eight minutes left to win his personal bet.

"Do you know Lord Wesford?"

The unexpected question lifted his brows. "Why do you ask?"

"One of my friends is enamored of him. Our rendezvous reminds me of Priscilla who's forever sneaking away to meet him."

"Wesford can't keep his mouth shut," the earl said, rebuke in his tone; the man was the worst cunt hound and gossip in London. Seating her against the pillows on his bed, he added, "You might tell her that."

"Unlike you."

"Unlike me. A gentleman doesn't discuss the ladies he knows."

"Intimately."

"Yes, intimately."

"Well that's a relief."

"I already told you as much."

She smiled. "That's right. How kind of you. You're going to give me pleasure and with the exception of closing your bet at Brooks's nothing of this little episode will be bruited abroad."

"Yes and yes."

"So assured."

"I have a certain reputation apropos women and dueling," he modestly said.

"Then I should consider myself very lucky."

"You should," he said. "Derby might have won the cut of the cards and he's notoriously crude. Now get under the covers. It's warmer."

While she scrambled under the crimson silk coverlet, with one eye on the clock, he quickly disposed of his clothing—a procedure with which he was well acquainted.

# Chapter 7

She watched him undress with undisguised curiosity.

He seemed not to notice, discarding his clothing with dispatch: black coat and dark waistcoat, neckcloth and shirt of steel-gray to be less distinguishable in the night, boots and stockings. He was pressed for time and also eminently accustomed to women's interest in him. Clothed or unclothed.

"You're very muscular," Felicity murmured, surveying his powerful torso with an examining eye and considerable admiration. His muscles were steel hard, his shoulders broad, his arms brawny, his tall, athletic form honed by more than amorous sport. "Do you box? My brother is forever talking about celebrated prize fights and his sparring bouts at some boxing saloon."

Albion looked up, his fingers on the top buttons of his black breeches. "I do on occasion. I prefer pistols."

"Have you shot many men?"

"Could we talk about this later?"

"Sorry. I'm unfamiliar with boudoir conversation. I suppose I should be flirtatious."

He laughed. "A little late for that, I'd say."

"Oh, good, then I may be frank. Will this take long? I'd like to be on the road soon. In case Papa takes notice of my absence."

"I'll do my best to speed things up," he replied as frankly. "It depends on you."

"Why?"

"Because I don't want to hurt you," he said, stripping off his breeches.

"Oh my," she said in a very small voice, her wide-eyed violet gaze on his monstrous, upthrust erection. "Are you sure about—that is . . . oh *my!*"

Christ, she truly was a tyro. "I promise you it won't hurt," he calmly lied, moving toward the bed—*or not excessively he hoped.* Virgins were not his area of expertise. Unless this seduction moved with more dispatch, however, neither one of them was going to win the monkey. With that look of apprehension in her eyes, she was going to require more time to reach a degree of irrepressible frenzy where nothing mattered but quenching sharp-set desire.

On the other hand, he decided, climbing into bed, nothing ventured, nothing gained. And it wasn't as though he was unfamiliar with this game.

So he exerted all his charm and considerable artistry in hopes of swiftly bringing the lady to a panting point of no return. First, he kissed her on the mouth, gently and then not so gently before moving to kiss her in other equally pleasurable locations. He kissed the pulse at her throat, the swelling curve of her breast, her nipples at some length until they were jewel-hard and her breasts were rosy pink and quivering. Then, dipping his head lower, he trailed kisses down her stomach to her pale mons and lower still until he gently spread the soft, slick tissue of her sex with his slender fingers and explored her pulsing flesh with his tongue. She shuddered under his touch, softly moaned as he licked her virgin cunt, as he stroked and nibbled until she was breathless with longing and her squirming hips gave evidence of her feverish need.

"Please, Albion, enough, enough," she finally cried, clutching his head and pulling upward, his hair coming loose from its binding in the process. "Please, please, I don't care if it hurts."

With four minutes left he wasn't sure he cared either. But as a sop to his conscience, he lifted his head, brushed his hair away from his face, and met her gaze. "Are you certain?"

"Yes—yes . . . yes," she panted. "Mount me Albion or I'll mount you!"

She'd seen too much of the breeding sheds at Langley stud, he decided, her blunt language a novel departure from the sultry endearments customary at times like this. "I'll have to think about it," he dissembled, coming up on his knees and smoothly settling between her outstretched thighs in a ripple of flexing muscle and well-placed finesse. "Maybe I will and maybe I won't," he added, carefully positioning himself before swinging his hips back in a smooth, fluid motion. "It's not for you to say."

"Don't you dare change your—"

Her vehement protest ended in a stifled shriek as he burst through her maidenhead, instantly arrested his forward progress, and thought, *Thank God that's over.* Only partially submerged to allay her distress, he rested his weight on his forearms, and paused quiescent.

Felicity lay rigid, absorbing the shock.

A taut hush filled the air.

Would she allow him further access or was the painful assault too much?

"Is that all there is to it?" she said moments later, her voice wistful. "I liked the other part better."

Back on familiar ground, his seductive skills once again in demand, the earl gently said, "I can make this part even better than the other. You have only to tell me to stop if it hurts and I will."

She drew in a small breath and nodded.

He smiled faintly at her unsentimental affirmation. Not that he viewed this night with any more sensitivity. But he could give her pleasure at least on this her first foray into carnal relations. "Remember now, I defer to your wishes."

She offered him a small smile. "I can see why women adore you."

"Not yet you can't," he replied with a grin.

Her smile widened and amusement lit her eyes. "Such confidence."

He liked that she was playful once again. "Wait and see," he roguishly said. "I've been practicing a long time."

She laughed, he smiled, and then he went about the business that had earned him endless praise and gratitude from legions of women. Withdrawing marginally in order not to abrade Miss Belvoir's tender tissue, his gaze fixed on her face, watching for any hint of discomfort, he moved forward once again with exquisite care.

Her virgin flesh yielded slowly to his entry.

He exercised enormous control; he was capable of infinite restraint in any event. That and his stamina were his greatest assets in the boudoirs of the world.

Whenever he met resistance, he arrested his advance, gently kissed the nubile Miss Belvoir, and murmured charmingly salacious endearments in her ear—informing her what he was about to do to her, how he'd make her feel, that he wasn't entirely sure his cock would fit—that perhaps she was right after all—she couldn't take him all.

Of course she wasn't right; his lascivious words further excited her, he slipped in another small distance, she gasped at the exquisite pleasure, and so it went.

A virtuoso performance by a master.

For the pleasure of an innocent young maid newly awakened to carnal delight.

At last, when his rock hard cock was buried to the hilt in her silken passage and Miss Belvoir's rapturous sigh warmed his throat, Albion met her heated gaze. "Is this part better now?" he softly inquired.

"Oh *yes,*" she whispered. "Please do it again."

"Like this?" Slowly withdrawing, he entered her once again with superlative languor until he filled her completely.

Several moments passed before Felicity found breath enough to speak and when she did, a slight quiver vibrated in her voice. "I never knew anything could feel quite so *wonderful.*"

"Allow me to show you further wonders," he murmured with the faintest of smiles.

She gazed up at him—every restive nerve in her body palpitating wildly—and like so many women before her, she purred, "You're amazing . . ."

"We try," he pleasantly replied and settled into a slow, deliberate rhythm guaranteed to please even more. She hardly moved whether from inexperience or by her own choosing, and, eyes shut, she softly moaned on each deep downstroke. Her warm palms rested on his shoulders, but lightly, without pressure or strain. And a few moments later, to his astonishment, the young lady beneath him quietly climaxed.

Either she was the latent nymphomaniac he'd been hoping for

or he was better than he thought because he'd won his bet by a full minute.

Which put him in an uncommonly good mood.

Her eyes slowly opened while he was congratulating himself. "Could we do that again?"

The longing in her voice was clear. "It's up to you," he kindly said.

"Then I would definitely like another of those marvelous"— she paused.

"Orgasms," he offered.

"Yes, yes, as many as you please." Rosy pink and flushed with satisfaction, she lazily stretched. "If you don't mind."

He felt her slick cunt tighten around his cock as she stretched and with his impressive erection still at full mast he was more than ready to oblige her. Also, her sweet eagerness was so uncommon in his world that he was motivated by a rare chivalrous impulse. He was not chivalrous as a rule; his privileged life served rather to promote selfishness. Nor were aristocratic men inclined to domesticity or genuine affection in their relationships with females. Or most of them at least.

As it turned out, he obliged her several times.

Not that he minded. She was a hot-blooded little puss, quick to learn and enchantingly orgasmic.

After a considerable interval of allowing the lady her pleasures, when she was no longer quite so voracious, Albion contemplated climaxing himself. But he was wary of virgins, more particularly ones like Miss Belvoir who were so damned cooperative. He didn't care to risk impregnating a young lady who may or may not be in the market for a husband. Whose family may or may not be an accessory to such a plan.

"That was ever so glorious. Thank you again," she finally whispered, her gaze half-lidded, her voice drowsy. "You're even better than I'd heard. Perfect, really. Absolutely perfect."

"My pleasure," he automatically said as her voice trailed off. Dropping a light kiss on her cheek, he gently withdrew from her greedy little cunt, rolled away, and idly gazed at the tester overhead.

Postcoital moments always required a certain tact; women disliked men who fucked and immediately decamped. In this case, they were leaving together, but it still wouldn't do to abruptly quit the bed and order her to dress.

But before he could utter some bland, urbane courtesy, he heard the soft, gentle rhythm of her breathing and turned to find Miss Belvoir fast asleep beside him.

He smiled. *Too much of a good thing for an innocent miss.* Relieved of further courtesies, he swung his legs over the side of the bed, came to his feet, strode, handsome and naked, into his bathroom reminiscent of a Roman bath, quickly masturbated, and even more quickly dressed. Returning to the bedroom, he rolled Miss Belvoir to one side of the bed, bundled up the bloodied sheet, cut off a lock of her hair with his pocket knife, and scrawled a quick note to Kit asking that the required evidence be delivered to Brooks. He also added a few lines of warning to his cohorts: should word of Miss Belvoir's denouement be disclosed, the perpetrator would answer to him on the dueling field although the potential for rumor spreading beyond his immediate colleagues was not without precedence in the incestuous ton. He blew out a small breath. *Time enough to deal with that should it become necessary.*

Shoving the two items into a leather bag, Albion left the bag and note on his writing desk. Then crossing the bedroom and sitting room, he opened the door into the hallway and ordered his chaise and four in a carrying voice.

Returning to his bed, he wrapped Miss Belvoir in the coverlet and lifting her into his arms, vacated his apartments. Perkins was waiting in the corridor and kept pace with Albion as he moved toward the stairs, responding to the earl's numerous orders with his usual calm. As the men descended the wide staircase, Albion added in a considering tone, "Perhaps you should bring up a maidservant when you come. I know we don't have the ideal lady's maid in my bachelor establishment, but do what you can. And don't forget—Lord Talmadge is to be given those items on my writing desk."

Perkins looked pained at the earl's reminder. But like any good valet, he only said, "Of course, sir. As you wish."

"Bring up my dueling pistols when you come."

Perkins didn't so much as raise an eyebrow although his impulse was strong. He merely asked, "Which ones, sir?"

"The silver chased rosewood Mantons. They shoot true." In the event he had to face an irate male member of Felicity's family. "Follow us as soon as you may."

"Yes, sir." Perkins decided that it would do well to see that the postilions were also well armed. Having cared for the earl since his youth, Perkins knew his master well. The young lady in the earl's arms was naked; she was also obviously a lady. The possibility of trouble was not insubstantial. He'd warn the coachman to be on alert.

Several servants followed the men, conveying the earl's luggage. Reaching the base of the stairs, Albion crossed the entrance hall to the open door where Sanders was waiting.

"Should anyone inquire about my whereabouts," he said, "tell them you are unacquainted with my plans. I'm for Newmarket as you know. My friends are privy to that fact as well. And for others, they may search for me as they please."

"What of—"

"My parents?" To Sanders's nod, Albion said briefly, "Use your best judgment."

"Yes, sir." Sanders knew what that meant. Evade—if possible or as long as possible.

"Should my father prove difficult, give me warning."

"Of course, sir."

Albion smiled. "It won't be the first time, will it, Sanders?"

"No, sir." *Or the tenth.* "Should the marquess be in temper, I'll send Timothy."

"Excellent." The young groom was a consummate rider. "Tell Tim to take his pick of my stable. By the way," Albion said with a wide smile, "my racers are going to win at the Spring Meet. Every last one of 'em. What do you think of that?"

"I believe you'll enjoy yourself at Newmarket, sir. As always."

"Indeed," Albion softly said with a glance for the lady in his arms. "Perhaps more than usual this time." With a nod, he turned and walked outside where the luggage was being tied into the boot of his carriage.

A footman held open the door of the post chaise, the green lacquer gleaming in the light of the flambeaux blazing above the entrance. Crossing the pavement, the earl placed his boot on the step, bent his head, and entered the chaise, taking care not to wake his guest. Lowering himself onto the seat, he settled Felicity on his lap, rested her head on his shoulder, and leaned back against the padded black velvet upholstery. The footman shut the door, a signal for the coachman to ease the four matched chestnuts away from the curb. With a snap of the whip, the team briskly entered the street and soon the carriage was moving full tilt through the night streets of London.

Felicity slept soundly in Albion's arms, not even waking when they left the city and turned onto the Cambridge road. The horses were given their head and the chaise bowled along at a smart pace.

In good spirits with the Spring Meet imminent, the earl lounged back in the seat, his long legs braced against the sway of the coach, a fine brandy within reach in his pocket flask. A basket of food had been sent along should he or the lady require sustenance. Barring accidents or lame horses, they should arrive at his race box by cock crow.

# Chapter 8

They only stopped twice to change horses; the earl's stable master had arranged to have teams from Albion's stable in readiness at Harlow and Saffron Walden. His bloodstock was first rate and unlike post horses they were capable of running long distances.

Felicity hadn't stirred at their first halt, but when they stopped at Saffron Walden she came awake enough to drowsily murmur, "Are we there?"

"Not yet. We're changing horses."

Her lashes fluttered faintly. "How long before Newmarket?"

"Another two hours."

"Oh good. There's time."

"Go back to sleep, poppet." The earl spoke in a careless drawl, his mind on the races.

"But I'm awake now," she said with purpose, bestirring herself.

The crimson coverlet fell away from her shoulders as she sat up, revealing her ripe, curvaceous charms, her peaked nipples indicating a certain sexual readiness. Albion not only understood what she meant by *there's time* but suddenly found himself in agreement. "You have a fancy for more?" he asked with a generous smile.

"Who wouldn't? It's most agreeable."

"Like winning at piquet?" he teasingly suggested.

"No, dear Albion, like pleasure piled upon endless pleasure as you very well know. This could become quite a lovely addiction." Her light brows rose. "Must I wait?" She wiggled her bottom against his pronounced erection and smiled. "It doesn't seem so."

"I warn you, once the races start, even these"—he trailed his fingers over her lush breasts—"won't entice me. I have my own addictions."

"Perhaps we could do both at the same time: watch the races and—"

"No."

"How rude you are." She pouted prettily. "You must have a private stand. Why *can't* we do both?"

"Because you can't afford the scandal. Now behave or I'll leave you at my race box and you won't see any races."

"Have I mentioned how I dislike authority of any kind?"

"I gathered as much," he drily said, "when you were packed and waiting for me in your bedroom."

She looked at him, a question in her raised brows. "You don't *mind* pleasuring me, do you?"

"Not when I have time." Race week was frenzied and his bet was won.

"Like now, perhaps?" she sweetly inquired.

He laughed. "Very well, poppet, like now."

"And more than once please."

He looked amused. "Demands—so soon?"

"I said please," she disputed. "And consider, it's your fault that I've become fond of lustful pleasures. You're responsible for awakening my desires."

"Responsible?" His voice was sharp. "You asked for this bargain as I recall."

"Now you're angry. I didn't mean to provoke you when—"

"You want to fuck," he cooly finished, wondering again if Miss Belvoir was as naive as she appeared.

"I do apologize," she whispered, flushing under his punishing gaze.

Either she was an actress of note, he decided, or he was jumping to conclusions. Not that either mattered when his erection was pressing into Miss Belvoir's soft bottom and good judgment was fast exiting the scene. "Apology accepted," he said, his voice gentle, his outrage forgotten, his smile propitiatory and much used in situations like this. "Now, why don't you unbutton my breeches and we'll see how many times you can climax."

Her mouth formed a breathless O, her cheeks turned cherry red. "Thank you ever so much."

She spoke so softly he had to strain to hear her. Good God, such gratitude struck him with contrition. "Here, let me do that," he kindly offered, brushing aside her fumbling fingers and sliding the gold buttons free. Knowing that she'd been well used short hours ago, unsure whether a virgin might be harmed in some way by such unremitting intercourse, he asked with unfailing tact, "Tell me, my dear, are you feeling any aftereffects from our earlier dalliance? I wouldn't want to cause you further distress."

"No, no aftereffects. Should I have?" No longer fainthearted with the earl's temper restored, she spoke with her usual candor.

He shrugged. "God knows."

"Because you don't consort with virgins."

"You're the first."

She was surprised the wicked earl had scruples. "But twenty thousand was at stake."

He smiled faintly. "So I recalled on waking yesterday."

"To my good fortune," she remarked, smiling back. "I'm on my way to Edinburgh thanks to you. Now if you don't mind," she added in the decisive tone he was beginning to recognize, "could we do something other than talk?"

He laughed. "Don't be shy."

"Why should I be when you're obviously interested"—she wiggled her bottom—"and I am as well?"

"A word of warning, my dear, for your future amours. There are men who don't like outspoken women."

"Are you one of them?"

Amusement sparkled in his eyes. "Would it matter if I was?"

"Not unless it interfered with putting this"—she shifted her position on his lap, slid her hand into his opened breeches, and ran her fingertips up his rigid erection—"inside me and from your notorious reputation I rather doubt you'd hesitate at this late stage regardless what a woman said."

"You're well informed," he blandly noted.

"Your exploits are the subject of much discussion among my friends."

"Good God, have they nothing better to do?"

"We are not allowed your freedoms, my lord. Although now I know why you're so much in demand," she murmured, grasping his upthrust penis and sliding her hand downward. "He's not only gorgeous in size but you've trained him well."

It took Albion a moment to reply, the pressure of her fingers adding inches to his erection, subverting intellect for primal sensation. When he spoke, he ignored her comments and said instead, "Do you think you can take him all?" Not that he didn't have his own answer to that question.

"Since I've been thinking of little else since I came awake, I'd be more than happy to try and quickly if you please."

"I'm sorry I didn't climb up your wisteria earlier," Albion said with a grin, feeling an affinity for a vixen with such frank desires. "You're a hot little piece."

"If I had known how magnificent the pleasure I might have climbed down and set myself in your path. In truth, Albion, I'm vastly pleased it was you who"—

"Won the cut of the cards for your virginity?"

A thrilling little frisson raced up her spine at his careless prodigality.

"You like that? Being put on the block?"

"No—yes—oh Lord, I don't know. Just don't make me wait," she pleaded, the throbbing between her legs a hard, steady rhythm. Taking his face between her hands, she met his languid gaze and impatiently said, "Do you hear?"

"I hear," he quietly answered, her heated whisper curiously enticing. Lifting her easily, he swung her around so she was facing him and her legs were straddling his thighs. With one hand under her bottom, he raised her to her knees, deftly positioned the head of his cock in the crease of her labia and politely said, "You decide how fast or slow—how deep."

She smiled. "Because you don't consort with virgins."

"Because of that," he softly said.

"Dare I be outspoken or will you take umbrage?"

He acknowledged her question with a fall of his eyelids. "I'll let you know if you go too far."

"Then I'd like to feel you inside me"—she began to lower herself down his rigid erection–"all the way to Newmarket."

*Christ, she didn't want much.* Gazing down at the pink and white miss, he smiled. "That's a bloody long time."

She didn't hear him because she was swiftly plunging down his cock, putting to rest any concerns he might have about her tenderness. At the same time, Felicity was recalibrating degrees of happiness and delight in a purely physical sense. When she came to rest on his thighs a second later, suddenly neither was capable of thought. She was firmly impaled, he rooted deep inside her, fierce, explosive ecstasy was strumming through their nerve endings and nothing mattered but wild, promiscuous feeling.

Albion recovered first, less prone to emotion after playing the game so long. "I can feel the sway of the chaise—can you?" he whispered, his hands at her waist to steady her, the delicious friction as he rested inside her fiercely arousing.

"Among other things," she purred, shifting her hips in a delicate undulation. "Just stay right there. Don't move. Don't, *don't!*"

But he did, flexing his hips and driving deeper, her wild cry construed as approval by a man who'd honed his amorous skills to a fare-thee-well.

A hush fell, the creak of the chaise and pounding of hoofs unheard.

Intent on his next movement, Albion was awaiting the lady's convenience.

Felicity was trying to restore breath to her lungs. She finally did and lifting her head from the earl's shoulder, she said, half breathless still, "Can one die of bliss?"

A smile lit his eyes. "It gets better."

Color flooded her cheeks. "Truly?"

"I swear," he said.

"You don't know how grateful I am," she asserted with feeling, "that it was you and not any of Charlotte's disgusting choices"— she trembled—"who introduced me to—"

"They will never touch you, I promise." The poor thing had been frightened half to death by her stepmother's vile plans.

Prompted to a gallantry he rarely exerted, he quietly said, "You're on holiday, darling. You must only think happy thoughts, experience pleasure, and smile at me from time to time." At which point, he raised Miss Belvoir to the crest of his erection, held her gently by the waist to slow her descent, and settling into a gratifying rhythm, soon brought his traveling companion to experience not only pleasure but a soul-stirring climax.

In the remaining miles, he obliged the lady several more times, her charming appetite for sex putting his legendary stamina to the test. Miss Belvoir panted and purred and repeatedly screamed in orgasmic release, after which she invariably blushed for having so forgotten herself that she gave raucous vent to her feelings. "Oh, dear, they heard didn't they?" she'd whisper after the fact.

"It doesn't signify," he'd reply, his jaded soul captivated by her guileless passion. "The coachman and postilions know better than to listen. Did you enjoy yourself?"

She'd declare her gratitude with artless exuberance and he'd be told he was splendid or superb or utterly magnificent or some such thing.

Her smile would be very close and lush, her shapely form warm under his hands, his cock buried in her sweet cunt, and he'd be feeling a certain degree of splendor himself.

When they reached the outskirts of Newmarket, however, Albion lifted her off his cock, set her on the seat beside him, and kissed her gently. "Until later, darling. We're here." He raised the window curtains and surveyed the quiet street. "Does the town look familiar? I expect it does if your mother raced thoroughbreds."

His voice was easy and level, his expression bland, as if they were no more than passing acquaintances rather than partners in frenzied sex for the past many hours. His attentions had clearly shifted elsewhere.

He'd warned her of his passion for racing and now that they'd arrived at the holy grail of the turf, it was to be expected that she'd been displaced by more important priorities. It wasn't as though she was indifferent to the sport; she understood its allure.

And he was her savior of sorts, after all.

So she gathered the coverlet around her and gazed out the carriage window, pragmatically resigning herself to a lesser role in

Albion's schedule in the coming days. Dawn had broken, a golden light bathed the town in morning freshness. "It's been years since I've been here," she noted as the chaise sped through the deserted streets. "Much has changed. Perhaps we could do some sight-seeing."

"I wouldn't recommend it unless you want to be named my latest light o' love. Servants talk. It's a small town. My acquaintance is large. Until you reach the safety of your aunt's establishment your reputation is in jeopardy."

"Maybe I don't care."

"Maybe I do," his lordship said with conviction. "I don't ruin young maids."

"Publicly."

He rolled his eyes. "Your father should have kept you on a shorter leash."

"Or certain men shouldn't have come into my bedroom with the object of seducing me."

"Impertinent chit," he grumbled. "I should spank you."

"I'm not sure I wouldn't like that a great deal," she murmured, giving him a sidelong glance from under her lashes.

With a groan, he distanced himself from the little nymphet with the tousled red-gold hair who was infinitely desirable and much too greedy for sex. Staring out the window, he tried to think of something other than his rising cock.

"I like that you're always ready," she softly said, her gaze on the swelling bulge in his breeches. "Perhaps we could pull down the curtains for a minute."

"Don't say another word," he muttered, watching shops and dwellings pass by. "We're nearing my race box and I have no intention of walking past my staff looking like this."

She smiled. "Maybe if you thought of something else it might help."

"Maybe if *you* thought of something else it would help even more," the earl said, turning from the window with a frown.

"I can't," she whispered.

He softly swore at the longing in her voice, at his own irrepressible response to her passion. Even while decrying his lack of restraint, he reached up, rapped on the ceiling, and called out, "Pull over Will and give me ten minutes." They'd just arrived at the northern reaches of town, the countryside opening up before them.

The chaise had no more than come to a stop and the coachman climbed down when Felicity let the coverlet fall away. "You're ever so nice, Albion. Thank you again."

"You're hard to resist, sweetling." He suppressed a sigh. "Although I don't know why I try."

"It's only a few days." Her answering smile was sunshine bright. "Does that make you feel better?"

"Lie down," he directed, his fingers on the buttons of his breeches, "and I'll show you what will make me feel better."

She immediately complied and gazed up at him, flushed and glowing. "There's no question why you're such a favorite with the ladies. Does every woman respond to you with insatiable desire?"

"I wouldn't know," he politely lied. "Although if you don't mind," he added, adjusting himself between her legs on the wide seat, "this will have to be the last time."

Her eyes flared wide.

"In the carriage," he quickly said.

"Oh good. You had me worried."

"Worry no more," he whispered, sliding into her, the little chit more tantalizing than he would have wished, his desire for her beyond the ordinary. He had no explanation for his enthusiasm or none he cared to acknowledge.

Then she twined her arms around his neck, raised her hips into his downstroke, and reflection gave way to reality.

One booted foot braced against the opposite seat, the other on the carriage wall, he favored the lady's hot-blooded desire in a hard, steady, ungentle assault, neither noticing nor caring that the little chit was meeting his hammering frenzy stroke for stroke.

In short order, as the earl buried himself to the very depths of my lady's sleek passage in a savage thrust, her scream rent the air. He recognized the high-pitched orgasmic wail, a familiar sound in his life. But what he did next, he rarely did, and never with a female unschooled in the ways of the world.

The first orgasmic freshet rippled downward through his body, driven by rash impulse and perhaps necessity after so long, the explosive force surging and swelling as it went until his semen burst forth and he poured, gushed, flooded the maidenly Miss Belvoir's cunt with his long pent-up ejaculation.

Seconds later, his forehead braced against the window, he silently cursed himself for a fool. Even as a callow youth, he'd known better than to take such risks. Damn and bloody hell!

Felicity moved beneath him, breaking into his brooding thoughts and getting his breath back, he raised his head. "Forgive me," he said with palpable reserve. "I didn't mean to treat you so roughly."

"You needn't ask my forgiveness. Really," she added, meeting his restive gaze. "You gave me enormous pleasure as usual."

He softly sighed, consciously dismissed useless regret and eased away from her. "Let me find something to wipe you off."

Dropping onto the opposite seat, he pulled out a handkerchief from his breeches pocket and quickly set himself to rights. Reaching under the seat, he opened a compartment, rummaged inside, and extracted a small table linen stored there for outdoor dining. "This should do," he gruffly said, tossing it to Felicity.

"Don't be angry."

"I'm not."

"Sulky then."

"I don't sulk, but keep it up and I might," he muttered, not inclined to discuss his irresponsible actions. "We should find you some clothes."

"It might be wise. Not that anything about this situation is in the least wise."

He looked at her with a touch of impatience. "Is this where I say, 'We should have thought about that before?'"

"Or where I reply, 'In contrast to my options, you were very much the lesser of evils.'"

His smile broke through his frown. "That doesn't sound like a compliment."

"In your case, Albion," she said, returning his smile, "it most certainly is. You are excellent in every imaginable way. Women discuss lovemaking ad infinitum so I understand my good fortune."

"And you always just listened," he said with amusement.

"I needn't anymore."

The earl's brows rose a little. "I hope you don't name names."

"I wouldn't have thought you so modest."

He shrugged. "It's nobody's business, that's all. I'll get your valise," he said, becoming weary of a useless conversation, his driveway over the next rise. "Which one do you want?"

"The red leather case," she said, as capable as he of urbanity.

Reaching out, he turned the latch, shoved the door open, jumped to the ground, and called for his men.

# Chapter 9

The Earl of Albion and his companion alighted at his race box, if not band box fresh, at least suitably attired.

While grooms and footmen attended to the horses and luggage, the young couple moved across the raked gravel drive to the main entrance sheltered within the vaulted base of a soaring clock tower.

Her hand resting lightly on Albion's arm, Felicity gazed at the sprawling Tudor structure with its ivy-covered red brick walls and three stories of leaded glass windows sparkling in the morning sun. "How grand a structure! My mother's Newmarket property was a cottage compared to this." She glanced up and grinned. "You really are rich. Everyone says so but I didn't understand just *how* rich."

"If you need money you should have said so." *Or he should have known.* The quid pro quo of amour was universal, only the currency changed. "How much do you need?"

"Having seen your house in town and now this, I suppose whatever I might ask for would be the merest bagatelle to you."

*The little chit was more calculating than he thought.* "Why don't we do our negotiating inside where you can convince me in more comfort," he sardonically said, surprised at his annoyance that she was just another scheming tart.

She stopped abruptly at the mockery in his tone. "Do you think I want your money?"

He met her gaze. "Don't you?"

"Does every woman want your money?" she asked, staring back.

"Some want my title too," he pithily noted.

"What a cynic you are."

"With good reason, I believe, is the appropriate phrase."

She smiled faintly and her voice when she spoke held a derisive note. "Allow me to calm your fears. I brought my pin money, a not ungenerous amount—particularly since I've not had an opportunity to spend any of it the past month. So are we finished here? Or need I be plainer? I want nothing from you but an escort to Edinburgh."

His sudden smile was replete with charm, his dark gaze the devil's own in seductive allure. "Nothing more than that?" he said soft and low. "Are you sure?"

"Damn you, Albion. Of course I want more!"

"Perfect," he said, pulling her close and kissing her lightly without regard for servants. Then taking her hand and resuming his progress, he cheerfully said, "We're well matched you and I."

"You're embarrassing me," she hissed, struggling to pull her hand free.

"We're out in the country. Who's to see?"

"Your servants."

He shot her a look. "You can't be serious. Morning, Rothby." He smiled at his steward who'd come out to greet him. "You're up early."

A solid-built, middle-aged retainer, Rothby kept his gaze on his master; the earl's women were always politely overlooked. "We've been expecting you, sir."

"How are my racers? Doing well on their training gallops I hope."

"Very well, sir. Chambers tells me Golden Pride is tearing up the track."

"I knew he would. I'll be out to the stables directly. I don't suppose cook is up yet."

"Everything is in readiness, sir."

"Good." Albion escorted Felicity into a vast entrance hall where he greeted his waiting major domo, Bagley, and Mrs. Carr, the housekeeper with casual familiarity. He inquired about their families, listened to their replies with genuine interest, mentioned at the last that they would change before breakfast. "Have a maid servant sent upstairs for the lady," he directed, then glanced at Felicity. "I expect you'd like to refresh yourself."

She nodded, not entirely sure what the code of conduct was for a transient paramour in Albion's establishment.

"A bath perhaps?"

"Yes, please." While he was unconcerned with their audience, she couldn't but notice the many servants observing them.

He held her gaze, her chastened tone unlike that of the out-spoken chit he'd been fucking the last two hours. "Say what you like darling. No one cares."

"Then I would like a bath and food in that order and quickly," she briskly said.

He grinned. "That's better. I thought you'd turned bashful."

"I was trying," she replied with a flashing smile.

"You needn't. Come." Moving across the imposing entrance hall manned with liveried flunkeys, they approached a wide oak staircase. "I'll show you upstairs and after breakfast, we'll go to the stables and you can see my splendid racers. You'll be impressed."

"When can we ride them? Soon I hope." She glanced up at him as they mounted the stairs. "I'm impatient."

"You're always impatient," he murmured, his dark gaze amused. "But my racers aren't available until after the meet. I have mounts aplenty in my stables though. We'll go out later in the day."

Reaching the top of the stairs, he paused for a moment. *Did he want her in his suite?*

"Anywhere will do, Albion," she said as if reading his mind. "I don't wish to impose."

He laughed. "Now you tell me."

Her gaze narrowed faintly. "I haven't heard you complain."

"I don't believe I've had time to do anything but service you, my little jade."

"And you've found that oppressive?" she silkily murmured.

"Not at all. You suit me well." A simple acknowledgment that summarily clarified issues of privacy. "Allow me to show you to my rooms."

He left her at the door to his apartments in the care of the maidservant who'd run up behind them. "I'll see you at breakfast." With a graceful bow, he strolled away.

Driven by hunger, Felicity hurried through her bath with only a cursory glance at the marble splendor of the earl's bath chamber. The young maid serving her was cheerful and chatty, not in the least flustered to be ministering to a female guest. The earl must bring women here often Felicity concluded with a twinge of anger—after which she immediately took herself to task for such folly. She was no more than a passing fancy to Albion; she'd do well to remember that.

Now what to wear? she bracingly thought, taking refuge in the practicalities. Rising from the tub in a sluice of scented water, she stepped out onto a sumptuous Turkey carpet.

The maid toweled her dry and wrapped her in a peony pink silk dressing gown of indeterminate origin—another reminder of Albion's prodigality. He must keep a wardrobe at the ready for female visitors.

His hospitality was to be admired, she peevishly thought.

A loud clearing of the maid's throat interrupted her fretful musing.

"This way, mum, if you please," the young girl repeated, waving Felicity into the adjacent dressing room where she found that her gowns had been unpacked and were hanging in a large wardrobe beside Albion's clothes. His tailor must find him a lucrative client, she decided, surveying a great number of coats—mostly black—although some were of colored silk for evening wear.

Had she known that no other woman had been given access to his wardrobe she would have been gratified. But she didn't and querulously wondered instead how many women had preceded her in this bedchamber.

The maid cleared her throat again, Felicity chided herself for acting like a silly schoolgirl and set about choosing a gown. She decided on a daffodil muslin morning gown, dressed with the help of the maid, then sat at the earl's dressing table while the maid pinned up her hair in a froth of curls.

"Jewelry, mum?" The maid glanced at Felicity's open jewel case on the dressing table. "Perhaps that string of pearls or the citrine necklet, mayhap those grand emerald ear-bobs."

*Did the earl like his ladies bejeweled. Did it matter in the least*? "What would his lordship prefer?" she heard herself ask, apparently incapable of censoring her thoughts.

"I wouldn't know, mum. He don't say what he likes or don't when it comes to ladies' jewelry, although he's always ever so nice to"—she paused—"everyone, mum," the young maid diplomatically finished.

Felicity flushed with embarrassment or anger, she wasn't sure which. But she *was* certain that it would be unwise to fall under the spell of a man who was a byword for inconstancy and vice no matter how seductive his allure. Unfortunately, in defiance of logic, a frisson of excitement coursed through her body at recall of his amorous skills.

"Are you cold, mum? Would you like a wrap?"

"No thank you. A bit of a draft touched me," she calmly lied, then vexed when she had no right, she calmly inquired, "Does the earl often entertain guests in his suite?"

The young girl hesitated. "On occasion, mum," she carefully replied. "When his lordship has a right large house party."

"I see." Albion's servants were well disciplined to give nothing away. Not that it made the least difference she decided, striving to maintain her objectivity. But out of a niggling pique, she firmly said, "No jewelry this morning. Now if you'll give me directions to the breakfast room. I'm quite ready."

She made her way after numerous turns through a rabbit warren of passageways to a sunny room at the back of the house where she found Albion at breakfast, deep in conversation with Rothby and another man. The earl had bathed, his hair was still damp, his handsome face tipped slightly toward his steward.

As Felicity entered the room, he looked up, quickly came to his feet, and put down his napkin. He crossed the room to meet her, looking very much the country gentleman in buckskins and a coat of umber wool. "Very pretty, my dear," he said with the careless charm he exercised so effortlessly. "That pale yellow is very becoming on you. Come sit down." He waved her to the table, signaled for a lackey to serve her, and politely inquired as he pulled out her chair, "Coffee or tea?"

"Chocolate, please."

"Chocolate for the lady," he instructed a servant who materialized at his side. "Forgive my lack of attention," he added, addressing Felicity in a quiet voice, "but I'm being apprised of the condition of my racers. Enjoy your breakfast."

He returned to his seat across the table and continued his conversation, asking questions, nodding at his answers, looking up once and growling, "Harvey bought Louder's black? Bastard." Scowling, he almost imperceptibly lifted a finger and when a servant immediately appeared at his side, he said, "Brandy. Quickly."

Felicity saw the men seated on either side of him stiffen and she wondered at the extent of the earl's temper. But a moment later, Albion leaned forward in his chair and smiled at his two companions. "It's not your fault Harvey's a prick," he said in the way of an apology. "We'll just have to see that Golden Pride runs his best. Who's up on him? Farley? Good. He has the best hands in the business. Which race? The first of the afternoon?" Leaning back in his chair, he took the glass of brandy offered him, drank it down, and handed it back to the footman. "Another," he said and entered into a prolonged discussion about the races scheduled on the morrow, the horses entered, and what instructions would best serve his jockeys.

Sometime later, as his two companions rose to leave, a flunkey came in and whispered in his lordship's ear. Albion listened for a moment, then abruptly came to his feet. "If you'll excuse me," he said to Felicity, his face without expression, "a business matter requires my attention."

A woman's voice raised in dissent echoed faintly through the open door.

With a grimace, he tautly added, "I won't be long."

She watched him stride away and was grateful she wasn't about to face his anger.

Rothby and his stable master, Chambers, followed Albion from the room and Felicity was left alone in the large, sunny chamber, save for the liveried servants who stood awaiting orders. Mildly intimidated by the sizable staff, she surreptitiously surveyed the palatial room under their watchful gazes, taking note of the resplendent gilding on the creme-colored paneling, the numerous Montrose portraits looking down from their ornate frames, the fine furniture of recent date. The room had been transformed from the original Tudor design, the east wall now composed entirely of soaring French doors reminiscent of the Gallerie des Glaces at Versailles.

A shrill cry disrupted her musing, the two words, *our child,* shattering the silence of the breakfast room. Shocked and embarrassed, her breathing momentarily arrested, Felicity went motionless, not certain how to react to the disconcerting outburst. Should she get up and leave? Pretend she hadn't heard. Ask for more chocolate?

Saved from a decision by the sudden appearance of the housekeeper bustling into the room, her breathing resumed.

This had nothing to do with her.

*Nothing* at all.

"His lordship thought you might like the paper," Mrs. Carr explained with unruffled calm as she reached the table and set the *Morning Chronicle* before Felicity. "He asks that you wait for him."

Were irate female intruders so commonplace the staff dealt with them unperturbed? So it appeared. "Tell his lordship I await his pleasure," Felicity said with what she hoped was a bland smile.

"Yes, miss." With a bob of her head, the rotund little lady dressed in tailored black silk rustled away. A moment later, the sound of the door shutting behind her reverberated like a thunderclap in the stillness of the room.

Felicity nervously picked up the paper and began to read, or attempted to read, her gaze largely unfocused with her thoughts in turmoil, with so many watchful eyes on her. As she pretended to peruse the news, Felicity debated whether to make her way to Edinburgh without Albion? Would her reputation be more or less compromised if she traveled alone? Was it even possible to withstand the horrors of a journey on the mail coach with all the vulgar scrutiny or worse? It wasn't, of course, she understood, which was the reason she'd chosen to solicit the earl's help in the first place. Profligate though he might be, he would honor his agreement to safely convey her to her aunt's.

So she'd do well to be agreeable until she arrived in Edinburgh.

And continue to bear in mind that Albion's personal affairs were none of her concern.

"Thank you for waiting."

She looked up to see Albion strolling in, his smile charming as ever, his expression once again bland, the anger gone from his eyes.

Taking his seat, he nodded to a flunkey. "Bring me a brandy." Turning to Felicity, he smiled. "Is there anything of interest in the paper?"

"Did you pay her off?" Tact was never her strong suit.

He hesitated a fraction of a second. "Yes, and the child's not mine although I suppose every man says as much."

"I suppose they do."

Ignoring her icy tone, he took the glass offered him and raised it to Felicity. "To better days," he sardonically murmured and poured the contents down his throat.

"Tell me how the child's not yours," she tersely said.

He set his glass down. "It's none of your business."

"I know. Tell me anyway."

"You have no manners," he returned, coolly.

"Surely that's no surprise at this late date."

He held her heated gaze for a moment. "Bring the bottle," he ordered a flunkey before returning his attention to Felicity. "If you must know," he said with a long-suffering sigh, belligerent females not without precedence in his life, "the lady and I haven't been friends for nearly three years. It's impossible for me to have fathered her child—who, by the way," he added with a lift of his brows, "looks to be about six months old, is very sweet, and bears a close resemblance to Tarleton who *has* befriended her of late."

"But you're richer."

"But I'm richer," he gently agreed. "My steward is giving her a bank draft for two thousand." His gaze took on a sardonic cast. "I hope you approve."

"I don't know if I believe you."

"I don't care if you do or not," he said with brutal frankness. Glancing up at a footman who arrived with the brandy, he held out his hand. "Now do you want to go riding?" Uncorking the bottle, he lifted it to his mouth and drank a long draught.

"You drink a great deal."

"That too is none of your concern. Are we riding or are you going to sulk? I warn you, I'm unmoved by female sulks. Consider too," he said, smiling faintly, "I have some of the best horse-flesh in England."

"You're incorrigible," she muttered.

"You've known that from the first. Now, do I go riding alone or do you keep me company?"

She bridled indignantly, exhaled, and finally said, "How can I refuse?"

"How indeed," he drawled.

"If you fall off drunk," she warned, intent on having the last word, "don't expect me to pick you up."

He laughed. "Would you care to make a wager on our riding skills? First one over the highest fence wins."

"How much?" She tried not to smile.

"Whatever you can afford to lose," he answered with a roguish wink.

"Fifty guineas."

"Done. Do you have riding clothes with you? If so, how long before you're outfitted?"

She jumped to her feet, her heart pumping with excitement. She loved riding above all else. "Ten minutes or less. It's some distance to your apartments or I'd only need five."

"Oh ho, a woman after my heart. Can you actually change in five minutes? Another fifty says you can't."

"Don't move. I'll be right back."

With a glance at the clock, he lifted the bottle to his mouth, and watched her race away pell-mell from the room without regard for propriety or manners. Miss Belvoir was most unusual, he pleasantly reflected. She had no missish airs, her sexual appetite matched his, she wasn't inclined to pout overmuch, and she had a passion for horses one rarely found in the opposite sex.

A shame she was of good family.

Otherwise he'd be inclined to set her up in a cozy love nest and avail himself of her many charms from time to time.

Time to time, of course, the operative phrase.

Because the world was full of willing women.

And he liked variety.

# Chapter 10

When Felicity reappeared in the doorway and moved into the breakfast room, Albion set down the bottle he was holding, slid upward in his chair, and regarded her with an unhurried appraisal. "Very nice," he said. "And under ten minutes." He made a small circle in the air with one finger. "Show me the whole."

She stopped and gracefully pirouetted.

"Do you dress this way often?" he softly asked, regarding her with distinct curiosity.

"Meaning?"

His gaze sharpened at her pert response. "Perhaps the question should be instead, do you prefer this attire?"

Her red-gold hair beneath a tricorne hat was tied at the nape of her neck with a black ribbon, her feet were shod in top boots, her slender legs encased in buff breeches, her voluptuous breasts confined beneath a plain linen shirt and a riding coat of blue cloth with silver buttons.

"I do when riding at home. You may stop scowling. It's merely practical."

He was unaccountably relieved when he wouldn't have considered himself so righteous. "Should I call you Frederick and Felicity?" he drawled, libertine impulses quickly reasserting themselves.

Taking off her hat, she swept him a bow. "Whatever pleases you, my lord. But I'll have my fifty guineas."

He dug in his breeches pocket and tossed a bill on the table. "Come closer," he softly said.

She recognized his tone. "You like young boys?" she asked, walking toward him.

He smiled. "I like young ladies who dress like young boys." With the veriest glance, he dismissed the servants.

In the brief interval before Felicity reached the breakfast table, the room emptied. "Are they that frightened of you?"

"No, I just pay them well." Adding more bills to that on the table, he pointed to them and smiled. "What say you to five hundred more to take off your breeches? I've never fucked a beautiful boy."

"Much as I'd like to accede to your wishes, my lord," Felicity sweetly replied, "I'm more intrigued with your offer of prime horseflesh."

His astonishment showed only fleetingly. "You amaze me, Miss Belvoir. I've never known a lady to turn down five hundred guineas. Or," he added with a slow smile, "prefer horses to me."

"I expect you amuse yourself with those of a certain set, my lord. I'm a country lass. Horses are always my first choice."

"I'll have to see if I can change your mind," he said with the assurance shaped by notable success in the boudoir.

"I rather doubt you can once I detect the smell of the stables."

A gleam of amusement and understanding lit his eyes. "I know what you mean, damned if I don't." Coming to his feet, he offered her an elegant bow. "Allow me, my fine sir, to show you my noble steeds."

He guided her through his extensive stables with obvious pride and she inspected his splendid horses with a connoisseur's eye, appraising and praising, comparing the bloodlines with those her mother had bred. She was pleased and excited to once again be witness to such a glorious display of racing stock and she reminisced briefly about the years when her mother's stable had competed with the best. "I shan't sleep a wink tonight thinking of the race meet tomorrow," she said, her eyes alight, exuberance in her voice. "I'm quite giddy at the prospect!"

"There's a little matter of being recognized," he gently reminded her. "With your mother's love of racing, surely there will be people here you know."

"Not when I'm dressed like this." Stepping back, she dramatically flung open her arms. "Behold your new page."

He surveyed her small form doubtfully.

"Don't look at me so, Albion," she fretted, dropping her arms. "You *promised.*"

He hadn't of course. He'd been very careful not to. But her bottom lip began to tremble and he had an aversion to female tears. "Very well," he reluctantly agreed. "But only if you're circumspect."

She launched herself at him in an untrammeled flying leap—which didn't bode well for the prospect of circumspection. Throwing her arms around his waist, she tipped her head back and offered him a dazzling smile. "You're an *absolute, absolute* dear! I don't know how I can *ever* repay you!"

He rather thought he knew how she could, but under the eyes of his trainer and stable lads, he instead gently extricated himself from her grasp. "Come, let's find you a mount and we'll ride out to the gallops."

She made him an elegant leg. "Your servant, my lord."

"As to that, my young page," he quietly said, "you may serve me *after* our ride."

"I know." Her limpid gaze held the artless allure of a young Aphrodite. "I can tell."

He grinned. "How in hell did you manage to stay chaste so long you wanton little tart?"

"I never met you."

Albion raised his brows, opened his mouth to speak, thought better of it, and in lieu of a subject fraught with liabilities, changed the conversation. "I have a nice filly you'll like. This way." He indicated the direction. "She's from Eclipse's line and can outrun just about anything."

She cast him a sidelong look as they moved down the passage between the stalls. "Anything? Why haven't I heard of her?"

"She doesn't race until next season. And at the moment, my black might offer her some competition."

Felicity grinned. "Care to wager? "

"Are you sure you can afford to?"

"Of course. I just won fifty guineas."

He laughed. "You're damned entertaining, Miss Belvoir."

"You're a pleasant diversion as well, your lordship. Even on short acquaintance," she added with a playful wink. "Now about our little competition. Why don't we say two hundred guineas?"

"You must be good." He smiled. "Or reckless."

"Both."

Damn the chit's directness was appealing. Unlike the women he dallied with who flattered and cajoled in varying degrees for sundry reasons. "You're different," he said, half musing.

"From all the coquettish women you know?"

"Yes."

She grinned. "I'll take that as a compliment."

"It was meant as one," he replied, his voice velvet soft.

"I *do* hope you're not changing your mind about riding," she briskly remarked, looking at him askance.

*Christ, he was—damned little temptress.* "No," he smoothly returned, disturbed with her perspicuity, more disturbed with his ungovernable passion for the little chit. "Ah, here we are," he said with relief.

In short order, Felicity was put up on a chestnut filly by the name of Primrose, who had the best set of legs and feet Albion had ever seen; in another year she'd be taking all the race purses and plate.

Albion's black was a brute of a horse with a tremendous stride who liked to win and always had—coming first in every important race the last three years. Tarquin had been retired to stud recently, but racing was still in his blood.

Once mounted, they passed through the stable yard and out to the horse walks leading to the Heath. The Newmarket gallops were consecrated ground: smooth and green as a manicured lawn, lovingly cared for, a training ground for racehorses since ancient times.

As they approached the Heath, Albion came to a halt on a small rise overlooking the broad expanse of bucolic countryside. A light breeze blew from the east, portending rain, but the sky was still free of clouds, the sun brilliant and warm. Resting his gloved hands on the pommel, Albion surveyed the landscape alive with horses and jockeys going through their paces. "What do you think? Does the sight please you? This scene always evokes profound feeling in me. It's my church without walls as it were, the only faith I believe in."

"Well put," Felicity agreed, gazing down on the training canters and gallops that had once been so much a part of her life, had been her mother's passion as long as she could remember. "The lush green of the downs, the familiar bustle of activity, the magnificence of the bloodstock bring back a flood of memories. I've been away too long." Her voice caught for a moment and when she turned to him her eyes were wet with tears. "I feel as though I've walked from prison into the sunshine of the world again."

"Your stepmother should be flogged," he growled.

"Most would agree. Except Papa of course," Felicity added with a sigh.

"She must be damned good in bed," Albion muttered.

"I expect she is. And Papa was very unworldly and susceptible. Now, if you don't mind"—Felicity shot him a telling glance—"I'd prefer talking about something more pleasant."

"I'll race you to that tree on the horizon," Albion quickly offered, never one to miss a cue from a beautiful woman.

Before he'd finished speaking, Felicity had sent her little filly off like a bullet and the race was on. Light in the saddle, her hands lighter still on the reins, Felicity rode like the wind, her hat flying off before she'd gone fifty yards, her cry of delight echoing behind her.

Albion's black set a true gallop right from the start and, moving easily, drew up to challenge the filly. The pair raced together for about a half mile and then flashing a grin at Albion, Felicity tapped Primrose lightly with her whip. The gallant little horse galloped away with the beautiful, easy action of a free runner and the big, long-striding Tarquin dug in and swiftly matched her pace. Neither horse showed the slightest sign of weakening despite the long distance and blazing speed.

The last mile turned out to be an all-out sprint for the finish.

First Albion then Felicity took the lead, the accomplished riders vying for supremacy.

But in the end, Felicity swept past the tree first or Albion let her win or *perhaps* he let her win. It was that close.

After reining in Primrose, Felicity slid from the saddle and Albion followed suit, taking her reins and putting the horses out to graze. Both riders were still breathing hard, as if they'd run the course themselves, and when Felicity dropped onto the grass in a sprawl, Albion joined her, pulling of his gloves and stretching out full-length beside her.

Turning her head, Felicity said, "You let me win. Don't say you didn't." Her quelling look stopped his protest. "Really, Albion, you needn't be so chivalrous. You're already much too wonderful and unbelievably kind," she muttered, restive under her deepening infatuation for a shameless rake. "Say something vicious so I'll hate you instead."

"I don't want you to hate me." His dark gaze was very close and as restive as hers. "I want you to fuck me."

"Oh God, please, don't say that—don't, don't, don't," she whispered even as a perverse rush of desire raced through her senses. "We can't. Not now, not here. People are within sight. What if someone should ride up?"

Rising on one elbow, Albion scanned the distant horses and riders and turning back, blandly smiled. "Did I mention the gallops are almost over? Everyone should be gone in ten minutes."

Her gaze instantly narrowed. "You knew all along," she hotly said. "But then you've done this countless times before with countless women I expect. Or do some of your lovers take issue with making love on the grass?"

"I've never asked them."

She blushed furiously at his mild reply and her misplaced resentment. "How gauche of me to take you to task," she said with chagrin. "You must think me terribly rude *and* naive. You see, you *should* have said something awful to me so I wouldn't have been so stupid."

He had been watching her with amusement. "Darling, say what you like, do what you like, scold me if you wish," he added, carelessly brushing her cheek with his finger. "Chastise me at will."

"So you say because women never do," she answered, fretful and moody when she had no right. "Men order the world to their liking with unquestioning authority and a good deal of overbearing presumption," she grumbled, discontent overruling practicalities like their very new acquaintance.

"I plead guilty to the collective indictment of my gender," he gently said, not unaware of the discrepancies. "I'd be happy to apologize if it helps."

She snorted. "Am I supposed to be appeased with that nonchalant offer?" Quite unintentionally she'd taken up the gender argument. But then she'd been cruelly used in recent months and was much put out by what she considered the restraints imposed on her sex. "I spurn your apology," she scoffed.

Albion grinned. "As would my mother. You two would get along."

Felicity lifted her brows. "I hardly think we'll meet."

"That may be, but only because she's in Paris. As for the rest, Maman is very independent. Papa married her out of hand after she stopped his chaise one night on Hounslow Heath. She was playing highwayman on a dare and very nearly shot Papa dead when her pistol went off." His smile was benign. "We are not a conventional family."

"Our family, too, was unconventional," Felicity said with a sigh. "Papa very happily kept to his books, Maman occupied herself with her stables, and my brother and I were allowed to do very much as we pleased. I was regarded as somewhat of a hoyden"—her brows lifted faintly—"in my former life."

Albion smiled. "Why am I not surprised?"

"You'd be bored to tears if I were a proper young lady," she said with unflattering frankness.

"If you were a proper young lady, my wager would have been won in your bedchamber, I would have been back at Brooks within the hour, and I wouldn't have had time to be bored," he tranquilly replied, immune to aspersions on his character.

"Personally, I find this more gratifying," she noted, ever candid and pragmatic. "I expect you do as well."

He didn't immediately answer, not in the habit of discussing his feelings. Or more to the point—his ambiguous feelings. "Yes," he finally replied, opting for bland consent. "This is more gratifying. Now, in the interests of augmenting that gratification," he added with a smile, habits of a lifetime coming to the rescue of earnest emotion, "what would you say, my young page, to kissing your master before ministering to his—"

His smile abruptly disappeared. He'd heard his name faintly

in the distance. When the cry rang out again—louder this time—
Felicity flinched at the sound.

"I *told* you we'd be seen," she whispered in dismay.

"I'll take care of this," Albion firmly said to allay the panic in
her eyes. "You're with me. You're safe." Sitting up, he squinted
into the sun and softly swore. "Devil take it." His lip curled in
disgust. "I don't bloody believe it."

"Oh God, it's my parents, isn't it?" Coming up on her elbows,
Felicity nervously scanned the distant Heath.

"No, it's worse. It's bloody Harvey," he grumbled. "What the
*hell* does he want?"

Her alarm instantly disappeared, relief washed over her in a
tidal wave, and she lapsed once again into a comfortable sprawl.
"Surely you know." She'd overheard the conversation at breakfast. "Louder's black won widely last season. He's come to stake
his horse against your Golden Pride."

"Couldn't it wait until tomorrow?" Albion said with asperity.

"I don't understand how he knew you were up here."

Albion jerked his head toward their horses silhouetted against
the horizon. "Tarquin's size is unmistakable. I should have teth-
ered the horses out of sight." He suddenly frowned. "Harvey isn't
acquainted with you, is he?" he asked, concerned for her anonymity.

Felicity shook her head.

Albion's brow cleared. "In that case, we'll just brazen it out.
As my page you needn't speak unless I give you leave."

"Yes, master." Her gaze was misleadingly innocent. "Your
wish is my command."

"Vixen," he said with a lazy smile. "See that you obey me as
dutifully once Harvey's gone. Now—sit up, my pet, we're about
to go on stage," he quietly added before coming to his feet and
turning to the approaching horseman. "To what do I owe this
early morning pleasure, Harvey?"

"I caught sight of your brute of a horse." The viscount brought
his mount to a halt and waved his whip in Tarquin's direction. "I
understand he's standing stud and has sired eight promising foals
already. I don't suppose you'd be willing to sell him?"

"I don't suppose so." Albion cooly surveyed the burly man.
"Now if you don't mind, I'm presently occupied, you're intrud-
ing—*and* you're blocking my view."

At Albion's pointed rebuff, Harvey's gaze shifted to the earl's companion and after a slow, comprehensive appraisal, a leer creased his fleshy face. "I didn't think your taste ran to boys, Albion."

"The lad's my page. Unlike you I don't fuck my pages."

"Alas, we can't all be so fastidious."

"Or in your case, even slightly fastidious—your recent revels at the docks a case in point."

"Is nothing private anymore?" the viscount observed with patent insincerity.

"Not when your orgies occur in public taverns."

"My word, Albion. You're frightening your little page with talk of orgies," the viscount silkily remarked, openly ogling Felicity who had turned pale under his coarse inspection.

*Christ, the prick was scaring Felicity.* "I'll stake five thousand on my bay tomorrow," Albion abruptly said. He wanted the bastard gone.

"Ten," the viscount replied without shifting his lecherous gaze. "Your page has such *lovely* blond hair and enchanting eyes. Unusual—that shade of violet; quick remarkable." His attention was fixed on Felicity. "You wouldn't be interested in selling him would you?"

"Not to you. I'd sooner shoot him."

"My, my," the viscount softly mocked. "Perhaps we should ask the lad whether you hold his life too cheap."

"Maybe we should ask him if he'd rather I shoot you?"

"Ecod, Albion. No servant is worth such unhealthy choler," Harvey drolly remarked, contemplating Felicity's ashen hue with amusement. "I rescind my offer. Now, do we have a wager at ten?" the viscount indolently inquired, turning to the earl.

"Yes, ten. Now get the hell out of here," Albion said. "Or stay at your peril."

Of the opinion that Albion was more interested in returning to his pleasure than putting a bullet through anyone, Harvey suavely smiled. "Until tomorrow then. Is Farley up for you?"

"As always. You have Chetly I hear. Good luck. You'll need it."

Suspicion arched the viscount's brows. "You don't like Chetly?"

"I like him well enough. I just don't trust him."

"He's the best in the business," Harvey pugnaciously retorted.

"I agree. Now, are we finally quit of your company?" he said with impatience.

"We?" A sardonic sneer curled the viscount's lip. "Rousseau has much to answer for if even you've taken up his radical principles. Take care, Albion, or your authority in your household will be gravely subverted."

"I don't anticipate problems with my authority. I pay my staff too well. *Good day,* Harvey," Albion said, his expression uniquely unpleasant.

The viscount dipped his head, the faintest of smiles on his thick lips. "Good day to you, Albion. And good day to you my pretty little maid. When Albion tires of you have him send you my way," he said, wheeling his horse. "I'll show you some real sport."

Albion swore for a considerable time after Harvey rode away, consigning the viscount to hell in a surprising number of languages, taking time between curses to apologize to Felicity for Harvey's crude behavior. Apologizing as well for not being able to openly protect her.

"It would have given rise to questions. I understand," she said. "He's an enemy of sorts I gather."

"An annoyance more like. Not that the world wouldn't be the better for his absence. But he's too much of a coward to ever meet me with pistols drawn." Albion delivered another startling variety of expletives in emphasis.

Felicity was impressed with Albion's fluency, although his repertoire might not extend to ordering a meal or hiring a chaise. But curious, when his curses faded away, she asked, "How many languages do you speak?"

He looked bewildered for a moment, his thoughts focused on the ramifications of Harvey's visit. "Six," he absently said, adding more somberly, his brows drawn together with concern, "Harvey's very likely to make trouble for you. I might send you north with Perkins for safety."

"I won't go," Felicity mutinously retorted. "I came to see the races! You *promised!* Besides," she said, her jaw set in defiance, "he doesn't know me."

"He might have heard about the wager," Albion muttered, dropping down beside her on the grass. "You had. Who knows how many others are privy to the gossip. Perhaps your parents have sent out the Runners by now. Bow Street could be hard on your trail. Be sensible. Let me send you north with Perkins."

"Kiss me and I'll think about it."

"Little witch," he grumbled. "You're not helping."

"Harvey doesn't know me—really he doesn't. There's no way he can associate me with your wager even if he heard about it." She refrained from saying Albion had unleashed hitherto unknown desires she intended to gratify at least within the defined limits of race week. She said instead, "I'll be gone in a few days. I promise to stay out of Harvey's way."

"Nevertheless, he's dangerous. With the bad blood between us, you could get caught in the middle."

"I won't wear these clothes. I'll choose some other disguise. I'll be like a mouse in the corner at your race stand," she argued. "No one will even notice me."

"Somehow I doubt that," he drily said. The chit would turn heads even dressed in sackcloth.

"Let me stay please, *please!*" she entreated. "You won't be sorry."

"I'm already sorry." After Harvey's parting remarks, all bets were off apropos Felicity's anonymity.

"No, you're not." She reached out and brushed her fingers over the prominent bulge in his breeches. "You like me," she softly said. "*He* likes me even more."

Albion didn't move, or breathe, or so much as twitch an eyelash as he called on every bit of willpower to curb his hotspur desires. "You *are* damned likeable," he said through clenched teeth, vowing to toss the seriously compromised Miss Belvoir into his coach the minute they returned to his race box and send her off to her aunt in Edinburgh.

"Thank you," she blandly replied, as if accepting a trifling compliment. "Personally, I find *this*"—she trailed her finger up the impressive length of his engorged penis stretching the soft buckskin of his breeches—"*extraordinarily* likeable."

He sucked in his breath as his cock swelled larger.

"Oh look, how *huge* he's gotten!" She looked up, her smile sweet as candy. "I do wish I could feel him deep inside me. I'd be *ever* so grateful."

Having lived a life of considerable license—some would say of unbridled license—Albion was ill-equipped to long withstand temptation. "Damn you, you enticing little jade," he growled, better judgment abruptly jettisoned to the demons of lust. Swiftly coming up on his knees, he shoved her back with the flat of his palm, and roughly spread her legs with one hand while unbuttoning his breeches with the other. "You're nothing but trouble," he muttered, transferring his attention to the buttons on Felicity's breeches. "What the fuck am I going to do with you?"

"Give me what I want," Felicity tranquilly replied, helping him slide her breeches down her hips. "And keep giving it to me until I can't move or you can't—preferably me if I'm allowed to be selfish."

"Any other orders?" he muttered.

She lifted her foot so he could pull off her boot, aware of his heavy breathing, confident of the current tide of events. "Why shouldn't I ask for what I want when I have only a few days to enjoy your gorgeous cock." She raised her other foot.

He frowned, his gaze unreadable. "Why not," he finally said, tossing her second boot aside, quickly stripping off her breeches, jettisoning all the heretical complexities for the more immediate pleasures of the flesh. "It seems I have my work cut out for me."

"I'd be more than willing to help in any way," she purred, easing her thighs wider as he settled—booted, spurred, and minimally disrobed—between her legs. "Although I understand you hold several records in terms of endurance and stamina. Don't look so surprised. Your dedication to carnal sport is much heralded in female circles. In fact, I fully understand how"—She got no further.

Albion rammed his cock into Miss Belvoir's very receptive cunt.

She gasped.

He caught his breath.

And for a shuddering moment only raw, overwrought sensation held sway. Too raw, too overwrought—disturbing. Albion resented the violent sensations this outspoken chit provoked.

"Hurry!"

He drew in a breath, hard, through his nostrils. "You want me to hurry?"

She met his gaze, hers as heated as his. "Yes, now!"

While he was always more than willing to accommodate his lovers, they didn't as a rule give him orders. "Yes, ma'am." His voice was melodious, his gaze intent, disconcerting, his manner of doing her bidding his own. He took her like a sailor on shore leave—quickly, selfishly, crudely, without thought for anything but an expeditious orgasm that would put an end to his unrestrained, headstrong passions. But damn the chit, she climaxed first like the little tart she was and taking offense when it had never mattered before who came first or at all, he inexcusably retaliated and ejaculated in her.

An incredibly stupid act he understood a heartbeat later.

For the second time.

She was damnably hot-blooded, he was unspeakably reckless, or vice versa he decided a moment later, because she was thanking him in phrases like *everlasting bliss* and *heaven on earth* and it was impossible to stay angry with such a grateful little wanton.

"You're entirely welcome," he whispered, as if he wasn't facing a potential paternity suit. "And forgive my ferocity. It won't happen again."

"I don't mind. I suppose I shouldn't say so, but being dominated is terribly arousing." She smiled up at him as he rested above her, his weight only lightly felt. "You're very powerful and large—all over," she said, her voice suddenly softening and dropping in volume. "Umm—I can feel you everywhere, inside and out, mostly inside which is ever so delicious."

"You feel hot." His voice came from deep in his chest, a low guttural sound. "And slick as silk. I wouldn't be surprised if you were ready to climax again."

"You would know," she whispered.

But she shifted her hips in the faintest of undulations that made him think: *she's a natural.* His smile was very close and wicked. "I think I'll make you wait this time."

"You could try." A sultry challenge accompanied by a sorceress's smile.

"Fifty guineas says I can."

"Do you bet on anything?"

"Pretty much, although I've had good luck with you—win or lose."

She laughed.

"I felt that. Very nice. See what you think of this." He slid his hands under her bottom, pulled her into his erection, and plunged deeper with exquisite deliberation until he met the entrance to her womb.

She softly gasped, her eyes went shut, and she lay motionless as the fierce pleasure vibrated through her body. Long moments later, she opened her eyes and smiled. "You're going to lose your fifty guineas."

He shook his head. "You're going to beg before I'm done with you."

She practically climaxed on the spot and if he hadn't quickly withdrawn she would have.

"There now," he quietly said when she'd stopped quivering. "Are we ready for more?"

She glared at him. "I hate you."

"No you don't."

"I *should* hate you."

He smiled. "That's different and you're probably right."

"But not just yet."

"No, not for three days."

"I may not last. I may die of rapture first."

"That wouldn't be very useful for me."

She smiled. "Am I useful?"

"Very."

She raised her hips slightly. "Then perhaps you could return the favor."

Their ideas of favors given, received, and returned in full measure kept them on the Heath for several hours. Albion gave up any pretense of caution apropos paternity; an aberration that would have been unforgivable if he hadn't been reduced to the level of brute lust.

Felicity had no means of evaluating the inexplicable craving that disallowed the possibility of satiation. She had never conceived of either desire or its fiery conclusion in terms of such shocking, incomprehensible wonder. But a child of impulse, she gave herself up to the glory and in truth begged as Albion had predicted—over and over and over again.

Until finally, gasping, she pushed him away. "Wait—wait!"

"No," he said, because he'd long ago lost control, he was approaching another orgasm and he'd barely heard her in any case.

"Damn it! Stop! Stop!" She pounded on his chest with the strength of desperation.

He brushed her hands away without interrupting the hard, pounding rhythm of his lower body.

Turning her head, she sank her teeth into his arm.

He jerked back at the sudden pain.

"Stop!" she screamed.

He glanced down, her voice finally registered in his fevered brain and with a furious oath, he rolled off her just as he climaxed.

She watched his seed spurt in a wide trajectory as he held his erection away from his stomach and arched his back against the explosive delirium racking his body. She saw his angry scowl as well but didn't care—damn him!

He was still glowering when he sat up a few moments later, grabbed his shirt, wiped himself off, and shot her a black look. "I'm ready to go whenever you are."

"You're a brute."

"Yes, and you're the randiest female I've ever run across. Don't blame me."

"I am *not* the randiest female."

He'd been reaching for his breeches and turned back. "The randiest, Miss Belvoir, bar none—and I should know."

"That's not very polite," she pettishly said.

"It's even less polite to stop me mid-orgasm."

"How was I to know that?"

"You couldn't tell?"

"I'm afraid I'm not as experienced as your other—"

"Randy tarts?"

"How dare you!"

He drew in a breath, got up, and shoved one leg into his breeches. "A word of advice, Miss Belvoir." He shoved in the other leg and pulled the buckskins up his lean flanks. "When you've fucked a man for hours, it's a little late to play the demure maid. That's best done before." He swiftly fastened his buttons.

"Thank you. I'm sure you know of what you speak."

"I do." He leaned down and picked up his jacket. "Do you need help dressing?"

"Certainly not!"

Leaving his jacket open over his bare chest, he grabbed one of his boots and put it on. "Then I'll fetch the horses." He pulled on his second boot.

"Maybe I'll stay here."

"Get dressed or I'll haul you back naked," he said and walked away.

By the time he came back with the horses, his temper had cooled along with his frenzied nerve endings, the chit was dressed and waiting, and damned if she didn't look desirable as hell. "I apologize." His voice was much kinder. "You will find men who are interrupted in the middle of an orgasm can be hot-tempered. I apologize as well for being such a brute. For that I have no excuse." He shrugged, his hair laying loose on his shoulders stirring with his movement. "It's out of the ordinary for me, so," he said with a faint smile, "I expect you're to blame. I mean that as a compliment, a most profound compliment. You are a rare jewel, Miss Belvoir."

"Felicity," she said, smiling back. How could one remain angry with a man who offered such lavish praise, was as beautiful as Albion, and more to the point offered such exceptional pleasure. And she rather liked being called a rare jewel. "You are excellent at delivering the most gratifying orgasms, my lord. Once I rest, I'm sure I shall be wanting more."

He laughed. "I must have done something to please the gods. Come, give me a kiss."

She stood on tiptoe and gave him a chaste kiss. "Until later."

"I wait with bated breath," he teased.

Then he tossed her up on Primrose, mounted Tarquin, and the young couple so well matched in carnal desires, slowly rode home in quiet companionship.

# Chapter 11

While the Earl of Albion and Miss Belvoir were otherwise engaged, Harvey had ridden into town and stopped at the Jockey Club Coffee Room to socialize and more importantly, dispense his newest bit of gossip. With the training gallops over, the Coffee Room was teeming with owners and breeders, young bucks and old hands—all animatedly discussing the next day's race card, the merits of various horses, and the latest on-dits.

Harvey's recent purchase of Louder's black stallion, Negus, was generating a flurry of wagers for the morrow's race with bets running high—the odds nearly even between the champion black and Albion's bay. Harvey added to the furor by announcing his sizable personal wager with Albion to some acquaintances at the door and the news quickly spread through the crowd.

Scanning the throng, Harvey spotted some cronies and, making his way through the crush, joined them at a table in one of the alcoves. His friends were sharing the contents of a punch bowl rather than drinking coffee, reason enough to seek their company. After assuaging his thirst with a long draught of the potent brew and assuring them all that Negus was in fine form, Lord Harvey leaned back in his chair and casually remarked, "I chanced to meet Albion out on the Heath where he was enjoying the company of his pretty young page."

Every man jack's gaze rounded on him.

"Needless to say he didn't wish to be disturbed," Harvey drolly noted.

"You must be foxed." Lord Howard arched one brow. "Albion would no sooner take up with a boy than Prinny. Both those young cunthounds wouldn't waste a glance on a lad."

Harvey smiled. "She's only dressed like a boy."

A communal *Ahhh* wafted through the air in acknowledgment, Albion's reputation intact.

"So who's the bit o'fluff?" an old wag drawled.

"Is she bought and paid for or a chit with a pedigree?" the Avery sprig lazily queried. Albion amused himself with democratic scope.

"Devil a bit, I wish I had his good looks," a Yorkshire baronet groused. "Albion has only to stand still and women cluster around him like bees to honey. As for a pedigree, he don't care so long as the pretties spread their legs."

"This one was no lightskirt I'd warrant," Harvey said. "She could still blush."

"And a beauty for cert if Albion's mounting her." Captain Sydney raised his tankard. "I'd be willing to take seconds."

"I already put in my bid," Harvey rebutted. "You'll have to take thirds."

Lord Banbury snorted. "As if Albion would accommodate you, Harvey. He'd sooner see the wench locked in a nunnery."

"Or sent home ruined."

A sudden silence greeted old Napier's remark.

"What do you know that we don't?" Banbury silkily inquired, his piercing gaze on the white-haired baron.

"Only that Belvoir's daughter is missing. She'd been locked away and now she's disappeared. Talk is she was part of some wager between Albion and his friends." The elderly roue smiled faintly. "A wager over a virgin."

"Albion don't fancy virgins," Lord Mortimer's heir bluntly declared.

"Maybe she wasn't," a man standing on the periphery of the table suggested. "Word has it Albion can smell willing cunt a mile away."

"Did I mention twenty thousand was at stake in this sporting venture?" Napier divulged with a sly smile.

Harvey leaned forward, his attention suddenly focused on Napier, his eyes like slits. "Describe this Belvoir chit."

Napier shrugged. "Can't." Nor did any other man at the table have cause to know a virgin.

"Does Belvoir have the Runners out?" The possibility of scoring a victory over Albion galvanized Harvey's attention. Ruining young ladies of quality might be an outrage even the shameless earl couldn't shrug off.

Napier shook his head. "Don't know. My man heard the tale third hand from a groom who knew a groom who knew a groom. The tale *might* be only salacious rumor. Now I have five thousand to wager tomorrow," he said, the question of virginal chits of little consequence compared to the coming race. "Reassure me that your black with Chetly up will win tomorrow—or should I bet on Albion's bay? Chetly can be unreliable."

Irritated at having Albion's opinion substantiated, Harvey bristled. "Do what you like. I'm not your bloody keeper."

"Farley was thrown last month," one man pointed out. "From what I hear, he's not completely recovered yet." At which point, the relative merits of both jockeys as well as the two thoroughbreds took over the conversation. Disagreement was loud and vociferous, considerable drink adding both confusion and spice to the arguments. Thanks to male priorities, rumors of missing virgins quickly gave way to more important matters having to do with hazarding large sums on the ponies.

Obsessed with the notion of humbling Albion, Harvey soon excused himself from the conversation and made his way to a quiet corner in the adjoining club room where he had a footman bring him writing materials. After briefly debating his message, he put pen to paper, addressed his note to Lord and Lady Belvoir and began without salutation.

*You might wish to pay a visit to Lord Albion at Newmarket in regard to your missing daughter. She's been seen in his company.*

He signed it: *A well-wisher.*

Harvey didn't care whether the chit with Albion was Belvoir's daughter or not. Even if she wasn't the missing virgin, he suspected Albion's amorous holiday would be rather violently disrupted. The thought brought a wicked smile to his lips. He would

have been willing to pay a small fortune to witness the con-
tretemps—but, alas, he would have to content himself with at
least disturbing Albion's little rendezvous.

Or with luck, ruining his gilded future.

If the chit was Belvoir's virginal daughter, he doubted even the
powerful Marquess of Pembroke could save his son from an expeditious marriage.

Sealing the missive, he handed it to a waiting footman. "Have
this carried to London immediately." He offered the servant
some bills to defray the cost of a messenger. "When he returns,
have the man bring me word that the letter was delivered. Understood?"

Regardless that Harvey was loathed by the Jockey Club staff
for his abusive manner, nonetheless, a nobleman must be obeyed.
That didn't necessarily mean the footman was required to carry
out his lordship's orders with dispatch.

Nor did he.

Harvey's note arrived at the Belvoir home well after midnight.

Which meant it wasn't delivered to its addressee until Charlotte woke slightly before noon the next day. Since Lord Belvoir
was away from home searching for Felicity, the letter was conveyed to his wife with her breakfast tray.

After picking up the folded sheet of paper, Charlotte scrutinized the rough script and wondered if she should open it. While
her husband was agreeable in most matters, he never discussed
his business affairs with her.

Yet—*Lady* Belvoir was plainly penned on the address.

"Who brought this?" She held up the letter and looked at her
maid, a slight frown on her comely face.

"The night porter received it very late, my lady. He didn't recognize the messenger."

"That will be all, Watters."

Charlotte waited until her personal maid closed the door behind her. The prissy old woman was a long-time member of Lucien's household and while she'd prefer a new maid her husband
didn't agree. And one had to prioritize one's battles with a husband after all; there were more important issues than maids.

Like getting rid of his defiant daughter.

And seeing that he substantially increased her allowance.

After that, she could turn to lesser matters like replacing Watters.

Once alone, she ripped open the seal on the letter and quickly read the brief note. Then she set the missive on her tray, leaned back against her pillows and smiled an exceedingly satisfied smile.

*What splendid news. She'd never thought to look so high as Albion. Perhaps her stepdaughter was a clever little baggage after all.*

*Imagine the Belvoir name linked with the illustrious Montroses!*

*Just imagine! she gleefully reflected, having Albion as a son-in-law.*

*How very convenient.*

Now then, she pragmatically reflected, what should she wear to face her future son-in-law? Her new azure silk she decided. It showed off her figure to advantage and the color matched her eyes.

Quickly tossing back the covers, Charlotte bellowed for Watters and in short order she had the household in a frenzy. She must look her best today, her bags must be packed, the carriage brought round, a note left for her husband. There was no need to explain more than that she was off to Newmarket for the races with a party of friends. Lucien disliked parties in any event, nor would she appreciate his company when she surprised the unsuspecting pair.

There was no question in her mind that she was infinitely more capable of handling the situation; Lucien was too lenient when it came to his daughter's outrageous behavior. Hadn't it taken her considerable amorous exertion to convince him that a bit of discipline would do the awful girl some good. She wasn't about to take the chance that Felicity would dissuade her father from the *proper* conclusion to this scandal. And God knows the little tart might.

Marriage was the only remedy of course. She had every intention of seeing that the Belvoir and Montrose families were united in holy matrimony. For any number of reasons, the least of them Felicity's happiness. The Montroses' enormous wealth primarily, their exalted title secondly, and not to be discounted, the fact that Albion would become a member of their family.

A very *close* member.

Naturally, she expected him to resist, but he would find that she was not a woman to be trifled with. She doubted very much that he'd want his parents to weigh in on his disgraceful behavior. When it came to seducing an innocent young maid, there were limits even for a man as rash as Alex.

And so she would warn him.

# Chapter 12

The day at the races was all that Felicity imagined and considerably more in terms of sybaritic pleasure. Albion barred admittance to his private race stand, posting two burly footmen at the door to turn away his raucous friends. They all took noisy issue with their unaccountable exclusion and on one particularly rackety occasion Albion had to go outside and personally send them away. His rumpled clothing caused ribald comment from his inebriated chums, but it also brought understanding—of a sort. To their irreverent proposal of perhaps sharing in Albion's amusements—a circumstance not without precedence among the wild young bloods—he offered a terse, baffling reply. "I don't share."

Which of course was completely untrue.

But then he followed up that gross fabrication with a more alarming statement. "If anyone chooses to argue, I'd be more than happy to meet them at dawn next week."

The door was slammed in their faces and since no one chose to die on the dueling field over some fille de joie that Albion had taken a fancy to, the rowdy throng dispersed.

Albion bent to kiss the nape of Felicity's neck when he returned to the viewing balcony. "They won't be back," he whispered, sliding his arms around her waist and leaning into her. "What did I miss?"

She glanced at him over her shoulder. "Templeton's jockey smashed into Mercer's chestnut on the straight and nearly took him out."

"But Johnny Fife whipped him off," Albion said.

She smiled. "Of course. Did you threaten your friends?"

"Of course," he mimicked.

"I do adore you when you're masterful," she purred. "Not," she added with a grin, "that I don't adore you every other way too."

"Speaking of every other way," he murmured, beginning to unbutton his breeches. "I might let you scream this time."

She spun around in his arms. "Don't you dare."

"It's up to you."

"No, it's not and you know it."

He smiled. "Are you saying I'm in charge?"

She didn't answer for the space of two heartbeats. "Perhaps in some ways," she allowed and then she smiled too. "At least for three days. I suggest you take advantage of the situation."

"You don't have to tell me twice." In truth, horny as he was, Albion wouldn't have been able to keep his hands off her—a circumstance he realized deviated sharply from normal custom *and* didn't bear close scrutiny. Fortunately, there was little or no time for reflection that day for he was kept fully occupied accommodating his companion's ravenous appetite for sex.

Their passion for racing as well as their lust were happily fulfilled by an arrangement that allowed the earl to fuck his lovely companion as she leaned against the balcony rail and watched the races. Since they were both relatively clothed should anyone choose to look up, it wouldn't have been apparent that Felicity's skirt and petticoats were tossed up in back and Albion's breeches were unbuttoned. In all respects, the couple appeared to be nothing more than conventional race goers while, in fact, they were engaged in the most delectable sexual intercourse.

Albion was consistently in rut, Felicity was insatiable, the races thrilling to behold, the fortuitous convergence of pleasures a phenomenon of unspeakable delight. The young pair explored rapture with an unquenchable gluttony that blotted out all but exquisite physical sensation and the narrow field of green grass and racing bloodstock. It was as perfect a day as an imperfect world allowed, or to fevered brains and lustful sensibilities perhaps unequivocal perfection.

The earl's thoroughbreds won all their races, although Albion found himself experiencing a profound sense of triumph quite apart from the thrill of victory. He couldn't remember when he'd enjoyed himself more. And so he told Felicity between kisses and the slow, lazy rhythm of his lower body sliding to and fro inside her. "You're unbelievable," he whispered. "Hot and silky sweet. I'm bewitched you little witch, horny as hell and considerably richer in more than money. You deserve at least half my winnings— probably more," he rasped, gripping her hips firmly, flexing his legs and plunging deeper, holding her captive with his rigid cock.

"No—no," she protested, breathless in the throes of passion, another orgasm hovering, mounting. "I can't . . . take . . . your money."

"Take it or I'll stop." He began to withdraw.

"Yes, yes," she gasped, at the mercy of her frenzied craving. "Whatever . . . you . . . want."

He drove back in, burying himself to the hilt, knowing full well what he wanted. More of the lush, liquid heat surrounding his cock. More of the hot, greedy cunt that lured him. More of the tantalizing witch who made his life sweet.

"Tell me you need this," he growled, ramming his cock a modicum deeper, as if brute force would wrest from her an answer commensurate with his own gut-wrenching desire. His nostrils flared. "Tell me!"

"Yes, yes, always—always," she cried, shameless in her need, so overwhelmed by longing she would have willingly promised him anything. "God, please, stay, stay—don't go, please—*don't!*"

But he did briefly before plunging back in, her blissful sigh imprinting itself on his willful soul with a jarring smack. When it shouldn't. When he'd never felt anything so ridiculous. When it didn't matter in the least, he quickly decided, relegating the disconcerting feeling to quixotic vanity, focusing instead on bringing them both to orgasm again. Competently as it turned out—and frequently, his sexual talents well honed—his orgasmic frenzy his habitual remedy for unwanted reflection.

It was twilight when they left his race stand, the track largely deserted, Albion's coachman was asleep under the carriage, the sky a pale lavender streaked with the trailing vestiges of a golden sunset.

Sweetly naive and only human, Felicity couldn't help but enjoy Albion's charming attentions. "Today was the absolutely best day of my life," she whispered, resting in Albion's arms as they were driven home. "The races and sex and you all together were utter *bliss!*"

He was mildly unnerved to find himself in agreement, but in his experience passion was fleeting—along with Miss Belvoir's sojourn in Newmarket. So he comfortably replied, "I agree. It couldn't have been a better day."

Felicity's eyes suddenly filled with tears and in a stricken tone, she whispered, "Kiss me—now, now, *now.*" All too soon her holiday in paradise would end.

He couldn't see her face as she lay against his shoulder, but he heard the tremor in her voice and when in the past he would have flinched at the woeful sound, he willingly obliged her. Shifting her in his arms, he kissed her gently like one would a fretful child, soothing her misery, whispering sweet love words that were almost true between kisses, promising her another day at the races because he knew how to beguile a horse mad young lady sniffing back her tears.

He was gratified to feel her relax in his embrace and a moment later, she drew back and smiled up at him. "How do you do it? How do you know how to make me happy?"

He couldn't say he knew a thousand ways to please his lovers. "It's easy because you make me happy too," he said instead, mildly surprised at his honesty.

"Thank you."

Her face was uplifted and shining, her violet eyes quite the loveliest eyes he'd ever seen, he thought, when they glowed like that. "No, thank *you,*" he said in another instance of rare earnestness. Then, not completely lost to all reason, he grinned and added, "Good God, I'll be spouting poetry next."

"Not unless it's about horses," Felicity sportively warned, knowing they had come very close to blundering into the realm of affection.

"There once was a filly from Araby," Albion sportively intoned. "Who—"

"Stop, stop," Felicity said with a giggle. "Kiss me instead."

He did, then he pulled her closer. Felicity snuggled against his chest and the return journey passed without further forays into dangerous emotion.

When the carriage came to a stop at Albion's race box, he lifted Felicity down, took her hand, and moved toward the house. Moments later, the door was opened for them and on stepping into the entrance hall they found Rothby pacing, a distraught Bagley at his heels, the scent of disaster in the air.

"Problems?" Albion asked. Any number of difficulties could have arisen from his newest liaison.

"Yes, sir," Rothby nervously replied. "Bagley summoned me, sir, when a visitor—"

Albion frowned. "Is it my father?"

"No, sir. There's a woman in the green drawing room who threatened to call in the local magistrate if I didn't allow her to wait for you. I thought you'd prefer—"

The strain across Albion's shoulders vanished. "You did the right thing. Thank you, Rothby. I'll take care of this." Anyone other than his father was manageable. "The green drawing room you say?"

"Yes, sir."

"Why don't you go upstairs, darling," he quietly suggested, taking in Felicity's anxious expression, releasing her hand. "God knows what it is, but you needn't be involved."

"May I disagree," a melodious female voice replied from across the hall. "She's very much involved. How lovely to see you again, Alex."

Albion recognized the voice and as he turned and saw the familiar figure he thought—*so that was the Charlotte who married Felicity's father.* She'd changed very little in eight years; she was still in the full bloom of her looks, a glossy bijou of a woman with a stone-hard heart to match.

"You know her!" Felicity hissed.

"We've met." He was standing perfectly still.

"You were a darling," Charlotte said with a gratified smile, having heard the umbrage in Felicity's voice. "Such youthful enthusiasm."

Felicity glared at him.

"Acquit me," he muttered. "I was sixteen." *And Charlotte had been between twenty-six and two thousand.* He shot a glance at the hovering servants. "Why don't we discuss whatever we have to discuss in private. Or," he added, with little hope of success, "if you'd rather wait upstairs, I'll speak to your stepmother alone."

"I don't think so," Felicity replied in blighting accents.

"I'll explain later," he said under his breath.

"I have no interest in your explanation," she icily retorted, advancing stiffly toward the doorway where her stepmother waited.

He should walk away. Last week, he would have. Two days ago, he would have. Had he not always avoided any claims on him? *Fuck.* He dubiously took note of Felicity's rigid spine, perceived with foreboding the smug smile on Charlotte's face, knew he'd be caught in the middle when all hell broke loose. For another second, he didn't move. Then ignoring the conventional wisdom having to do with stepping into the lion's den, he thought, *What the fuck. How bad can it be?*

"You're looking very handsome, darling Alex," Charlotte whispered as he approached her.

"You're looking troublesome." He conveyed brisk impatience. "This isn't some Drury Lane farce, Charlotte. Keep it in mind."

"I defer to your judgment," she sweetly replied. "Although some might say your entire life would serve as scintillating entertainment at Drury Lane. I particularly recall that day at Hampton Court when you couldn't wait until the concert was over. The Countess of Denbigh still teases me about that."

"Jesus," he disgustedly said. "Do you mind?"

Charlotte glanced at Felicity who stood waiting in the drawing room. "Perhaps she'd like to hear of your many exploits?"

"If you dare, I swear, I'll strangle you."

"My, my, such vehemence, darling. I remember that lovely temper of yours. Always so sexually gratifying," she purred.

He swept past her with a look of noticeable animosity, moved into the room, and dropped into the nearest chair. He waved Felicity to the chair beside him. "I expect we're going to be lectured."

"I'd rather stand," she curtly said.

*Perfect. Two women in a temper.* Repressing a sigh, he slid down on his spine, stretched out his legs, and shuttered his gaze.

Charlotte closed the door, leaned back against it, and surveyed her companions for a lengthy moment. She knew she looked her best. She wanted Albion to see what he'd been missing.

He looked; it was only natural for him. He even recognized the mantua-maker's style; Madame Derain knew how to glorify a bosom.

"What the hell are you doing?" Felicity hissed, as if she had the right.

"Nothing," he said, like every man would in the same situation.

She swore at him, he scowled, and Charlotte sweetly intoned, "Now, now, children, we have more important matters to consider. We have a notable little scandal on our hands." She folded her hands at her slender waist and smiled, enjoying her position of command. "I'm more than ready to listen to any suggestions you might have to rectify this unfortunate situation."

"Go home, Charlotte," Felicity snapped. "Leave me alone."

"Alas," Charlotte murmured with nauseating drama, "if only circumstances allowed. But I'm afraid your father is searching for you as we speak my dear. And, darling Alex, I felt it necessary to apprise your parents of your latest iniquity, so they too might be traveling this way." Her smile was gloating. She rather liked having these two young creatures at her mercy. She had not the remotest expectation of her demands being refused. "Now, I believe we have a great number of things to discuss, beginning with your betrothal—which to my mind should be announced forthwith."

Nothing in Albion's lounging pose stirred.

"Such reticence, Alex," Charlotte jibed.

"You overstep," he said flatly.

"I have no intention of marrying him," Felicity declared. "There. Are we clear? You have no authority over me, nor any right to be here. I suggest you leave. Or would you like me to tell Papa of all your crude attempts to marry me off to the grossest peers in England?"

"My heavens, such rebellion," Charlotte mocked, lazily tucking a curl behind her ear. "Does Albion's presence give you courage? You weren't so brave before."

"It wasn't worth the effort," Felicity tartly replied. "I had no intention of marrying any of those pigs."

"I see," Charlotte placidly replied, her former plans unnecessary, the new bridegroom much superior.

"Good. Then you can also see that it was completely useless for you to come here." Felicity's fists were clenched at her sides, her temper barely in check. "My life is my own."

"May I point out to you both," Charlotte pleasantly observed, unperturbed by the antipathy she faced, "that this little arrangement of yours could put Albion in prison. I believe there are laws against abduction and rape."

Felicity drew in a sharp breath that displayed her flaunting breasts to advantage, the charming sight instrumental in making a disagreeable conversation more agreeable, Albion decided. You couldn't help but admire a young lady of such strong convictions, refreshing independence, and—well—clearly voluptuousness.

"I came with Albion of my own free will," Felicity hotly declared, as if confirming Albion's thoughts. She cast a loathsome glance at her stepmother. "And so I will avow in court or elsewhere."

"There you have it," Albion drawled, his teeth showing in a rather saturnine smile. "Now what, Charlotte?"

"You ask me—*what?*" Charlotte's azure gaze was clear and unruffled. "I believe the answer to your question is that you have ruined a young maid, Alex. The purdah I imposed on Felicity will be nothing to that which society will inflict on her. She will be completely ostracized. Can you live with that, I wonder?"

"Don't listen to her," Felicity rapped out, turning on Albion. "It was my decision—you hear? I would have found someone else to take me away if you hadn't. I never would have married any of those horrible men. Never in a million years." She swung around and faced her stepmother. "As to being ostracized, I doubt the Duchess of Devonshire or Lady Foster or Lady Melbourne have realized such a fate. On the contrary, they're welcomed in the highest circles. So save your threats."

"You have to admit she's right," Albion said. All the ladies cited lived grossly unconventional lives. "Furthermore, the Montrose name still carries considerable weight in society," he added in his most ordinary voice. *Did she really think that he could be coerced into marriage?*

"There. You see, Charlotte. You might think twice about challenging the Montroses. Or my father," Felicity coolly asserted. "I'd be more than happy to tell father about every vile thing you've done to me and I've been keeping score. I'll be sure to mention your friendship with Albion as well. How do you think Papa will feel about him sniffing around your skirts?"

"Christ, Felicity, grant me some sense."

"It doesn't signify," she airily remarked, although the snappishness of his reply afforded her considerable satisfaction. "I'd appreciate you telling her to leave."

"Consider it my pleasure," Albion said, swiftly coming to his feet and walking toward Charlotte. "You've outstayed your welcome, Charlotte, if ever you had one." He stopped before her and looked down from his great height. "Now either retire under your own power or I'll have you carried out."

She checked for a moment before her gaze turned derisive. "Don't threaten me, Alex. You'll rue the day." Her lips, shapely and red, parted in a smile. "This all could have been resolved in a civilized manner. As for you, you little hussy," she murmured as if in afterthought. "I have half a mind to have you whipped for embarrassing your father and me."

"That's enough," Albion said wearily. "Get the hell out."

"You insolent young cub." Her eyes were suddenly bright with resentment: of his arrogance and impudence, his unrivaled beauty and wealth that allowed him so much. "You haven't heard the last of this foolhardiness. Don't think you can walk away, Alex, like you always do. You will pay dearly this time. Do you hear?"

He smiled tightly, a spark of anger in his eyes. "You must leave," he said stiffly. "Or I may not be accountable for my actions."

"Lay a hand on me," she threatened, "and I'll see that you hang."

He went still, then turned to Felicity. "Is she fucking insane?" Felicity rolled her eyes.

"Don't roll your eyes at me you little strumpet!"

Albion took a step forward; for a big man he moved with stealth.

"Don't," Felicity hissed.

"Then it's time she goes." Striding away, he jerked open the door a moment later and called out to Rothby and several footmen standing outside. "Some help here," he ordered, knowing he'd best not touch Charlotte in his current mood. "Lady Belvoir is retiring to her carriage."

"Don't you dare lay hands on me!" she cried as Rothby and the footmen approached her. "I'll have you arrested for assault! I'll have you all thrown in gaol! You'll rue this day Alex!" she screamed, as she was half-carried from the room. "I shall inform your parents of this *outrage!*"

Albion's stomach tightened. All else he could ignore. But not that. His father was sure to be displeased. "I'll be right back," he said and strode away. Perhaps he could still control the damage. His father might not have been home to receive Charlotte's message. He'd talked about going to Paris. If there was a god, he'd gone.

A groom had run to fetch the Belvoir carriage and before it was brought round from the stable yard, Albion caught up with Charlotte in the drive. "Be sensible, Charlotte. There's no advantage to you in pursuing this matter. You'll only make trouble between Felicity and her father. Why not forget that you were here?"

"Why don't I see that you marry that little tart you're fucking instead," she snapped, livid with rage, not within shouting range of sensible. "How like you, Alex. Even at sixteen, the world was yours, wasn't it? But this time you've gone too far. And so I will tell everyone in London."

"I wouldn't recommend it." His voice was tightly constrained, his gaze cold as ice.

"Fic to your recommendations," she archly replied. "Do you think I care one whit what you want?" Her bitter smile was that of a woman scorned. "In fact, I'll take pleasure in informing the world of your little peccadillo. I doubt it will impact your life with your illustrious family and odiously large fortune behind you, but it will destroy the little doxy who's been warming your cock."

"Christ, Charlotte, consider the embarrassment to your husband, if not to Felicity. You have to live with him."

"You needn't concern yourself with my marriage." Her gaze was scathing. "I can handle Lucien."

He briefly wondered how a woman like Charlotte, very much

the merry widow for years, had snared a man of Lord Belvoir's temperate character. "Very well. If you choose not to be reasonable, allow me to give you fair warning. If you hurt Felicity, you'll answer to me. It's not an idle threat."

"Marry your little bed mate. Then you won't have to worry about her being hurt." Charlotte smiled insolently. "But that's not what you want to hear, is it? Then, remember this, you arrogant cub. You ruined her whether she came of her own free will or not. *You* did it, not me."

"You misjudge the situation, Charlotte," he tersely said. "Now go home, keep your mouth shut, and all will be well."

"I'm surprised you kept her after your wager was won," Charlotte snidely noted. "She must be an inventive little slut."

The Belvoir carriage arrived—just in time.

Albion was about to strike a woman for the first time in his life.

Turning, he wrenched open the carriage door and forcibly thrust Charlotte inside. Slamming the door, Albion glanced up at the driver, the violence in his gaze enough to make the man quail. "Lady Belvoir is leaving. If you come back, I'll have you all shot."

The driver whipped his horses off as if the devil were on his tail and the coach and four careened down the drive at a breakneck pace.

"I'm sorry you had to deal with her," Felicity said, coming up beside him. Even watching from the doorway, Charlotte's voice had been shrill enough to reach her ears. "And you're not at fault no matter what she says. I practically forced you to take my virginity. You know it's true," she added as he was about the speak. She smiled. "You know how demanding I can be."

"Both of us perhaps," he said with an answering smile.

"The point is I'm not sorry for anything that's happened, except that our holiday has come to an end. It's time I go north with Perkins if he's still available. Charlotte will be back."

"With your father."

"Yes. I hope I haven't caused trouble with *your* parents."

"No, of course not," he lied. "But why don't I escort you to Edinburgh?"

She smiled. "You're afraid of your father."

"Let's just say he won't be pleased."

"You'll be lectured about seducing a young lady of quality I suppose."

"Virgins will be the issue and the interview will be unpleasant." He softly exhaled, then touched her hand. "At least we had one glorious day at the races and my horses will compete whether I'm here or not. I suggest we leave within the hour."

She grinned. "In a hurry? Will he beat you?"

"I'd prefer that. No, I'll be subjected to his frigid disapproval. If only Maman wasn't in Paris, she'd mitigate his temper. He adores her. Come, now, your wicked stepmother has drastically altered our plans. Would you like something to eat before we leave?"

"I'd prefer a bath," Felicity said with a flicker of her brows.

He dipped his head. "I won't join you or we'll never leave."

But once he escorted Felicity to his apartment, he ordered Perkins to pack and then swiftly bathed himself. It wasn't until Perkins entered his dressing room as he was slipping into his coat that he knew he'd made a mistake in delaying their departure.

Albion met his valet's impassive gaze. "He's here?"

"Yes, sir," Perkins replied. "In the library."

"Have Miss Belvoir informed that there will be a slight delay. Tell her I'll come for her shortly."

"Yes, sir. Would you like me to tell her—"

"No. Don't mention my father."

# Chapter 13

While Albion had been expecting his interview with his father to be unpleasant, it was more disagreeable than he was prepared for. When he walked into the library and the door shut behind him, the Marquess of Pembroke was seated in a chair by the window, holding up a glass of Madeira to the light. The marquess neither acknowledged his son's entrance nor arrested his examination of the russet-colored liquid for some lengthy interval while the earl remained standing by the door.

In no rush to shorten the silence, the marquess took a sip of the liquor, tasted and swallowed it with maddening deliberation before setting the glass down on a small table at his right hand, the several rings on his fingers catching the light in an iridescent shimmer. A product of an era when en grande toilette was in vogue, Pembroke favored more sumptuous attire than his son and was elegant in rich burgundy velvet, the lace at his throat embellished with a diamond that would have been vulgar on anyone less distinguished. Taking out a jeweled timepiece from his embroidered waistcoat pocket, he snapped open the enameled lid, checked the time, shut the lid, and returned it to his pocket.

His temper rising, Albion shifted his stance.

The marquess at last turned to his son. "I saw the Belvoir coach taking Lady Belvoir away as I arrived. I couldn't help but notice her scowl. I surmise she was not successful in her undertaking."

"No sir," Albion curtly said.

The marquess regarded his son with cool disdain.

"No sir," Albion said more respectfully.

The marquess's heavy-lidded gaze so much like his son's narrowed slightly in acknowledgment of the remedied tone. Then he crossed his legs, took another leisurely sip of Madeira, swallowed, and set the glass down while Albion waited in increasing discomfort. When he finally deigned to speak, he softly said, "I understand you've been amusing yourself more indecorously than usual. I confess, I hadn't thought it possible."

"I can explain."

The marquess smiled thinly, his lean face an attenuated version of his son's handsome countenance. "You feel an explanation will suffice to resolve your tasteless actions and the accruing gossip? Gossip by the way that will cause your mother distress. I deplore it when you make your mother unhappy."

"I beg your pardon, sir. I should have had a care for Maman."

Pembroke studied his slender fingers for a moment before looking up. "I believe we've had this conversation numerous times before. I'm beginning to find it tedious."

"I'm sorry, sir."

"I'm not sure platitudes will suffice this time," the marquess said with a disturbing finality.

"If I could explain, sir."

"You mean you don't have a young lady of quality residing here with you?"

"No sir, I mean, yes sir I do, but it's not as it seems."

The marquess surveyed his son, his brows faintly lifted, his gaze bland. "She is still intact then?"

Albion flushed under the expressionless gaze. "Not exactly, sir."

"Ah, there are degrees to virginity? Pray enlighten me."

"The thing is, sir," Albion said, beginning to take a seat in the chair beside his father.

"I don't believe I've given you leave to sit."

Albion set his teeth and stood again. "She was being forced into a marriage she deplored, sir," he said stiffly. "I contrived to help her."

"And win your wager in the bargain."

"Yes, sir."

The marquess softly sighed. "So you're telling me that you rather uncharacteristically contrived to save a damsel in distress. I find your chivalry surprising."

"There was twenty thousand at stake, sir."

"Of course. How could I forget. You bet on anything don't you?"

"Yes, sir. I believe it's a family tradition."

"I do not think, however," the marquess said with a dampening glance, "that abducting young ladies of quality, using them, and casting them aside is a family tradition."

"Forgive me, sir. I stand corrected."

"As well you might." The marquess's cynical gaze surveyed his son. "This is not some small mischief this time, Alex. Miss Belvoir was unknown to you, she was in her own home. She was not one of your high-born tarts inviting you in for carnal sport."

"I understand, sir. Might I make a suggestion?"

"No. What transpired with Lady Belvoir before you drove her off? I imagine she recalled your youthful friendship."

Albion's eyes flared wide.

"It wasn't as though you were discreet or even nominally so. I refer to the Hampton Court impetuosity although I could go on."

"Please don't, sir."

"Your mother didn't like her. You were too young, she thought, for someone of Charlotte's shall we say appetites."

Awareness flickered in Albion's gaze. "You bought her off."

"I don't recall you being heartbroken."

"No," Albion said, smiling faintly. "I was busy at the time."

"As you have continued to be ever since. I understand youthful folly. I will not pretend to some false virtue or piety with a past like mine. The pertinent question, however, is what do you propose to do with this young lady?"

"I promised I'd take her to her aunt in Edinburgh after the races. She's horse mad too. Her late mother owned the Langley stud."

"I knew her mother. A regrettable death."

"We were about to leave, sir."

"There is one more question?"

Something in his father's voice occasioned fresh unease. "Yes, sir."

"Apropos this modern notion of er—degrees of virginity, I have an old-fashioned question? What are your plans should the young lady find herself with child?"

The sudden silence brought a frown to the marquess's brow.

"I'm not sure that will happen, sir," Albion finally said.

"Not sure or certain?"

"I couldn't say, sir."

The marquess didn't speak for some time and when he did, his voice was so low Albion had to strain to hear him. "I have never forced you to do anything you didn't wish to do. Nor will I begin now. However, you are my son and a Montrose. I request you not lose sight of your responsibilities to your name, nor, under any circumstances, cause heartache to your mother. That is all."

Albion couldn't quite contain his sigh of relief. "Thank you, sir."

"One more thing. I believe I'll talk to this young lady before you go."

"Must you? I mean, yes sir, I'll tell her."

"Alone."

Albion flinched. "As you wish, sir." But halfway to the door he turned and smiled. "I like her, sir. You will find she's not in the least ordinary."

His son took obvious delight in the lady. The marquess was surprised he let it show. But soon enough, Pembroke discovered the accuracy of his son's characterization when Felicity strode into the room with the easy gait of an expert rider and without so much as a curtsy or introduction immediately launched into an explanation. "I beg you don't blame Albion, your lordship. This was all my idea. He was planning on seducing me, quickly departing, and collecting his twenty thousand wager. But, instead, I made him sign an agreement to take me to Edinburgh or I wouldn't relinquish my virginity. It was my doing entirely. Absolutely and completely," she announced resolutely.

The marquess surveyed the plain-speaking young lady fashionably dressed in apple green muslin. "Knowing my son I expect he wasn't difficult to convince," he drily said.

"Oh no, my lord, on the contrary, he was at first reluctant," she frankly replied, immune to the marquess's cool contemplation, bent on defining what she perceived as a reasonable arrangement between two people with unique priorities. "But of course there was twenty thousand at stake and you must admit that is no small sum to sacrifice. Especially since I was wholly willing so long as he agreed to take me to Edinburgh."

The phrase *wholly willing* raised the same warning flags in the marquess's mind as Felicity's initial willingness had for his son. "Might I ask," Pembroke carefully posed, watching her intently for any deviation in her remarkable aplomb, "whether this agreement of yours waived marital rights?" Ingenious females of every stripe had been in pursuit of his son for years.

"Not precisely, sir, but it was understood. Neither of us is inclined to marry. I expect you know that about your son," she said with a certain small emphasis. "As for myself, I have no interest in a husband despite my stepmother's machinations—which was what really drove me from London. Also, my aunt in Edinburgh has been a widow most of her life and loves it dearly. Every female doesn't want marriage, although I'm sure most do. Not that I might not consider marriage *someday,* but I'm only twenty and I have any number of things I wish to do first." She paused to take a breath in her galloping monologue. "I do hope I have taken the onus off your son. In truth, I gave him no choice. I *had* to escape, you see."

"I quite understand," the marquess replied, no longer in doubt about Miss Belvoir's motivation, mildly astonished at her stunning candor. "Come sit down," he said, indicating the chair beside him, "and we will discuss this dilemma."

"Thank you, sir, but Albion is in a hurry—as am I," she quickly added at the lift of the marquess's brows. "Not to put too fine a point on it, sir, but my stepmother is bound to return and make trouble."

"I see that you are a woman of spirit like your mother," he gently said. "I knew your father less well. He was more bookish than I, while your mother and I shared a passion for the turf. A passion my son inherited as you did your mother's I hear. Now, as to this—er—friendship between you and my son. Alexander will do the honorable thing if required. He is my son after all. He knows right from wrong. Perhaps your stepmother will be satisfied with such a promise."

"Oh no, your lordship! Don't even suggest such a thing! I couldn't allow it! Please, think no more of such lamentable redress as marriage between us," she said earnestly. "It would be horrid, sir, and that's a fact."

The marquess regarded her fixedly for a moment. "You have no personal regard for my son?" *Was it possible when all of Alex's lovers coveted the title of wife? Even the married ones.*

"Oh, of course, sir. How could anyone not adore your son," she cheerfully replied. "He is quite extraordinary as you must know. But I only needed an escort to Edinburgh and Albion's wager conveniently coincided with my requirement. Our bargain was limited to race week and the journey north."

*Time would tell he supposed whether a marriage was necessary.* "Very well, but I must warn you, my child. I cannot stand between you and your father if it comes to that." He smiled faintly. "But for now I suggest you go with my son who is apparently waiting anxiously. And I will do my best to extinguish any gossip concerning your sojourn in Newmarket."

Felicity grimaced. "I'm not sure that's possible with my stepmother determined to fan the flames of scandal."

"Leave her to me," the marquess quietly said. "I'll talk to her."

Felicity grinned. "I have to admit, sir, I would dearly love to witness that conversation."

"I've found that such conversations are best done in private," he murmured with a fleeting, sardonic inflection. "As for now, I suggest you go with my son. He will see you safely into your aunt's care."

"Thank you, sir. You're most understanding."

"I sympathize. I once had cause to deal with your stepmother." He shook his head when she began to speak. "It was long ago, my child. Before you were out of the schoolroom."

The door was suddenly flung open and Albion stood on the threshold, a look of determination on his face. "I'm taking Felicity to Edinburgh, father, whether you like it or not."

"Miss Belvoir is of the same mind," the marquess calmly replied. "I would offer you children my blessing but I rather think my stock with the gods was depleted long ago. I will instead wish you safe journey. You will take armed postilions with you, Alex." Albion was his only child and dear.

"Yes, sir. All is in readiness." He strode to Felicity's side and held out his hand. "Primrose and Tarquin will come along," he said with a smile, "should you wish to ride part way."

"How wonderful! I would love it dearly," she said, taking his hand. She turned back to the marquess. "Thank you so much, sir."

Albion bowed to his father, affection in his gaze. "As always, sir, I'm in your debt."

"I am not so old to have forgotten the indiscretions of youth," the marquess said with a small smile. "But if I might give you both some advice—I'd suggest a little less visibility wouldn't be out of hand—at least for a fortnight."

"I shall be well out of sight in Edinburgh, sir. Virtually a recluse," Felicity promised.

"I will do my best, sir." Albion offered him a rueful gaze. "I wouldn't want to lie to you."

The marquess dipped his head. "I appreciate your honesty, although I find Miss Belvoir much more accommodating. You might take a page from her book, Alex."

Knowing full well what her book contained when it came to accommodation, Albion grinned. "Yes, sir. I'll try, sir."

This scene of fond affection was abruptly and violently shattered by the shrill sound of Charlotte's voice raised in umbrage, followed by a more moderate, masculine tone and the accompanying tattoo of footsteps drawing near with deplorable speed.

Albion swore, Felicity turned ashen at the sound of her father's voice. The marquess rose from his chair and moved toward the door. "I'll deal with this," he said with perfect composure. He pointed to an adjoining door. "Go," he softly said. "Wait in the study."

# Chapter 14

The Marquess of Pembroke stood alone by the windows when Bagley opened the door and Charlotte pushed past him and stormed into the library.

Bagley's announcement of, "Lord and Lady Belvoir," was obscured by Charlotte's shout, "Where are they?" She swiveled, surveying the book-filled room. "If you let them escape, I'll see that you—"

"For heaven's sake, Charlotte," Lord Belvoir brusquely said, coming up to his wife and taking her arm in a steely grip. "Be so good as to sit down or return to the coach if you can't control your temper."

Charlotte stared openmouthed at her husband; he'd never addressed her harshly.

"Might I offer you a chair, Lady Belvoir," the marquess smoothly interposed. "And perhaps a glass of Madeira. It's quite excellent. Whatever my son's shortcomings, his palate is superb."

"This isn't a social call," Lord Belvoir said stiffly, road weary and much put out. "I understand my daughter is here. I have come for her."

"If I might have a private word with you first," the marquess suggested.

"I don't see the point." Lord Belvoir was not a man easily ruffled, but he'd also never had to scour the countryside for a runaway daughter. His expression was as grim as his voice.

"I require only a moment of your time and then I will bring you to your daughter." The marquess indicated a doorway opposite that taken by his son and Felicity. And calmly waited.

"Good God, Lucien, she's *your* daughter! Tell him *no!*"

A muscle twitched along the baron's jaw and without looking at his wife, he said, "After you, Pembroke."

The marquess preceded Felicity's father into a small sitting room, splendidly decorated à la Grecque and rarely used in Albion's bachelor home. "Please, sit. I wished to speak to you man to man," he obliquely said, rather than disparage the baron's wife. "I thought we might better deal with this awkward situation."

"I apologize for Lady Belvoir," Lucien remarked, having regained his composure. He sat in a sleek chair of pale wood and gray satin. "She is quite agitated I'm afraid." He softly exhaled. "We met on the outskirts of Newmarket and well—she is gravely upset with Felicity."

"I understand." The marquess sat opposite Lord Belvoir in a larger chair with gilded lion head armrests. "Lady Belvoir's er— lively temperament has caused some little strife between her and your daughter I understand. At the risk of interfering I wanted to call your attention to that discord should you be unaware of it."

"Felicity never said a word to me of any disagreements." Lord Belvoir paused as if digesting the information, his high brow creased in thought. "Nor did Lady Belvoir other than in the most general way," he added in a musing tone. "She wants only the best for Felicity you understand. In fact, she's offered various proposals to improve my daughter's prospects for her debut into society."

"A new marriage brings inevitable changes in a household," the marquess said as tactfully as possible. "Perhaps in the process of adjusting to those changes, misunderstandings occurred between your wife and daughter."

"Charlotte *has* taken a firm hand in Felicity's upbringing," Lord Belvoir allowed. "Very generously I might add." He abstractly rubbed his forehead with his fingertips. "Although I may have been rather inattentive to my daughter. My late wife always dealt with the children you see."

"Which is only natural," Pembroke suavely replied, rather than say that Lucien should have taken his head out of his books long enough to notice he had a family. Not that Arabella Belvoir, nee Winthrup from the long line of Winthrup thoroughbred breeders, hadn't been more than capable of running a household and a renowned stud by herself. Her expert management skills might partially excuse Lucien's lack of due diligence, but it didn't alter the result. "Nevertheless, I think you'll agree," the marquess diplomatically remarked, "we have a problem on our hands."

Belvoir squared his jaw. "I am here to resolve it. I will take my daughter home."

"She was hoping to visit her aunt in Edinburgh."

Lord Belvoir was taken aback. "She told you that?"

"Yes. Again, at the risk of interfering, perhaps a short separation between Lady Belvoir and your daughter might well serve? A time to reflect as it were," Pembroke delicately added.

"No, I would rather Felicity come home," Lucien firmly replied, placing his palms on his knees and sitting up very straight. "I would also prefer your son have no further contact with my daughter. There is no way to tactfully put this, Pembroke, but he is not the sort of young gentleman I approve of."

"I understand," the marquess said imperturbably. "I'm afraid my son has inherited the Montrose wildness."

"Just so," Lucien replied a trifle grimly, leaving unsaid any allusion to the marquess's reprehensible past. Motivated to action by that unsavory memory and its corollary effect, Lord Belvoir rose to his feet. "If I might see my daughter now."

There was a curtness to his demand and a note of determination that the marquess understood rendered further conversation useless. "Of course," he said. "If you'll follow me."

He conducted Lord Belvoir to the study. As the two men entered the room, Pembroke caught his son's eye and nodded his dismissal before turning his gaze on Felicity. "Your father has come for you, Miss Belvoir."

Albion opened his mouth to protest, but Felicity softly said, "Please. I'd rather speak to my father alone."

"I'll be waiting outside," the earl quietly said. "We'll go wherever you want to go."

"Thank you," she whispered and turned to her father. "Hello, Father."

The baron waited for the door to close on the Montroses before speaking, his gaze on his daughter a mingling of puzzlement and doubt. "I should ask why you did what you did but I'm not sure I want to know."

"It's not easy to explain," Felicity replied. If he wanted details, she was willing to elaborate.

But he didn't ask for an explanation. He said instead, "I'm astonished at this madcap flight of yours. It's shocking and lamentable."

"It wasn't a whim, Father."

At which point Lord Belvoir avoided the significance of Felicity's reply, chose to express further dismay at his daughter's behavior, and the conversation progressed in the same obtuse fashion. After some minutes, finally weary of the senseless exchange, Felicity told her father that she was thoroughly opposed to her debut and would prove unyielding on that point. He didn't reply immediately, by nature a man of deliberation. But when he spoke, he assured her that she need not participate in the Season if she found it distressing. Felicity thanked him for his understanding and went on to say that she preferred a quiet life to that being urged on her by her stepmother. Her father said she was quite free to decline any suitor, that Charlotte had only meant to offer her assistance. Felicity said she knew Charlotte's intentions were of the best and so it went—respectful and meaningless. The crux of the problem—Charlotte—was left largely undiscussed and completely unresolved.

When Lord Belvoir insisted Felicity return home, she agreed, rather than face a bitter confrontation that would only cause further offense. She would be free of all constraints in a twelve month; she could afford a temporary truce.

Felicity had said what good-byes she intended to Albion while they'd waited in the study and she had no wish to repeat what would only be a painful conversation. Their bargain had been clearly defined from the start; they both understood.

She smiled and waved at him as she exited the study with her father.

He raised his brows in query.

She shook her head.

And that was that.

But Pembroke followed the Belvoirs out to the carriage and

took Felicity aside after her parents entered the carriage. "I did what I could, child, but he's your father. I'm sorry."

"I'm quite resigned to our arrangement." She gave him a lying, sensible answer. "Papa has agreed I need not come out this Season which is a great relief. Nor do I have to deal with any suitors I dislike. Papa is not unfeeling but he has other obligations," she said with a rueful smile. "He deserves his own happiness."

"If possible."

She shrugged. "You forget that Charlotte deals with Papa quite differently. He doesn't know the whole. And should he find out the truth someday, I don't want to be the one who shattered his illusions."

"No, indeed. That would be an unfair burden for your young shoulders. Unfortunately men will be men," the marquess noted. "I wish there were a better excuse."

"A twelve month will quickly pass and I will have my own independence." Felicity glanced at her father who was waving her in. "Please offer my thanks to Albion again. Despite his wicked reputation," she said with a smile, "he is not at all the callous rake but exceedingly kind in every way."

"I agree," the marquess said with an answering smile. "But then I'm partial." He lightly touched her cheek. "God speed, child."

# Chapter 15

While the ton chattered like magpies about the abduction and the subsequent amorous interlude disrupted by Miss Belvoir's irate father, the young couple in the eye of the storm resumed their former lives.

Not that anyone expected anything different from Albion. His relationships with women were always fleeting.

As for Miss Belvoir, it was fortunate that Albion had been her abductor or she would have been completely beyond the pale. With a few well-placed threats from Pembroke along with Albion's propensity to deal with his detractors on the dueling field, the young lady was saved from the insults and overt discourtesies that would have been directed to anyone less well protected.

Albion promptly embarked on his former dissolute path. He reappeared in his old haunts, took up with his wild friends and adoring lovers, gambled too high, slept too little, and in general amused himself with his usual indiscretion.

Truth be told, he was relieved that he hadn't been obliged to break off the connection with Miss Belvoir. He disliked the inevitable, awkward good-byes and the little miss had been becoming too attached to him—an all too common occurrence in his life. With the exception of what would have been an entertaining journey to Edinburgh in the company of a very passionate young lady, he had no regrets that the curtain had come down on their adventure.

As for his friends' initial crude comments concerning the abduction, Albion brought those jests to an abrupt end with a few pithy warnings. Not that anyone was under any illusions about what had transpired between Albion and a female guest at his race box in any case.

The only real question was whether the scandalous liaison would bear fruit?

Which fascinating topic gained strength in the coming days, further titillating the ton, causing everyone to check their calendars and begin counting the days. This potential consequence of Albion's wager became the juiciest bit of gossip in club rooms and drawing rooms, effacing even the shocking rumor that the Prince of Wales was considering a morganatic marriage with Mrs. Fitzherbert.

Naturally, every licentious tidbit concerning her Newmarket tryst was relayed to Felicity with gleeful malice by her stepmother who continued in private to castigate her at every opportunity. Charlotte decried not only Felicity's disgrace but that which she'd brought on the family—her diatribes always delivered well out of earshot of Lord Belvoir of course.

Pembroke had kept his word as well. "I make a wicked enemy," the marquess had said among other things in his meeting with Charlotte, the soft venom in his tone enough to make her blood run cold. "If you speak of this I will destroy you."

While Charlotte was checked from publicly spreading her tale, at home Felicity was obliged to listen to her stepmother's constant criticism. Not that she hadn't long since become hardened against Charlotte's carping. What she found harder to ignore were the sly glances from members of the ton who knew full well what several days in the company of the Earl of Albion entailed. She would have preferred outright comment to the lascivious glances directed her way on the rare occasions she went out in society. Since the fashionable world had been warned off by the Montroses, however, no one dared confront her.

In this unique bubble insured by her powerful protectors, Felicity occupied herself in the company of her friends. Not that they all weren't curious about the details of her abduction. Particularly Henrietta.

She arrived on Felicity's second day back in London, sailed

into her sitting room, and breathlessly exclaimed, "Tell me every-thing, you clever girl! I want to know what he's like, how he acts, more to the point is he really as stupendous and glorious as rumor implies? Or you can tell me later," she'd quickly added, taking note of Felicity's melancholy expression. Sitting down beside her friend on the window seat, she patted Felicity's hand. "Really, darling, you needn't tell me anything."

"I *shouldn't* even be here," Felicity said depressingly. "I should be in Edinburgh at Aunt Lucy's. But Papa wouldn't allow it, thanks to Charlotte's interference." She grimaced. "Father doesn't under-stand in the *least* what a gorgon he married."

"How dreadful. What are you going to do?"

"Do? Sit here for a year until I gain my mother's inheritance," she said with resignation. "After that," she added, brightening, "I shall instantly leave."

"I envy you," Henrietta had said. "With three sisters and a brother, my portion isn't very grand. My fate is to marry some younger son and make do with gowns three seasons old."

"Come live with me. I'm going to buy a farm, breed racing stock, and never talk to Charlotte again."

Henrietta smiled. "It sounds ever so nice. I could help you with your accounts. I'm excellent with numbers."

"We'll have to see if I *last* a year. I might slit my wrists before-times if Charlotte persists in her *viciousness.*"

"I'll keep up your spirits if you do the same for me. I'm not at all sure my coming out won't be dreadful with Mama already hounding me that I must put myself forward in order to form an eligible connection for the sake of the family coffers. With my younger sisters next in line, Mama constantly reminds that I can-not fail to take this season."

"Nonsense. You're beautiful. You'll have all the young bucks at your feet. Trust me, you can look higher than a younger son. As for myself, I intend to remain in retirement for a tedious twelve month."

Before long, however, the daunting prospect of an entire year under her father's roof with her stepmother berating her at every turn served to alter Felicity's plan of a secluded life. She couldn't hide in her rooms forever, nor did she wish to openly engage in battle with Charlotte or worse, fall into an abyss of despondency over Albion. Her father was under the impression a certain normalcy had been restored to his household; there was no point in disturbing the tranquility of his domestic arrangements to no good purpose.

So as much as her situation and Charlotte allowed, Felicity contrived to set her own course. She began going out occasionally, primarily to private parties in the homes of her friends, driving out to the country to ride at her cousin's home, attending a few concerts where she was certain not to find Albion. Her infrequent forays into society allowed her to maintain her sanity, distract her from her all too prevalent thoughts of Albion, and remind her that life was for living. It would never do to fall into the megrims over a heartless, heedless, too handsome rake given over to selfishness and every form of vice.

Or so she resolutely maintained in the light of day. At night, however, alone in her bed, what was indefensible fell away, rationalization and reason decamped, and she missed him to the marrow of her bones. She fought against the mindless longing that only worsened and deepened and would not be dislodged no matter how refined her mental arguments. She told herself over and over again that she was a fool, that every woman he'd ever known adored him.

But logic and common sense always lost out against the power of love.

And sadly and undeniably, she knew she loved him.

In contrast to Felicity's limited social schedule, Albion was conspicuous in society, appearing at numerous drums, routs, and balls that in the past he would have avoided like the plague. His hostesses were ecstatic; he was after all, the most eligible bachelor in the kingdom. Nor could anyone fault his suave charm when he chose to exert it. As for his tall, elegant form, stark good looks, and rakish air, it went without saying that he added a certain careless dash to any gathering.

He would generally arrive late, greet his hostess with well-bred grace, pass the required time with her in trivial, harmless conversation that would invariably bring a smile to her lips, then excuse himself and make for the card room. Long after midnight he would return to the ballroom, and drink in hand, find a convenient vantage point from which to survey the throng. He spoke to those who came up to him, smiled now and then but discouraged lengthy conversation, more interested in the frequently replenished brandy in his hand. Mildly interested as well, although his dark gaze held a faint hint of boredom, in the glittering array of beautiful females in attendance, all of whom—whether demurely or blatantly—were vying for his attention.

Only when well into his cups would he make his way through the crowd to some comely young lady who was trying not to look too eager. His bow was always exquisitely graceful, drunk or not, and after humoring her with the requisite flattery and suavely accepting the familiar coquettish replies, he'd escort her to his carriage. And shortly after, to a soft bed—somewhere, anywhere.

If he hadn't been notorious for avoiding society events, his presence wouldn't have caused such a stir. If his various lovers hadn't added to the tittle-tattle with lavish praises for his virility, wildness, and indefatigable prowess, the rumors might not have been so lurid they reached even Felicity's semicloistered hermitage.

But she did hear from Henrietta who gently said, "Knowing Charlotte, you're going to be told this sooner or later." She went on to give a measured, restrained account of the stories.

Even braced by Henrietta's forewarning, Felicity was surprised at the degree of despair she felt. Ever pragmatic, however, she immediately took herself to task and forcing a normal tone said, "Thank you for telling me. Although I certainly know better than to harbor feelings for a self-indulgent profligate like Albion. It would be foolish and more to the point, useless. He is what he is." *She'd always known.*

Henrietta exhaled in relief. "Good. I've been worried whether to tell you or not."

"Better you than Charlotte."

"That's what I thought."

"But Lady Grenville," Felicity said with a groan. "She'll tell everyone, everything."

"She already has. She must have been keeping one eye on the bedroom clock because we all know now that he can keep it up for—"

"Stop. *I* don't want the details."

"Sorry, darling. It was just so—well—unbelievable. Did I mention my new blue gown? You'll have to see it."

Felicity laughed. "I would love to hear about your new blue gown."

Henrietta grinned. "No you wouldn't, but I'll tell you anyway."

But a few days later, after rational measures failed to mitigate her stark ache of longing, Felicity realized that some stronger remedy was required. She couldn't bear the thought of the endless months in which she'd pine for a man whose indifference to all but his personal pleasure was legendary.

To that end, she determined on a new course. She would capitulate to Charlotte's interminable prodding and agree to receive some of the men who had been calling on her. Why not? Was not Albion socially engaged—with a vengeance apparently? Meantime, she seemed to have acquired even more suitors than before. Evidently her friendship with Albion had only added to her allure. In the male world, she had become the equivalent of a femme fatale with the stamp of approval from the ultimate libertine.

So she commenced sitting through numerous visits from a variety of men, some young, some old, some rich, some richer, all surveying her with lecherous, hopeful eyes. Practicality notwithstanding, she found the visits dreadful, for no matter how handsome or well bred, accommodating or suave, not a single suitor came within an ocean's width of Albion's glory and charm. She silently suffered through the dull, miserable conversation and utter boredom in order to please her father, avoid Charlotte's unending badgering, and she supposed to keep from going completely mad. She even began keeping a list of the fulsome, unctuous compliments paid to her or rather to her licentious reputation and giggled over them with Henrietta.

In the tedium of her new venture, she discovered she was able to rise above her misery and survive the loss of the man she loved. A very stupid love as she well knew, although that knowledge didn't in any way detract from Albion's fatal attraction. But a kind of stubborn resolve sustained her in her unhappiness, along with the certainty she would soon be independent.

In the small, incestuous confines of the haut monde, the sudden influx of suitors to Belvoir House didn't go unnoticed by the Earl of Albion. He would have had to have been deaf, dumb, and blind to be oblivious.

At first he ignored the goings-on, then he turned to drink, after which he rarely drew a sober breath and slept even more rarely. Not that his lack of sleep diminished his sexual competence, nor his increasing need for the oblivion sex afforded. In fact, the ladies he favored with his company decided that Albion had a new, exciting flair for novelty, which fact caused considerable grumbling in the male establishment when the rumors surfaced. As if Albion's virtuoso talents weren't already a source of considerable resentment.

In the full grip of his search for lewd sensation, for something or anything to fill the emptiness of his world, Albion managed to turn a blind eye to Felicity's social schedule for nearly a month. Until one night, he climbed out of the Countess of Waldegrave's bed without so much as a good-bye, walked out, and disappeared. Some said he left for the Continent. Others that he was fishing in Scotland or was it Ireland. His father knew where he'd gone though; he'd had a watch on his son from the moment his drinking had turned destructive.

The marquess saw that his son had his favorite retainers at his refuge. Perkins was sent up the next morning, followed by additional servants from his London home. In the course of the next fortnight, Albion gradually stopped drinking. He became engaged in his thoroughbred stud, enjoyed the spring weather, the new foals, the company of his trainers and neighbors in Surrey. He rose early to watch the morning gallops, ate a hearty breakfast on his return to the house, worked with his steward in the morning, his trainers in the afternoon, and went to bed early and alone.

The routine calmed his discontent, the distance from London made it simpler to forget, his race horses focused his attention, his occasional wild rides temporarily eased his chafing resentments.

Another two weeks passed in the country, if not ones of complete content, near enough to soothe his frustrations. He had examined and dealt with the consequences of his unwelcome desires, of what a continuing relationship with Felicity would entail. He would eventually be caged, his privacy gone, and worse—his freedom. He would not give up everything for lust.

And so his life would have continued in a kind of reliable purgatory if not for the small item in the *Times*.

If it was possible for one's heart to stop, his did.

He read the few lines over again, not quite believing his eyes.

But there it was, from a trustworthy source: The betrothal announcement of the Honorable Felicity Belvoir and the Earl of Ancaster. Fuck, Scotland was a long way off, he bitterly thought, then threw the paper in the fire and closed his mind to it.

But as the wedding date approached, he became increasingly testy and ill-tempered. Perkins avoided giving offense by remaining largely mute. The staff went about their duties in dread of their sullen, inebriated master. His trainer expected any day to hear that the earl was selling off the stud. His steward didn't disagree.

It was two days before the wedding when Albion left, saddling his horse himself and riding off without a word to anyone. He rode hard for London, stalked into his house in a vile mood, retired to his study, and slumped in a chair, mindlessly stared into the fire, a brandy bottle in hand.

He looked up when Kit walked in, but didn't speak.

"I heard you were in town," Kit said. "You look drunk."

Albion cast him a sour glance. "So?"

"So I should think you'd be in a better mood since you've eluded the ball and chain," his friend replied, walking over to the drinks table. "There was talk you might be forced into marrying the Belvoir chit if she started increasing. Now, it's not your problem," he said, pouring himself a healthy bumper of brandy.

Albion scowled. "Don't tell me she's—"

"How should I know? I'd say not if Ancaster is marrying her. His stiff-necked father wouldn't allow a bastard as future heir. Aren't you going to offer me a chair?"

Albion waved toward a chair and sank back into his gloom.

For the next half hour Kit regaled his friend with all the latest gossip, receiving in return monosyllabic replies or none at all. Until he finally said, "What the hell's eating you?"

"Nothing. I'm tired." Albion was not, in fact, perfectly fit after weeks of drinking deep.

"You look like hell. When's the last time you slept?"

Albion shrugged and drained the bottle.

Kit came to his feet and held out his hand. "Another? I need one."

The earl tossed the bottle at Kit.

Catching it easily, Kit walked to the liquor table, poured two drinks, and turning back, found himself alone, the study door open wide.

# Chapter 16

A short time later, Albion invaded Belvoir House, roughly shoving aside the butler and footman who tried to stop him. With a murderous look on his face, he glared at them. "Where is she?" he growled, his voice raspy with fatigue, the dust of the road still on his clothes, an alarming wildness in his eyes.

Then he caught sight of Ancaster's walking stick with the goshawk crest on the hall table and strode away without waiting for an answer. Leaving visibly-shaken servants in his wake, he ran up the stairs, paused for a moment on reaching the main floor corridor, then turned right and began stalking his prey. He systematically opened one door after another, indifferent to the consequences, too drunk to care, the focus of his mind coldly centered until he smelled the perfume—sweet, expensive, pruriently arousing—and came to a sudden stop.

He'd been without a woman a long time; it took him a moment to stifle his cravings. After violently summoning his intellect and once again in command of his body, he reached out, turned the knob, and opened the door.

Felicity looked up at the sound and forgot to breathe.

Albion stood on the threshold, swaying slightly, his riding clothes much the worse for wear, his hair wild, a gauntness to his face, the devil in his gaze.

She was suddenly conscious of an overpowering joy.

Ancaster was seated much too close to Felicity, Albion decided, damn his poaching soul. "Get the hell out, Ancaster, or I'll shoot you," he growled, sliding his pistol from his coat pocket and dangling it in his fingers.

"Christ, are you ever sober?" Freddy Ancaster didn't move.

"Occasionally before breakfast," Albion drawled.

"You can barely stand."

"The devil I can't." Albion opened his arms in a lazy gesture, the cocked pistol sweeping the room. "And I can shoot out your eye from a hundred paces drunk or sober. So I suggest you get the fuck out."

"Damn your insolence," the slender young earl snapped, suddenly goaded too far. "Name your seconds. We'll meet in the morning when you're sober."

Albion softly sighed. "Are you deaf? I don't care to wait. I'll likely be just as drunk in the morning." Slowly raising his pistol, he sighted in on Ancaster's head. "What really puts me out of humor is where you're sitting."

"There's no need for violence," Felicity quickly said, picturing Ancaster lying on her carpet in a pool of blood with Bow Street Runners after Albion and her life in complete ruins. She offered Freddy a dazzling smile. "Let me talk some sense into Albion. He's obviously foxed."

"Hush, darling," Lord Ancaster said sternly. "I'll deal with him."

"I certainly shall not hush!" Felicity retorted. Jumping to her feet, she ran to Albion. "How nice of you to call."

He waved her past him without reply, not entirely sure why he'd come, not entirely sure what day it was or week for that matter. But beginning to think he might smile again.

"This way." Felicity pulled the door shut behind them, locked it, and nodded to her right. "Unless you want to see Charlotte."

"Christ no." Slipping the firing pin back in place, he shoved his pistol in his pocket. "I'm very drunk by the way."

She started walking briskly, ignoring the pounding on the door that commenced behind them. "Too drunk to drive me to Edinburgh?"

"Or Gretna Green?" Keeping pace, he gave her a sidelong glance, warm and wicked and sinfully alluring.

"Perfect," she sweetly replied. "I'm already packed."

Seized with a kind of lunatic joy that overlooked exhaustion and a less than perfect mental acuity, Albion grinned. "Always resourceful aren't you?"

"I found I couldn't actually marry a wet-behind-the-ears sprig like Ancaster."

"That harridan of a stepmother made you do it, didn't she?"

"She and Papa both. Between Papa's sad, disapproving looks and Charlotte's relentless persecution I was worn down. And Freddy's sweet in his own way. I thought I could do it. I suppose we all go to the devil in our own way."

"Tell me about it," he bitterly said.

"You don't *have* to marry me."

He frowned at her snappish tone. "I bloody know that."

"I'd be perfectly content to go to my aunt's in Edinburgh. I was going there tonight anyway." She would not beg a man who had been hunted since his youth by every miss and mama in the ton.

"My chaise is more comfortable than the mail coach," he said, ignoring her pettishness along with the pertinent issues that had kept him drunk for so long. "You don't *need* your luggage, do you?"

"No," she said. "But I need Molly."

"We'll send for her. I promise," he added to her measured gaze. "I would have shot him, you know," he said apropos nothing, his teeth flashing white in a boyish smile.

"I could tell." His smile warmed her heart. "I thought it very *romantic* of you."

"Oh Christ," he said. "Do you want me to propose?"

"Heaven's no. It's enough that you came for me."

He liked her practicality more than anything. Well, not more than *anything* which was the reason, he supposed, he was here. "At least we'll put all the scandal to rest."

"It *would* be nice if your child was legitimate."

He dragged her to a stop, indifferent to their circumstances, to the uproar rising behind them. Standing very still, he scanned her from head to foot. "You're with child? You don't look it."

"It's still early on."

His fingers tightened on her wrist. "When the hell would you have told me?"

"I hadn't made up my mind whether I would or not."

His nostrils flared. "Consider the matter resolved as of now."

"You may recall," she said with equal fervor, "I don't take orders."

"In this you shall. It's *my* child," he said sharply.

"*Ours.*" She stared back at him militantly.

"Yes of course, you're right," he smoothly said.

"You don't mean it."

"Certainly I do," he heard himself say with surprise. "Did you think I'd allow a child of mine to go nameless?" *He was becoming more moral by the second.*

"How should I know what you thought? And you must admit your life of excess hardly suggested you would greet news of a child with delight."

He grinned. "I believe I've experienced an epiphany."

She snorted, then her eyes widened. "Oh hell—there's Charlotte bearing down on us. I suggest we slip through that door and make our escape for I don't have the least wish to see either her or Ancaster."

He glanced over his shoulder, saw the descending horde with the Baroness Belvoir in the lead, and pushed Felicity toward the door. "We can continue this charming discussion in my chaise."

"Unless we find something more interesting to do," she sweetly said because the man she loved was looking at her with the most provocative and familiar impropriety.

He laughed, reminded of the lovely Miss Belvoir's enchanting spontaneity within the confines of a carriage. "Minx. What am I going to do with you?"

"Entertain me," she purred, "as only you can."

"Damn it," he said with a sudden scowl, "if you said as much to Ancaster so help me—"

"I never even let him kiss me. You spoiled me for other men," she said. "Now, apropos such things," she added, "and at the risk of disturbing this lovely moment, I will insist on equal fidelity from you."

He came to a sudden stop in the moonlit garden. "You can't be serious."

"But I am. Edinburgh will suit me as well," she pointed out. "You need not alter your life for me."

"Perhaps we could come to some understanding. Other couples do, hell, most couples do."

"Sorry, no." Even in the moonlight she could see the incredulity in his gaze.

"You can't mean it."

She took a small breath because she might be throwing her life away. "I do."

"Jesus," he grumbled. "You want too much."

"I'm sorry. It's the only bargain I'll accept."

He didn't immediately answer but when he did a small smile accompanied his reply. "You always did drive a hard bargain. On the other hand, the reward more than compensated as I recall." He dipped his head. "Very well, I'll do it. Although I warn you, I might wake up sober tomorrow and rue the day."

She held his gaze. "You have to be sure."

"You can be sure for both of us."

"I'm serious."

He looked at her quizzically for a moment before his gaze softened. "Very well, I'm sure. I've been miserable without you and no amount of liquor or—well—anything else helped. Now are we done haggling?"

"Haggling?" Her eyes flashed.

"Allow me to reword that," he said with a grin. "I believe we were discussing my complete devotion to you." He lightly brushed her cheek with his finger. "I love you minx. Stop scowling. We'll be in Gretna Green soon and then you may ring a wifely peal over my head whenever you please." Taking her hand, he began walking again.

"I was so wretchedly unhappy I almost wrote to you a thousand times," Felicity said, thoroughly appeased with the word *devotion* echoing in her ears.

"I almost abducted you again a thousand times," Albion declared. "And I would have if I wasn't in horror of—"

"Marriage?" she helpfully supplied.

"What else," he frankly replied.

"I'm glad you finally came for me."

"I am too. Damn Ancaster though. He has his nerve."

"He's quite pleasant."

"No reason to marry him."

"I eventually discovered as much."

"Don't ever think of walking away from me like you did him, for I'll tell you right now, I'll drag you back no matter where you go."

"My goodness. Should I be alarmed?"

"Not so long as you stay where you ought," he muttered.

"You disarm me with your tender sentiments," she sardonically noted.

He shot her a wicked look. "I was thinking about disarming you the way you like best. What do you think? Do you feel like screaming?"

She could feel the flush rise on her cheeks. "I don't always scream."

He knew better than to argue with the conversation turning on a subject sure to hold his interest. "Maybe we should remain in London tonight and leave in the morning."

"I'd rather stay ahead of pursuit if you don't mind."

But as they reached Albion's chaise waiting behind the mews and he pulled open the door, a voice inside pleasantly said, "I was beginning to worry. What took so long?"

"Good God, Hugo," Albion said, handing Felicity into the carriage. "What brought you here?"

"Your father of course."

"Felicity, this is Hugo Digby, my father's chaplain and favorite chess opponent," the earl said, giving orders to his driver before climbing in and taking a seat beside Felicity. "So, to what do we owe this pleasure?"

"Compliments of your father, sir." Reverend Digby handed over a document. "A special license. He thought you might have need of it."

"Perfect. I was trying to convince my darling wife-to-be to avoid the open road tonight. There, darling, you see, we are relieved of a lengthy journey. Say whatever words you have to say over us, Hugo, to tie the nuptial knot."

The reverend cleared his throat.

"What?" Albion held the chaplain's gaze.

"Perhaps Miss Belvoir would prefer a less hasty ceremony."

"On the contrary—"

"Her parents are in hot pursuit," Albion explained.

"Very well." Reverend Digby took a small book of Anglican liturgy from his pocket and by the light of the carriage lamp conducted the marriage ceremony between Cavendish Square and Albion's house.

As the driver pulled up to the curb and brought the carriage to a stop, the earl shot a jaundiced look at the chaplain. "I suppose my parents are waiting at home."

"Yes, sir."

"Tell them we'll call on them tomorrow. Not too early mind. It's my honeymoon night."

"Naturally, sir. As you wish."

Albion laughed. "Only because father agrees."

"He wanted me to convey his and your mother's congratulations on your marriage," Digby diplomatically replied, rather than answer.

The carriage door was opened by a servant. "Thank you for your assistance, Hugo. We'll see you tomorrow. My driver will take you home."

Albion helped Felicity alight, lifted her into his arms, moved across the pavement, and up the small bank of stairs. "I believe it's customary to carry the bride over the threshold," he murmured. "Are you happy?"

"Yes, very."

Something in her voice brought him to a stop and as the door opened before them and light flooded out onto the stairs he curtly ordered, "Shut the door." Turning back to Felicity, he bent his head to better see her in the dim light. "What's wrong? I can fix anything short of saintly matters."

"I'm so happy it frightens me."

He laughed. "Thank God, I thought it was something serious. We're going to be happy, you and I. Get used to the feeling. Tomorrow we're going to my racing stud and we're going to stay in the country forever. What do you think of that?"

"I think it sounds like paradise." He could radiate happiness as few men could.

"Only if you're with me there," he softly said. "Only then."

"And the baby."

"Jesus, I forgot. We'll have to make the house bigger, add a nursery, and whatever else babies need. You tell me and we'll do it."

"Just love me."

"Of course. Always." He grinned. "Now that I've become reconciled to the notion of love and marriage. And knowing your greedy appetites, I rather think the role of husband will be extremely satisfying."

"Starting now?"

"Ah, ever bashful and demure."

"As if that's what you want."

He laughed. "Hell no, it's you I want."

She pointed at the door, he kicked it, and as it was quickly opened, he carried the new Countess of Albion over the threshold and across the hall, accepting congratulations because the staff always knew everything before he did. Taking the stairs at a run, he walked down the corridor and into the bedroom where the newlyweds had first discovered a singular and, in Albion's case, unprecedented pleasure.

The kind that beguiled the senses and blindly overlooked reason.

The kind that transformed rakes and enchanted young maids.

The kind that inexplicably turned into love.

# A Storm of Love

## Terri Brisbin

# Chapter 1

*Near Kilmartin Glen, southwest Scotland, 1083 A.D.*

Breac peered up at the darkening sky and wiped the rain out of his face. For the fifth time in only minutes. The storm swirled, throwing winds in his face and dowsing him in waves of rain that soaked through the layers of woolen plaid. His chances and plans of returning to his home in less than three days faded even as the daylight did. Hell!

His luck in finding the healer near Dunadd had been unexpected, for 'twas rumored that she traveled through the Highlands during the summer months, gathering plants and seedlings for use in her concoctions. He reached down and touched the pouch tied carefully to his belt. Concoctions such as the one he now carried back to heal his sister from the strange, lingering fever that struck her down.

Pushing on through the boggy ground, Breac tried to force his way along the washed-out path, but his steps became slower and slower. The unrelenting rain would, he feared, be his undoing this day. Finally, accepting the futility of making it any farther before night fell completely, he began to search for a dry, or drier, place to seek refuge from this storm. He spied a clearing ahead and made his way there, hoping to be able to see more once he reached it. Just as he approached it, Breac reached up to push a low-hanging branch from his path and stopped, searching for a good place to seek protection from the storm on this higher ground.

A copse of trees with thick and heavily leafed branches offered him exactly what he needed. Without heavy brush at their base, the canopy they formed above the ground would keep him mostly dry. Creeping in between the trunks, he kicked the pile of damp leaves from beneath him and slid down, using one of the trees at his back as a guide. With his tightly woven wool cloak wrapped around him, Breac might keep the worst of the storm away. Some time passed as he dozed in and out of a light, fitful sleep, one filled with dreams, nay nightmares, of his sister's death.

Breac reached up and rubbed his face, frustration and sadness filling him once more at the thought of his failure. Fenella was his responsibility. He'd sworn to his mother that he would care for her and protect her, and instead, he'd failed. Releasing a deep breath, he knew that he was her only hope now and he would not fail her again. When the rain began to ease a bit, he thought about getting a few more miles behind him, but the winds did not relent and without the light of the moon, it would be impossible to see his path until morn.

Leaning his head back against the tree's trunk behind him, he closed his eyes and sought sleep once more. No more than several minutes could have passed when the sounds of someone approaching grew louder . . . and closer. Others traveling in this same dismal weather? He knew not, but decided to stay in his place and let them pass, if they did, without bringing attention to himself.

Two men, riding horses, broke through the last of the bushes surrounding this clearing and stopped. One of them, the younger one by looks, lifted a large bundle from his lap and dropped it on the ground. The sounds made when it hit the ground told him that it was alive.

An animal of some kind? Breac slowly pulled himself up to stand, but stayed within the protection of the trees as he watched the younger man climb down from his horse and push the bundle with his foot. It rolled several times as he kicked it across the clearing to the brush at the edge. A cry or grunt echoed with each kick. Breac waited.

"Are ye awake then?" the man asked as he reached down and, using his dagger, slit open the cloak or sack that enshrouded the person within. He gripped both sides and tore it, pulling it free and dumping a bound, naked woman on the wet ground.

A woman? Aye, clearly one, whose feminine curves were not hidden by gown or cloak. Gagged, with her hands tied behind her back, she struggled weakly against those bonds.

"Go ahead, Keegan," the older man called out from his place on top of his horse. "Finish this."

From the seriousness of the tone used when giving the order, Breac expected the younger man to kill the woman, but the younger one put his dagger back in his boot and held out his hand. The older one tossed a large cudgel to him. Rolling her on her back with his foot, he positioned himself over the woman and lifted the club.

"This time you should heed his warning and not return to the village," he said swinging the heavy weapon over his head. The woman began to struggle under his foot and he leaned more heavily on her until she stopped. "This time, you will not be able to come back."

Breac was within an arm's reach before he even decided to intervene, grabbing the club from the young man and throwing it into the trees. He took hold of this Keegan's cloak and tossed him aside, away from the woman, where he could watch both of the men.

"You should not interfere in something not of your concern, stranger," the older man warned. "Her lord has exiled her and she disobeys his orders. He has the right to punish her and we carry out his orders."

Breac could not think of whose lands were nearby or which lord would order such a thing, but he shook his head.

"Who orders such a thing?" he asked. Glancing over at her was a mistake as he realized in a second for her eyes were wild with terror and her naked body shook in fear and cold. "I see not the brand of a whore on her breast. No fingers or hands are missing befitting a thief. What crime has she committed against her lord to earn this kind of punishment?"

He knew he had no standing, no legal right to stop their actions, and he had no doubt they did act on the orders of their lord. But something in her gaze drew him into this and forced him to step where he most likely should not go. The two drew swords then and faced him, one on foot, one on horse, and he knew he was no match for them. But he stood his ground, keeping them on one side and her on the other. Needing to ease the situation or end up dead like this unknown woman would be, Breac held his hands up to show he was not going to fight them.

"It seems a waste of an able-bodied woman when I need a slave to work my farm," he said. Nodding at her, he made his offer. "I will take her and make certain she never returns here." He tugged at his belt and breeches with an obvious gesture, leered at her nakedness, and then smiled. "She will not have the strength to go very far when I finish with her."

The men understood his meaning and so did the woman, for she struggled once more against the ropes binding her legs and hands, managing only to dig herself deeper into the layer of mud at the edge of the clearing where she lay. He could see the doubt in their expressions but he waited, not offering any more words that could sway them or seem overly anxious. He only hoped, for some reason not clear to even him, that the look of disdain for their assignment and exhaustion on the man's face won out over any qualms of handing her over to him. Finally, the older one nodded.

"Take her then and make certain she is never seen any farther south than the standing stones again." He pointed off to the south toward the rings of ancient stone pillars that stood like silent sentinels along the glen. So, her lord governed the lands south of Dunadd then? Breac nodded, but Keegan objected.

"How do we know he will keep his word, Callum? If she returns, it will be our backs that will bear the whip. I say we at least do what our lord ordered—break her legs to make certain she cannot come closer than this." He put his sword back in the scabbard but picked up a large rock as his weapon.

Holy Christ in Heaven! Breaking her legs as he intended to do was as much a death sentence as simply killing her. She would never walk again and the wounds would no doubt fester. Her end would be tortuous and filled with fever and grievous pain. What sin could she have committed to warrant such a brutal punishment? He appealed to Callum, hoping the older warrior would agree.

"I have nothing to give you but my word and I give that as my solemn oath. This woman will never return here or any place south of the stones."

She whimpered again, but he would not look at her. Meeting Callum's gaze, he waited for his answer. He would deal with her once these men were on their way.

"Where is your farm, stranger?" Callum asked.

"More than three days walk from here, many miles north and east of An t-Oban Lotharnach," he exaggerated, wanting the soldier to be comforted by such a distance. He thought Callum would not agree, but then he called Keegan off and the younger man dropped the rock and returned to his horse, muttering his unhappiness with every step. Breac held his breath, hoping this tentative agreement would stand. Callum leaned over and said something under his breath to Keegan, the words he could not hear but they seemed to quiet his objections.

"She is yours now," Callum called out. "Stand by your word or I will find you."

He watched as they left the clearing, heading back in the direction from which they'd come. He didn't move until the sounds of their departure disappeared into the sounds of the storm around him. Any daylight faded quickly and he must handle her before it was too dark to see anything.

Breac reached down and drew his own dagger from its place in his boot and walked toward her. She struggled now, but could not go anywhere but deeper into the mud tied as she was. He stood over her and shook his head in disgust. Then, with blade in hand, he bent down.

# Chapter 2

She could only hope it would be a quicker death than the one Donnell had ordered for her. Aigneis had no chance against this giant of a man, not trussed as she was and exhausted from the brutal ride to wherever this place was. Donnell had claimed to love her and to accept her but now he ordered her death without a moment's hesitation. To fit his needs and to accomplish his goals.

Offering up a prayer to the Christian God, for the old ones had long ignored her pleas, she closed her eyes and waited for the dagger to do its work. After committing as many sins as she had, it did not surprise her that no god would help her. The prick of the dagger into her skin as it sliced through the rough ropes at her ankles shocked more than hurt her.

Aigneis opened her eyes to find the man reaching for her now. Ah, his promise to use her would happen before he killed her and to do that her legs needed to be freed. Unable to watch, she closed her eyes tightly and tried not to struggle and make him angry. Angry men were more dangerous and more likely to add pain to the punishments they wrought. Keegan was one of such men.

Yet again, his actions surprised her, for instead of spreading her legs, he grabbed her at the waist and turned her. When she thought he would position himself at her back and take her from behind, the prick of the dagger scratched her skin again, this time at her wrists. Her hands and arms were without feeling from being tied so tightly for so long and fell useless at her sides. She could not even lift them to defend herself now.

The man rolled her onto her back once more and just as he reached for the thick gag stuffed into her mouth, her arms and hands burned with feeling again. Like a fire racing through her body, her skin and muscles came alive again and she moaned against the rough cloth at the intense pain of it. Before she knew it, the dagger sliced again and he tugged the cloth out of her mouth.

Why did he draw this out? Why did he not simply strike and end it? His touch was almost gentle as he lifted her muddy hair from her face and touched the place across her cheeks and mouth where the cloth had been tied so tightly. This was worse than pain or facing his anger, for it made her damned soul think there was still a chance for life. And there could not be that.

Or could there?

He seemed neither inclined to take her body or her life just then. Once he'd released all the bonds, he stood and lifted her slowly to her feet, supporting her from behind with his strong arms around her. The mud made his efforts more difficult and he stilled for a moment when one of his hands slipped along her skin and cupped her breast instead. Waiting for the inevitable, Aigneis could not believe when he moved his hand back to her waist and stood with her.

"You must move around," he said, his voice gruff with the effort it was taking him to hold her up. "The ropes could have damaged your limbs and lying on the cold ground will not help." When his hand slipped a second time and he let out a harsh curse, Aigneis flinched and waited for him to strike. Instead he placed his large hands around her arms like the gold cuffs she used to wear when she was . . . She shook her head to try to clear her thoughts.

He stood at least a foot taller than she and, because of the hooded cloak or cloth he wore, she only caught a glimpse of his true appearance. With the rain and wind blowing in her eyes, she could only hear his voice and feel the strength in his arms as they held her and in his legs as they supported her.

He began walking forward, forcing her legs to move. She wanted to curse him for it as the painful burning crept down now to her feet, making every step an anguishing one. They'd struggled through more than a dozen paces before the pain lessened and her legs began to support more of her weight. Just as she was able to take a few steps on her own, she felt her body tumbling down. Her scream echoed through the trees.

The icy cold of the water as she hit forced her breath from her body and it surrounded her, pulling her under and down. Aigneis struggled against the cold and the water, trying to hold her breath as she fought to find her way out. Did he mean to drown her like some unwanted dog? Her flailing hands grasped onto his strong arm in that instant and instead of holding her down, he pulled her above the surface. Gasping, she clung to his arm, hoping to get a chance to fight back.

"Hush now," he said softly as he lifted her out of the water. "You were caked with mud and bleeding from a wound I could not see." He smoothed her hair back out of her eyes, treating her with a gentleness that belied her new position—slave to him as master.

"Are you going to kill me?" she asked, trying to calm both the fear and the awful coldness that now shot through her.

He released her with a dark frown and fumbled in the leather bag he carried over his shoulder for something. She drew back as far as she could, but his tall form blocked her way. With the stream at her back and trees forming a row on either side of them, she stood trapped within his grasp. Instead of a weapon, he drew out a garment and shook it out.

"Wring the water out of your hair and put this on," he ordered. "Though 'tis summer and the air can warm, that stream starts high in the hills and never does."

It was a shirt, a long one that ended at her knees when she managed to get it over her head, after twisting her hair to release as much water as possible. The front gaped, exposing her breasts and much of her stomach to his gaze. Since he'd seen and touched her naked body both covered in mud and clean, she thought that was the least of her troubles.

Until she noticed the glint of lust in his gaze as he pushed the woolen cloak from his head and stared at her.

'Twas almost as though covering some of her nakedness was more appealing to him than seeing every inch of her skin. It lasted only a few moments, before he swallowed and nodded at the sky.

"We have precious little daylight left. We should see to your leg and find a drier place for the night." His voice was even and almost comforting. He held out his hand as he backed a few paces from her. "Come."

Whether the exhaustion of the last weeks finally took control or the insanity that Donnell accused her of having set in, she knew not. Aigneis knew only that she could fight no longer. She met the man's gaze as he nodded and motioned with his hand to follow him. Lowering her eyes, she now noticed the gash on her leg and watched as the blood trickled down over her ankle and dripped onto the already-soaked ground beneath her.

She knew not if the storm had strengthened around her, but her sight grew dark and hazy and her ears buzzed like the time a swarm of bees had attacked her. Squinting, Aigneis noticed that the man seemed farther away and . . . grayer, as if all the color had left his hair, his eyes, his skin.

"Do not."

His voice stern now, he warned her against . . . something. Shaking her head in confusion, she felt as though back in the stream with the water rising around her. She reached out her hand in his direction, hoping he would pull her from death once more, but her world went black before he could.

Her pale face turned ghostly white and her eyes rolled back into her head. Breac tried to get her attention when he noticed the changes begin, understanding what would happen next, but she lost consciousness as he watched. Lucky for her, he needed to take but one step to catch her before she landed in the mud again. He leaned over and scooped her into his arms while yet trying to figure out the reasons for his actions of the last several minutes.

Breac carried her back to the clearing and sought out the rough shelter of the copse where he'd left most of his provisions. Holding her slight form against his chest, he eased back down to sit on the ground. Once there, he tugged most of the length of his woolen cloak from around him and wrapped it around her. Then, as the last rays of the storm-covered sun faded, he shifted her in his arms and waited for her to wake. He must have drifted into sleep for the next thing he knew, she scrambled away from him, dragging his cloak with her. The other trees acted as a boundary and when she reached them, she could go no farther.

He stood then, stretched his arms and legs to get rid of the stiffness from sitting too still for too long, and searched his sack for his flint and the few pieces of dry kindling he always carried. Without a fire he could not see her in the darkness. Or more importantly it seemed, she could not see him. He could hear her terror in the rate of her breathing.

"I will try to start a fire," he explained. "Stay where you are."

Breac ignored the sounds of distress from her and got some of the kindling burning. With that faint light, he was able to find some drier branches and start them to burn. They didn't need a fire for the whole night, just long enough for him to see to her wounds and for them to settle in. Everything else could be managed in daylight, hopefully a drier one than this one had been. It took a short time, but soon he had a fire burning well enough to see their small shelter.

And the woman.

She sat huddled against a tree, wrapped in his cloak, watching every move he made. Her pale-colored eyes were wide with fear and she worried her teeth over the fullness of her bottom lip every time he gazed at her. Though her skin was the color of the pearls that his lord's wife wore in a necklace, he knew from seeing her naked that it bore darkening bluish-purple bruises that had not yet shown their true color or size. It was her hair that fascinated him though, the hue of burnished silver with flecks of some darker shade through it. And, cut off as it was only a few inches from her scalp, it began to curl as it dried.

Breac's body reacted then, remembering on its own the pleasing shapes and softness of her body and ignoring the clear signs that she was older than him. Desire at this time was unseemly, even for a man who'd not had a woman in many weeks.

He crouched down, searching in his bag for the oatcakes and cheese he carried. Finding it he broke them in two and held out a portion of each to her. Trying to banish the desire that flowed through his blood now, he turned away after she took the food from his hand. That she took the food and then shifted back as far as she could bothered him in some deep way.

Breac waited for her to eat the cheese and then handed her a skin filled with ale. She accepted it the same way she accepted the food—a quick grab for it and then out of arm's reach. The action should not surprise him; it was an act of fear and, after witnessing what must be only a small part of the treatment she'd received from the men and their lord, it was one he could understand. So, like gentling a wild animal, he would accustom her to his presence. At least for the night.

He had no inclination to bring her to his home and his farm, no matter what story he told to get her released to him. The tasks of seeing to his sister and overseeing his own land and those that his lord owned were too important to be distracted by this woman. No matter that her gaze held a measure of pleading in it each time she looked at him, and no matter that his blood stirred for her in a way he'd not felt for a woman in a long, long time.

So wrapped in his own thoughts and his own arguments about her fate that he did not notice her approach, he startled when she held the skin out to him from just a foot or two away.

"My thanks," she whispered, as she stepped away once more.

"Come closer," he said. "The flame is meager and you cannot feel its heat from over there."

He watched as she stood, wrapped his cloak more securely around her body, and then took a hesitant step forward. She silently slid to sit nearer to the small sputtering fire, but remained as far from him as she could. The night had fallen deeply around them, the sounds of rain grew fainter as the minutes passed in silence. Putting the skin up to his mouth, he drank a mouthful before meeting her gaze.

"What are you called?" he asked.

The low flames sputtered and crackled and he waited for her to answer. What surprised him was the tone of her voice when she did speak.

"Aigneis," she said. Her voice was deeper than when she was terrified and her name flowed like the melody of some unsung song, touching something deep within him. Heat and warmth and comfort flowed through him in that moment, with just one word.

Her name.

"Say it again," he found himself almost pleading to hear it again.

# Chapter 3

"**M**y name is Aigneis."

Her exhaustion lulled her into revealing her name and, worse, it came out in *that* voice. The one she kept hidden from everyone. One of the few remnants of her time in the land of the Sith, it had the most unusual effect on others, especially men. This time was no different. Her captor shifted as he sat on the ground and his eyes glimmered in response.

Aigneis cleared her throat and pitched her voice a bit, nearly whispering now so that it was not as evident. It was the reason the men assigned by her husband kept her gagged—he knew its effect and had warned them. She could, he claimed, tempt the angels from the heights of heaven to the depths of hell with that voice. And though it had tempted him to many, many things, he believed she could overpower the will of men and bend them to her bidding. 'Twas not true, but it did not stop him from believing it or from spreading it as truth and making his people fear her.

"Where are you from?" Breac asked, his eyes intent on hers as he did, as though he was anxious to hear her speak.

Mayhap he was?

Uncertain about revealing anything else to him, she looked away, hoping in each second that passed that he would not challenge her silence. She watched as he lifted the skin to his mouth and drank from it another time. Just as she thought he would not speak again and as the pain in her body from being manhandled for days reached a level that made it impossible to ignore, his strong voice called out to her.

"I am called Breac," he said. He leaned toward the flames, revealing more of his face to her.

In addition to the strength in his voice and in his body, his face was chiseled by masculine angles, with a straight jaw and nose that showed a previous break. Instead of making him look weak, it added a sort of dangerous appeal to his looks. The thing about him that shocked her the most was his age.

Aigneis had lived almost thirty years, but this Breac appeared to be at least five or mayhap even seven years her younger. He wore his black, shoulder-length hair pulled away and tied at his neck. His beard was trimmed close, unlike most men who let their beards grow wild and bushy. But it was his eyes that caught her attention.

Not that their dark brown color was anything apart from ordinary. Nay, 'twas not their color, but the stark sorrow that lay deep within them when he was not paying attention to hiding it. The sorrow was so strong and so clear that it made her heart, one scarred by deception, betrayal, and loss, hurt at the sight of it. Aigneis held out her hand for the skin, thirsty from so many hours without nourishment or drink.

"What are your plans for me?" she asked softly. She did not wait for his reply, for her thirst threatened to overwhelm her, as did the pain piercing through her body and the exhaustion. Tipping it back, she drank several mouthfuls before realizing how little was still left and stopped. "Am I your slave now?"

She watched as a shiver pulsed through him and lust shone once more in his gaze, but only for a moment before he controlled it and banished it.

"I need no slave," he answered. "Come morning, I will take you farther north and release you."

Of all the things she expected and steeled herself to hear, that was not one of them. Did he speak the truth? Would he chance her going back to her . . . lord and bearing such retribution from Donnell's men? As though she'd spoken her word aloud, he shook his head.

"I know not what happened to bring you here," he began. "And in such condition"—he paused, throwing a glance at her cropped hair and his clothing—"but you would be wise to seek a new place and a new life, far from whichever lord you offended."

Considering how many she'd offended in her life, his advice was both warranted and wise, but he had no idea. Even her lord husband, who'd married her because of the bargain her father struck upon her return from the land of the Sith, had no idea. 'Twas the chest filled with an unimagined wealth in gold that convinced her father and her husband to uphold their betrothal and to keep her. Until now.

Her body grew heavy even as her heart did when she dared to think of her ultimate sin. However, she knew this pain was from the beatings and the torturous ride here, bound and held on the back of a horse. She was about to ask his leave to sleep when he spoke again.

"Let me see to that gash and then seek your rest," he said. "The rain is letting up and I will leave at first light." The deep sorrow filled his gaze once more, yet unlike when lust crept in, he made no attempt to hide or banish it.

Aigneis handed the skin back to him, sliding back a few feet. His care was quick and efficient and soon the wound on her leg was clean and wrapped. Then she lay down on her side and curled in a ball. The woolen cloak wrapped around her smelled of his scent—masculine, leather, and something else—and she tried to stay awake long enough to watch him, yet uncertain of his plans. But the heaviness in her body and heart and soul took control and dragged her into a fitful sleep.

Sometime in the night, she awoke, whether from the cool air that settled around them making her shiver or his voice, she knew not. Breac mumbled in his sleep, his words sounded like prayers.

Prayers for Fenella. Fear that she could die. Fear that she would die before his return. All repeated over and over, disturbing his sleep but not waking him. Was Fenella his wife? She suffered from some illness and his guilt was clear from his words. Was this something from his past or the reason for his journey and his haste? He settled deeper into sleep as she thought on calling his name to rouse him from it.

Then later, as she shivered against the cold, Aigneis began to wake. Before she could force herself to sit up and wrap the cloak anew in hopes of better protection from the cold, she was surrounded by a soothing and comforting heat. Lulled back into sleep, she did not remember hearing anything else until his voice called her name again.

"Aigneis," he said. "You must wake now."

Only on his second call did she realize that he spoke her name and that his voice came from behind her. Startled that he was so close, she opened her eyes and tried to sit up. His weight on the cloak yet wrapped around her stopped her. His arm, resting across her waist, held her in place. His warm breath on the back of her neck teased her body and she shivered against it.

He lay next to her! Aigneis began to push him away, but he clutched her tighter.

"Hush now," he whispered against her ear. "You lay shivering in the night and I thought to ease your discomfort." Breac lifted his arm once she stilled and then rolled to his feet away from her. "And to keep myself warmed as well," he admitted.

Aigneis scrambled to the other side of their small enclosure and tugged the cloak loose. Pushing her hair out of her face, she realized that he stared at her. His shirt gaped open again, this time though the bruises that covered her skin were visible to both of them in spite of the day's weak light.

Gathering the edges together, she stood and picked up the cloak once more, her body aching with every move she made. Before she could even try to replace the cloak over herself, he took it from her and wrapped it around her shoulders.

"See to your needs at the stream." His voice was brusque. "I . . . we have a good distance to travel before night."

Aigneis did not argue or even comment, she simply followed his instructions and walked away from their shelter, back through the trees where he pointed. With each step her feet and legs screamed and her back tightened in pain. Her mind had lost the ability to make plans and she only knew she would not lie down and die here as Donnell had ordered and hoped. She must live. She must live to seek her sons.

Breac tried to focus on the tasks he needed to complete in order to get on the road, but his gaze followed the injured woman as she walked away. He'd seen the bruising begin to blossom on her skin and, as his shirt slipped and exposed her, there were few places he saw that were not marked in some way. Now it was not surprising that she'd flinched as he held her close in the night.

She never stopped, in spite of the pain clear in every step she took. This Aigneis continued to walk toward the stream as he'd ordered and never once looked back or hesitated. The sun's light grew stronger with each passing minute and just before she entered the shadows of the trees he saw that her hair was silver, streaked with black.

The length of it spoke of a humiliating punishment, a public sign of the loss of status or honor, and he wondered at it. A disobedient female serf, an unfaithful wife or leman, any willful or offending woman could be dealt such punishment—a beating and the loss of her hair. The way she dealt with her pain and her uncertainty, for he could read that in her gray eyes every time he looked at her, spoke of honor and strength.

She disappeared into the trees and Breac turned back to his task, quickly gathering and packing away any items he needed. The skin of ale was nearly empty so he carried it down to the stream to fill it for their journey. When they reached the next village, he could use a few of his coins to buy more and to buy food.

Breac pushed through the last branches before the rushing water and stopped. He thought she'd walked straight to the water's edge but her path had taken her a different way and she stood in front of him now facing the flowing stream. He watched, holding his breath as he did, as she eased his shirt off her shoulders and down. If he only saw the feminine curves of her body, narrow waist and full hips, he would have been rock-hard in an instant. But the sight before him made his stomach turn.

Not a place on her skin was unmarked.

Lash and cane marks marred her back and buttocks and legs—bruises there and every other possible place from fists or some other weapon. Though none other than the gash he'd wrapped broke the skin, these were evidence of great anger and the need to inflict as much pain as possible. She knelt down slowly and bent over to scoop some water onto her face and arms and he closed his eyes.

He'd seen discipline. Hell, he'd been the recipient of a beating or the lash more than once for disobedience to his father or to his lord, but never had he seen such treatment inflicted as this. Breac moved back as quietly as he could, determined not to add to her humiliation with his gawking. When he was free of the trees, he walked back to the two sacks of his supplies and waited for her return.

Breac thought of his choices and was not satisfied with any of them. He could not fight her battles, whatever they were and no matter the impulse to do so, because he needed to return to his sister as soon as possible. His hand moved to the precious herbs still wrapped and packed safely with the pouch at his waist. Every delay in this journey was a risk to her survival, every hour increased the chances that she would not recover.

From the injuries he saw, Aigneis's ability to keep pace with him was not possible. Her stiff and painful gait across the clearing and down to the stream made it clear she would be a hindrance to his journey home. And though his sister teased him about his tendency to take in stray and injured animals, this was one injured creature he could not.

He also knew that if . . . when his sister recovered and found out that he had abandoned such a one as Aigneis, he would see disappointment in her eyes and could not bear such a thing. So, he either had to not let Fenella find out or . . . he needed to help Aigneis. He wavered between the choices, convincing himself one way and then the other until she walked into the clearing.

Her chin lifted as she spied him watching and she struggled to keep her steps moving smoothly. If he hadn't seen the marks and the injuries, he might even have believed what she tried to fake. When she met his gaze, he nearly stopped breathing.

Her eyes, now visible in the growing light of day, were like something otherworldly. Almost an exact match in color to her hair, an unusual shade of silver, they seemed to reflect the sun's light back at him. And her skin . . .

He'd seen the places covered by his shirt and cloak, but the skin on her face seemed to glow in vibrance, making her look younger than the age he thought her to be. Aye, he'd noticed the difference in their age, with her having at least five more years than he did. In spite of that, she seemed younger now.

She walked up to him, remaining more than an arm's length away, and nodded. "I am ready."

So she was, but was he ready to begin this journey? If she

could display this bravery in the face of a completely unknown future, surely he could?

With an offered prayer that she would not be a distraction from his true task at hand and that whatever caused him to intervene was not a case of scattered wits, he positioned his leather sacks over his shoulder. As he gave a final tug on the straps, he thought he heard his sister's laughter.

Without another word, he nodded back at Aigneis and began walking.

# Chapter 4

It took little more than twenty paces for all his good intentions to fall apart. She could not walk at his pace, not because he was taller and had longer strides, which he did, but because her feet were bare. As he cursed himself for such obvious stupidity, he thought on how to best remedy it. She already wore his spare shirt and his cloak and he had not another pair of shoes or boots. In the end, it was Aigneis who sorted out a solution.

Soon, with the bottom of his shirt torn into strips and wrapped around her feet, they walked north away from the glen.

She never complained and never slowed unless he did, but Breac could read the exhaustion in her eyes, those luminous eyes that seemed to show her emotions. But he found himself easing the grueling pace he'd set for most of the morning and watching from the corner of his eyes for any sign she could not continue.

And cursing himself as he did.

When she stumbled for the third time, he stopped.

Wiping the sweat from his eyes with the back of his hand, he looked up at the sun and knew it was almost at its highest in the sky. There was another eight or so hours of light, another eight or so hours of walking, left in this day. One glance at Aigneis told him she could not do it. Breac handed her the skin with the last of the watered ale.

"There is a village another hour's walk from here," he said, still not certain of what he would do. "Can you make it there and we will stop for food and rest?"

She swallowed another mouthful from the skin and gave it back to him. "I will," she answered.

Not "I can," but "I will," as though sheer force of will would drive her along. And, from what he'd seen of her this last day, he was certain it would. Breac slung the skin over his shoulder and nodded, more confused about her than before.

And more confused over his path.

From her bearing and the softness of her hands, he knew she was noble. She had not worked the fields or labored as a good-wife in a croft. She had lived with others doing the work for her, yet she had been exiled. Nothing made sense to him about her.

The lust and desire he felt at times he could understand—he was a man with needs of the flesh and eyes in his head to see her womanly form. Sleeping next to her in the night, his body reacted as it should—he woke hard and ready to couple with the woman at his side. His prick did not need to know more than that she was there.

His mind though struggled with the confusing knowledge, or lack of it, about her. The most vexing thing was his reaction to her and this fierce growing need within him to protect her. Breac must make a decision about her by the time they reached the village or he would lose too many hours today.

With at least an hour of time to think on the matter, he stood and began walking along the rough road, expecting that she would follow.

Aigneis kept her gaze on his back and took one mindless step after another along the road. She would recover, she knew she would, but each time she was injured, it took longer and longer. Every year away from the Sith, her body returned back to its human frailty. And she'd noticed the biggest changes after seven years.

Her obvious health and vigor gave Donnell hopes for a child, a son, an heir to his and his father's lands and power. Though he knew it not, she believed that the ease with which she'd borne children, sons, for the Sith prince would happen again with Donnell. Seven years they tried and failed and his disappointment became sharper and angrier with the passing of each year.

Part of her hoped for children, to fill the emptiness within her for the ones she'd lost. Part of her was pleased she did not conceive when faced with Donnell's bitter anger and unfaithfulness. Then, three years ago her husband began his pursuit of a new wife and his plan to rid himself of Aigneis. The worst betrayal was her father's support for breaking the marriage contract.

Tears gathered in her eyes and she wiped them away. The Sith prince had warned her about Donnell, but Aigneis did not heed the warning of what was to come if she left the Sith world. Taking in a labored breath and letting it out slowly, she brought her attention back to the road . . . and to the man before her.

She knew he watched her as they walked, discreetly so that she would not notice, but she had. The cant of his head as he led her down the road belied his seeming inattention to her. And each step he took that did not leave her behind made her wonder more about this Breac.

Most men, nay all men, she knew would never have stepped into the situation that presented itself to him in the middle of nowhere. Facing down armed men on a mission from their lord? Saving a stranger, a woman, from a fate decreed by her rightful lord? Staying at her side with no reason to? She shook her head. This Breac was different from any man she'd ever met and part of it was some sense of his deep and abiding honor.

Even now, when his purpose, whatever it was, should take him swiftly away from her halting steps, he waited for her and adjusted his pace so she was not left behind.

Aigneis thought on his actions and the words he'd spoken in the night as they walked toward the village ahead. Fenella. Sick. Dying. The thought of this woman dying terrified Breac and tore his heart apart. Again, his honor was clear in his actions.

Thinking about him was easier than considering her own life, her own sins, and her own future, so she did that as they walked. About an hour later, he finally stopped and held out the skin to her to drink.

"Finish it. The village lies ahead and I will get more," he said as though in answer to her unspoken question. She lifted it up and drank every drop she could squeeze from it.

He took it from her. Lifting the two other sacks from his shoulder, he placed them on the ground and motioned for her to sit. "It should take me about an hour to return," he began to explain. "Stay here, out of sight, and you should be safe."

"Wait," she said, as she placed her hand on his arm. "Why are you helping me?" He startled at both her touch and her question. Then she dared to ask more. "Who is Fenella?"

He drew back quickly, stumbling over a small rock in the path behind him. Regaining his balance, his eyes took on that stark, empty expression of guilt and sorrow. "How . . . ?"

"You spoke her name in your sleep," she said, shocked at the extent of his sorrow. "Is she the reason for your relentless pace?"

Aigneis thought he would answer. However, he opened and closed his mouth several times as though trying to make words come out before he turned and walked away. She thought to call out to him, to offer an apology to him, but within seconds, his long legs had carried him too far for him to hear her.

Unless she used the voice.

Not strong enough and not ready to reveal any more of herself to this stranger, she sat and watched him leave. Only when she spied his leather sacks did she feel comforted that he would return . . . for them.

Taking hold of them, she carried them deeper into the shadow of the trees, found a dry spot, and lay down there. Using one sack to pillow her head, she drew his cloak tightly around her and curled up to sleep while she waited. Only through sleep could she recover her strength and, if he was going to leave her on her own, she needed that strength.

When she next opened her eyes, she found him sitting nearby watching her sleep.

Breac held out a chunk of bread to her and she sat up, untwisted the cloak from around herself, and reached out for it. He did the same with a piece of roasted fowl and a small wedge of cheese. And she ate whatever he handed her, famished from both the walking since dawn and the healing that was happening within her. She stopped only when he did and washed it down with a long drink from a new skin of ale. Her stomach had not been full in many, many days and it felt wonderful.

"Fenella is my sister," he said without preamble. "She is ill and I must return."

"What is wrong with her?" Aigneis asked. "Has she seen a

healer?" She looked around for something to wipe her hands on, but there was none. "How old is she?"

Her curiosity was rising as her strength did. 'Twas not a matter of her concern, but she was touched that he explained himself. Most men she knew . . . She shook her head.

"She is the reason for your haste and I delay you from her," she said, finally putting some of the bits and pieces of knowledge and observation together. Climbing to her feet, she nodded at him. "My thanks for your help and for the food."

Doubt crept into his expression now, his dark brown eyes wide and staring at her. He held out a bundle to her. Clothing it seemed.

"Get dressed. Then we can speak on this."

Aigneis took the bound pile of fabric from him and turned her back. Tugging the string free from it, she found a shift, a gown and tunic, and, more surprising, a pair of stockings and soft leather shoes. The last item was a square piece of material to cover her head. With barely a glance back to see if he watched, she dropped the cloak, shrugged off his shirt and dressed in the clean garments.

Folding the fabric into a triangle, she wrapped it around her head, catching the wild curls under it and securing it at the nape of her neck. 'Twas not the jeweled circlet and fine linen veil she used to wear, but it covered the evidence of her shame and made her feel safe again. Aigneis turned back to face Breac and found him staring at her.

He'd seen her skin!

The look on his face, eyes widened in disbelief, spoke of his shock. The frown that followed told her he was trying to figure out what he'd seen only this morning and how it could be healed now. The shake of his head demonstrated how he could not believe it.

She waited for the next emotional step—the one that usually followed the disbelief, the shock, and the inability to understand.

Fear.

Hatred.

Anger.

Aigneis was tempted to close her eyes so she would not see his. To this point, he'd surprised her with his reactions to finding himself in the middle of something not of his making or concern. The intervention, the protection, and the way he saw to her needs were not what she was accustomed to facing. Now was the time when he would react as all other men did when faced with the reality of her.

Aigneis held her breath and waited and watched for the inevitable to happen.

# Chapter 5

The bruises.
   The lash and cane marks.
All nearly gone.
Had he only imagined them there and now saw the truth? Or had they disappeared in just hours?
How?
She'd moved quickly and he'd turned away to give her some measure of privacy, but not before catching a glimpse of her legs and her back. Now, instead of the angry red and purple criss-cross markings of punishment, her skin was nearly unmarred, nearly perfection in its creamy whiteness. Instead of a damaged victim, a woman stood in her place.
Breac considered himself a man with some intelligence, not the wisest or most knowledgeable, but he was known for his logical thinking and common sense. That was why Lord Malcolm appointed him as overseer to the village and consulted him on matters about the crops and supplies. Neither of those skills or that position helped now in the face of this incredible situation. When he met her gaze, he could see that she watched him and waited for some reaction.
"How?" he asked, the word escaping before he could stop it.
Part of him wanted to tear off her clothes to see if he mistook the shadows she stood in for changes to the color of her skin. Part wanted to run, run back to his village and to his sister and forget

he'd met a woman such as this. But the part that won out was the man inside him who had seen the real pain and shame and fear in her gaze and the true injuries to her body and discovered that he wanted to banish both from her forever.

"How?" he asked again.

She looked away then and would not meet his eyes. Her hands twisted in his shirt and cloak which she held tightly, positioned almost as he would a weapon before him. She shrugged.

"I know not."

Aigneis may not know the whole of it, but the guilt now lacing her expression said she knew some of it. And she was not going to reveal what she did know.

He swore not to allow her to distract him from his purpose and this new aspect about her threatened his will more than anything else she'd done or said. Fenella lay dying, a certainty if he did not return with the medicaments in his bag, a possibility even if he did return. So, even fascination and intrigue could not sway him from the decision he'd made on the way to the village.

Even fascination and intrigue wrapped in the feminine curves of this woman before him.

"I spoke with the blacksmith of the village. I know him from other dealings in the past and he is a good man."

"The blacksmith?" she stuttered.

"Aye. Once you recover . . ." he stumbled over the words now. "He will see you to his cousin who lives north of here and will offer you a place to live. You will be safe there while you decide about your future."

The words rushed out of him and he could see their effect on her. Like more blows raining down on her, she flinched with his attempt to separate their paths, one from the other. Then he watched her gather the shards of her pride around herself and nod in reply.

Aigneis folded the torn and dirty shirt and cloak and handed them back to him. Then she packed up the leftover food into one of the sacks and waited as he did the other. She did not say anything as he led her down the path back to the village. Her steps seemed less labored than earlier though she rarely met his gaze or said a word at all.

He tried to convince himself of the rightness of his decision.

They were strangers. He'd managed to save her life. He had his own responsibilities to which and to whom he must return as quickly as possible. She could not be part of his life.

Breac walked on, trying to use those words to convince his heart that he was making the right decision, but he knew only that his heart was not listening.

Aigneis understood his reaction—she'd seen it before, whether in her father's eyes or Donnell's or his men's or many others when faced with the strange remnants of Sith left in her. Most were not as honorable as Breac though, for he made arrangements for her even though he could not or would not take her with him. And though they were strangers and he'd done more than her own family had for her, she had no claim on him or his life.

So, she would honor his actions by letting him leave without question or argument. Without begging to stay with him as her heart wanted to do. She shook her head in disbelief at the very thought of it.

Aigneis had followed her heart's desires twice in her life, and the cost turned out to be dear—first her sons to their father's curse and then her own life to her husband's needs. She would not do it again, no matter that he seemed honorable or good. It would not last when his wishes and needs exceeded hers.

And when that happened, she feared the possible cost of such a betrayal. What did she have left to lose? Her soul?

So, she kept her thoughts to herself and walked along the road behind him—more comfortable in the clothing and shoes he'd brought and in less pain than earlier, but more uncomfortable for knowing the truth of it.

He was just like the other men in her life.

'Twas hard to think of him like that when she noticed he still slowed his pace so she could keep up with him. And when he kept glancing back to make certain she was following. And especially when he waited for her so they could enter the village side-by-side and without her trailing like a serf.

Soon, within shockingly few minutes, she found herself standing at the smith's cottage, watching Breac leave her behind. Aigneis had learned how low her husband had sunk in his attempts to rid himself of an unwanted wife and how low her father had in order to keep as much of her gold as possible for his own use. But this hurt her in some way she could not describe.

She only knew she was not content to stay and let him leave. His honor demanded he get back to his sister, but there was nothing to keep her from following him. And when she remembered his frantic whispers in the night that spoke of his fears for his sister's life, Aigneis knew she wanted to be there to take the pain from his gaze and his heart when his sister did not survive.

She could not explain how she knew that, but she did. And she suspected that he did, too. So, she found herself back on the road, trying to catch up with him before the distance became too great. An hour later, she walked along the road as it curved sharply and spied Breac coming toward her. Aigneis stopped and waited for him.

The doubts struck within minutes of leaving the village . . . and leaving Aigneis behind. Breac knew, he knew, it was the right thing to do, but something forced him back to get her. He did not own her, nor did he have any claim on her. He knew both of those things well. His heart whispered other things to him.

Finally, his practical part won out, deciding that he would ask her to come and care for his sister. It made sense. He would not have to worry about her care if Aigneis was there. He would not have to hire others to see to her during the days when he spent his hours at his duties for Lord Malcolm. He did not fool himself about the other reasons, the ones he did not think but felt through his flesh and bone.

He wanted her.

The vitality she offered. The curves of her body. The scent and creaminess of her skin. Everything about her tugged at him like an unseen cord, pulling him to her.

Even now, the thought of the way she felt against him in the night made him hard. The memory of the full breasts and hips that he saw as she dressed. The riotous silver curls—covered now—that begged him to pull off the kerchief and run his fingers through them. The mouth that could utter words and a name in a way that made him feel it instead of hear it.

All that and more and the intensity of it shocked and worried him. Not usually a man to be controlled by needs of the flesh, the power of his desire for her was something new.

He'd turned and was heading back to the village before he ever made the decision. Breac did not see her until he almost walked into her as she stood by the road. Puzzled to find her there and not in the village, he noticed she carried the sack of additional clothing he'd purchased from one of the villagers for her. Her expression gave no clue as to her thoughts or feelings as she stood there watching him approach.

Her presence answered part of the request he planned to make, for she would not be here following him if she did not wish to accompany him home. Would she?

"I . . . ," he said, pausing as he tried to put the words together for the rest.

"I . . . ," she said at the same time, pausing as he did.

Breac laughed at the simple irony of it and she smiled.

Holy God in Heaven! When she smiled . . . he lost his breath and his mind at the splendor of it. Though none of her features, other than her eyes, could be called beautiful, when those did sparkle, they lit up her face with a radiance he could feel in his own heart.

"I know you are confused and have many choices to make about your life, but would you consider coming with me to care for my sister?" He blurted out the whole question at once. Breac could not remember feeling so nervous about anything as he did over this. His stomach tightened, his mouth dried, and he held his breath as though her answer would determine his next one. "I can pay you," he added, as though it would help.

She smiled again at his offer and nodded. "You have paid me more than enough already," she whispered. "I would come and care for her, as long as you have need of me. 'Tis the least I can do for you, Breac."

His body reacted then, both to her smile and to her words and to the sound of his name on her lips, as visions of their two bodies, sleek with heat and sweat, entwined in passion, flitted through his thoughts. He could feel his thrusts into her womanly flesh, hear her cries of completion, and even taste the saltiness of her skin as they coupled. Breac cleared his throat and pushed those thoughts away. He was not asking her to be his leman, only a companion and caregiver to his sister.

"Can you walk?" he asked. "We have far to travel." His question sounded stupid even to him, but he needed to say something to banish the images of heated embraces that still threatened.

"I am feeling much stronger now," she replied. "I do not think I can keep up with your long strides, but I will try."

The silence between them as they began was companionable, and he did not try to comprehend the improvements in her condition. He just accepted them because they could not be explained. He did need someone to help with Fenella and he sensed she would be able to help in ways he could not yet understand.

"Tell me of Fenella," she said after they'd walked for another quarter hour or so. He noticed that she kept her voice low and in one tone, but pushed away any thought of questioning her about it.

Breac felt his spirits lightened as he spoke of Fenella, her kind personality, the responsibility he had of her since their parents' death, the sweetness that everyone remembered about her, and many, many other things. When he thought he was finished, she asked about the illness and he went on. Some of the revelations were easy things to speak of, some were not, but he continued until he had no more words to use about Fenella.

Aigneis had not spoken other than to ask him more questions; the rest of the conversation had been one-sided. For the first time since she'd fallen ill, he'd spoken to someone else about his beloved sister and shared his hopes and his fears.

The miles moved by quickly and, although he slowed his pace, they made up much distance over the hours. Though clouds built in the sky, it did not rain, and Breac offered a prayer of thanks for that. If the weather held clear for another two days, he could be home.

After stopping for another meal break later that afternoon, Breac began planning for the coming night. As they moved north of the glen and further inland away from the coast, the air grew a bit drier, giving him hope for an easy night. Watching as the sun dipped lower in the sky, he began searching for a sheltered place where they could sleep.

The road followed the path of the stream and they walked uphill as it meandered into the highlands toward the lake that would lead to his village. When the road leveled once more, he found a clearing in front of an outcropping of rocks, almost like a small cave, and decided to use it for the night. Within a short time, as the day's light faded, he'd built a fire, cleaned out their stone shelter of remnants of brush, and prepared a place to sleep within it.

Aigneis offered to set out their food, so he decided to take advantage to the closeness of the water. He'd not washed in days, not his usual custom, and his skin itched from the dampness of the rain and the dirt of the road. He took the soiled shirt she'd worn along with him and, after explaining his task to her, he headed for the stream.

# Chapter 6

Aigneis watched as he strode away from the shelter. Deciding not to take out their food until he returned, she did sort through it and choose something for them to share. She noticed that one of their skins was empty, so she made up her mind to fill it before it was full dark. Following the path he had but turning uphill just as she reached the water's edge, she dipped the leather skin into the rushing water and let it fill.

She only then realized that it felt good to be needed and useful. After so many years of being made to feel like a burden to others and forced to know she was unwanted, knowing that she could help and would help, brought her a satisfaction she'd not felt in a very long time. And by the time she was not needed by Breac and his sister, her mind would sort through her choices and accept one.

Aigneis stood with the heavy skin in her hand and lost her balance, stumbling and landing on her bottom. She managed to keep her grasp on the skin so it did not float off downstream in the water. Laughing to herself, she began to climb to her feet but the sight before her stopped her. Some yards downstream, blocked by some brush, Breac stood.

Naked.

He walked out of the bushes to the water's edge and crouched down to wash his body.

Aigneis' own body reacted to his male form by sending waves of heat then ice through her veins.

His strong arms connected to a wide muscular chest that was covered with black hair, which tapered down below his narrow waist and hips before covering his prick. His thighs were like tree trunks, even more muscular than his chest. She thought his body closer to the Sith prince's, when in a human form, than to her husband's, and her entire body warmed as she thought about touching the curls on his chest and stomach and . . .

He turned then and she glimpsed his back. It was no less impressive than the other part of him, with each limb and back and buttocks covered in muscles that rippled as he moved. Her mouth went dry as he bent over, splashed water on his skin, and then rubbed it to clean himself. She'd felt those muscles, that strength, as he'd lifted her, held her on her feet, carried her from the stream, and then when he'd lain with her in the night.

What would it feel like to couple with such a man? To feel his strong hands running over her skin and to have him push his hardened . . .

Shaking herself free of such gawking and fleshly thoughts, she scrambled to her feet and walked back to the shelter. Her face grew heated and the place between her legs grew both heated and wet as she remembered his form, his flesh, and his strength. That heat threatened to burst into flames when he walked back from the stream wearing only his trews.

Aigneis tried not to notice the way that garment lay loose over his hips, or how his stomach rippled as he leaned forward and tossed his other wet clothes over bushes to dry. Or how his arms flexed as he reached up and tied his hair back with a thin strip of leather. He finished and approached and Aigneis realized the food was not ready!

She quickly opened a cloth on the ground and placed the roasted meat, cheese, and last chunk of bread there. He reached down for the skin she'd dropped and hefted it in his hand. She could tell the moment he noticed it was filled and then when he realized what she had done and where. The heat of embarrassment crept further into her cheeks and it was all she could do to keep from covering them with her hands.

They ate in silence, as she considered about this situation. She'd coupled with a man, well, a male, when she thought it was for love and with her husband when she knew it was for duty, but her thoughts today involved neither of those. Donnell's disavowal of their marriage was accepted by everyone, except her, and it meant they were no longer man and wife. But Aigneis had been faithful to her vows and had given her oath to remain his wife until death.

Men of noble status always had a leman, and 'twas not unusual at all for them to couple with women other than their legal wives. Some of higher and royal status even had concubines, but women were expected to do their duty, accept their husbands' attentions, and bear his children.

She gazed across at Breac as he ate. She'd not asked him about a wife. She never thought to ask such a question of him, with his attention focused on his sister. He wanted her, 'twas clear in the way he looked at her, but would it be as leman? Would she supplant someone else in his bed? Somehow, she could not imagine him taking a mistress while married.

"Do you have a wife?" she asked. Better to know than to be surprised later.

He choked on the food in his mouth and had to cough several times to clear it and be able to breathe. "Nay," he finally said. Drinking some water, he finally felt as though he could speak. "Though once my sister is well, 'tis something that Lord Malcolm would like to see accomplished."

Breac could see her thinking on his words and wondered what she would ask next. He thought her silence through dinner had been out of embarrassment that he knew she'd spied on him at the stream. But this question bespoke of more personal matters.

"Is your lord interested in your marriage because you are serf? Or family mayhap?" she asked as she tossed the last of her bread in her mouth and chewed it.

"Family," he answered. "Though a distant connection, I am cousin to his wife and serve him as a freeman. He would like me to marry and settle permanently with him."

Some indefinable emotion passed over her face for an instant and then it was gone. She settled back into silence as they finished their food and packed the rest away for their journey on the morrow. He never claimed to understand the way women behaved or thought, but he suspected she wondered about the coming night.

As did he.

He saw her as she ran away from the stream and knew she'd been watching him there. Her perusal since his return and through their meal included moments of plain scrutiny as well as secret glances at his body and his face. 'Twas her body's reaction that told him she thought about tupping—for each time she looked at him, a blush crept into her cheeks or her breathing grew shallow or, more telling than those, her nipples tightened into peaks he could see pressing against the gown and tunic she wore.

Breac turned his attentions back to preparing for sleep. He banked the small fire so that it would continue to burn low for a bit longer and then took his cloak and spread it next to the fire, under the cover of the rocks. He sat down and watched her fidget with the sacks of supplies and food and the skins until she'd arranged them and rearranged them several times. Holding out his hand, he made his offer.

"Lie with me," he said softly.

The first reaction she had was that her blush grew stronger until he thought she might burst. Then, she glanced from him to the cloak and back again three times. Her question made him laugh.

"To sleep?"

"We did so last night and you came to no harm," he said.

Though his body and especially his cock clamored for more than sleeping next to her, his honor would not permit him to demand her favors. He did not force himself on women. And this woman had been forced too much already by too many men and he did not want her to count him among them and their ilk.

Aigneis walked over to him and took his hand. He assisted her as she sat, then again as she lay down next to him on the cloak. The last thing she did was to pull the kerchief from her head, freeing the mass of curls that he wanted to touch. Holding himself under control, he moved in closer to her and then drew the free edge of the cloak over both of them.

Within moments it seemed, she fell into a deep sleep, barely moving, barely breathing, as he lay behind her with his body afire with desire for more than sleep. If she were awake, she would have no doubt of it from the size and hardness of his cock, so mayhap 'twas best she slept.

But it took a long time, with much effort, for him to quiet the raging need within his body and force it to sleep. All the miles walked and sheer physical exhaustion could not compare to the enticement she offered, if she offered, and his body stood ready for any sign from her. The soft snore that escaped her though was not the sign he'd hoped for; it served to calm him down quickly.

When next he knew it, the night's darkness was full upon them and he could feel that she'd rolled away from him. Then he noticed that she watched him through eyes that seemed to glow and glimmer. The soft touch of her hand on his face surprised him, but her words shocked him to the core.

"Lie with me, Breac."

If he mistook her meaning, the way she caressed his face, touching his mouth and outlining his lips, and then sliding her hand down his jaw and neck onto his shoulder, convinced him she did not mean to sleep. Her fingers slid onto the bare skin of his chest and she swirled them in the hair there, teasing and tickling in a playful way. But once she spoke again and her voice pierced through him, he did not feel playful at all.

"Couple with me, Breac," she said in a breathy voice that spoke of desire and pleasure and need and passion.

How did she make him feel it in his blood with just words? How was it that the sound of his name on her lips drove him to madness? Her fingers now traced the edge of his trews and, with as loose as they were, she could have slipped inside to touch the length of him easily. His hips thrust forward toward her before he could decide to do it. He prayed her hand would slip inside.

She moved closer then, leaning up on her elbows and nearer to him. He struggled to control the growing beast within, but her scent and the nearness of her body let it break forth. As though she knew, she laughed softly and the throaty sexual tone made him growl in reply. And then he moved.

First he guided her hand where he wanted it to be and then he pulled the rest of her into his arms and took her mouth in a kiss that inflamed him more rather than satisfying his need. She responded by wrapping her fingers around his flesh and sliding it as he slid his tongue into her mouth and tasted her deeply. He nearly lost his breath as she slid her hand lower and touched his balls. Cupping them, she massaged the length of him and then encircled his cock with her fingers once more.

Breac drew back then, releasing her mouth and hearing her draw in a ragged breath. Before he reached over to loosen the laces of her tunic and gown, for he wanted to feel her skin against his, he paused.

"Do you do this out of obligation?" he asked, while his thoughts could still be coherent. "Is this because I saved your life?" The rational part within him did not want her gratitude and the irrational part only wanted to bury himself to the hilt in her heated flesh.

"Would it matter to you?" she asked, her voice surrounding him and making his skin heat.

"Aye." His answer an honest one, for he did not want her gratitude. He wanted her desire.

"This is for pleasure, Breac, not gratitude," she assured him. Then she leaned her head back and laughed softly, the sound of it echoing through their shelter and out into the night. "Pleasure me, Breac."

# Chapter 7

Aigneis meant it.

For once in her life, she desired a man not her love, not her husband, not someone who could claim her life or her heart, just someone with whom she could share a moment or two of pleasure. When he disclosed his plans for a wife, a burden was lifted from her, for she was neither interested nor able to be such a woman for him.

First, she was married. Though abandoned by her husband and family and expected to accept the decision, Aigneis knew she could never again take marriage vows with another man until Donnell died.

Second, she was too old for him. Protected yet from the ravages of age, Aigneis would soon show signs of her true age as the touch of the Sith wore off and she became what she was—a woman of nigh onto thirty-and-five years old.

Third and worst for a man seeking a wife, she could never bear him children. If her true age did not soon prevent it, something done by the Sith prince would. Aigneis knew in her soul that she would never bear any man's children again since she had born those of the Sith.

Once those matters had sorted themselves out in her thoughts, she knew that she could provide for him something he needed and would need in the coming days—a place to release his torment and grief and passion while he dealt with his sister's coming death. And in exchange she could share some moments of pleasure before she left him to the life he must have and she to whatever fate intended.

He moved quickly then and she found her garments not unlaced and loosened, but pulled as one over her head, leaving her only in her shift and stockings. Then, but a moment later, even those were gone, and she felt the heat of his skin against hers and moaned at the intensity of the feeling.

And he was only just beginning.

Aigneis smiled then as he stripped off his trews and covered her with his now-naked body. Wrapping her arms around him, she ran her hands over the strong muscles of his shoulders and back and then down farther, cupping his buttocks and holding him tightly. Instead of quickly spreading her legs and entering her as Donnell did, Breac began to ease down her body, suckling and licking her neck and shoulders and on and on until he reached her breasts.

She gasped at the touch of his mouth on the tip of one and then the other. She arched as he drew it into his mouth and teased it with his teeth and tongue. Aigneis lost control, holding his head close and urging him to do it over and over and over. He laughed now. The masculine deepness of it made her ache within for his flesh to fill hers. Still, he crept lower until she could feel the heat of his breath on her stomach.

What did he mean to do? Surely not . . .

She felt his large hand slip between her legs and then the touch of a calloused finger along the throbbing cleft there. Her legs opened for him and he slid one and then two fingers deep within, rubbing against a sensitive spot near the top that made her cry out in pleasure.

And still he did not enter her.

Aigneis ached inside, something tightened and tightened and she could only feel. He brushed her hands away when she tried to reach his prick, laughing again, as he relentlessly caressed her.

"Breac," she called out, infusing her words with every bit of the voice she could. "Take me, Breac. Take me," she commanded.

Whether the power of the voice or the strength of his arousal and desire, she knew not, but finally he moved into the cradle of her thighs, lifted her legs around his waist, and thrust in until he could go no deeper. Her breath rushed out at the power of his strokes and every muscle of her body from deep inside out to her skin spasmed at the same time.

As she keened out her satisfaction, he began to take his. Slow then faster. Shallow then deep and deeper still. Even paced then without pattern. He took her breath away with the way he filled her time and time again, over and over until she found herself on the edge again and yet again. His young hard body and hungry prick would not be conquered until he wished to give in, so she opened to him, allowing him to do as he wanted and allowing her own body to respond until she'd given everything she could.

Breac must have known, for he laughed wickedly and then rocked himself deep within her, and once more, until she felt the hot release of his seed deep in her body.

Aigneis waited for him to withdraw and move away, but he remained buried inside her for some time—long enough for her breathing to return to normal and the waves and waves of pleasurable throbbing to calm within her. Breac eased from her, but held her close, turning them onto their sides and wrapping his leg around her to keep her there.

It did not take long for the relief brought by that kind of pleasure and the exhaustion that she barely held at bay to return and drag her into sleep. Held tightly in his arms, warmed by the closeness of his body and overwhelmed by the passion she'd just tasted, Aigneis fell deeply asleep.

Breac lay awake before the first glimmers of sun crossed the line of dawn. He heard the morning song of the birds in the forest around them just as the first note was sung. And he held her as she slept. For all that his body was exhausted from the miles traveled over these last five days and the release he experienced deep within her body, Breac could not find sleep.

He'd lost his mind in the night as she offered herself to him and he feared her reaction when she woke. He had taken her, and in spite of the fact she begged, nay ordered him to it, he worried about the vigorous way he'd done it. Worse, if she woke and gave him any sign of wishing to repeat it, he would plow her as deeply and as thoroughly this morn as he had last night.

He did not recognize the ravening beast that must live within him and crave fleshly pleasures, but he knew it would rouse for her at the slightest provocation. She shifted in his arms as though sensing his attention, but she did not wake.

He took advantage of her being asleep and the growing light to search her skin for the marks he knew had been there. Now, there were fewer places where he could see the remnants of bruising and they were lighter than the previous morning when he saw her skin. How had she healed in so little time?

It seemed too unbelievable, but when he considered some of the stories told of the Old Ones and the Sith who'd lived down the glen from the dawn of time, he wondered if it was too far-fetched to think it linked to something Otherworldly. Even the healer whom he sought told stories about the old ways and the power of the Sith.

The biggest practical question he had for her was about her past—who was she and who was the lord she'd offended. And what would she do now.

Breac watched her face as she slept and could not stop himself from reaching out and touching her hair. The curls were soft under his fingers and they made her look younger than he thought her to be. The color was different from other shades of gray he'd seen, for it glimmered when the sun's light touched it instead of being dull and colorless. When he moved his hand away, she gazed up at him.

He had so many questions to ask her, but feared she would continue to avoid answering them. Now, the morning after such a joining seemed a good time to pursue some questions.

"Is it dawn so soon?" she asked, separating from him but remaining close enough for him to feel the heat of her body, and she his.

"Nearly. The birds will begin their morning song soon," he said. One did just as he said it and he smiled. "Like that one."

"How much farther to the lake?" she asked, sitting up and searching the ground around them. She did not ask him often and did not complain at his answers.

"About eight hours traveling to reach the southern end. I need to reach it by dark, so we can take a boat in the morning," he explained. He remained as he was, unconcerned with his nakedness as she stood and began picking up the clothing that was flung in

172 / *Terri Brisbin*

nearly every corner of their shelter. His trews, her gown and tunic, her shift and stockings.

As she walked to retrieve the garments, he examined every inch of her skin he could see. Not a sign of injury. No sign of lash or cane. Nothing. She noticed his attention and sat at his side.

"Did I imagine it then?" he asked. "Were the bruises only a trick of the light?" He reached out and touched the skin on her shoulder where a large handprint had been . . . and now was gone.

"No," she said with a shake of her head. "You did not imagine it." She tugged her shift over her head and into place. The gown and tunic followed.

"How does it happen? I want to understand," he offered.

"I know not how it happens, Breac. I heal. I heal quickly."

She seemed irritated by his questions. As she pulled first one then the other stocking on and tied them in place, she shrugged. "I cannot explain it."

She would not explain it, for he could read that expression in her eyes and it spoke of knowing exactly how it worked. And why it happened as well. So, although she trusted him with her body for comfort and pleasure, she did not trust him with her past. Since they'd known each other for less than two days, it wasn't something he expected her to do.

"Can you heal others?" His first thought when she revealed even this little was of Fenella.

"Nay," she said tersely without even sparing a glance at him. Had she tried and failed? Was her exile due to that?

"How many years have you?" he asked, hoping she would answer a nonthreatening question after refusing the other.

She stood and moved away, searching for and finding the shoes he'd bought for her. Aigneis sat on a rock and tied them in place, without saying a word. Just when he thought she would not answer him, she spoke.

"How old do you think I am?"

He'd watched her walk around the sheltered area. He'd seen and touched her body, and though tempted to say as old as him, Breac knew she was older. He climbed to his feet now, pulled on his trews, and stared at her from a few paces away, searching for clues.

"I have twenty-and-five years. I think you are older."

She nodded her head in reply. Finished dressing, she began to walk away.

"How many years, Aigneis?" He followed her as she set off for the stream. "How many years?" he called out. She mumbled some number and disappeared into the trees.

He'd heard the number, but shook his head in disbelief. Most women of that age in his village were already grandmothers. Or widowed. Or married again if they'd survived that long. Yet she survived and somehow managed to look fifteen years younger than the age she said. It could not be.

Breac decided he would ask no more questions of her. If he could not or would not accept her answers, it made no sense to pursue them. In spite of what happened between them, she would stay with him, with them, until Fenella recovered and then be on her way. He would find a wife and settle in as Lord Malcolm's overseer.

She returned from the stream and he took his turn there. After she commented that it would take her nine hours to walk what he could in eight, they ate quickly, packed up their supplies, and began walking.

Hours later, after the sun peaked and dropped from its highest point in the sky, Breac realized they would not reach the lake by nightfall. 'Twas not because of Aigneis, for she kept up his hard pace through the entire day, but just because he'd misjudged the distance he had left. Still, they should reach the lake in the morning, with time enough left in the day to reach home by dark tomorrow.

"You should go on without me, Breac," she said. Her soft voice coming from behind as he stood in the road both grieving his mistake and trying to accept it. "Surely you can reach the lake on your own."

He turned to look at her and realized she was in earnest. "And that will gain me what? I will still have to wait until morn to hire a boat." He shook his head. "And I will worry with each step about your safety and whether you will find the way there."

The admission surprised him because he'd spent the day convincing himself that there was nothing between them except a shared need for physical release. Yet he realized he spoke the truth to her. He had invited her to come home with him, so she was his responsibility and he could not abandon her now.

"I will not hold you up in the morn," she promised as she took the sacks from him to unpack their food.

They worked well together, having gotten into a pattern each time they stopped. She would set out the food, he would refill the skins from the stream. As had happened last night, she set out their bedding while he gathered wood and made a fire. Soon, in a short time, their camp was set and night was falling.

Breac watched as her eyes drifted shut for a moment and then opened widely as she fought sleep. Then again, but this time they remained closed longer before opening. Her ability to fall asleep was different from his, for he tossed and turned for a long time each night before finding rest.

"Aigneis," he whispered, trying to get her attention without startling her. He stood and put the remains of their meal back in the sack and tucked it away before approaching her. "Aigneis? 'Tis time to sleep."

She roused long enough to take his hand and let him see her to the covered ground next to the fire. He laid down first and helped her down to lie at his side. Once settled side by side, she rolled toward him and nestled in his arms as sleep took her.

He did not sleep then, so that a few hours later when she woke from this deep rest, he was yet awake. Breac was too restless and wondered why she'd awakened.

"I would heal her if I could, Breac. I owe you that much," she said quietly. Sliding away from him, she stared at him as though willing him to something.

"I think you would," he admitted. Reaching out and touching her cheek with the back of his hand, he stroked it gently.

He did believe she would if she could.

There was a sadness in her gaze now as she met his, but she offered no words to explain that either. He climbed to his feet.

"I will be back. I need to . . . walk a bit," he said.

She said nothing, only watching him with those silver gray eyes as he walked toward the stream. He suspected that nothing would help him sleep this night. All he could do was to count the minutes until the sun rose and he could be on his way home.

Breac never saw her stand and follow his path.

# Chapter 8

Fenella was dead.

Aigneis shivered as she thought the words—the words, the declaration, that troubled her more as they moved closer to his village and his sister. Even if forced to it, she could not explain how she knew, but it was, she feared, the truth.

And it would destroy this good man.

His restlessness was palpable to her as he struggled through the night before the day came that would see him home. Even now, as he walked away because he could not identify the real reason for it, she could.

Once back among her family and away from the Sith, Aigneis discovered she had some talents or skills. Coming with no regularity or explanation, sometimes she could see things that were not around her. At first she thought she was dreaming while awake, but later she realized that these were visions of a past or present or future event. She could hear things—sometimes people's thoughts unspoken rang inside her head. Sometimes the truth of a matter would echo around her, clear to no one else but her.

And she healed. When she first noticed it, she had tried to use the living force that seemed to pulse through her at times to aid others, but there never seemed enough to work on any other person, only her.

It took her a long time to realize that these too were remnants, but not of her time with the Sith. These were shadows of the powers the Sith prince had gifted her sons with before their births and his curse. Her body must have absorbed some of it as it passed through her to them, but not enough to do anything but drive her mad.

And so she watched others around her suffer and die and fail because she knew only enough to know such power existed, but not enough to use it. As though losing her sons was not a terrible enough punishment, this too was another one given to her by the Sith.

Now, she knew, *she knew*, that Breac's sister had already passed away and there was nothing she could say or do. And once he discovered the truth, he would blame himself for more than he was responsible for in this.

Aigneis followed him down toward the stream, realizing there was only one thing she could do to comfort him—give him release from the tension within and make him rest so that he faced the trying day alert. He would lose many nights of sleep in the coming days to grief, but she could make this be a restful one.

She owed him that much and more for giving her a second chance to live.

Aigneis closed her eyes and took a deep breath in and released it. What she planned would be the last time she drew on such power, but she did not grieve the loss of it. Indeed, it had caused much trouble for her and she would be glad to be rid of it, and for such a good cause as this. She undressed then, tossing her clothing aside and standing in the chill night air naked. Tiny gooseflesh rose on her skin and her nipples and breasts tightened in response to the coolness around her. Raising her arms up, she faced the small sliver of cresent moon and began to sing.

Not human song, but the song of the Sith.

As the sound and tones in her mixed and came forth, she chanted the old words and sent them out to Breac. Not many people could harness Sith song, but she had been able to, much to the delight of the prince and the consternation of his queen. She did not truly understand whatever words she sang or how it truly happened, but her body and soul could use them to call forth pleasure or desire or more.

She used them now to call Breac to her in the night. With the power of such song, she could offer him pleasures of the flesh that would empty him of the restlessness in his soul and body and allow him rest. Though the Sith prince enjoyed such pleasures, she'd never been tempted to use this song with Donnell. Now, the pain in Breac's heart spurred her to offer it for what would be the last time.

He walked toward her now, unable to resist such a call, and she waited for him. When he stood before her, she moved around him, stroking him and touching him and preparing to comfort him and ease the coming pain. With no resistance from him to slow her efforts, she unlaced his shirt and trews and tugged them from him. Within moments, he stood as naked as she.

His body was magnificent, young and strong and in his prime, and even now it responded to the call in the song. His prick thickened and lengthened, standing forth from the nest of dark brown curls at its base. The song came from within her, swirling sounds in the air, glimmering like fireflies around them.

Aigneis reached up, standing on her toes nearly, and kissed him. His mouth was firm and hot beneath hers and soon he took over, sliding his fingers into her hair and holding her head close as he plundered her mouth. Like the movements he would make with his prick, he slipped his tongue in and out, tasting and feeling, until they were breathless.

The song still poured forth from within her.

Breac released his grasp on her and she moved down over his skin, kissing and licking his chest, suckling on his male nipples until he gasped, and then kissing her way down the rippling muscles of his stomach. She smiled as his breathing grew ragged. She felt his hands on her head once more, his fingers flexing through her hair, massaging her scalp, while gently pushing her toward his erect flesh.

Aigneis knelt before him, bracing herself on his strong legs, and took his prick in her mouth. He whispered her name through clenched teeth as she slid down him, taking the length of him deep into her mouth and throat. Her fingers teased the sensitive sac beneath his shaft as she pulled back and slid down again, and again, until he was calling out her name into the silence of the night around them.

His moan when his release happened filled the night air and she suckled him for every drop of it. She had barely swallowed it when he took her by her arms and pulled her up and into his embrace. She laughed as he took over and spread her legs around his waist, walking to their bed. Then he knelt down, laying her on the cloak, and kissed her body the way she had his.

Aigneis's song continued as he spread her legs and, though ready once more, he leaned down to use his mouth there. Now, her cries mingled with the other sounds of the night as he kissed and licked and suckled the flesh between her legs, bringing her to release several times before stopping.

Before she could breathe again, he moved forward and filled her, thrusting his hardness in as far as he could and then out again. Her muscles spasmed and she shook at the power of his flesh to bring her to satisfaction so quickly. Barely had the inner walls of her woman's core finished, then he began anew to torment and touch and thrust his flesh into hers, making her scream out from the pleasure.

Aigneis felt the end of the song approaching, so she changed it as he spilled into her body. She sang of oblivion and rest and his body relaxed against hers as the song ended. The last words vibrated through them as he fell asleep, still buried deep inside her body . . . and her soul.

Easing him to his side, Aigneis clutched the cloak and pulled it over them. She gave into the call to oblivion and fell into a deep and dreamless sleep.

Strangely, it was she who awakened first in the morning and eased from him. Dawn's light had not yet pierced the darkness of the sky, but she could not sleep any longer. Gathering her clothes, she went to the stream, saw to her needs, and was dressed and ready to go before he showed any sign of rousing. Then, as the sounds of the coming day began around them, he opened his eyes.

"Good morrow," he said in a voice husky from sleep. His body reacted in its normal way, hardened and ready to tup. He glanced down at it and shrugged as he climbed to his feet. "I will be ready in a moment."

She'd shaken out his clothes and handed them to him on his return. Aigneis handed him a chunk of hard cheese and the last of their ale and watched as he consumed it in moments. With everything packed and ready, she stood and waited for him to lead. He surprised her by taking her hand in his.

"I had the strangest dream," he said, staring at her as he spoke. "Did we couple in the night?"

She nodded. "Aye."

"Are you . . . well?" he asked, clearing his throat.

The shadows of the shared passion remained in his memory but not the details. He must think he rode her too roughly?

"I am well, Breac," she said. "Worry not."

"Come," he said, still holding her hand. "The lake is not so far away and we can make it there in an hour or two."

They walked hand-in-hand for a ways and in silence as they headed to his village. By the end of the day, he would know the truth and suffer for it.

Aigneis searched within herself for the words of a song, for the way to begin, but could not find them. Whatever understanding had been there was gone now and she had no song left within her. Though she frequently cursed the powers she seemed to have, a sharp pang shot through her now.

Regardless of the limitations of it or her lack of understanding of it and regardless of her anger over having it at all, the song had been a link to the Sith and to her sons and it was gone.

As they walked toward Breac's destiny with the truth, she wondered if she would ever find them.

She kept pace with him and they reached the southern end of the lake sooner than he thought they would. He used his coins to buy some food and hire a boat to take them north and, before nightfall, they approached his village.

She felt his anxiety as the boat came to a stop at the dock. He barely waited for the men to tie off the ropes before jumping out and lifting her over the side of the boat. Then he took her hand and led her through the village. Though many called out to him, he did not slow or stop to speak with them, or to answer the questions that she could see in their gazes about her.

Aigneis did not need the powers of the Sith to read the truth in their eyes—Fenella was indeed dead. And Breac was about to discover it.

At first, he identified people and places as they passed but once they reached the edge of most of the cottages, he stopped speaking and simply walked. When she struggled to keep up with him, she released his hand and let him run as he wanted to see his sister. By the time she caught up with him, he was already entering a large cottage that stood apart from the others.

Aigneis waited outside while he went in, and noticed that others had followed them from the village. She heard Breac call out to his sister and then again before he came back out to where she stood. The tears gathering and burning in her eyes fell on their own the moment he looked at her and realized the truth—his beloved sister was dead.

# Chapter 9

Breac stumbled as the truth struck him and he would have fallen over, but for Aigneis at his side. Even as he struggled to avoid believing that Fenella was dead, she clutched his hand and squeezed it as the villagers, many of his friends, approached. From their silence, he understood their confusion over what to say.

"Fenella?" he asked, wanting some explanation. His mother's friend Daracha, whom he left in charge of Fenella's care, walked closer and put her hand on his arm.

"I am so sorry, Breac," she said softly, her voice cracking in sorrow as she said the words he dreaded to hear. "The fever took Fenella while you were gone," she explained.

*While you were gone.*

Those words damned him forever. His sister who depended on him died while he was gone. Images of her calling out for him, alone, frightened, sick, flashed in his thoughts and the pain nearly tore him apart.

"Lord Malcolm comes," Seumas, the miller, called out.

The gathering crowd stepped back to allow Lord Malcolm to approach him. When Breac would have bowed, Lord Malcolm took hold of his shoulders and held him up straight.

"Cousin," he said, embracing him before all. "Breac, your cousin Gaira sends her greetings to you in this terrible time of grief. She said to make sure you knew that she has had mass said for Fenella's soul each morn since her passing."

It should offer him some comfort, the efforts to pray for his sister's immortal soul, but in the face of losing her, it did not.

"And Gaira had her buried in the graveyard next to our chapel, in respect for your kinship."

Again, the most proper and unexpected regard for his sister's soul and burial and Breac waited for the pain or anger or something to strike, but he felt only emptiness.

"Come to see Gaira on the morrow so that she can speak to you." Lord Malcolm extended the personal invitation, again, an unexpected gesture for their kinship was not so close as to warrant such treatment. With a nod at him and to those gathered around, Lord Malcolm left them.

Daracha and Seumas and his closest friend Ceanag approached and spoke of Fenella. The words flowed by, his grief striking so deep he could not even hear them. He knew they cared, but his mind and heart could not take it all in. He only realized that Aigneis was not at his side when he spied her standing near his cottage away from those gathered around him. Seumas's daughter spoke to him then. Beatha was close in age to Fenella and the two had been friends.

"Breac, we have our evening meal ready. Come, join us now," she invited. Seumas nodded.

"I am not hungry," he said, but they would not accept his refusal.

"Come and rest then," Daracha offered. "Go stay with Seumas. It is not good for you to be alone this night."

He turned and looked at Aigneis. She stood aside with her head lowered and shoulders slumping as though trying to disappear from view. "I am not alone," he said.

His friends turned as one and stared over at Aigneis, who still did not raise her eyes to his.

"Who is she?" asked Ceanag. "Why is she with you?"

"This is Aigneis of . . ." They'd not really discussed what they would tell people about her before their arrival and now the moment was upon him to explain her presence. "Farigaig," he finished, naming the village where he'd tried to leave her as her origin. "She is recently widowed and comes as companion and caregiver for Fenella."

The words explained the situation but there was much left unexplained. Now that Fenella did not need a companion or care-giver, other arrangements would be expected for this woman.

"Is she welcome in your house, Seumas?" he asked, stating clearly that she was under his sponsorship until things were settled.

"As you are," Beatha answered, taking his arm in hers and beginning to lead him back down the road to their dwelling.

He did not look back, as he let himself be led to his friend's house. Soon he found himself seated at table with a huge bowl of Beatha's stew and a steaming loaf of bread in front of him. Aigneis sat near the hearth, separate from the family, but where he could watch her. No one spoke to her or approached her throughout the meal, which proceeded quietly with an occasional mention of his sister and the recent illness that took her.

A short while later, understanding that he must face the inevitable, he thanked Seumas and his daughter for their hospitality and stood. He held out his hand to Aigneis and she accepted his help in standing, but dropped it as soon as she did. Silence filled the cottage, an uneasy one even he could tell, until they left.

She walked at his side back to his home . . . his empty home. Once they reached the door, he stopped, unable to step through it knowing his sister died there. He lifted the latch and pushed it open, staring into the darkened chamber before him.

"I cannot," he began, shaking his head. "I . . ."

Aigneis put her hand on his arm then. "'Tis fine, Breac." Moving around him, she stepped inside and motioned to him to enter.

Mayhap it was the darkness inside or Fenella's absence or some other thing, but Breac could not enter. He shook his head. "I cannot come in there, Aigneis. I will be back later," he said as he turned and strode away.

Aigneis recognized the stark expression of loss in his eyes, sure that hers had borne the same look when she'd lost her sons. Coming at him so quickly without warning, for he had to believe his sister would live or he would not have left her side, Aigneis understood his need to be alone.

He must stand high in the regard of his lord for Lord Malcolm to attend him personally with news of his sister's death and burial. And such an invitation as was made to him spoke of the respect he held in this village. Aigneis knew all of that because, as Donnell's wife, she watched as he doled out such regard and respect to the few he believed worthy among his men and followers.

But, for now, Breac needed time to accept his loss.

She closed the door and looked around the larger chamber. Someone had left a lamp burning so she took some kindling and used the flame to light a new fire in the hearth and two other tallow lamps. This first room held a table and some stools, the hearth in the center under an opening in the roof and a cooking area. Several trunks and a cabinet with some food supplies completed this chamber's furnishings.

Walking to the next room, she found two sleeping areas—one with a larger bed obviously for Breac and a smaller one, separated by a wooden screen where his sister must have slept. Again, several trunks lined the walls, most likely for storing their clothing and personal items. Though smaller than Donnell's main house in Ardrishaig, it was larger and more well kept than most cottages they'd passed on their way from the dock.

Unsure about whether to prepare for sleep or to wait for his return, Aigneis retrieved the sacks Breac had dropped at the door when he entered the first time looking for Fenella and unpacked the food. She hung the skins on a hook near the cooking area and put his clothing next to the pallet that must be his.

And she waited.

Several times she walked outside, peering into the darkness and listening for any sign that he was close by. Though she left the lamps burning for his return, most of the other cottages lay darkened and silent in the night.

After a few hours had passed with no sign of him, she sat on one of the stools and laid her head on her arms. Aigneis did not feel right about making herself welcome in either bed, but especially not Fenella's. And sleeping in Breac's arms on their journey here was one thing, but sharing his bed in his house was another.

The tension of this day, along with the sadness of Breac and his friends tired her and she found herself dragged into sleep. The loud knocking on the door was the next thing she heard.

Waking in a strange place confused her and it took a few moments to realize that she was in the very bed she had not chosen to sleep in—his—and someone was at the door. With no sign of

Breac in his bed, she climbed out and discovered she was fully clothed and alone in the cottage. He was not in the larger chamber and not responding to the visitor's call, so she lifted the latch and pulled the door open. The older woman who'd greeted Breac stood there, with several bundles and baskets in her arms.

"Good morrow, Aigneis," she said, walking in as though this was her home. "Breac asked me to bring these to you."

"Breac?" she asked, reaching over to unburden the woman of some of the things she carried. "Where is he?"

"At work in the fields down the road," she answered, pointing with her hand in a direction once she put the basket on the table. "The harvest will begin in several weeks and he wants to be ready."

She spoke as though Breac had shared his thoughts on the matter this morn. "You spoke with him this morn then?"

"Only about the food you needed," the woman said. "I am Daracha," she explained. "A friend to Breac's mother."

Since she knew nothing of Breac's family other than that Fenella was his sister and Lord Malcolm's wife was a distant cousin, she knew not if Breac's mother lived or had passed. Her lack of knowledge must have shown for Daracha offered, "His late mother."

Aigneis opened the bundles and looked in the baskets to find an assortment of root vegetables, flour, another sack of oats, another of barley, a jar of butter, another of cream, some eggs, and a piece of meat, though she knew not what kind. Foodstuffs enough for several meals for several days if she knew how to cook.

"The baker at the end of the lane will cook the roast and your bread if you bring it to him by noon," Daracha explained. "And he has been paid so no coin is needed." Gesturing at the empty bucket in the cooking area, she added, "The well is near the dock in the center of the village." Pointing in the other direction, she continued, "and the stream for laundry is on the other side of the village."

Aigneis nodded at each instruction, keeping track of each location given, though she knew not the first thing about cooking or laundry or the other tasks of being a goodwife. Her servants carried out those duties, putting her food before her when she was hungry, washing her clothes, and meeting her needs. The only thing she did well was sewing. And she could read, a task not many could do, whether man or woman, but one of which she was proud.

It had only been these last few weeks when, tossed out without her belongings or any gold or other means to support herself, she faced actual hardship. Before that, she had still remained a part of Donnell's household or her father's, though forced from her rightful place at the head table.

And when she agreed to accompany Breac here to care for his sister, she thought it would be simply assisting Fenella as she recovered, not cooking and cleaning for him. Then when she realized that Fenella had passed away, she'd not considered that he would want her as housekeeper.

Daracha left as quickly as she arrived, but not without several pointed and curious looks at her and her uncovered hair, before Aigneis was left alone with food to cook and tasks to complete. She found some cheese among the baskets, and some oatcakes already made, so she ate those to break her fast before attempting anything else. She would need fresh water, so she grabbed the bucket and walked to the well.

Though she crossed the paths of several other women, none greeted her. They watched her though, without meeting her gaze or appearing to, and nothing about her was missed. Though familiar with being scrutinized by others, she was not used to being the stranger. And without further explanations or introductions by Breac, she would remain a stranger to the villagers.

After filling her bucket and carrying it back to his cottage, Aigneis decided to try to make a stew like Beatha had the night before. Without a recipe, she did what she thought would work, cutting the piece of meat, chopping some of the vegetables, tossing it all in the large pot and covering it with water. Moving it onto the cooking rack, she let it cook the rest of the day, hoping it would be ready when Breac returned.

If he returned.

Since she did not think he would ask Daracha for so much food if he did not intend to return, she felt confident he would be back this evening. So she walked around the village, learning where things were, and then waited for Breac.

Just as night began to fall in earnest, she heard his approach and opened the door. He stood talking to Seumas and two other men she did not know outside the cottage. They all nodded to her and then the three left before much time passed.

Breac turned to her and she saw exhaustion and sorrow written on his face. He walked up to the door, pausing as though still not certain he would or could enter. She stepped aside and he walked past her with barely a look.

# Chapter 10

Breac had avoided his home for as long as he could this day. Though Aigneis probably did not remember, he'd come back in the dark of the night and carried her to his bed, after finding her bent over the table sleeping. He sat in a chair next to the bed but could not find rest himself. Before the sun rose, Breac was gone. He spent the day doing his duties, the ones he'd neglected when he left to seek help for his sister.

After seeing to the oversight of the coming harvest, he poured himself into some hard labor—felling some trees, repairing one of Lord Malcolm's barns, and moving large sacks of stored grain all in the hopes of being too tired to notice the empty place in his house. He glanced into the smaller chamber as he walked inside, an unconscious gesture, for Fenella always greeted him at the door.

Instead Aigneis stood waiting.

He'd not explained more than his initial introduction of her to his friends or even to Lady Gaira. If he was being honest, he'd not thought on her place here today. They would have to discuss it, but he had not the heart or will to think of the future. Luckily, his friends and the men who worked the fields seemed to know that he needed to focus on the work and there was little talk that did not involve the fields, the harvest, the supplies, or plans for the rotation of the fields in the spring.

But now, in the house where he did not want to be, in the silence of the coming night, he suspected there was no way to avoid it. She'd kept some lamps lit for him the night before and this night too, and as he entered, she took his cloak and hung it on a peg by the door.

"I made a stew," she said softly. "Are you hungry?" He was not, but he nodded, more to appreciate her efforts than in a need for food. "Sit then," she directed him.

She'd been almost invisible last night once they'd arrived here, head down, blending in and not speaking. And though he had liked it little, he could not muster enough strength to bring her into the conversations. Now she appeared quite at ease in his house, cooking something for his dinner, much in the way he'd seen to her needs along their journey.

"Why is your hair covered?" he asked, realizing that he preferred to see the wild curls than to see them hidden away. The kerchief that he'd removed when he'd carried her into bed was firmly back in place.

"Married women cover their hair," she said evenly, though he noticed the hitch in her voice.

Her voice.

It was different now, in some way he could not identify. The melody that seemed to run through any words she spoke was gone now and her words sounded like . . . words. He walked over to her and tugged the fabric off her hair. She turned as though ready to say something but she just stared at him.

Breac reached up and ran his fingers through her curls. For a moment a vision of her on her knees before him, sucking his cock, flashed through his thoughts and his cock hardened in anticipation of it. Was that a memory from that lost night? Had that been two nights before? He remembered being unable to fall asleep and taking a walk to ease his nerves, only to fall asleep then and have such vivid dreams of them coupling and pleasuring each other through the night.

He dropped his hands and stepped away.

She did not speak, but she did not cover her hair either.

Aigneis scooped some of the stew into a wooden bowl and placed it before him. It did not look or smell like the thick, aromatic meal that Beatha fed them last evening, but she was sure it would suffice. Unwrapping the loaf of bread she'd purchased from the baker, she sat down and waited for him to begin.

He dipped his spoon into the bowl and lifted the thin broth to his mouth. She had not figured out how to thicken her stew into the tasty gravy that Beatha had. Aigneis waited as he took the mouthful of meat and turnips in and chewed it.

And chewed.

And chewed some more.

The second spoonful held only the broth, which he swallowed quickly. Then he tore off a piece of bread and chewed that. Aigneis tried hers and found the meat inedible and the broth worse than she imagined old bathwater would taste. It was so bad she fought not to spit it back into her bowl.

"'Tis horrible!" she said, waiting for him to agree.

"The bread is good," was his only response.

"I did not make the bread," she admitted.

"'Tis good."

She put her spoon down and met his gaze. "I cannot cook."

There. It was the sad and awful truth.

"No, you cannot," he agreed.

Part of her was miffed that he agreed so quickly and part was relieved that she did not have to try to hide her inability and pretend to know. He stood and left without a word of explanation. Within minutes he returned, carrying a small pot in his hand. He put it on the table and after dumping the contents of their bowls back into the large cooking pot, he divided Beatha's wonderful stew between them. Only the slight slant of his mouth as a smile threatened told her he was not upset.

After their meal, he took care of the fire while she worried over where to sleep. But Breac never hesitated as they entered the other room, inviting her to his bed with a soft word and a warm embrace.

That night their joining was different from the other times. It should not have surprised her, but it did. He touched her gently and slowly, bringing her release, but without the wild passion that happened before. He drew out every caress and eased deep inside of her, moving at a pace that drove her mad with desire for more and for harder and for deeper.

He satisfied her several times before seeking his release and then held her close without a word between them until they both slept. In the morning when she woke, he was gone from the bed and the house.

Beatha arrived in the later morning, baskets on her arm and an offer to teach her to cook. Aigneis found out that Breac had secured her help, if Aigneis wanted to learn, and so she spent the rest of the day conquering a simple porridge dish. If Breac thought it strange to have his morning meal in the evening, he did not comment. He just ate it. The practice repeated each day for several more until Aigneis could make something resembling Beatha's stew.

Though they fell into a comfortable pattern, she knew that Breac had not yet accepted Fenella's death. Each time they entered or left the bedchamber, she noticed the sad glance toward the other pallet. She watched in the evening as they ate, and he gazed at the door as though expecting his sister to walk through it and sit with them.

But the clearest sign to her was that he never mentioned his sister by name. The few times she'd witnessed Daracha or one of the others try to talk about Fenella, Breac either changed the matter under discussion or he left, avoiding it completely. Like a boil that festers until broken, Aigneis knew it was only a matter of time before his grief came to the surface, but she had no idea of the powerful emotions he kept controlled . . . until he could not any longer.

Breac found that he actually looked forward to discovering what concoction Aigneis was making for their evening meal each day. He spent the days busy enough to avoid thinking on his loss and spent the nights wrapped around or deeply inside Aigneis's supple and welcoming body, sharing a passion with her that he'd never shared with another woman. The few hours between were pleasant ones, as she became skilled in cooking with the help of Beatha's expertise and offered him meals that filled his belly and lightened his spirit.

Aigneis seemed content in their arrangement, using her time to practice the one household skill at which she was accomplished— sewing and embroidery. Uneasy about taking Beatha's time up with teaching her to cook, she offered to sew and mend clothing for Beatha and her father. And she repaired his torn or worn-out clothing that he'd ignored for so long.

This exchange seemed to make her feel useful and ease some hurt from her life before, and he could not disguise his pleasure in having her happy.

She accepted his invitation to his bed every night and never turned from his touch or embrace. Nor did she hesitate to make her desires known and they explored the limits of pleasure in the dark of the night, never stopping until each one had a full measure of satisfaction.

His cock hardened as it did every day when he returned to his cottage and found her there. Breac smiled thinking of something he discovered last night when he took her from behind. His body readied itself for her endless sense of adventures of the flesh, and she had only to look at him to know they would not make it through any meal first.

Within minutes, and without a word of greeting exchanged, he had her pressed against the wall next to his pallet, her skirts flung up on her back, with his cock sliding between the cheeks of her butt from behind and his fingers touching her cleft from the front. Her body wept into his hands as he plundered her, rubbing some of the moisture on the sensitive puckered opening and pressing the thick head of his cock there as though he would enter it. Her moans excited him and he ached to get inside her body and spill himself there.

Pressing his hand on the small of her back, she arched lower and his cock slid inside her tight channel, the muscles of the opening gripping every inch of his hardness. It was more intense than anything he'd felt before and he eased himself in deeper. Rubbing his fingers over her nether lips, he felt her body tighten around his. He thrust in and out, in and out, slowly until the tremors began within her. As she cried out and her channel spasmed around him, he pushed her to find her release with his fingers against the sensitive bud between those swollen lips.

In those final moments of pleasure, he leaned over her and bit her on the tender area between her neck and her shoulder with his teeth, claiming her body as his, marking her with his mouth as a stallion did a mare in heat.

It took awhile before either of them regained their senses, so complete and intense was their joining. Their breathing slowed and they fell together on the pallet in a heap of entangled limbs and bodies, waiting for their bodies and their passion to cool. She still lay unmoving several minutes later so he offered to get some ale for them.

Breac stood and climbed from the pallet, wobbling on his feet from the exertion and excitement they'd shared when he noticed that the screen separating his part of the chamber from Fenella's was gone. As he walked toward the other room, he realized her pallet was gone as well. A coldness settled over him as he turned back to face Aigneis.

"Where is the screen? Where is Fenella's pallet?" he asked quietly. Though the words were soft, he could feel the rage building within him.

"We spend so much time in this chamber, I thought it . . ."

"*You thought?*" he interrupted. "*You* . . . thought?"

She slid off the pallet and walked nearer to him. He stepped away. "'Tis been more than a fortnight since . . ."

"It was not your decision to make," he yelled. "It is not your house or your place to make decisions."

Like some insanity that lay dormant and then breaks free, Breac could feel the grief and anger over his sister's death boil to the surface in him. Even the way Aigneis's face lost all its color and she flinched at his words did not ease it.

"What is my place then, Breac?" she asked, her soft tone goading him more.

"Your place is on that pallet with my cock in your mouth or between your legs or in your arse," he snarled. Even feeling his rage overflow did not stop him. "Do not think it is more than that. You warm my bed and get a place to live in return."

He pulled the door open and strode out. He could not breathe in there and his head felt like it would explode at any moment. But his heart! His heart pounded in his chest and his blood raced through his veins. Rage heated him and pushed him on, and even knowing that his target was the wrong one did not stop him.

"The worst part of this is that we caused her death," he yelled at her. "While I was busy sniffing after you and swiving you by the side of the road each night, she lay here dying. If I had ignored you, she would still be alive," he leveled the accusation that had tormented him for weeks.

He panted then, unable to take in an even breath. Aigneis moved around him, keeping close to the wall, watching him as though afraid he would strike her. And, at that moment, and in spite of the terror he saw in her eyes, he did not know what he was capable of doing.

She flung open the door and ran from him into the night.

Breac fell to his knees and screamed out at the pain that tore through him. His sister was dead because of him and his weakness. If he'd gotten back sooner, he could have saved her. Instead, he'd sacrificed her for a stranger. His grief and his guilt surged up and he sobbed it out until he had no more tears left.

# Chapter 11

Aigneis had never felt terror like she did at that moment. The terrible power of the guilt and grief he'd held inside exploded in a horrible flash aimed at her. And even knowing that it would happen in some way did not lessen her fear. She ran from his cottage, down the road until she could not run any farther. Then, turning into the woods, she held onto a tree for support and wept for their losses.

She'd begun to believe he was not like the other men in her life, that he could be trusted, that he would not hurt or betray her when this happened. Even understanding the power of grief, she still understood that something had changed between them in that instant, that he had expressed some grain of truth about his feelings for her, and they were not the ones she felt for him. Though she would now grieve for losing something special between them, she knew it was better to find out the truth about him now before she fell . . . in love with him.

Aigneis fell to her knees as the truth sank in—it was too late for her after all. She had not learned.

She pulled her legs up and curled around them, rocking as the disclosure shocked her. There was no choice now—she must leave. But without coins, she could not support herself or find a place to live. What would she do now? How would she live? How would she ever have any hope of finding her sons now?

The night passed slowly and no matter how she thought on it, she could not find a way out. Sometime before dawn, she collapsed into a fitful sleep, unable to face the turn her life had taken.

Breac wiped his face and looked around the chamber. The door still stood open as she'd left it as she ran. He'd never done something so cowardly before as this—setting an innocent woman as his target and abusing what little faith he'd established between them.

If there was any guilt, it was his.

If there was anyone in the wrong, it was him.

Climbing to his feet, he realized that she had turned his house into a welcoming place. She had learned to cook to please him. She had taken him into her body and eased his grief without words, and she had never asked for a thing in return, not even a promise of a future.

He needed to find her and try to undo the damage he'd wrought already. Aigneis could not go far, for she'd crept out without even her shoes. Mayhap she sought refuge with Seumas and his daughter? He would go there first and try to come up with a plan if she was not there.

Seumas knew nothing of her whereabouts but patiently answered his questions about Fenella's last days, seeming pleased that Breac finally spoke of his sister. They talked for some time and Breac explained what had happened earlier and how he'd blamed Aigneis for missing the chance to help his sister.

Armed with the correct knowledge of how and when Fenella had died, he knew he must find Aigneis. With full moon's light, he followed the road down almost a mile before finding signs of someone nearby. Then her soft snore gave her away and he discovered her curled up next to a tree, sleeping. Though this time it was not the deep sleep she usually fell into, but a fitful one in which she mumbled and cried.

Breac sat at her side, easing her against him, and waited for her to wake so he could ask for her forgiveness.

Though not warm, Aigneis awoke feeling not as cold as she thought she would after spending a night sleeping on the ground. Her back and her legs ached and she shifted around trying to get comfortable. The sun's weak light barely crept over the horizon when she finally gave up trying to sleep and forced herself to face this day.

After a brief respite during which she simply lived and enjoyed a short time of a pleasure with no promises or commitments, Aigneis knew she must face the reality of what her future would hold. And she must find a place to live.

Opening her eyes, she pushed her hair away from her face and began to stretch, moving muscles that did not want to move. That was when she realized she did not lay on the ground, but against someone. She scampered away before his identity had even become clear and she found herself facing Breac.

Easing farther away from him, she knew this was not the raging beast she'd seen the night before. Still she could not trust that he would not become that beast again.

"I am sorry," he said, in a gravelly voice.

She did not speak. When she did not, he continued. "I am sorry for making you my target when I was angry with myself," he said. "I am sorry for not listening to Seumas and Daracha and Ceanag and even Lord Malcolm when they told me I should let myself grieve for Fenella. I am sorry for being exactly like the others in your life who failed you and blamed you instead of themselves."

She gasped at his words for they were so close to her truth it frightened her. How had he known?

He held out his hand to her, but she was not certain she should take it. "Please come back," he said.

His eyes held the glint of guilt now, but she sensed it was not about Fenella but about his treatment of her. "And her death? Do you still blame me for delaying you and causing it?" He flinched at her words and she waited for him to explain.

"Seumas told me that she died within two days of my leaving. Lord Malcolm wanted to send someone after me, but I had not told him my destination or path. Once I left here, I could not have returned in time to be with her at the end."

"Oh, Breac," she cried, crawling back to him and accepting his embrace, while wrapping him in her arms. "I am so sorry you were not there with her."

"Daracha said she never woke from her sleep. That she slipped away quietly," he whispered. "At least I can content myself that she was not alone and not in pain."

They sat quietly together for several minutes until he leaned back to look at her. "Come back with me, Aigneis."

She could hear both a request and a plea in his words and thought on them. This incident had awakened her to the dangerous feelings growing between them, ones that would not survive what he must do—choose a wife, marry, and have children. Now that he was accepting his sister's death, his lord would begin to press him to do so. And since she could never be the woman he chose and she could never stand by and watch it happen, she must find a new life before it happened.

She stood and waited for him to join her. "For now."

"For now? What does that mean?" he asked. "I know you are angry and that I terrified you, but I can promise it will not happen again."

"You did terrify me, I will admit that," she nodded. "But this just made me realize that my place is not with you and that you must choose a woman soon who will stand with you."

"Aigneis . . ."

She lifted her hand and placed it over his mouth to stop him. "Make no promises, Breac."

"Come back with me?" he asked again.

Aigneis nodded and they walked back to his cottage together. Instead of leaving her to carry out his duties that day, he remained there and spent most of the day with her, rearranging the bedchamber as she'd started to do.

Their days fell back into the comfortable pattern of the last weeks, but Aigneis was ever mindful of the future that moved toward them. Breac laughed off several attempts by men in the village to negotiate betrothals with their daughters. He even managed to ignore Lord Malcolm's advice about a suitable wife, but Aigneis knew it would not be long now that he was coming to terms with the loss of his sister.

The summer ended and the harvest progressed well. Aigneis grew stronger as did their feelings for each other. He brought her to gatherings and introduced her to the villagers openly and without shame. He made no pretense of her being a housekeeper—she was his lover, his mistress, and he showed no sign of taking a wife. But when Breac brought up the subject of marriage to her, she knew it was time.

Aigneis just could not figure out how to leave her heart and soul behind and still live.

# Chapter 12

A servant answered Aigneis's knock and led her to the room where Lord Malcolm waited. After dismissing the woman, he gestured for her to sit and she did. In the months she'd been here, he'd never spoken to her directly, so she could not imagine what this summons to his hall meant. The fact that he waited for Breac to be away from the village did not bode well for her.

"Can I offer you some wine or some ale, Lady Aigneis?" he asked, holding out an empty cup to her.

She began to answer and then realized his address to her. She could feel the blood drain from her face as she waited for the rest.

"We met about ten years ago, my lady. I attended Lord Donnell's court to celebrate the marriage of his nephew to my cousin."

Aigneis closed her eyes, remembering the occasion but not the man before her. There had been so many there as Donnell showed off his wealth and prestige during a wedding feast that went on for days. She opened her eyes and watched him. When he held out the cup now it was filled with wine. She took it and drank it, the first time for such a rich drink in months and months.

"I know the sad circumstances regarding your marriage," he said softly. She could not tell if he was being sarcastic or sympathetic so she continued to wait in silence for him to make his point or his demands. "Your husband believes you are dead and would not be pleased to discover you yet live. Too many complications."

"What do you want, my lord?" she asked, tiring of this game.

"I want you out of Breac's life," he said plainly.

"I am not part of his life, my lord," she explained. "I have no intentions of remaining here."

"I want to arrange a betrothal that will insure he will stay here and work the lands for me. As long as you are here, he will not allow it."

"Have you told him your wishes? He makes his own decisions without counsel from me."

"I must have these things settled. Either you leave or I will tell him the truth about the woman he thinks he loves. And that truth would ruin any chance of a life together with him when he discovers the lies and betrayals of your past, *Lady.*"

Aigneis's stomach rolled from the heavy wine and from the thought of the way her past could be twisted and used against her. Lord Malcolm could make it unrecognizable just as Donnell had in order to make his case of divorce against her. She would rather walk away from Breac than see the same hatred and fear in his eyes that had filled Donnell's and her father's and so many others when faced with the truth about her.

She nodded and stood, dropping the cup on the table without regard to damaging it. Her heart screamed in pain, but she would not change her mind in this.

"I can make arrangements for another place for you to live. A quiet village on my cousin's lands in the north."

He was willing to be gracious in victory and she was willing to accept it. "What do I tell him?" she asked.

"You can tell him whatever you like, it matters not to me." He turned to face her now. "Be ready in a sennight to leave," he ordered.

She shook her head. "He returns on the morrow and I will be ready to leave then," she said. The sooner the better and the less chance of changing her mind in the matter, she decided.

"Very well, then. On the morrow."

Aigneis left without another word, shocked that her legs moved so smoothly and that she didn't fall to the ground in pieces. The rest of that day and the night moved as a blur before her eyes. She sat on the stool at his table waiting for his return so that she could bring this to a close.

202 / *Terri Brisbin*

She heard his voice as he called out to someone down the road and the tears began to flow. Then his footsteps as he approached, the time when her body would ready itself for the passion he would bring to her. This time, her heart beat so heavily in her chest she could not breathe. When he lifted the latch, she took in a ragged breath and prepared to tear her heart and soul apart.

Breac missed her. This was the first time they'd slept apart or been apart since that night he accepted Fenella's death and he did not like it. It was more than just the pleasure they gave to each other; it felt like he'd found the other half of his heart and soul in her.

He fought to keep from running down the road to his cottage and to be the laughingstock of the men in the village for his lack of control when it came to her. But he did not care, for she had grown to be more important to him than anything or anyone else. And though she had not shared her past with him, he believed she did trust him and would open up to him soon.

Breac opened the door, wondering if she would greet him as she had two days ago when he found her naked on the table, offering him a feast he could not refuse. He laughed as he lifted the latch and entered.

Something was horribly wrong.

It took only one look at her face to know it and his stomach rolled at the sight of such desolation. Then it was gone and some horrible mask of emptiness covered her.

"Aigneis, what is wrong?" He dropped his bag at the door and strode over to her. Taking her by the shoulders, he pulled her into his arms. She was shaking.

"I have some news," she stuttered.

"What kind of news?"

"Lord Malcolm has found me a place to live in his cousin's village. I leave today."

"Do you jest?" he asked, leaning away to watch her face as she spoke. "There is no reason to do such a thing."

"Breac, we both know that you need a wife. You said so when you invited me here—it was only until the matter of your sister was handled and then you would marry."

"The *matter* of my sister?" he asked, feeling as though he was being manipulated but he could not see all the strings yet.

"I am an impediment to a marriage."

"Who has told you such a thing?"

"There is not a woman in this village, or a man for that matter, who does know the true nature of our relation . . . involvement," she said. "And no woman will accept a betrothal while your leman lives with you."

"I offered you marriage," he said, feeling the cold emptiness open within him. What had happened to cause this?

"That was not our agreement when I came here and I beg you to accept and honor that arrangement now."

Silence filled the room and the space between them grew and grew though neither one had moved an inch. Sounds outside alerted him to the arrival of others. She flinched at the knocking yet she never looked away from him. He placed his hand on the door latch.

"I have never forced a woman to do anything she did not wish to," he said, "and I would not start now." He pulled the door open to find four of Lord Malcolm's men waiting there.

He thought she would leave without saying another word, which would be bad, but the words she did say were worse, much much worse.

"Thank you for saving my life, Breac. And thank you for teaching me that I could trust again."

And then she was gone.

"What did you say to make her leave?" Breac asked in a tone that did not carry the least bit of respect for his lord as it should.

She'd left two days ago and he finally realized he could not let her go. Whatever had happened led back to Lord Malcolm and he would find out the reason for her hasty departure. It did not take an idiot to realize that she loved him, he'd known it in his own heart for months, and to see that she was being forced to leave him. He would find out the reason and then go and get her.

Lord Malcolm had not answered yet, so he asked again.

"She wanted to leave, Breac. I gave her the chance for a new life." He knew it had not happened that way, but it did not matter.

"I am ready to pledge myself in your service, my lord," he said. "And to expand and improve the farms in your three villages."

Lord Malcolm's face brightened, for this was exactly what he'd been negotiating with Breac to do and what Breac had resisted. "Excellent!"

"As soon as I bring Aigneis back and she accepts my offer of marriage."

"She will not marry you. 'Twas her choice."

Breac stood silently, waiting to play his true weapon. They both knew the stakes here, but only Breac knew how important Aigneis was to his happiness and the price he would pay to get her back.

"Either you accept her as my wife or I will walk away from here and the flow of gold you earn from the sales of your crops will end."

Because of drought or flood, most of the farmland for miles had not been yielding strong crops for a number of years except their lands because of Breac's knowledge of the land and his planning and management. Malcolm had become much richer for it and could become richer still if the pattern continued.

"It matters not, she will not have you," Lord Malcolm answered now, too confident in the matter.

"Then you agree?" he pressed the question.

"Aye."

With a curt nod, Breac was on his way. He'd already bribed the knowledge of her destination from one of the stewards and he could catch up with them before they reached the coast.

He would catch up with them and bring her back with him.

# Chapter 13

This trip was made in more comfort, Lord Malcolm had provided a wagon fit for his wife's use to Aigneis. Even though two servants along with four guards kept her cared for and protected, she was more miserable than after being beaten by Donnell's men.

And it was for Breac's own good and safety . . . and happiness. If Donnell found out that he'd interfered in his punishment of her and saved her life, he would take his revenge against Breac and his lord with the backing of the king and his soldiers. But the worst threat was that Malcolm would tell Breac about her life, and she believed he would do just that.

She prepared herself for his anger when she told him she was leaving, but there would be no way to prepare herself for the hatred and the fear she would see if he learned about her years in the land of the Sith and her lost sons. Or the rest. He could simply not understand it all and he would hate her or grow to hate her over time.

'Twas better this way.

And she continued to tell herself that with every passing mile, hoping that she would come to believe it in time. Now, two days later, she was no closer to believing it than she had been two days before.

They would leave the mountains soon and then head north

along the coast for three more days, where Aigneis would disappear forever and she would take a new name.

They came to an abrupt stop when someone called out about a block in the road ahead. But it was neither rocks nor a mudslide that halted their progress. Breac stood in the road before them. He approached the soldiers leading them and spoke with them in a low voice. They glanced back at her several times during their exchange, but she could only see him. Thrilled to see him again and terrified over what it meant, she waited until he approached her.

"You said you trusted me," he said, standing close so that no one else heard their words.

"Breac, please do not do this," she begged.

He took her by the arm, waved the soldiers and others away, and guided her back a distance where they could have some privacy.

"I need to know what you hide. What do you fear telling me? Why can you not marry me?"

She could not utter the words, so he asked again. "Please tell me, Aigneis. You owe me at least that for saving your life."

"I cannot marry you because I am already married, Breac," she said, giving up any hopes of resisting his pleas of hearing the truth.

He gasped as she said it. "The man who ordered you lamed was your husband?"

"Aye, I was married to Lord Donnell of Ardrishaig."

"He is a powerful chieftain in the south," Breac said. She still hesitated in revealing the whole of it, but he urged her on once more. "With a new wife . . ." He'd heard of the new marriage then? His expression showed his confusion.

He said she could trust him. Could she? She'd lost him already, so mayhap it was worth the risk?

"I was betrothed to Donnell when I was but a girl and was intent on marrying him until I met someone else," she began. "On my father's lands in the western isles, I fell in love with a man. I thought him a man, until his true nature was revealed to me."

"His true nature?" he asked quietly.

"A Sith prince in human form, seeking a mortal lover. By the time I knew the truth I gave my pledge to him and he took me to his home."

It sounded absurd, but it was the truth. She thought he would scoff, but he nodded, accepting her words.

"It was a wondrous place, but I discovered I did not love him and wanted to return to my home and the man I should marry. When he refused, I managed to escape but it was too late."

"Too late?" Breac frowned. "Did he catch you?"

"Aye, and at the worst possible moment. I was in labor when he found me." She paused as the feelings and fear washed over her again. "But worse than being caught was his anger at my betrayal. He cursed the bairns," she heard her voice hitch and tried to continue, but could not.

Breac took her in his arms and held her, comforting her in a way she never thought to feel again. "Hush now," he whispered.

She shook her head. "Nay, I must tell you the rest before I lose my courage." He released her but stood close.

"Because they are half-Sith, they have gifts, but he cursed them to lose their humanity as they use their powers. I begged him for mercy but he was too angry at me to lift the curse. I cannot tell them the truth or he will destroy us all."

"You are here, so you must have escaped?"

"He let me go after he took my sons," she whispered, the pain so deep it cut her in two. "I did not even hold them. He took them away as they were born and gave them to others to raise because he said I was not worthy."

The tears flowed then. She was unable to stop them. She'd told no one the whole story until now and had bottled up most of her guilt and grief inside. "I returned to my father along with gold, paid by the Sith as the price for my sons. That much gold convinced my father and Donnell to accept the betrothal as it was and to accept me, as damaged as I was."

"Did they know? About your sons?" he asked, taking her hand in his and entwining their fingers so she could not move too far from him. He could feel her desolation and loss and could not believe the pain she bore.

"Nay, I dared not tell anyone. I came back changed—living in their land gave me a vitality I could not explain. I did not age as usual and during the months I spent there five years had passed here. I never get sick, I . . . ."

". . . heal quickly," he added.

"And there's more than that. I believe that I have a bit of whatever gifts or powers he gave our sons."

"You know things, do you not?" It made sense now to him. He'd suspected for some time.

"And I hear things . . . and the healing. I think those are the powers he gave them too."

"How old are they?"

"If they are here, in the mortal world, they will have ten-and-three years now." He could see her thinking about them even now.

"Because of my youth and my obvious health, Donnell thought I would bear him children easily. With the gold to soften his bruised honor, we married and he set about trying to get heirs."

"It never happened?" Breac could see where this was leading. "In all these years?"

"I think my womb will not bear mortal children after bearing them for the Sith," she said. He sensed that this disclosure was more painful than the others for her. "I have never shared that with anyone else, Breac."

She did trust him, but he could feel her fear. As though she waited for the worst of it.

"After seven years, he gave up. It infuriated him that I still looked so young compared to his appearance. And that I could heal and never be sick. Worse, he hated me for the powers he glimpsed within me. He turned his family and mine against me, claiming a deal with the devil prevented me from having children. He offered my father some of the gold if he did not object to me being set aside for a new wife."

"And your father agreed to this?"

Breac was gaining more insight into the terrible damage wrought to this woman by others. Everyone in her life had failed her and betrayed her. If he walked away, he would simply be another added to her list.

"Enough gold will ease the roughest of roads. So Donnell announced that due to my sins, I was barren and he divorced me. I objected but my father signed the papers. When I would not leave, he had me taken from my home. When I returned . . ."

"He declared you exiled, shamed you by cutting your hair, and throwing you naked into the street."

She looked away then, but not before he saw the shame in her eyes. He reached out and cupped her chin in his hand, lifting her face until she met his gaze. "It is not your fault."

"Ah, but it is, Breac. I could not love the Sith prince as I promised and he took my sons. I could not love Donnell as I'd promised and I remained barren until he banished me. Now, married and barren I have nothing to offer the man I truly love. Except . . ."

He understood the conclusion she was drawing and shook his head. "But I do not wish to be free of you."

"You will as the Sith power continues to fade from within me and I become the mortal woman I truly am."

"So I too will age. Would you get rid of me because my beauty or form fades?"

"You jest over something too serious. Each passing year sees me older and older. You will be saddled with an old woman if I were to stay."

"Aigneis, you are being too noble in this. I need no children. I will keep you without the vows of marriage if you will stay. I will not hate you because you are older than me. None of this is a barrier to me."

"Every man wants children, to say otherwise is a lie," she said furiously. She had been held accountable for sins and the failings of others, too, for so long, so knew no other way. "What must I do to make you see the truth between us?"

He could see it in those luminous eyes of hers—she wanted to take what he offered but the fear and the past kept her from accepting him. Then he realized that he must offer her the same thing she offered him—freedom.

"You are right, Aigneis," he said with more than a little fear making his heart race. He could lose her forever if she didn't want to try to trust him. "I do not wish to marry you."

"You do not?" Her voice shook and her face grew pale.

"I want to keep you for a year. At the end of the year, if you are not happy and still do not trust me, you are free and I will not trouble you again."

"A year?" she asked. "Not a lifetime?"

"Aye," he nodded. "Only pledge me a year."

He knew the moment she overcame her fears and decided to

give him a chance to prove himself. And he did not mind her doubts because he was sure of his love for her and hers for him, even if she was not . . . yet.

And Breac intended to keep her for a lifetime, no matter his bold statement. He would just prove it a year at a time until she realized it too.

# Epilogue

*Southwest Scotland, 1091 A.D.*

He was not even certain he'd closed the door. Breac had been traveling on Lord Malcolm's business for nigh on a sennight now and only just arrived home. Within minutes, nay seconds he thought, she stripped him of his clothes and was having her wicked way with him. Once she straddled his hips and began inching her way down his shaft, seating him deeply inside her, he cared not if the door was open or closed.

Now he was truly home where he wanted to be.

He reached up and covered her breasts with his hands, rubbing his thumbs over the nipples until they were tight buds and she moaned. Aigneis rocked her hips, creating the most wonderful friction against his cock. He could not help but to thrust deeper into her tightness.

She enjoyed being in this position and he did too, for it freed his hands to tease and pleasure her as she mounted him. But now, after too long away, he wanted more. Before taking control, he slid his hand between the wet folds of flesh and found the small bud that would make her scream. He placed one hand on her neck and pulled her down to kiss him while he stirred her passion and rubbed that bud until it hardened as he did.

She panted against his mouth and, from the slickness between her legs and the tremors beginning deep within her, he knew she was close. Releasing her neck, he gripped her waist and rolled her under him, now able to plow her more fully. If she objected she said nothing, but only met his thrusts with a roll of her hips against his. His sac tightened and she tightened around him and then he felt his seed release and she cried out and milked him of every drop.

Breac rolled just enough not to crush her and waited to catch his breath so he could share the news with her.

"I think I will keep you for another year," he said, laughing.

"And what convinced you to do that this time?" she pushed the curls from her face and kissed him once. Once he'd mentioned that he preferred her hair shorter, she cut it herself the way he liked it.

"Your warm welcome could have been it."

"You are so shallow if a simple tupping will convince you," Aigneis teased.

He leaned up on his elbow and kissed her. "And my performance was not enough to keep you in my bed for one more?" Before she answered, he continued. "Then I shall have to try to impress you with my news."

Their search for her sons had been unsuccessful, but they'd not stopped since she revealed their existence to him those eight years ago. With no idea of where to even begin, they went back to see the healer near Dunadd, who'd told him the story of a woman caught by the Sith and taken to his lands under the fairy hill on Mull. And now, he'd learned . . .

"Tell me," she whispered excitedly. He could almost hear the lost song of the Sith in her voice sometimes when she spoke of her sons or the Sith prince.

"A friend on Mull spoke of a young man who counsels a chieftain there. There is talk of visions and knowledge not of the mortal world."

He watched as tears gathered in her luminous gray eyes and she tried to blink them away. "Do you think it is possible? Could he be one of the three?"

"I will send someone there to learn more before we get our hopes up again."

She sighed loudly. "So, I guess I must keep you again for another year."

Breac kissed her to celebrate her declaration, her eighth since that day long ago, and to mark his hopeful news. Soon they were lost in passion again. His last thought was that one day he would tell her she was keeping him forever.

# Stealing the Bride

## Mary Wine

# Chapter 1

*Scotland, 1554*

"Ye're all the same with yer promises of sons, but I've had a bellyful of talk."

Hayden Monroe slammed his tankard down on the table so hard a measure of ale sloshed over the rim. He gave the mess no mind but aimed his displeasure at the rows of guests sitting at his table. In spite of the fact that he'd invited them, he was not sold on the idea behind issuing the invitation. It didn't sit well on his mind. Now that he was being forced to listen to them try to sell him a new wife, he was convinced that he'd been insane to agree to welcoming them all into his home.

"Get ye gone. Supper is finished."

He dropped back into his large, X-framed chair, a dark expression covering his face. As much as he detested the business at hand, he could not dismiss the fact that he must face the issue of finding a new wife.

"Simply agree that ye will wed my sister Arabella and we can send the rest of these chattering women home." Craig Buchlan's eyes glowed with anticipated victory.

Argument erupted along the table. Men who had just broken bread together began shouting at each other, the volume of their voices increasing with every word. Hayden felt his disgust double.

"I said enough! Listen to the bunch of ye, turning on one another. I've no stomach for it. Go. Hopefully the bright light of morning will help us remember that we are all kinsmen."

Hayden closed his eyes, certain he was too young to feel so old. He ran a hand through his hair and listened to the sounds of chairs being pushed back from the table. His guests didn't go quietly; they grumbled about his temper but at least they went.

"What did I do to offend ye, Lord God?" He looked up at the ceiling of his castle home. It was a sturdy roof, fine and modern.

Hayden's eyes strayed to his abandoned tankard. It too was quite a remarkable show of wealth, made of solid silver, along with every plate gracing the high table. The precious metal shone in the candlelight, but the sight of his belongings did not bring him any pleasure. They were cold and devoid of life. None of it was what he wanted. Wearing the title of laird was nearly breaking his shoulders with the expectations of his clan. His neighbors saw his lack of a male heir as an excuse to raid one another. He'd been trained by his father to use his sword well but it seemed that becoming laird meant he had to fight the battles of the Monroes without that weapon.

It hadn't seemed difficult. He'd wed Ruth, the girl his father contracted, never knowing what a struggle it was to negotiate a bride from among those who felt he should wed their kin.

He wished he still didn't know but the ache behind his eyes reminded him that he'd spent three days trying to select his next wife. He'd never missed his father so much.

He missed his wife more.

Sweet, delicate Ruth from the Kavanagh clan. She'd been too young to die. He snorted. No one was ever really ready to die but his bride had been so happy about their coming child, her cheeks blooming every day that her belly swelled larger and larger. She'd never feared the birth; only winked at him when he made sure the priest added a new prayer into the daily mass for her well-being. It wasn't their first child and Ruth had glowed with confidence, just like so many other women who never rose from the bed they birthed their babes in. Reminding him that she had delivered his children before.

Six months later, his face was covered in the beard he'd refused to shave on the morning he heard that his wife was dead. He reached up and tugged on the lengthening strands.

"I know a way to help ye get what ye want, Laird Monroe."

Hayden straightened up and jerked his head around to stare at the single man who hadn't fled in the face of his displeasure.

"Ye have a death wish, Laird Leask? I told ye and the rest of those bride peddlers to be gone from me sight." He didn't want another wife, didn't want to feel such guilt when he was forced to bury another bride who tried to give him children.

The castle was as still as death . . . the servants wiping their silent tears on the sleeves of their shirts and chemises. His first born daughter had followed her mother into death's embrace only a day later, leaving him with no reason to shave because there was no soft baby cheek to worry about scratching when he kissed it. No little chubby hands to be concerned with offending with rough whiskers. Nothing at all to draw him out into the sunlight. There was only a burning resentment for the fact that the fever that had taken both mother and daughter from him had somehow decided to pass him over. The church told him that was mercy but Hayden called it a curse. He didn't want to be left behind alone with the memory of his daughter's laughter and his wife's sweet voice as she sang to her child. The bed chamber they had died in was too full of their memory for him to consider using.

"There will be no peace until ye marry and have children to secure yer borders."

"I know that, Leask. Why do ye think I am suffering through these suppers that remind me of a slave auction?"

His neighbors would raid one another more and more often until life became as uncivilized as it had been a century ago. He must marry and soon. He was the last of his father's sons, the third to wear the lairdship, and that fact only made his neighbors that much bolder for they saw him without an heir. Soon they'd begin trying to rip land away from the Monroes and he'd have to defend it. Blood would be spilt, a great deal of it.

"Except that I am not interested in peddling ye a bride."

Hayden grabbed his tankard and took a large swallow. "Then why are ye eating at me table, lad? I have no patience for men who waste me time."

"Or a lot of guests that want to impress ye with how many sons their mothers bore."

Hayden chuckled. "Exactly, lad, which is why I told the bunch of ye to leave me to find what peace I may."

Dunmore Leask stood up and moved closer. He scooped up an abandoned tankard on his way to the chair sitting next to Hayden. That was a bold move and no mistake about it. Leask might be a laird, but his clan was one-tenth the size of the Monroes. Whichever woman he might have been thinking to offer up as a prospective bride didn't have much hope of competing with the other men Hayden had just evicted from his hall because her dowry would not be worth as much. If he chose her, the clan would think he was a poor laird for not getting the best offer he might. Life had been so much simpler as a third son; he'd even thought to marry a lass he loved. Those days were gone, carried away with the sweating sickness that had taken his brothers before it stole his family away as well.

Dunmore Leask sat down and took his time getting comfortable. "I do nae plan to ask ye to marry my sister before she gives ye a son."

Hayden frowned. "I don't need any grief from the church, man. It's peace that I'm seeking by looking for another bride."

"Ye need a son for that."

"Aye." He may have barked the word but there was no disguising the longing in his voice. He was weary of the gloom in the house even if he knew well that another bride would not replace Ruth. He could but hope that a new wife would help banish the specters that seemed to inhabit the corners. Even if he didn't love her, there might be affection between them after a time, and later children to love between them.

None of that would happen if he was riding the border putting down invasion.

"I have a sister who is strong in spirit and body."

Hayden took another mouthful of ale. "Of course ye do, man. Ye and all my neighbors delight in coming to me home to sup on me fine plates and fill me head with nonsense about how yer female relation is the one who will give me clan their next laird. Right after I give ye the use of me men to secure yer land, that is." He fixed Dunmore with a hard look. "I'm bloody sick of promises.

It's empty prattle, all of it. Only fate knows who will have the pleasure of watching his children grow up."

"I am willing to alter the order of things."

Hayden felt his anger dissipating as his curiosity was aroused. "I heard that and it's sure to bring the wrath of the church down on us both. Do ye fancy a day in the stocks, then?"

"Ye want a bride and I want an alliance with the Monroes. My sister does nae have enough gold coming with her to gain yer attention above the others here."

A low growl shook Hayden's chest. "So ye want to offer her body to me, man? I'll have that of any girl I take to wife. It's a wee bit of a requirement if I want children."

He bit back a snarl because any man who treated his sister in such a manner was no friend of his.

"I propose a bit of courting instead of negotiating for days on end. It's spring and fine weather. Come and meet my sister, and if the pair of ye find interest in one another then we'll start talking about handfasting."

"The church forbids handfasting, lad." Hayden tried not to sound too hopeful. It was a fact that he liked what he was hearing. It was also a fact that his mother would likely rise from her grave and fill his sleep with nightmares for listening to such an idea. A pure girl deserved marriage from a man. It was the Christian thing to do, the honorable thing, but he was sorely tempted. If by nothing else than the chance to escape the walls threatening to crush him.

"I was thinking to be a bit more practical. The Leask do nae bring ye the same sort of riches ye might get with another clan, but we also are nae so large that the church interferes with traditions that are a thousand years old. What's the harm in meeting me sister and finding out if she's the sort of woman ye might be content to wed? If ye do nae care for her, ye gain a few days of peace before returning to my fellow lairds and their demands."

Hayden rubbed his beard, trying to control the urge to jump at the offer like a hungry hound. He had an appetite for what he was hearing, all right. Maybe it was wrong to not offer for the lass first—the church would tell him that sure enough—but wasn't keeping his retainers alive more important? He hadn't agreed to any handfasting. Leask might offer but there was no sin in not answering the man about that end of the arrangement. He could meet the girl; there was no sin in that. But the girl might be eager to tempt him beyond just a meeting.

Her clan might cry foul if he was left alone with her and she claimed he'd had her. Laird Leask painted a pretty picture of peace and relief from the bride negotiations but that might be nothing but a clever ruse to get him close enough for the sister to cry rape. It wouldn't be the first time a laird was snared by such means. The church held a great power over its people. If a girl cried rape, he'd have to settle accounts with her family, and he could well imagine that wedding the girl would be the demanded settlement.

"Tell me, Leask, is yer sister the sort of woman who sees no harm in bedding a man not her lawfully wed husband?" His thoughts turned dark. There might be even more reason why Dunmore was willing to let his sister lie with a man who wasn't her husband. She might be a light skirt, and if that was the sort of woman he wanted, he'd go to court.

Leask smiled at him. A slow parting of his lips that flashed his teeth.

"My sister is strong willed and would try to rip my throat out if she heard what I just said to ye about handfasting."

Hayden snarled. The sound even startled him because he hadn't realized how much he was liking what his companion was saying.

"Ye are wasting me time and trying to lead me on a merry dance."

Dunmore Leask remained comfortably seated in the face of Hayden's displeasure. That took courage or stupidity, and maybe a measure of both when ye considered the topic and how tender his heart was toward it.

"Strength breeds strength, Monroe. My sister will not marry at my command. She will nae walk in here to yer hall, an example of submission, because wedding ye will bring a strong alliance to our clan."

"Then why are ye talking to me?"

Dunmore leaned forward and Hayden was too interested not to do the same. He was hungry, hungry for what Dunmore was tempting him with. He was happy to marry and please the church, but the moment he married all attention would be focused on his new bride. If she failed to conceive quickly, there would be more raids along the borders. If she produced a daughter, those raids would push inward. It would bring war to every soul looking to him to lead them. Handfasting was different. No one would worry if his mistress kept her smooth waistline. Everyone would assume the girl was drinking some concoction to keep her womb empty. The idea beckoned to him even though he knew he should reject it.

"It's un-Christian, man." Hayden forced the words out. "Besides, ye said she would nae obey ye. I think that makes her wiser than both of us."

Dunmore chuckled. "Aye, that's Elspeth right enough. If ye want her, ye'll have to impress her." He leaned further forward. "But just think, Laird, wouldn't ye enjoy being allowed to court a girl instead of choosing one sitting at this table? Come and meet her. If ye are the man I think ye are, ye'll enjoy charming her. Do nae expect it to be a simple task. Elspeth is a maiden because she is proud. Too proud to be led around the back of the stable by smooth words and a winsome grin."

It sounded simple but he was suspicious. Dunmore Leask shrugged in the face of Hayden's stony silence.

"Unless, of course, ye prefer to sit here listening to your other guests tell ye how many sons their fathers sired. I suppose that is one way to select a bride. I agree that it would make the wedding day quite an exciting moment, while ye wait to see what lies hidden beneath her face veil."

Hayden scowled at his companion in response. Dunmore chuckled and took another long drink from his tankard.

Hayden felt the rise of something inside his chest that he had to think long and hard on to identify. It swelled up and began to boil, sending raw need coursing through him. It had been so long since the idea of bedding any woman excited him that he sat in stunned silence, just enjoying the burn while his cock stiffened behind his kilt. The Leask lass was a far cry from the noble-blooded mares his other guests were offering. The clan was small but they had courage, and that snared his interest.

Proud? He could admire that in a lass, maybe even be attracted to it. He wanted to meet her, meet the sister to see if she had the same fire the brother did.

"Ye're right about one thing, Dunmore Leask, yer idea is better than sitting through any more of these suppers. I will meet yer sister."

"Ye are worse than a peddler of French boy sluts, Dunmore! A horrible excuse for a brother."

Elspeth turned in a swirl of her wool skirts, her eyes bright with temper. She should have been born with red hair, not the blond locks covering her head. At least men knew not to toy with a redhead. Her blond hair invited moments like these from her brother. He thought her meek and mild like the color of her hair.

"And ye know what a French boy slut is used for, Sister, so do nae pretend ye are so delicate and unable to stomach this conversation."

Elspeth propped her hands on her hips.

"I am nae a slut, Dunmore. My body is pure."

Dunmore lifted one finger and pointed at her. "Which is why ye are worth something more than our money will get for ye. We are talking about Laird Monroe. A man of his wealth and importance will nae have what any other man has tasted. He can demand a noble-blooded bride."

She tossed her head again, lifting her chin in defiance.

"Let him. I have not ignored passion's call so that ye can decide who shall pay my whore price. The man wants to come and dally on the green grass of spring before collecting his dowry fortune that comes with a blue-blooded wife. He'll use me to prove his seed is good and then toss some words of how much he values ye out before riding back to his castle."

Dunmore cast a quick glance behind them to make sure her voice wasn't drawing curious eyes. That only made her madder. He closed the distance between them and hooked her arm with one hand. She was slender, but not petite by any means. Elspeth dug her heels in, refusing to be moved so simply. Her brother would know that she meant it when she said no.

"He had two children with his last wife, so his seed is nae doubted. Don't be hating the man for something he is nae intent on doing. I am talking about getting ye a husband far above any that ye might have aspired to with the meager dowry yer clan can afford."

"No man comes to see a lass like me without thinking he's going to be getting all of me. Our clan is nae powerful enough to make him worry about offending us if he leaves me with his bastard."

Dunmore let her go, his face full of frustration. She crossed her arms over her chest. "Then what shall ye have, Brother? Naught but another mouth to fill."

"Ye are nothing like the other girls he has wed. Their noble blood was thin, but yers is strong, Elspeth, and no Leask woman is considered stained for bringing a new life into this world. If ye have a child, it will be a member of this clan. Conceived during a handfasting."

Elspeth felt her eyes go wide. "That is an old custom and ye know the church frowns on it. We'll both end in the stocks if Father Simon Peter hears even one word about handfasting. Even England is once more a Catholic nation with Mary Tudor sitting on the throne. Keep talking about handfasting and even being laird will not save ye from being shamed by the church for it."

"Handfasting is a Scottish custom and one that has been honored by our ancestors." Her brother's face clouded with pride. "We're Scots, not English, and handfasting is Scottish. It does not diminish our faith. The church makes changes to suit its needs, like saying that nuns and priests can't marry, in order to keep all their land and money. But there was a time that they did wed and they were still devoted to God. Chastity is about keeping money in hand, and I propose a handfasting between you and Monroe to gain ye a better husband than I can get ye with coin alone."

Elspeth began to pace. She'd always known the day would come when her brother returned from some clan with an offer of marriage for her. She snorted. At least she had assumed it would be marriage. She had spent her time dreading that she might wed an old man when she should have been fretting over being offered up like a tart just because the man was laird of one of the most powerful clans in Scotland.

But Hayden Monroe was powerful, so much so she felt her throat tightening as if there were a noose around it. There would be plenty of her own kin who would eagerly dress her up in the finest dress she owned and present her to him. Never mind that her honor would be forfeit. Even if her brother spoke the truth about the changes in the church, it did not change the times they were living in. She'd be judged by the priest sitting up at the church in his dark robes.

"I've not remained pure to whore it away, Dunmore. 'Twas something I was saving for the man who would respect me for it."

Dunmore lowered his voice. "Monroe does value yer purity. The man has his pick of all the daughters in Scotland, and he is riding here to meet ye."

"Because ye promised him that I would spread my thighs for him."

Dunmore frowned at her but Elspeth glared back at him.

"What I promised him was that ye are no meek lass, and ye are not, Elspeth. Ye have steel in yer spine and courage the same as any Leask man. But if ye want the greatest reward, ye shall have to be willing to earn it."

"I never thought to marry above where I was born." She didn't care for how meek her words sounded. The church would approve but her pride didn't.

"Fine, Elspeth, if ye have outgrown yer boldness, so be it. Simply tell the man to go back to his land. That ye will not have him. I'll find ye someone else to wed."

"That would be rude since ye have invited him here."

She closed her lips because her brother shrugged in response to her argument. Men. They were so foreign to women. She often wondered just what God had been thinking to create it so that they needed each other to produce children.

"Remember, Elspeth, William Wallace didna do what those that came before him did. He employed new ideas and strategies and defeated the English because of his modern thinking."

"We are not talking about battle here, Brother. Besides, I wouldn't be the first woman to ripen with a bastard and be denied a wedding. What of my child? It is not an easy thing to be called bastard."

"Monroe will wed the mother of his child. The man is still wearing a beard in mourning for his family."

That shocked her. Since the man had invited his neighbors over to negotiate for a bride, she would have expected him to shave and move on.

What sort of a man longed for a woman and daughter that fate had stolen from him? A son she might understand, but now she felt a tender stirring inside her chest. Maybe the man didn't want to get married any more than she did, but was being pressured by his kin. That was something she understood.

Dunmore shrugged. "Besides, I did nae promise him ye'd handfast."

"Ye did nae? In truth, Dunmore?" That tender emotion stirred again, this time stronger. Could it be that the man wanted to meet her and discover if there was anything between them? Now that would be too much to hope for. It would mean he was not ruled by lust for coin and land.

Dunmore cuffed her gently beneath the chin. "I told him that ye are wild and proud of yer purity."

Elspeth snorted at him. "Now yer back to praising me for holding tightly onto my virginity. What happened to yer suggestion of handfasting?"

"Be who ye are and meet the man. If he does nae please ye, I'll negotiate a contract with the Setons. There's a second son in that clan I think would have ye with what ye come with." He held up his hand to still her next comment. "But Monroe is still coming here to meet ye, so ye can hide above stairs if ye're too worried about not being able to remain a maiden just because ye've been in the same room with him."

Elspeth frowned at him, but her brother clearly thought his plan a sound one. She battled against the urge to feel defeated but it was becoming harder, especially when she noticed her brother's men peeking around the edge of the wall to see how she was taking the news.

*Oh, fie upon it.*

With her own mother gone, there was no woman with enough position to force her brother to see reason.

"I am going riding to think the matter through," she announced in a firm tone. "And I am taking yer horse, not some tired-out mare."

That drew a frown from her brother. He adored his stallion, but so did she. At least there would be some enjoyment from the day's events. Her brother didn't care to share the prized animal but she was going to take what enjoyment she might.

"You will nae." Dunmore crossed his arms over his chest. "It's time for ye to stop straddling a horse. No man wants that in a wife. I should have forbid ye that years ago."

Elspeth narrowed her eyes. "I'm asking for a bit of time to think it through. 'Tis nae much of a concession to let me ride out on a horse that has some life in him. Seeing as how ye told Monroe how untamed I am. Ye can't very well have the man showing up and seeing me walking along on a mare with my legs hanging down sidesaddle. Why, such is the very definition of submissive. Nothing wild at all about that."

Her brother snorted. "I hate the way ye turn my own words against me. All right. Off with ye."

Her brother grumbled but she didn't remain to listen to him. The urge to escape was pounding through her, urging her toward the open land beyond the walls of their tower.

She loved Dunmore's stallion. Elspeth slowed down when she entered the section of the stable where the animal was housed. She never approached it too quickly because a wise person didn't startle such a powerful beast.

The power in him fascinated her. There were plenty of people telling her to stay well away from the stallion, but she didn't listen to them. It felt as if something drew her to him. She reached out and touched his velvety coat with her fingertips to judge his temper, and it felt as if fire raced down her arm and into her body. The animal tossed its head, pulling on the leather that held it in the stall.

"Aye, my beauty, that is exactly what I was thinking of—getting out of here."

Pulling the saddle from where it rested over a rail, she secured it on top of the horse. Reaching for the knot that held the bridle, she untied it and wrapped the reins around her fist.

"Do ye nae think that is wee bit too much horse for ye, lass?"

The stallion's front hooves came off the ground and he let out a shrill sound. Whoever had snuck up on her reached for the bridle but Elspeth pulled down on the reins, controlling the horse before her unwelcome company got close enough to do it. Stroking the stallion's muzzle in a soothing motion, she peered over the thick neck of the animal at her company.

"Nae. 'Tis not the first time I have ridden him." And she didn't care if she was being prideful in telling him that.

"Is that a fact?"

He sounded amused by her claim. There was only a small bit of daylight left and most of it didn't make its way into the stable with its small windows. Whoever he was, he stood tall enough to have to watch the ceiling or risk knocking his head on one of the thick beams that supported the roof.

"It is nothing ye have to take my word for. Stand there and ye can watch me mount him."

She was not going to waste the last of the day debating with a stranger when she had her brother's permission to ride his stallion. Tugging on the reins, she led the horse through the doorway and out into the yard. With a carefully placed foot, she used the power in her legs to gain the saddle. The stallion danced with excitement, snorting in the evening air. But she felt the eyes of the stranger on her. She shouldn't care what he thought, not when there were far more important matters for her mind to dwell on today.

Still, she couldn't resist the urge to look behind her. He stood just outside the stable door and his head was even with it. The evening sun touched him and set his hair aglow. It was dark but with copper hiding beneath that dark sable mane. He had it pulled back from his face but the back of it rested on his broad shoulders. Even his beard had a touch of copper in its dark hue, and the sun lit it. But it was the way he watched her that drew her attention. Something flickered in his eyes that filled her with confidence. There was no hint of disapproval for the way she sat atop the horse with her thighs gripping the saddle. In fact, it looked as though he approved of her approach to riding the stallion. Many would not. Half her own clan warned her that riding astride would make her sterile. The other half was quick to tell her that no man would have her to wife if she insisted on acting so dominating. For the moment she didn't care. Quite possibly, that would be the best solution because then she would never have to marry and answer to another man. Dunmore was bad enough. The only thing that drove her toward considering Laird Hayden Monroe was the fact that her brother would marry soon and his bride would consider herself the mistress of the tower. An unwed sister wouldn't be wanted, which meant she had important things to think on.

"As you see, I know what I am about."

"It does appear that way, but it does take a wee bit more to impress me than just sitting there." His gaze moved over her, touching on the way her knees pressed into the sides of the horse, and a flicker of approval lit his eyes. "A lad of ten could do as much as you've shown me."

"Oh, I plan to do much more, sir."

And she hoped that he enjoyed the sight of her riding away from him, the arrogant man. There was something about the way he watched her that made her quiver. A hint of command in his gaze that told her he was accustomed to getting what he wanted from everyone he met. Especially women. She was the laird's daughter, even if her father had been a poor laird. Most of her kin never looked at her as this man was doing. As if she were a woman that they found pleasing.

She shook the odd feelings aside, blaming Dunmore for opening her thoughts up to lying with a man. Now she couldn't seem to control the urge to contemplate surrendering to passion.

Setting her heels into the belly of the horse, she leaned low over his neck and smiled when she felt the powerful beast begin surging beneath her. Excitement filled her and the wind began chilling her ears and nose as the animal gained speed. Her heart accelerated and soon all she heard was the pounding of the hooves and the thumping of her heart. Everything else fell away behind her. The evening chill failed to bother her. Her heart was beating fast enough to keep her skin warm and her breath coming in small pants. The noose she'd felt tightening around her throat finally loosened, giving her release from the sensation that she was being choked by all the expectations surrounding her.

A flash of lightning ended the ride as the stallion reared up into the darkening night, his front legs pawing at the air in front of him. Elspeth laughed and tightened her thighs around him. When his hooves hit the dirt she took the impact easily, the smile on her lips never wavering.

"All right, I'm impressed with ye, lass. I've seen full grown men tossed by a startled stallion."

Her lips pressed into a hard line and she jerked around to stare at her company.

"I was nae trying to impress you. I don't even know who ye are." She felt the return of the pressure about her neck. "'Tis the truth that I wish ye were not here. I was riding out to think some matters through. Important ones."

He sat very confidently atop a horse that was finer than the one she rode. It was obvious in the subtle darkness of the coat and the more noble lines of the animal's face. The saddle was richer too, with decorative tooling applied along all the edges. Its quality bespoke a man with money and position. It would seem that her brother's plan had hooked the interest of Laird Monroe quite well, for the man had ridden in right on his heels. Elspeth struggled to draw her next breath, her throat tightening to the point that it was painful.

"You didna waste any time coming after my brother, Laird Monroe."

He grinned, a smug little parting of his lips almost hidden by his beard. Another flash of lightning illuminated him and made both their mounts dance. The scent of rain filled the air and thunder clapped loudly above their heads, but the man sat as content as might be, unconcerned about the rain beginning to soak him.

"I am not in the habit of wasting time, Elspeth. I agreed to come and meet ye, so here I am."

"Nor are ye in the habit of being polite, it seems."

One of his eyebrows rose, giving him an arrogant look. He pressed his knees into his stallion and guided the animal closer to her with a firm hand on the reins.

"Because I used yer name, lass? Well now, yer brother told me ye were nay the sort of girl impressed with ceremony and titles."

"My brother told you several things you'd be better off not counting on." Elspeth suddenly wanted to know what his face looked like beneath that beard. She scoffed at herself for thinking it, annoyed that she couldn't keep her thoughts on the conversation.

"Is that so?" Something flashed in his eyes that drew an answering flicker from deep inside her. She raised her chin, giving him nothing kind in her expression. But the eager looks on the faces of her brother's men returned to needle her. The man in front of her was powerful; insulting him was not wise.

That didn't mean she was set to do what he wanted. Hand-fasting was sure to gain her nothing. She would have to think of a way to send him away without offending him.

"I came out here to think things through, and I've no had any time to do that just yet."

"So I can leave, is that the way of yer thinking, lass?"

Her horse was nervous with the lightning still making jagged lines across the sky.

"Aye. For the moment. 'Tis nothing against ye."

He grunted. "Well now, Elspeth, I do believe ye are living up to the very image yer brother painted of ye." His face darkened. "But I've come to meet ye and a bit of surly temper will nae send me packing."

"Ye're too accustomed to people pampering ye if you think I am being surly."

"Pampering?"

He nearly choked on the word, bringing a smile to her lips. Elspeth shrugged.

"Do you mean to imply that yer position does nae bring many to you who do naught but agree with anything ye say?"

The rain began to soak her, a full downpour with no softness to begin it. Wild and harsh, the weather whipped against them, soaking her to the skin in moments. It suited her mood and she didn't even raise the hood of her cloak but left it draping down her shoulders while the rain wet every inch of her head.

"You certainly don't suffer from that need." He sat as content as she in the rain, no hint of dislike for the cold water bathing him. It soaked his shirt, where the front of his doublet was unbuttoned. The fabric plastered itself to his form, allowing her to see the firm ridges of muscle that coated his chest. Apparently he was a man of action. That was in his favor, but it was not enough to gain him hers.

"As if I care what any man thinks of me." Elspeth kneed her mount and the animal needed no further urging to break into a full run. She did not mind the rain; however, her brother's horse falling sick would mean trouble for her. But she did not mind taking a care with the stallion. Riding such a magnificent creature meant thinking of its health too. That was the bond that yielded trust between horse and rider. It was getting colder by the minute, so she would have to take the animal back to its dry stable.

The ride back to the stable was very different from the one away from it. A strange awareness invaded her mind, interfering with her normal enjoyment. She couldn't become one with the beast, couldn't seem to forget that Hayden Monroe was behind her. She could hear the faint pounding of his horse's hooves breaking through the thunder to tease her ears. For certain, men had flirted with her in the past, but this was different. She was acutely conscious of the fact that he was trailing her, actually chasing her for the purpose of bedding her.

That was a wicked thought if ever there was one. It bled through her like scarlet wine spilled on a cream-colored table linen. You knew it would be impossible to remove completely, yet couldn't help but watch in fascination as it was streaked farther across the fabric.

She wanted to turn her head and look back, but that would only encourage the man. It would be the same as hoisting a flag of surrender. What did it matter if he was well muscled? She needed to recall her mother's words and the teaching of the church, because handfasting was considered pagan.

That was what she needed to do. She knew it and still part of her wanted to know Laird Monroe better.

Elspeth snorted at herself. She gained the path that led to the tower and growled when she noticed the green and yellow flags of Monroe sticking to the stone of the walls. Even soaked with rain, they still stood out, announcing the presence of the powerful laird.

But what enraged her was the looks she gained when she entered the yard. People poked their heads out of windows and doorways. All of them looking at her expectantly. Her cheeks heated when she realized that they were wondering if she was still a maiden. Many of them looked at her dress, seeking out any little telltale sign that she'd already surrendered to Hayden Monroe.

Well, she would not be.

And that was that.

# Chapter 2

They gained the stable and she was forced to slide from the saddle. The yard was already muddy, making her glad she had good boots to protect her feet. A man like Monroe would have a stone courtyard, with thousands upon thousands of small rocks hauled up to his castle to keep the rain from turning the courtyard outside his home into a bog. It was a task for which a smaller clan such as the Leasks did not have the resources.

At least the stable was sturdy and dry. The stallion was happy to be led through the doorway and toward his stall. He snorted and shook the water from his head. Elspeth heard Monroe behind her and peeked back at the man. Slight amazement hit her as she caught him seeing to his horse with his own hands. For so powerful a man, the sure strokes of his hands drew her attention. He was no stranger to the task and even appeared to be enjoying it. No boy appeared to relieve his laird of the chore, which meant the man had either told his people to leave them alone or he always saw to his own stallion.

"Ye find it surprising that I tend to my own horse, Elspeth?"

She frowned at the use of her Christian name. But a little ripple of sensation traveled across her skin leaving gooseflesh behind. He chuckled at her pout, clearly enjoying her annoyance.

"I suppose ye believe that the laird of the Monroe clan would be above doing chores, but I'll tell ye something, lass—any man who will nae rub down his own stallion does nae deserve the trust of that animal."

"I agree."

Her own hands were moving along the flanks of her brother's horse, and even if her fingers lacked the strength of a man, she would keep at the task in spite of the ache that often invaded her joints. It was how she showed the animal he was more than just a beast of burden.

Monroe nodded. "'Tis a point of honor to look after good Hector here. I'm longing for the day that I can teach me son to honor the same tradition."

"Ah, of course, the reason ye are here." Her voice sounded hurt and she struggled against the feeling because it shouldn't make any difference whatsoever why the man was on Leask land.

"Well now, lass, would ye prefer that I came to meet ye because of the number of sheep yer brother offered me to take ye?"

"No." She rubbed a little too hard, gaining a snort from her brother's horse. "Why did ye name yer horse after a hero who fell before the end of the battle?"

"Because he carries me, and all men have flaws, lass." Monroe stopped working and looked over the back of his horse at her. "I have desires that distract me and I'm no fool enough to say otherwise."

"What ye want is a sin. The church could have us lashed for even talking about handfasting, ye know."

He laughed, the sound deep and brassy. With a final pat on Hector's flank, he stepped around the animal. Elspeth felt him nearing her. Her belly tightened and her eyes were glued to him in fascination.

"Lads and lasses have nay stopped surrendering to their passion. We Scots are too lively for that to ever happen."

"Ah, and now we're to the root of what ye want, aren't we? Surrender. 'Tis so easy for a man to ask that of a maid."

She turned her back on him and went out into the rain once more. At least the icy droplets cooled her skin and sent a shiver down her back that had nothing to do with Hayden Monroe. It was disgusting the way her thoughts were becoming so wanton.

But she shivered again and again, the chill of the spring night making itself known. Rushing up the stone stairs that led to the double doors of the Leask tower, she then darted inside before Armelle the housekeeper caught her dripping water across the floor. The hallways were dim with only a few candles set to burning along their lengths. There would be a fire in the hearth in the hall but Elspeth turned in the opposite direction. Let her brother welcome their guest and entertain him. She wanted to dry her hair.

There were two sets of kitchens at Leask tower, one built in back of the great hall and a second one that faced the yard. Elspeth headed toward the smaller kitchen. Now that it was dark, it would be deserted but the coals in the hearth would still be hot. Picking up a log from near the hearth, Elspeth pushed at the thick layer of ash sitting in the fireplace. It looked cold and dead but she could feel the heat teasing her chilled nose.

The end of the log easily moved the soft ash to reveal a softly glowing bed of embers. Pushing the wood into it she reached over to pick up the bellows that hung from the stone side of the chimney. Pulling it open to suck air inside, she aimed it at the wood and closed the bellows. Air rushed into the hearth making the embers glow brighter. The heat increased, warming her cheeks, and the wood crackled just a tiny amount. It was wasteful to use a log here where only she might enjoy its warmth, but she craved the sanctuary enough to shoulder the guilt.

Just one log wasn't too greedy. She worked the bellows some more, smiling when the wood crackled. A few more moments of patience and a small flicker illuminated the hearth. Elspeth fed it a few smaller branches to make sure the log would burn.

"Exactly what I was thinking, lass, to warm my fingers in front of a fire."

Elspeth jumped. She swung around, landing on startled feet that lacked balance for the first moment. She righted herself quickly, shooting a glare at Hayden.

"I did nae invite ye here."

"No, yer brother did."

He was already halfway into the small kitchen and the expression on his face announced the fact that he wasn't impressed with her temper. The man moved too silently; it had to be unnatural. She looked down at his boots and wished she hadn't because she enjoyed the length of well-muscled legs that smoothed into strong calves. His boots were knee high and she gained a glimpse of bare skin above them where the pleats of his kilt were shorter.

"But I'll confess that I was too weak to resist his invitation since my own home was full of men trying to peddle their sisters and daughters to me."

His comment deflated her anger. Her jaw partially dropped open and a hint of merriment danced in his eyes. She looked away, jerking her head to the side as she realized he was watching her, intensely studying her with his keen gaze. But the moment her eyes were focused somewhere else, all she wanted to do was look back at him.

"I thought ye sought another wife. That is the only reason Dunmore made the journey to yer home."

He frowned, his expression darkening. "It's nae a home, not at the moment." Each word was edged with pain. He walked farther into the kitchen and sat down on the floor in front of the hearth. He closed his eyes and allowed the heat from the fire to warm his face. Nothing moved for long moments except for the flicker of the flames casting their orange and scarlet light over his features.

"At the moment Rams Court is naught but a place I protect. Without my family, it is nae a home."

Elspeth reached for him, the pain in his tone too much to ignore. Her fingertips made the briefest of contacts with his shoulder before she jerked them back. Heat shot down her arm as white-hot as the lightning that had sent the storm breaking around them out on the hills. She had never been so aware of a single touch, never thought that anyone might be.

He turned his head sharply when her motion gained his attention.

"I'm sorry . . ." she stammered as she tried to cover up her actions. "About yer family."

She couldn't ignore the fact that she found his grief genuine.

That was a surprise indeed and one that held her silent while she stared at him. He allowed her to gaze into his eyes for a long moment before shrugging.

"So ye see, Elspeth Leask, 'tis the truth that I used you as an excuse to avoid doing me duty."

"Doing yer duty?" Amusement coated her words. Hayden raised one dark eyebrow in response.

"What? Do ye think that being hounded to marry is something that only happens to women?"

He chuckled, the sound rich and strangely attractive. Elspeth felt her cheeks warming and it had nothing to do with the small fire flickering near her. This was a blush and it stunned her because she couldn't seem to recall ever blushing for a man before.

"I suppose I never did think about the fact that men get pressured into wedding."

"Well we do. I've nae run away from anything in my life before but I confess that I willingly abandoned my own castle to escape from the pressure to choose another wife from among parchments and pleading from their kin."

"Well, you did nae run away from it completely." Her voice became softer and her blush brighter. She suddenly realized that they were very much alone. She'd been alone with men from her clan before, but Hayden was different, and she was keenly aware of him. Sensation flirted over her skin softly like the heat from the fire, awakening hundreds of little points that responded with enjoyment.

"That's true enough."

He reached out and cupped her chin. It was such a gentle touch, and she remained still, fighting against the urge to lean into it more. Somehow the idea that he wasn't using his greater strength to claim her made her want him that much more.

"Yer brother said ye took his horse to go and think about me. I must say I find that an interesting idea, Elspeth."

"Ye are using my name on purpose now."

His fingers began smoothing along her jaw, stroking her skin in delicate circles that sent the most delicious sensation through her. Beneath her stays, her nipples drew into hard points, heat spreading over the delicate mounds until they were warm and willing to be uncovered with no concern for the evening chill.

"Maybe I am."

She offered him a soft snort. Both of his eyebrows rose before he looked up and laughed. His hand dropped away from her face, making her almost sad. But the sound of his brassy amusement sent her lips twitching up into a smile.

"Yer brother warned me that ye were no simpering lass. I see Dunmore is nae given to muddying his words."

"Ye may depend on my brother to tell ye whatever he thinks without any worry for how it will strike ye. Some call him blunt, but I consider it better to know exactly what he means instead of sifting through honey-coated words." Her skirts were still wet and beginning to stick to the skin of her legs. Being so aware of her body made the feeling annoying. "But I'm being a poor hostess to nae offer ye a pint of ale."

Elspeth stood up and her dress fell in heavy clumps around her because most of the fabric was still wet, making the wool stiff. She was conscious of Hayden's gaze on her. She discovered herself fighting the urge to look back at him.

"Yer brother invited me but I find the idea of ye playing hostess a bit more pleasing than having him interrupting us."

"We're merely sharing a fire. At least the fact that ye are here will keep me from feeling too guilty for using the log."

She searched through the kitchen, looking for the mugs that were stored away for the night. This kitchen had pottery and wooden dishes, the silver finery residing in the main hall. Elspeth turned two earthenware drinking vessels over and held one beneath a tap set into a small cask. The flicker from the fire's flame danced off the pale brown ale that poured into the mug. She switched to the second mug and smiled as her nose filled with the scent of the ale. It was yeasty and tart and it drew a low rumble from her belly. Supper had been served while she was out riding the hills. That wasn't unusual, at least not in the fact that it often happened that she was riding when the meal was placed on the tables. The fact that she was allowed to ride so freely was the unusual part. It was a freedom that Dunmore granted her, and it was a truth that most brothers were not so kind.

"Why did ye invite the clans to bride negotiations if ye are nae in the mood to wed? As laird ye could easily avoid the matter."

She handed one of the mugs to him and placed her own on the front of the hearth. Moving back to the work table, she flipped cloths back to see what they covered. A broken round of bread gained approval and another plate yielded some soft goat's milk cheese. Hayden didn't answer her until she returned to the fireside with the food. A smile parted his lips, rewarding her for bringing along the food. She'd done the same for countless men, every day that she could recall, but her hand trembled slightly tonight. She hurried to place the plate on the stones of the hearth so that he wouldn't see it shaking. It knocked against the hard surface and she turned to look at her ale mug to conceal her nervousness.

It was ridiculous to be so unsteady.

Yet she was.

"So why did you leave them? Most men like the dowry more than the wife."

He took a sip from his mug, making her wait even longer for an answer from him. She suddenly understood why he was as powerful as rumor told. This was a man who danced to no one's tune. He listened first, making sure that when he spoke, his words were the last ones that were heard. That sort of self-control she admired.

*Would he be that way in bed? Patient and slow?*

The blush returned to her cheeks and Hayden's attention settled on the spreading stain.

"If I were that sort of man, I'd be there and nay here. I prefer it here."

With her. That was a compliment. One that sent a quiver through her. A low rumble from her belly broke the tension of the moment. Hayden snorted and sat his mug aside.

"I've spent too many nights nursing a mug of ale." He picked up one of the rounds of bread and broke it. "Supping with a pretty lass is far better."

A ghost of a memory drifted across his face but he banished it quickly. Still, Elspeth found it heartwarming to see that he held tender feelings for his family.

*He might come to care for her . . .*

She was placing the cart in front of the horse. But she couldn't stop herself from looking at him and seeking out things that pleased her. His beard made it hard to see his features and she decided that it made him look far older than his years. His body was large and his shoulders coated in thick, hard muscle. She actually felt small sitting so near him.

"Common fare but I think it better than anything I ever sampled at court." He held out a portion of the bread that he'd slathered thickly with cheese.

"Ye're flattering me now." Elspeth took the bread but Hayden slipped his hand along hers and stroked the tender skin on the inside of her wrist while she held her arm so near him. She jumped and the bread went slipping out of her grasp.

Hayden caught it before the cheese-covered side touched the floor. He moved too quickly. She shivered because he was calmly sitting there to gain her trust. She pushed against the floor, intending to scoot back, away from his imposing presence. It was pure instinct to move and had nothing to do with thinking, only with the fact that she was suddenly keenly aware of how easy it might be for him to take what he wanted from her. There was a quiver in the pit of her belly that demanded action. So instead she stood.

Hayden was on his feet before her skirt finished settling. The bread was gone and her breath froze in her throat.

"I am flattering ye, lass. That's a part of getting to know ye."

He reached out and cupped her chin once more. The feeling of his skin against her own was too delightful to step away from. His eyes darkened almost dangerously.

"And I am wanting to know more of ye." Something flickered in his eyes, a flame that was near as bright as the one in the hearth. "I'm wanting to know what ye taste like."

His grip tightened just a bit as he leaned forward to kiss her. The kiss was neither hard, nor soft, but a tasting one as his lips slipped across hers in a delicate motion that sent pleasure through her. It wasn't her first kiss, but it felt more intense, deeper than the others, and maybe the knowledge that she might take him to her bed was making her body more receptive to his touch.

Handfasting . . . it was time-honored . . . and there would be no need to resist the desire beginning to lick across her skin. She could simply surrender.

Her eyes widened. Surrender was exactly what everyone wanted of her and she would not give it to them so simply.

"I do nae like yer beard."

He frowned and stroked his chin full of whiskers. "Many men have beards, lass."

"Well, I do nae like it against my face."

He stepped up close, moving fast, and she realized that she had grown too trusting of him. One of his arms slid around her waist to keep her near him. Her heart was pumping faster now, her lungs drawing in quicker breaths that brought his scent into her senses. She shivered, her body reacting without thought, but with enjoyment to not only the scent of him, but also the feel of his hard body against hers.

"Ye don't like it against yer face?" His voice had dipped so low, she had to lean closer to hear him. He blew out a harsh breath, the hand resting on the center of her back, moving in a sliding stroke, up and down. It felt too good to be true; no touch should be so enjoyable and yet it was. He leaned over and pressed another kiss against her neck, the skin surprising her with how sensitive it was. The impulse to tilt her head and give him full access to her neck for more kisses was strong.

"It is rough . . . yer beard that is . . ." She stumbled over her words trying to force herself to recall why she wanted him to stop kissing her. She pushed at him, her small hand looking impossibly overwhelmed by his wide chest and the greater strength it held. But he straightened up, leaving her neck hungry for more kisses.

"Then ye can shave me, lass."

"Me?"

He stroked her face, his fingers gliding over her upper lip and setting off another shiver.

"Aye, I can see how delicate yer skin is. There is nae a man besides me overlord and king that I'd cut me whiskers for."

From the doorway came the sound of footsteps. Leask retainers spoke to one another as they sought a mug of ale to cut the chill of the rain. Hayden released her, stepping back, and Elspeth frowned because she felt disappointed.

"I'll be finding yer brother now."


Elspeth awoke in a foul mood. She squinted at the morning light, realizing that she'd slept past her normal rising time. For the first time in years the bells calling the faithful to mass had failed to wake her. Missing service promised her a reckoning from Father Simon Peter, and it would not be pleasant because the priest would ask her why she had trouble rising from her bed.

Admitting that she'd tossed and turned for a good portion of the night due to the memory of Hayden's kiss was sure to gain her a penance that would take her a lot of time to complete.

Kicking at the bedding, she rolled out of her narrow bed. The shutters were still closed but the sun was high enough to shine in through the place where each side met.

Shave him? She would not.

Reaching for her hip roll, she tied it around her hips. The small undergarment was stuffed with all the bits of fabric that were too small to be used any other way, and it would help take up the weight of her skirts. She was always grateful for the roll when her wool gown became wet, tripling the weight of the wool. Next came her underskirt, and then she sat down to push her feet into her boots. They were fine leather, closing with antler horn buttons.

If she shaved the man, she'd be leaning over him, which would place her breasts mere inches from his nose. She snorted. Maybe that was his plan all along.

She stood up and caught sight of herself in her mirror. Without her corset, her breasts hung freely beneath the thin linen of her chemise. She could even see the ghost of her nipples through the worn fabric. New chemises were stiff until they had been worn for several months and washed over and over. She never slept in them until they were softened by time and use.

Would Hayden enjoy being so close to her breasts?

Her cheeks heated with a blush but her lips curled up with wicked enjoyment. She certainly would not be confessing that thought to Father Simon Peter.

But would he?

Picking up her under bodice, she walked to the mirror while shrugging into it. Her breasts hung like tear drops and the nipples were small little roses. Some of the other women had larger brown nipples, and she'd heard that such was a sign of better, richer milk.

But what did a man like?

She began to lace the front of the corset closed. Her breasts rose up, the tops swelling above the gently curving edge of the stiff garment. The corset kept her breasts from bouncing, sometimes painfully, while she attended to the chores that kept life comfortable.

The mirror showed her the plump swells and she leaned forward to see what Hayden might see if she agreed to shave him.

Her eyes widened, but more shocking was the thought that crossed her mind.

She wanted to know if he would stare at her breasts.

With a short hiss, Elspeth turned around and finished dressing. Her skirts had dried well overnight but they would not remain that way for long. She lifted the bar that kept the shutters closed against the wind, and opened them. Bright spring sunlight filled her chamber and the breeze carried the scent of new blossoms. Nae, her skirts would not be remaining dry today. Such sun would be needed to dry the washing.

Hurrying to finish, she tucked her hair into a linen cap to keep it from getting in the way while she worked. It rained often in Scotland, which meant you did the washing when there was a bright morning, or risked losing your costly sheets to rot when there was no way to dry them. There would already be many women down by the river.

She pulled the sheets off her own bed and hugged them tightly while heading to the kitchen. She tossed the sheets into a large basket that was mostly full of aprons and other things that need washing. Several baskets were missing, telling her that her fellow Leask women were all thinking the same thing. Searching the top of the long table that stood near the hearth, she scrapped together a swift meal with what was available. There was still hot cereal sitting in a large pot that hung over the coals in the hearth. Fresh spring honey was standing in a pottery jar, and when she drizzled it on top of the cereal, the sweet scent made her smile.

It also drew a rumble from her empty belly. She hadn't eaten last night. Her mind had been too full to worry about her belly. Full of thoughts of Hayden Monroe. It was frustrating but at the same time fascinating. She'd never met a man who drew her interest so completely.

Well, Hayden Monroe would have to wait. She was no princess or daughter of some laird who could keep an army of maids in his pay. There were chores to do and she agreed with her mother—a woman, even one who was high-born, should know every task that was needed to run a house. That way, she would not find herself being cheated by lazy maids or greedy merchants.

Grabbing her basket, she headed to the river.

The rain had filled the river to near bursting. It churned and roared while rushing down from the hills of the highlands. The current was dangerously strong, and the women scrubbing their laundry on the shore snapped their fingers at the children to warn them away from the water. Later in the season when there was not so much snow melting, the little ones would be allowed to scamper along the rocky banks. Today, they were banished up onto the banks where flowers and new spring grass were transforming the land.

"Someone missed mass this morning."

It was Birkita that spoke. She shot a gleeful smirk toward Elspeth. "Father Simon Peter was asking after ye."

Elspeth pouted, gaining a round of laughter from the other women. Every one of them had spent their share of time dealing with Father Simon Peter when the priest came looking for them.

"Well, I suppose the man needs to feel as though he's shepherding his flock."

"No doubt he feels ye need to know he's watchful." Birkita laughed again as she swung what she'd been washing in a wide circle by one end. Water sailed out while she swung it.

"I've no doubt of that man's devotion."

The women laughed again, but they all began to work instead of talk. The afternoon would bring time to enjoy one another's company, once the washing was finished and everything was laid out in the sun.

For now, Elspeth listened to the roar of the river and the slap of the water as she worked each dirty item over a flat rock. Dipping, scrubbing, and dabbing with some of the soap she'd made during the icy winter months. The water chilled her fingers because it had been snow only a day or two ago up in the highlands, but the sun was warm, keeping her back hot. Some of the women sang soft tunes that kept time with the washing.

Elspeth suddenly realized that everything had gone quiet around her. She lifted her head to look into the eyes that had kept her company most of the night. Hayden Monroe was even more powerful looking by bright daylight. He stood at the top of the bank, watching her with an unreadable expression. Birkita shot her a smirk before she and the other women found reasons to move farther down the bank, some of them climbing up the slope and disappearing altogether.

Hayden closed the gap between them, the pleats of his kilt swaying with each step. He had the garment belted securely around his waist, with the tail of the tartan pulled up and over his shoulder. A solid gold broach held it to the fabric of his jerkin, the Monroe crest clearly evident on it—one ram and a falcon that spoke of noble blood. But in spite of such a costly piece of finery, he wore only a knitted cap on his head, tipped to the side like any Leask man.

"I didna expect to find ye doing common chores, Elspeth."

"Why not? If ye wanted to meet that sort of girl, take yerself up to McDonald land. His sisters are pampered, I hear. They keep their hands soft as spring flower petals while the maids do the working. I am a Leask daughter and proud of being strong enough to do my share."

He chuckled at her. "Ye have a passionate temperament, Elspeth Leask. Father Simon Peter was kind enough to speak with me this morning about his fears that ye are being allowed to stray from the narrow path."

Elspeth rolled her eyes. "Well, I'll be facing him later. At least I'll have raw fingers to testify that I spent the day doing something he'd approve of."

Hayden captured one of her hands before she realized his intention. Warm and hard, his hand closed around hers with surprising gentleness. He raised her hand to study her fingers before he leaned down and placed a gentle kiss against the back of her hand. So simple and so often done in greeting, but Elspeth felt this kiss a hundred times more than any other. She tugged her hand away instantly, her face exploding with color. He released her or she never would have succeeded. Something flickered in his eyes that warned her he was not happy with her rejection.

"Ye enjoyed my kiss last night, Elspeth, so do nae be saying in the bright light of day that ye care naught for me."

Her fingers tingled, that single soft kiss sending sensation up her arm and down her body. She might be surprised by how quickly her flesh responded to his but she was not a liar.

"I said nothing."

"Only jerked away from me like I burned ye by kissing yer hand."

"It did burn." Her hand rose to cover her lips but too late. The admission had already escaped, exposing her internal dilemma. Hayden's expression transformed instantly, becoming one of hunger. She stared at it as he reached out to capture her hand yet again. This time, he gently rubbed each finger, chasing the chill from them with his own body heat.

"Did it now, lass? Well, I think we'll have to explore that."

Her belly tightened with excitement. A crazy jolt of anticipation ripped through her. No part of her remained untouched. It licked over her skin, awakening hundreds of spots that begged for a touch from the hand holding hers. Behind her corset her nipples became hard points that stabbed into the stiff garment containing them. Her breath froze in her throat and her lower lip felt dry. She ran her tongue over it and stopped when Hayden's gaze dropped to the path her tongue took. Hunger danced in his eyes, driving her excitement up another notch.

"Enough, I've work to do." Her tone was husky and foreign sounding. She swallowed, forcing down the lump that had somehow become lodged in her throat.

"Aye, I agree with that. Which is why I sought ye out, Elspeth."

She looked back at him to see him hiding behind an expressionless mask once again, but there was a challenge lurking in his eyes that warned her he was making ready to test her again. Her chin rose and her hands landed on top of her hips, pushing her elbows out. Hayden blinked and then tossed his head back and laughed.

The toad.

Wasn't that just like a man? To find amusement in a woman standing up to him.

"Get on with ye. I've tasks to see to."

She didn't care if her tone was surly or if Father Simon Peter would demand a full ten decades of Hail Marys said in penance.

Hayden lowered his face to stare at her. "Exactly what I wanted from ye, lass, to see to a task." He reached up and ran his hand over his beard. "I have need of yer delicate hands to rid me of these whiskers so I can kiss ye without complaint. And take a good long time about it at that."

"I've never shaved a man."

*Or discussed kissing one so plainly . . .*

He smiled at her but it was not a cheerful expression. It was full of wicked promise and that excitement warming her belly grew in response, spreading to her passage and the delicate folds of flesh hiding its entrance. No one had ever touched them but Hayden wanted to; she saw the intention burning in his eyes. It was dark and edged with promise. She shivered, her fingers tingling with the memory of just how gentle his hands could be, and then the folds of her sex tingled with longing to feel the same.

"I'm happy to hear ye have never shaved a man." There was arrogance in his tone that annoyed her. It was too confident, too sure of her will bending to his.

"And I did nae say I would shave you."

One of his eyebrows rose. "Well now, lass, if ye are too timid to try me, just say so."

"I am not timid."

He stepped up closer and she caught the scent of his body. It was strange the way she noticed what he smelled like. It wasn't a lack of washing that drew her attention to it. There was something very male that drew her interest. Like musk.

"Yes ye are, Elspeth, and I admire ye for that, for ye have kept yer hands on yer chores and away from men. Not many can claim that even if they declare it loudly."

She knew exactly what he meant. There were many who knelt in the perfect display of Christian obedience, but they met with their lovers once the Mass was finished.

Something behind him caught her eye. Elspeth looked between his arm and body, gasping when she realized that one of the younger children had ventured down to the water's edge. Too young to know the danger of the roaring river, the little girl was hopping among the rocks with an innocent smile on her face, the cool water beckoning to her with the heat of the day at its strongest. The women were all too far away to prevent the babe from making it past them. No one was watching the river bank in deference to her and Hayden.

"What is it?"

Hayden turned in a tightly controlled motion, but Elspeth was already darting out into the water. The child looked up as she jumped farther into the current. The moment she landed in ankle-deep water, it tore at her skirts, dragging her down to her knees and onto her face. The surging waters began tumbling the child like a branch, over and over while the little girl began screeching in terror.

"Elspeth, stop!"

Hayden roared at her but the child's cries were far more piercing. In the moments he'd taken to judge what was happening, Elspeth had run into the water with her skirts held high. The child kicked with all her might but the river was too strong, yanking her toward the rushing center that was foamy and white. Her white sleeves turned dark with mud, exposing the sinister nature of the flooded river. Elspeth threw herself toward the grasping hands, pushing hard against the muddy bottom of the river to launch herself after the girl.

She felt the small fingers clawing at her. Fingernails carved deep grooves down her forearms but it was the dearest pain she had ever endured. The river ripped at her skirts, the heavy weight of the sodden wool allowing the water to pull her along more strongly than it had the child. There was no way to escape as well as hold on to the delicate body clutching at her.

Women were screaming along the banks now, heads popping up from where they had walked up onto the banks. All of it was drowned out by the roar of the water. Elspeth kicked with every ounce of strength she had, but it was nothing compared to the pull of the water. Her feet lodged on a boulder for one moment, while the rushing current tore her skirt around the solid rock. Her thighs quivered, her strength threatening to fail her. Grabbing the child's small waist, Elspeth lifted her into the air and threw her to Hayden. He was only a few feet away, but still on feet braced wide against the fury of the water. He caught the child in a grasp that made her scream again, but he did not keep her. He sent her flying back to the women on the bank. Elspeth gained one glimpse of the child wrapping her dirty sleeves around her mother's neck. Relief surged through her in a thick wave one second before her legs crumpled and her body was sucked around the rock into the heart of the river.

# Chapter 3

"Elspeth!"

Hayden's voice was drowned out as the white water that looked so pristine closed its jaws over her like a steel trap. The force of it threatened to crush her chest as she was forced down, down into the swirling tempest. It sent her crashing into rocks and fallen trees without mercy, dragging her away after hitting one, and into another. It was also bone-numbing cold. It felt like a thousand tiny daggers pricking at her. Each second seemed like an hour, the agony lasting forever. Her lungs began burning for breath but the current held her down, refusing to release her. All around her were hundreds of bubbles, making it impossible to determine which way was up.

Strong arms wrapped around her, shocking her with how warm they were. Her head suddenly broke through the surface of the river, allowing her to suck in a breath. Hayden cursed next to her ear but his arms held her close while the river pulled them both along in its grasp.

"There, lass. Do ye see the bend?"

"No." All she saw was the white tops of waves, the sunlight turning them golden. There was another blinding jolt of pain as they were smashed against a submerged boulder. Hayden grunted, his huge body jerking, but he found the strength in his legs to push off the rock, sending them precious feet away from the center of the river.

"There is a bend in the river. If we make it to the shore, dig yer feet into the mud."

The roar of the water made it hard to understand him, but far worse was the chill. It was seeping into her mind, numbing her thoughts. He grunted as he shoved them off another rock and suddenly the shore didn't seem so far away. Elspeth kicked, pushing her feet against anything solid. Every muscle ached, resisting her demands that they work. She sucked in as much water as air, coughing when the water burned her lungs.

But the shore got closer. Hayden shoved her toward it, his body pushing hers toward the promise of safety. She felt the water turning and trying to suck her skirts along with it but Hayden refused to allow it. He dug his feet into the muddy bottom and growled while forcing them both out of the grip of the current.

They landed on their bellies like newly netted fish. Elspeth found that she lacked the strength to do anything but lie on the sand and pull deep breaths into her starving lungs. Her entire body quivered and the tiny pebbles that made up the shore poked into her face.

"I can nae believe ye took that sort of chance with yer life."

Hayden sat up, his chest heaving with the effort of trying to get them out of the water.

"You were too far behind me. The current would have taken that babe before ye got a hand on her."

He growled at her. The sound annoyed her, restoring enough of her strength to lift her head. "And do nae ye growl at me, Hayden Monroe."

He snorted and lifted one hand to point a finger at her. "What I'd like to do is give ye a spanking for acting so foolishly."

Elspeth felt her eyes widen with rage. She sat all the way up, staggering when she attempted to stand, but her anger gave her the strength to keep her feet beneath her.

"You will not spank me!"

Hayden rose up beside her, dwarfing her with his greater height. "If I thought ye weren't so chilled by that damned water, I would." His nostrils actually flared. "For ye're lucky to still be alive."

He clasped the sides of her head and kissed her. Hard and demanding, his mouth claimed hers in a kiss that held all of the tension of the last few minutes. Elspeth was suddenly desperate to return his kiss. She reached for him, wrapping her arms around his neck and pressing her body up against his. Hayden rocked back on his heels but held her steady while his mouth continued the hard kiss. He seemed to be seeking reassurance that she was alive, and she wanted to confirm the same. His hand slipped around to cup the back of her head while the tip of his tongue traced a path along her lower lip and into her mouth.

Elspeth shivered, moving her lips in unison and eagerly accepting the thrust of his tongue. She wasn't close enough. Pressing against him, she could feel the beat of his heart and it was suddenly the most important thing to touch. She pulled her hand down, sliding over the wet fabric of his shirt, her fingertips tracing the hard ridges of muscles that covered his chest until she found the source of the beat. Flattening her hand against him, she sighed as the steady beat of his heart filled her palm.

"It was a brave thing to do, lass. I know grown men who would have hesitated, concerned about their own lives." Hayden spoke quietly, his lips trailing down the column of her neck. She shivered again because his lips were warm and her skin so cold.

"Then why did ye threaten to spank me?"

She pulled away from him, but he held her against him with one solid arm around her waist. That didn't prevent her from glaring at him. His hand smoothed down from where it was resting against her lower back, over the thick cartridge pleating of her skirt until he was cupping one side of her bottom through the soaking wet fabric of her dress. Her cheeks suddenly heated up, chasing the chill of the water away.

"Ye might find that having my hand on yer bottom is something enjoyable, sweet Elspeth."

His voice was low and husky, hunger returning to his expression, but it didn't last. His gaze suddenly shifted to her head and he released her to pluck something from her hair. A broken twig with leaves still glistening with water was tossed to the ground.

"Even if it sounds strange, considering we're both soaking wet, I think we could use a bath."

"Aye." She suddenly felt as if there was sand beneath her corset, being ground into her skin with every rise and fall of her chest. "But where are we?"

Hayden looked up, turning to scan what could be seen. Nothing but rocky hillsides surrounded them. He grasped her hand and pulled her along behind him as he climbed up the steep slope of the riverbed where the earth had been carried away by the rushing water. Clumps of grass were perched on the edge, their roots the only thing holding them in place because the soil had been washed out in a wide bend sometime in the recent days. The river had changed course only recently, proving that fate had smiled on them today.

"Well, we're some fair distance from Leask Tower."

A pounding began on the other side of the hill. The hand holding hers tightened and Hayden forced her behind him.

"Get back over the bank until I know who is riding this way."

His voice was edged in hard command now. The tone of a man who expected to be obeyed.

Elspeth didn't get a chance to do as he ordered. Horses made the crest of the hill, their noses flaring from being ridden hard. Elspeth gasped as she recognized the horses carried men who wore the colors of the Dalry clan. They pulled up on their reins, turning their heads to stare at them.

"It would be Dalry retainers."

"Are ye feuding with the Dalry clan?"

Hayden drew in a stiff breath as the horses began moving again, this time bearing down on them. There were only a dozen of them, but that was far too many for the single sword strapped to Hayden's back.

"The Dalry clan keeps close with the English, too close for my comfort."

Which was as bad as feuding. A lump swelled up in her throat but she forced it down. This was no time to lose her nerve. There was part of her that wanted Hayden to approve of her, and that did not include cringing in the face of his adversaries.

"Well now, is this the man that didna invite me up to his fine castle?"

"Does that mean ye'd be interested in me marrying yer sister, Pherson?" Hayden's voice didn't quiver, it was full and brassy. Pherson Dalry leaned down and patted the neck of his stallion while studying Hayden with eyes as blue as the ocean. His men all smirked, enjoying the moment full well.

"Ye'd be lucky to have a Dalry bride." Thick pride coated Pherson's voice. Even sitting atop the horse it was evident that he was a large man. His gaze shifted to her and Hayden's grip tightened.

"Young Leask, ye are off yer land." He frowned. "And wearing enough dirt to plant in, too."

"One of the children went too close to the river."

The Dalry retainers all frowned, becoming serious. Hope flickered to life inside her. At least it looked as if their clan colors didn't matter when it came to the life of a child.

"So I had to fetch her out and got swept into the current myself. Laird Monroe had to pull me out."

"Well, that's a bit of pleasant news." Pherson didn't join his men in smiling in response to her tale. His eyes narrowed and Hayden stiffened.

"So we'll be leaving and getting back onto Leask land." She took one step and heard the sound of swords being drawn from their sheaths. Hayden pulled his too, and stepped in front of her, his wider frame shielding her. Horror flooded her as she realized that the numbers were too far out of balance for the outcome to be in question. The thought of watching Hayden fall hit her like a shaft being driven through her chest. She struggled to draw breath, that lump returning to clog her throat completely.

"Not so fast," Pherson Dalry declared.

Hayden stiffened, his body becoming a mass of tension.

"Leave the lass be, Dalry. She's on yer land because she risked her life for another. You and I can quarrel about the English another day."

"Aye, I'll agree with that."

Relief blossomed sweet and swiftly, but Pherson's lips lifted into a smile that chilled her once again. His blue eyes settled on her and the calculated look in them made her struggle for breath again.

"But I will be inviting the lass on up to me home. Seeing as how she looks like she could use a bit of hospitality."

"No thank ye." Elspeth stepped out from behind Hayden to speak her mind and the man pushed her back almost before she finished rejecting Pherson's invitation.

"Careful there, Elspeth Leask, I've delicate feelings." His men snickered, reveling that the man was anything but tender hearted. "Ye'll walk yerself over here or I'll fetch ye through Hayden Monroe, and that is a solemn promise."

His men abandoned their jesting expressions, becoming focused, deadly so.

"You'll stay behind me." Hayden's voice was low and deadly, but it was the sight of Pherson's men guiding their horses around them that forced her decision.

"I won't watch ye die, Hayden." She stood up on her toes to whisper in his ear.

"Ye will stay." He grabbed a handful of her skirt, but Elspeth jumped back and the wet fabric slipped through his grasp, forcing his hand down the length of her skirt until a full yard was stretched out between them. He shot a deadly look at her, but had to jerk his attention back to the men circling them.

A blade flashed in the afternoon sun and sliced through her skirt. She tumbled backward from the force of resisting Hayden's strength. The moment she stopped, a hand reached down and lifted her off her feet.

"Ye bloody savage!"

She didn't care about Father Simon Peter anymore and neither did Hayden. He cursed loud and profanely.

"Release her, Pherson, or I swear I'll begin a feud that will leave half yer women widows."

The man holding her pressed her over his horse so that her head was hanging halfway down the side of the animal.

"Now, lad, ye just called me a friend of the English, so what am I to do but prove that I am as Scottish as ye by stealing yer bride and holding her for ransom?" Pherson Dalry chuckled as the man holding her rode up close to him.

"I'll be waiting on ye, Laird Monroe. Take too long and I might take a liking to the lass."

Hayden snarled something that was lost as the Dalry retainers reeled their mounts about and took off. Without a horse, Hayden was left standing where he was, but Elspeth caught a glimpse of his fury. It was etched into his face, and even the bouncing of the horse didn't prevent her from seeing it.

He'd come for her.

At least she hoped he would. The fact of the matter did not

support her hope, though. She didn't have a rich dowry, and paying a ransom would take all that she did have. There was no contract binding her to Hayden and making it his responsibility to rescue her. Once his temper cooled, his men might well be able to counsel him into the wiser thing—riding back to Monroe land where he could begin the process of selecting another bride.

That made her heart ache. She wasn't even sure how it was possible to lament losing him when she had known him so short a time.

Would he come for her?

She prayed he would.

Hayden suddenly understood every cruel execution method he'd heard that was used in England.

Prisoners were boiled alive. Those who printed verses against the Queen were burned at the stake, and he felt the rage that would see a man signing his name to orders such as those.

But he wanted to beat Pherson Dalry to death with his bare hands.

Sheathing his sword, he turned and began running back toward Leask land. Stealing brides was Scottish but that didn't change the fact that he was going to wrap his hands around Pherson's throat for giving that order.

And that was a Scottish promise.

"You cut my dress."

Elspeth glared at her captor and resisted the urge to retch on his steps. That man was too fortunate because her stomach was near empty so her nausea had nothing to send up.

"Fabric is expensive."

"I know that. I've two sisters who remind me constantly by having their accounts come to me to be settled."

Pherson Dalry raked her from head to toe with his blue eyes. The man had a keen gaze but Elspeth discovered that she had no liking for the man at all. Let him think her shrewish. All that much better for him to long to be rid of her.

"Well, I have to wonder why you need to kidnap another woman when it sounds like you have no patience for the ones related to ye."

He smiled, his lips parting to flash even white teeth at her. "Well, because, little ruffled hen, I can nae be thinking what I'm thinking about me own sisters. That would be a sin."

Elspeth refused to be so easily shocked. She propped her hands on her hips and scowled at the man.

"It is still a sin and ye're a poor excuse of a man for trying to frighten me."

His smile faded, replaced by a pensive look. "Well now, maybe I wanted to test yer courage. Rumor has it ye ride that stallion of yer brother's with yer thighs holding ye in the saddle. I confess that I'm interested in seeing what manner of woman ye be."

She wished she could muster up some tears but her temper refused to allow her any expression save for a scowl. If she could weep he'd be finished with her, but her hands remained poised on her hips and her back straight and strong.

"Ye had plenty of time to come and meet me if that was yer wish. Do nae play me for a fool. Ye want to toy with Hayden Monroe and it has naught to do with what sort of woman ye might have heard I am."

"Maybe, lass, and then again, maybe I'm enjoying this fortunate turn of events. Every man overlooks an opportunity from time to time. Fate seems to be tossing ye into my hands and I plan to listen to her."

"Ye will nae be keeping me."

His expression hardened and he reached out to grasp her arm just below her elbow.

"Careful lass, ye seem to think me more English than Scot, but I'll warn ye just this once that I am pure Scot and I do nae ignore a challenge." His gaze lowered to her chest where the swells of her breasts were in sight beneath the stained fabric of her worn chemise. She cursed herself for not changing into a newer one that would have concealed more.

"Especially when that challenge comes from such a delightful package. I believe I'd enjoy proving my worth to ye."

Elspeth jerked against his hold but his grasp proved solid. Yet it did not pain her. He controlled his greater strength as expertly as Hayden did.

That comparison only made her long for Hayden even more. Her temper stirred and she became torn between directing her scorn at Pherson Dalry and being horrified that Hayden Monroe meant so much to her.

"Men are always so sure that women are soft hearted. As for myself, I find the lot of ye an annoyance."

She reached over and pinched his hand. "Get yer hands off me. My hearing works just fine."

An amused chuckle was her response but the man released her and offered her a mocking reverence that his men laughed at. Pherson turned to look at them and their amusement died.

Well, at least she would only need suffer his arrogance. Part of her was grateful that he was refusing to allow his men to make sport of her. A small amount of security against the imposing tower rising up in front of her. The Dalry stronghold was sturdy and impressive. Three towers that had curtain walls running between them to form a triangle. Behind them the hills rose at steep angles, making it impossible to bring a horse down the slopes. That left only the main approach to the fortification, and that was narrow and facing the first tower. With the curtain walls running back at an angle to the other towers, it formed a wedge that looked inaccessible.

"Well then, mistress, up inside with ye."

There was a challenge in Pherson Dalry's tone. There was also a hint of anticipation, as if the man would enjoy her resistance. Casting a look back at him, she noticed how much larger he was than herself, but there was no twist of excitement in her belly, only the warm flicker of frustration. She savored that frustration for it held off despair. But not completely.

Her gaze moved over the valley that led up to the fortress, and she cringed when she realized there was no way to force Dalry to give her up. The despair flowed freely around her attempt to ignore it, flooding her and reminding her that the most logical thing for Hayden to do would be to leave her.

# Chapter 4

Pherson's sisters were amusing.

In fact, they were by far the best entertainment that Elspeth could recall seeing in some time.

Tavia and Daracha were both beautiful. They knew it too. That was what made it so much fun to watch while they needled their brother in the most subtle ways—long looks from their eyes with flutters of lashes to complete the moment. They moved in an almost hypnotic fashion, their walk polished and perfected. The moment they entered the main hall, every man there turned to watch them. The sisters didn't rush but made their way down the main aisle looking as if they were striding into court.

They were certainly dressed for that role. Both wore damask. Fabric was expensive but damask was so pricey, noble families sometimes bankrupted themselves in order to outfit their sons and daughters for court. Tavia was a blonde with rare green eyes, and her gown was made of blue and topaz with velvet edging it. Her sister Daracha had the same coloring as her brother, midnight hair and blue eyes. She wore a dark green that was woven with sapphire blue and edged with sable brown.

They promenaded up the aisle with chins perfectly level and their slim fingers held in front of their stomachers to show off how long and lovely they were. Their hair was held up high on the top of their heads, leaving their necks on display, and the men

watching looked as if they approved. Both sank into deep curt-
sies, remaining there.

"Enough." Pherson watched his sisters from narrowed eyes.
They both stood and fluttered their eyelashes. Their brother
groaned.

"What are ye doing wearing those gowns? Ye're not at court
yet."

Tavia smiled sweetly. "Oh, but, dearest brother, we must practice walking and dancing in them. How else shall we keep from
shaming you?"

Pherson ground his teeth. "Well, I've got a guest for you to see
to so get those overpriced gowns off and save them for when ye
are at court. Take her to the bathing house since I do nae think
she'll fancy me doing it."

Elspeth snorted at Pherson. He turned and raised one eyebrow
mockingly.

"Would ye prefer to be my prisoner, lass? In which case, ye'll
think yer current condition clean compared to how ye will be in a
few weeks being kept in the dungeon."

"We do not have a dungeon, brother." Tavia offered her comment with soft tone.

Her brother snarled. "Why does every thought ye have sail
right out of yer mouth the moment you think it?"

Daracha lifted her chin and sent an innocent look toward her
brother. "Forgive us, brother, we were shocked to hear you threaten
a woman. You have always kept yer battling between men, and
we have never had reason to think you cruel toward a helpless
woman."

"She's not helpless. She jumped into a spring swollen river and
came out living, so don't be telling me she lacks strength."

There wasn't a single indication from either woman that their
brother's words either impressed them or not. They lowered themselves again, the damask fabric of their gowns puddling on the
hard stone of the floor with the stiff sound of silk. Elspeth couldn't
help but stare at the dresses; she could not hope to have anything
so fine, even for a wedding.

"Make yer choice, Elspeth Leask. Get ye off with my sisters or
I'll see to making ye comfortable."

She shot him one more hot glare before following his sisters.

At least the idea of bathing was a pleasant one. Now that she was half dry, she felt even more grit stuck between her clothing and her skin. Walking ground it against her in places, like beneath her waistband and stays. Her head itched and it was took great effort not to scratch herself as if she had fleas.

They cleared the hall and went down another set of stairs set near the corner. It was darker there, the light from the sun only having narrow arrow slits to enter through.

The scent of smoke was in the air, and Elspeth could see a slight glow coming from the fireplace set into the far wall. Daracha pulled a large apron off a hook set into the wall, and covered her expensive dress with it before taking a candle that sat in an iron holder near that hook. She carried the candle toward the fireplace and set the wick against the coals. It flickered to light, casting a friendly glow around the girl's face. She looked back at Elspeth.

"Men are pigs."

Tavia made a soft clicking sound with her tongue. "Now, sister, be just. I know many well-mannered hogs."

The pair laughed gently, their voices almost musical. Daracha carried the lit candle around the room, touching the flame to several other wicks. The chamber became cheerful with all four walls holding lit candles. The yellow and gold light revealed two overly large slipper tubs made of copper; one was large enough for two full-grown people. Her face colored with a blush as she considered what two naked people might do besides bathe. Elspeth stared at the expensive items and back at the damask dresses worn by the women.

"Yer brother is a pirate." There was no other way to explain such finery.

Tavia had donned an apron as well, and had set a log on the fire.

"Our brother is an uncivilized brute and for that we apologize." She pulled a chain set above one tub and water began falling from a missing stone in the face of the wall. It splattered into the tub, drawing a shiver from Elspeth. Just the sound of rushing water yanked her mind back to that moment when the white frothy water had clamped her in its jaws.

"But Pherson considers himself a patriot for keeping the sea safe. Calling him a pirate is a sure way to gain his disdain."

Elspeth stared Tavia straight in the eye. "He's a pirate."

Both girls suddenly laughed.

"Oh, ye are going to be wonderful fun to have about. Every girl that comes here to meet our brother is always so dull and proper. Of course they are mostly English-born ones." Daracha's eyes sparkled with merriment. She pushed two kettles of water over the fire and the small amount that was clinging to the outside sputtered and hissed when the heat connected with it.

"I am not here to provide amusement."

"Of course not and you must think us quite horrible to be so happy." Tavia sighed. "It's simply that our brother is by far the most arrogant creature ever born and we are weary of suffering his whims."

Daracha began pulling at the tie holding Elspeth's braid. Elspeth worked at the buttons on the front of her gown, eager to wash the grim off her skin. Pirated goods or not, she was going to enjoy that slipper tub.

"You certainly do nothing to sober him, what with yer stately entrance and lowering fit for a king."

Maybe she was foolish to taunt them, but Elspeth had never been one for polishing egos. She didn't know how to do anything but speak her mind.

To her surprise both girls laughed again.

"We continue to perfect it, just because he ordered us to learn courtly conduct." Tavia moved across the chamber on light steps that resembled dancing more than walking. "The smoother we walk, the more it annoys Pherson."

"Which he deserves for ordering us to learn to walk as if the only value we have is our appearance." Daracha pressed her lips into a tight line of disapproval. "That brother of ours never wonders what we have been doing to expand our minds. Instead he orders us to learn to glide when we walk."

"Men are so shortsighted. Concerned with things that mean nothing at all in a wife."

*Hayden liked her courage.*

Her simple and practical wool dress met with his approval also. Elspeth looked at the pile of her clothing now that she was pulling it off her body. There was nothing refined about it, but that had not kept Hayden from pulling her against him for a kiss.

Pherson Dalry watched Elspeth at her bath and raised a finger to his lips while staring at the girl sitting in the tub with her breasts exposed. Young, firm breasts that made his mouth water to taste them. The last bride prospect he'd welcomed had sniffled as she drew her inner robe off to show her body to him. Elspeth's eyes were not glassy with unshed tears but her cheeks were bright and her nipples hard with anticipation. Something stirred in him he'd not felt in a long time. It was warm and sliced through the years of duty his life had become. A laird had to keep his mind on so many things that he had lost track of the simple joy of affection. Elspeth Leask was thinking of the man she cared for and no mistake. He could see it in her eyes and it had the power to make him turn his back on her. He'd taken what he wanted when it came to goods and gold, but never when it came to a woman's embrace. But he'd negotiated it too many times to suit him. He was envious of Hayden Monroe, almost bitterly so.

For love was the only thing in life that no man could steal, even a pirate like himself.

"There now, sit by the fire and brush out yer hair. We'll have to find something pretty for ye to wear."

"Something sturdy will do just fine. I've no desire to impress yer brother." Elspeth made sure her tone was tart enough to cut through the way both sisters had of just doing what they pleased without waiting to see if she wanted it.

"Ah, but ye should be interested in blinding him. There lies the secret to dealing with men." Tavia offered her a knowing look. It was far different from the amused one the girl had worn until now. The façade was suddenly gone and Elspeth discovered that behind the pretty girl was a very confident woman.

"Be pleasing in all ways and men will never suspect that ye are also thinking."

Daracha brought her a chemise that was almost transparent. "This is silk and hemp from Egypt. I hear Cleopatra wore the same cloth. It does make one feel like a queen."

"She killed herself."

"But she loved and was loved in return." Daracha sighed. "I believe that once ye have loved, ye cannot live without it. That's why she killed herself."

The garment slithered down her body once Daracha released it. The fabric was a whisper against her skin. It was like the oldest chemise she had, translucent, and the candles flickers turned it into liquid gold.

*Hayden would like it . . .*

"Who are you thinking of?" Tavia was watching her from the other side of the room. A shiver crossed her neck when she realized that these sisters worked as a team. Tavia tapped her lips with one fingertip, drawing attention to them with the tiniest of motions.

"Ye're blushing and yer eyes are shimmering. Are ye in love with him?"

"Love?" Elspeth shut her mouth too quickly and her teeth clicked against each other, but her tone had been too high, exposing her true feelings.

Daracha made a soft sound beneath her breath and carried over two stockings. She knelt in front of Elspeth, looking too demure for how well the pair of them were dissecting her every motion.

"Yes, love. Yer eyes are shimmering when ye think of him. What else except love?"

"Does it matter?"

Daracha was intent on pushing the stocking up her leg but Elspeth grabbed it and performed the task herself.

Both Daracha and Tavia smiled, the smallest curving of their lips. Elspeth felt their gazes ten times more than any Father Simon Peter had aimed at her.

"I don't know what I feel, only that I detest yer brother for taking me away from Hayden."

Both sisters seemed to hang on her words, absorbing them as if they were savoring the idea, because they were starving for affection. Considering how their brother treated them, maybe they were. She suddenly felt remorse for being so cross with them.

"I was wondering if Hayden would like me in this chemise, but I don't even know if he still desires me. Considering that yer brother wants a ransom for me, I wouldn't be surprised to hear that he's returned to Monroe land and washed his hands of the matter."

"Ye doubt he will come to ransom ye?" Tavia sounded shocked. "If he fails to come after ye, he does not love ye, that is for certain."

Elspeth tried to keep the despair from her voice. "He has no contract to bind him to me." She looked around the room again, noting the fine things in it. "And it does not look as though yer brother will be content with any small amount." There were many trunks in the room, over a dozen, telling her that Pherson liked to collect everything he could from his victims.

"Ye are correct. Pherson never wants anything less than the best."

There was a note of annoyance in Tavia's voice. Elspeth considered the girl for a moment.

"Unless ye would care to help me out with yer brother . . . for the sake of proving that a woman can outthink a man."

Daracha looked up from where she had been studying what was inside a trunk. She lifted a pair of dainty shoes with dancing heels on them.

"Outwit Pherson? Now that is something we are always interested in viewing, but it does not happen very often."

Daracha brought the shoes to her and lifted a finger to her lips in caution.

"Keep yer voice low if yer intention is to scheme." She lifted the shoe up so that the light shone off the polished leather. "Do ye like these? I believe they will fit ye."

Now Daracha spoke in a normal tone but Elspeth was distracted by the shoes. They had heels on them and were a deep scarlet color. There was nothing practical at all about them but she adored them on sight.

Daracha smiled a wicked, knowing smile. "I hear Queen Catherine Howard had many pairs just like this."

Elspeth felt her eyes widen. "And she also lost her head."

Tavia waved a hand in the air. "She drew men's attention everywhere she went. Her failing was that she was too foolish to understand the difference between love and lust. Try them on."

They were a French fashion, something Anne Boleyn adored

too. Yet another woman who had lost her head over being too free with her affections.

But it was only a pair of shoes and she didn't have a husband to make jealous.

Elspeth slid her feet into the shoes and Daracha tied them closed.

"Now walk in them. They say the heels push yer bottom up, making it more attractive to the male eye. The English Queen Mary has forbidden them."

The heels felt decadent. Coupled with the silk chemise, she felt more alluring than she ever had. The silk flowed over her breasts, teasing her nipples until they drew into hard points that poked through the delicate fabric. Tavia laughed in a low, sultry tone.

"I believe ye need just the correct set of stays to go with those heels." Tavia opened another trunk and pulled something from it. Elspeth gasped when she saw it.

"Lovely, aren't they? My brother brought this back from a countess who clearly doesn't share the strict piety that her queen does."

The stays were made of emerald green silk. The candlelight illuminated the fabric, making it look like emerald fire. Elspeth reached out to run a single fingertip over the costly fabric.

"To think that there are women wearing such things beneath their somber black velvet court dresses . . ."

Daracha snickered. "An interesting idea, is it not?" She began to lace the stays into place around Elspeth. They lifted her breasts up and the neckline was lower than her practical linen ones. Now her breasts looked in danger of spilling out if she leaned over too far. But it was a clever deception because the garment held just enough of her breasts when she put them to the test.

*Now wouldn't that be the way to shave Hayden . . .*

The silk of the chemise only partially veiled her thighs, and the curls growing on her mons were a teasing hint behind the fabric.

"Now what are you thinking?" Tavia sounded almost hungry for the answer to her question.

"Hayden Monroe was set on me shaving his whiskers away and I was thinking . . ."

Daracha clapped her hands together, interrupting her with a gleeful laugh.

"Oh, you must wear this and do as he commands. What a punishment that will be for him to bear."

"Does that mean ye agree to help me escape this fortress?" Elspeth lowered her voice so that it remained between them. Daracha cast a look at her sister, the pair of them gazing at each other for a long moment. It felt like an hour but Daracha finally sighed and nodded.

"Pherson will be horribly cross with me for near a month. Possibly longer." Instead of sounding fearful, the girl's voice held a great deal of merriment.

"Unless he admires your craftiness. Yer brother looks the type to enjoy being trumped in grand style."

Tavia smothered a giggle behind a hand. "Maybe you should stay, Elspeth Leask. I believe it might be entertaining to watch ye twist our dear brother around yer whim."

Elspeth felt her hope sputtering and threatening to die, but Tavia giggled once again behind her palm.

"Oh, look at you. I was but teasing. I wouldn't be, mind you, if I didn't think yer heart was already taken." Tavia's voice became deeper and more somber. "Pherson so very desperately needs a woman who will love him."

"Ye would keep me here if ye didn't think I was in love with another?"

"Of course." Daracha laid a hand on her shoulder. "We may enjoy playing but we would never waste something he brought home unless there was love involved."

Pirates.

The sisters were very much like the brother. They both offered her unrepentant smiles while they went to searching through the trunks for more clothing. Elspeth bit her lip because she didn't need to chastise them when they were going to give her what she wanted.

What she wanted . . . Now that was what she truly needed to ponder. If she wanted Hayden Monroe, it was a sure bet that she would have to stop running from him.

And soon.

Other clans were willing to tie their female relations up in ribbons for him but all that idea did was make her more stubborn.

She didn't want him because he was Laird Monroe. That would make her as much a pirate as Pherson and his sisters.

*But you do want him . . .*

Her cheeks heated with a blush while the sisters brought her more common wool clothing to cover the decadent undergarments. But the silk was still there against her skin, reminding her of how much she could feel. It made her mind wander to the whispered tales she'd heard of lovers and the way they touched. Hayden's hands left trails of fire across her neck and cheeks. How much more intense would it be to have those same strong hands beneath her skirts and against her bare thighs?

She had to bite her lip once again to contain a soft sound of need from escaping.

"There. Ye look . . . quite boring."

Tavia smiled with her judgment. They had even brought her an arisaid, a length of fabric that was belted across the back of her waist and pulled up over her shoulder. At night it could be used to cover her head and provide warmth. It was a poor garment, for those who could not afford enough wool for a cloak.

"Come on before Pherson comes seeking ye." Daracha reached out and clasped her hand. The girl began leading her down another flight of stairs. The light from the bath house diminished until it was pitch black all around them. Daracha kept pulling on her hand and Elspeth placed her other one on the stone wall to help her maintain her balance. She shivered and her hearing became more sensitive now that her sight was inhibited by the darkness. Every sound began to echo, bouncing between the thick stone walls that the stairs descended through. The sound of water began in the distance and grew stronger.

They finally emerged from the base of the tower. Even though it was dark outside, it wasn't pitch black such as it had been in the stairway. The night was cloudy but there was a glow that seemed quite bright compared to where they had come from.

"Follow the river. There is a small gate down the hill that the servants use to return to the village when their service is finished. If luck is with ye, ye'll meet yer love on the road as he's seeking to reclaim ye." Tavia pressed a single coin into her palm.

"Of course if ye meet someone else, ye shall just have to accept fate's will." Daracha's voice sounded like an old woman did when the fire was banked for the night and there was no clergy about to keep the old Gaelic traditions from surfacing. That was when magic from years gone by was still toyed with.

"Fate's will?"

Tavia nodded. "Indeed, the will that ye belong to another."

Both sisters smiled and their eyes shone with excitement as though they wished her to be taken on the road by another marauder.

Pherson was one too many in her opinion.

"Go now. Someone will question us if we stay here."

Elspeth turned without another word. The heeled shoes were not going to be comfortable on the road but she dare not quibble with how the sisters chose to set her free. Gratitude seemed rather misplaced considering the excitement shining in the girls' eyes. They considered the unknown elements of the night to be things of fortune and not defeat.

Well, that suited them, she supposed. The river was rushing along at a good pace and she followed it to the gate the sisters had promised her. Hope filled her heart when the men guarding it didn't even look up from their game of dice. She passed through without trouble and into the night. She refused to fear, taking the advice given to her by Tavia and Daracha.

She would rely on fate's whim. But she added a prayer as well and pulled the arisaid up and over her head.

"Do ye truly think me so shallow?" Pherson Dalry emerged from the shadows. Tavia and Daracha stiffened but did not tremble. He tilted his head and watched the last traces of Elspeth in the distance.

"I have never thought ye two mindless creatures."

That sent both sisters looking to one another. Confusion surfaced in their expressions. Pherson shook his head.

"What I craved was for ye to grow strong. There are plenty of men that believe women should be naught but ornaments to enhance their lives. The dangerous ones are the ones that think having yer own opinions is the devil's work."

Daracha's eyes flashed with her temper. Pherson eyed her. "Always keep that hidden, Sister. That is the reason I've allowed ye to believe that I want nothing from ye but perfect poise. Why do ye think I allowed ye to have tutors that just happened to be able to school ye in things other than courtly manners when ye thought I was nae watching?"

"Ye wanted us to learn how to deceive ye." It wasn't really a question. Tavia knew she was correct; she was only unhappy about discovering she had been duped.

"I wanted ye to know how to survive. Ye'll both marry and have to deal with the unjust view many men have of women. With yer beauty, ye will both have to find a way to avoid becoming some greedy man's pet. What sort of a brother would I be if I failed to teach that lesson when it might mean the difference between life and death at the hands of some man that wants to label ye witches like old Henry did to Anne Boleyn?"

Daracha's eyes grew glassy. Pherson watched the realization sink into her. His life was balanced precariously. If he died, and that was a high probability, his sisters would be at the mercy of his aunt. She was a bitter woman who had coveted what his father had her entire life. His sisters would not do well beneath her rule.

"I'd naught have kept her, ye know."

Tavia shook her head. "I believe ye would have been tempted to, and she is falling in love with another."

Pherson looked into the night, along the path that Elspeth Leask had taken. "Her courage would have tempted me, but it was the love that would have seen me setting her free."

"Yes, love is something we all understand."

Daracha sighed and clasped her sister's hand. They both lowered themselves to their brother, meaning the respectful gesture for the first time. Pherson offered them a cocksure grin.

"Up the stairs with ye. Tonight is not for either of ye."

His sisters left and Pherson made his way downriver. His men allowed Elspeth through the gate and into the night. Some would label him ungallant for letting her challenge the unknown, but those were the ones who would never truly taste life. If you wanted the greatest reward, you had to take the most risk. He felt his lips split into a grin.

Aye he would have been tempted to keep her.

# Chapter 5

Elspeth tightened her grip on her arisaid and banished the ideas attempting to take control of her thoughts. Why had she listened to so many tales of specters and spirits that lurked in the dark? She was paying for every single moment of entertainment she'd ever gained from sitting by the fireside while the storytellers wove their words into tales that sent shivers down the spines of those listening.

Foolishly listening, for tonight it was costing her more confidence then she had to spare. Her fingers ached because she held them in a fist too tightly. The pain was enough to shatter the whispers trying to fill her mind.

Stories . . . naught but fictions.

She walked forward, drawing no true notice from the people hurrying to finish up their chores. The houses were closer together in the village but that gave way to small farms as she kept walking. The night wind picked up and an owl sounded off from its perch in one of the trees. The moon only made fleeting appearances between clouds moving with the aid of the wind. She toyed with the idea of seeking some place to hide, but found herself too nervous to stop while the towers of Pherson's castle were still in sight. At least the motion of walking kept her warm; she picked her feet up faster to fend off the deepening chill of night. Her nape tingled and she turned to see if someone was on the road behind her. Nothing moved and her ears strained to filter the night noises from anything made by men. Tension began to knot in her belly but her choices were walk or collapse in the face of her fears.

So she walked.

Pherson Dalry didn't fear the night. It was the truth that he felt at ease covered by its darkening folds. Next to a woman's embrace, there wasn't anything he liked better.

His lips split into a grin.

Well, he did have to confess to liking the way a woman wrapped around him when she wasn't wearing anything but skin. That was an embrace he was right fond of no matter how much the church preached against it. They didn't care for dishonesty either, so he'd simple say it the way it was. He liked women, liked being naked with them.

He eyed Elspeth Leask. She turned again, making his grin grow broader. The girl had instincts, even if she didn't have much experience using them when it came to playing stealthy games that involved escaping by night.

He hung back, using the strength in his thighs to gently squeeze his horse's sides and keep the stallion silent. Elspeth kept going and he pulled on the reins to guide his horse at a slow pace that would keep her in his sights.

No one outwitted him, not even his own blood.

"It's a fair nice sight to see ye so bristling with passion considering how lifeless ye have been, but I think ye are making the men a wee bit nervous."

Hayden snarled.

"Fair enough." Skene Monroe shrugged in the face of his laird's temper. Hayden shot him a hard glare.

"Don't tease me, Skene, I'm nae in the mood."

His captain nodded with agreement. "I noticed that. In fact, it's a grand thing to see because I was beginning to find it difficult to recall that ye were not an old man ready for his grave. That little Leask lass has awakened something that I missed seeing in ye."

"Ye're the only man I'd let say something like that."

Skene offered him a cocky grin. "Actually, it's more a matter of ye do nae want to take the time to thrash me."

"Aye, ye're right about that." Hayden wasn't stopping for anything. It had taken him too much time to meet up with his men, and the fact that they had already been riding after him didn't make him any happier.

"But the men were tugging at me to discover if ye plan to tell them to murder every Dalry man we meet. That is sure to be a mess and all. I think a few of the younger lads want to know if they need to be confessing that they are nae virgins in case they are riding to their deaths tonight. Now I didna want to be the one to mention this but a few of those younger lads seem to think that Dalry retainers might be able to out fight them. I figure we'll just have to be forgiving them on account of their youth."

Hayden rolled his eyes. Skene was a master of many things, and annoying him was one. The man didn't have any problem chatting away while riding. But Hayden cast a look behind him and noticed the tension drawing his men's expressions tight. He was riding hell-bent up onto Dalry land. His own rage could so easily translate into death for those bound to follow him. He normally didn't fail to notice when his men were uncomfortable. Dunmore was somewhere behind them, his men having been on the road before word was carried back to him that his sister was being swept down the river. The Monroe retainers had been waiting for him.

"I'm going to pay the damned ransom and marry Elspeth Leask so that I can place her on Monroe land where I won't have to worry about a rogue like Pherson getting his hands on her."

"Ah . . . well then, that's grand news." Skene sniffed. "Maybe you'd care to slow up just a wee bit, then. No need to kill the horses or make ye want to postpone yer nuptials because yer arse is bruised."

"It will be yer face that is bruised if ye do nae grant me some peace, man. Ye prattle like an old priest."

Skene smirked at him before pulling his horse up just enough to fall behind him and rejoin the main body of his men. Hayden forced himself to slow as well. He was pure Scot and proud of it, but for the time being he hated some of the cockiness that seemed bred into his fellow Scots.

He wanted to kill Pherson.

Slowly.

This was surprising considering he might have done the same thing, presented with the opportunity to rub a few of his neighbors' pride. Stealing a bride was rather common and considered slightly honorable. You ransomed the girl or married her, but Hayden discovered that he wasn't feeling so trusting in the tradition. It was burning a hole in his gut, the need to get Elspeth back.

He would have her back; there was no other option his mind was willing to accept.

Her mind began toying with her again. Elspeth heard horse hooves beating at the ground and shivered. There was so much tension pulling her muscles tight, she was beginning to become confused as to the root of each worry. Was it spirits? Or sinister druid spells left from a thousand years ago?

Maybe it was raiding highlanders bent on revenge.

She gasped when she saw the horses materialize on the road in front of her. She blinked her eyes, her heart increasing its pace to something so violent she wasn't sure she would survive.

Maybe that would be a blessing. To drop dead upon the road before the men bearing down on her had the chance to make any of her mind's imaginings into reality.

But she swallowed that urge, shamed by how cowardly it was. She was not a child to be startled by men who had yet to meet her.

They rode closer, the beating of their hooves shaking the ground beneath her feet. Time slowed to a crawl, each moment swelling into enough time to notice the rise and fall of the horses. She heard her own heartbeats and heard the smack of leather against leather as the riders' knee-high boots slapped against their saddles. She noticed the way they pulled up on the reins, the leader's elbow poking out as he used his strength to halt the powerful beast he rode. She smelled dust, churned up by the horses, as it blew over her in a cloud. The horses snorted, their chests heaving as they pulled in enough breath to support their midnight journey.

"Elspeth?"

Hayden's voice broke through the spell that had wrapped around her. Raising her face, she strained to find anything familiar about the man looking down at her. But the moon was hiding once again, leaving him cast in darkness.

He jumped from the saddle, landing in a slight crouch, but his legs took the impact easily. She felt his gaze searching her face, and the clouds shifted, illuminating him in silver moonlight.

"Sweet mother of Christ! What are ye doing on the road? Are ye insane, woman?"

He was angry again, the tone of his voice a perfect match to the one he'd used after they escaped the river's grip. It scraped against her frayed temper.

"I was on my way back to ye, but now that I'm hearing yer tone I'm thinking I was daft to take to the road for a man who does nothing but berate me for not collapsing every time life turns difficult."

She was yelling, and every single one of his men heard her. Elspeth propped her hands on her hips and jutted her chin out. Her feet were throbbing in the dancing heeled shoes and she was relieved to see him but she'd walk back to Leask land in the unpractical footwear if the man was going to try and lecture her.

Someone laughed behind her. Loud and long, Pherson Dalry walked his horse out of the darkness while snickering.

"By the Virgin's tits, Monroe, I think she's worth fighting ye for."

Hayden grabbed her wrist, his fingers grasping her quick as lightning before he tugged her forward and stepped in front of her. His sword was drawn with a scraping of steel against steel.

"I accept yer challenge." There was venom edging each word.

Pherson remained in his saddle, the moonlight revealing an arrogant smile on his face.

"If that's what I wanted, I would have kept her locked up. There was no need for me to ride out here if I wanted to fight ye Hayden Monroe."

"Ye've been following me." Elspeth felt her temper explode. She wanted to curse but realized that she didn't know any truly horrible words. "You swine! You allowed me to think I escaped."

"Well now, lass, I couldn't very well have ye out on the road alone even if I had nae intention of crushing yer little plan. It would nae do to have ye in peril out here."

"But—"

Hayden cut off her words with a hand cupped over her mouth. He took one long step backward to stand beside her and wrapped his arm around her head to seal her lips shut with his fingers. She snarled and struggled but her head was held in a solid hold.

"Skene."

Hayden barked that single word and slid his sword back into its sheath. He released her mouth but she didn't get the chance to blister his ears. The man hooked his hands around her waist and tossed her up into the air. Her throat closed up so tight, getting breath down it was too much. For an endless moment she was weightless, and then a strong arm grasped her around the waist, pulling her across a saddle.

"Take charge of my bride-to-be. I want a word with Laird Dalry."

"Hayden Monroe—"

Elspeth didn't get a chance to say anything further. Skene turned his horse and gave it the freedom to begin moving again. The stallion was eager, digging into the road and taking them away.

"Easy now, lass, there are some things men need to discuss among themselves." Skene cast a quick look down at her. "But I'll admit to wanting to hear that conversation myself. It's sure to be something worth hearing. Pity that the laird told me to take ye away. I can't be disregarding his wishes ye see."

"I am not his bride-to-be."

Skene chuckled and she felt it as much as heard it.

"Well now, lass, there's another conversation I believe is going to be very interesting." He sniffed. "I'm getting the feeling that I won't be hearing that one either. Poor night to be me it seems."

"Swine. The lot of you."

Skene didn't acknowledge her insult.

*Bride-to-be?*

Nothing had been decided. Nothing.

But her heart filled with joy. It flooded her, melting the tension that had been tormenting her for the past few hours. There was no thinking on it, there was only feeling.

Hayden swung back up onto his horse's back to face Pherson.

"What game are ye playing, Dalry?"

Pherson tilted his head to one side. "The same one I always do, to find the best profit."

"You think there is profit in allowing Elspeth onto the road? Are you thinking that I'll still pay you a ransom?"

"Aye, lad, I do."

There weren't many men Hayden would allow to call him lad, but his attention was snared by the topic of the conversation more than the needling choice of words.

"But ye can nae pay me enough for what I just allowed ye to see. That lass walked back to you without letting the night nor the fact that she was alone stop her. She was following her heart sure enough. Many might profess affection toward ye because of who ye are but actions tell a man the true facts. If ye say she is nae worth a ransom, I say ye are a foolish man to not notice the gem she is."

Hayden stiffened. He drew in a long breath and felt his anger dissipating. "Aye, that's true enough and I'll say it plainly." Knowing that Elspeth had come to him was priceless. The passion for life he'd lost was suddenly flicking brightly inside his soul.

"In that case, I like ye better than I did a moment ago, Laird Monroe, even if ye do spend a little too much time judging me. We both do what we have to for the sake of the people looking to us to keep peace on our land." Pherson gave a short whistle that drew his men out of the darkness. "But that does nae mean that I didna come well prepared to kill ye if ye proved too dim to understand what a treasure that lass is."

"I rode up here to kill you for taking her."

Pherson chuckled. "Couldn't help myself." He reached up and touched the corner of his bonnet. "Until the time comes when I need a favor from ye. You can count on it being a large one."

Elspeth paced back and forth in the chamber of a boarding-house. It was the best room in the house and she was all too aware of the fact that it was being provided because Skene had used Hayden's name.

With a sigh, she shook her head. There was no true way to stay angry. A yearning was eating at her to smile and embrace him the moment she set eyes on him once again.

That vexed her. No man should find it so simple to attract her or bend her to his will.

But wasn't that the way it happened for all the other Leask girls? The ones she had so often envied for their freedom to meet their lovers on spring and summer nights when it was warm enough to lie in the new hay. They sighed and claimed they could not resist when the right man kissed them.

Her cheeks heated.

When Hayden kissed her, she had enjoyed it full well. The heat flowed down into her body, touching off tingles of sensation as she contemplated lying in the hay with him. A longing to do exactly that overshadowed all of her frustrations with the man's arrogance.

"Haven't ye had enough walking for one night, lass?"

Elspeth startled and turned to look at the door. Hayden stood there, his body filling it. He must have ducked to enter because his head rose above the frame.

"Or may I hope that ye were pacing because ye were waiting on me?"

His tone was soft and full of tenderness. It sent more warmth into her heart because he sounded as though he hoped his words were true.

She was suddenly shy. Her emotions threatened to consume her and that frightened her far more than anything out on the dark road. A warm hand cupped her chin, lifting it until she met Hayden's gaze. What she witnessed there drew a soft sound of joy from her.

Need burned in his eyes so brightly there was no mistaking it. That was what the other girls were drawn to, that was what the church could not control.

"I was waiting on ye."

His fingers tightened and he moved closer, his gaze dropping to her lips. The delicate skin warmed with anticipation, her belly tingling with excitement. She rose up on to her toes to meet his kiss but he suddenly froze.

"I want to kiss ye, Elspeth." He released her face and disappointment hit her like a stone hurled at her chest.

"But ye made a request of me and I'd be a savage not to recall that." He reached up and ran his hand over his chin. Challenge flickered in his eyes. "Are ye ready to give me the service I came looking for this morning?"

"Why do you want me to do it?"

He reached out and captured one hand, his larger one curling all the way around it. Lifting it up, he pressed a soft kiss against the delicate skin of her inner wrist. Sensation raced up her arm and into her body, leaving a trail of gooseflesh. She quivered and fought to draw her next breath.

"Because I want to feel that same thing when ye reach out and touch me."

Elspeth had to swallow the lump clogging her throat before she could answer. "I will serve you."

Hunger glittered in his eyes, but she only gained a glimpse of it before he walked past her to the door. He pulled it wide and barked an order out into the hallway. Voices drifted up from the bottom floor of the house. His men would be sleeping down there, but for the moment the scent of food told her that they were keeping the maids busy. The women came up the stairs only a few moments later. One held a large bowl that had a cloth folded into it, and the other carefully carried a copper kettle that had steam rising from it.

"Skene."

The burly man appeared before the maids had time to leave the room. He blocked their path by standing in the doorway. Hayden turned to stare at her.

"Elspeth Leask, I want to wed ye and declare my intentions to do so as soon as we find a priest."

The maids looked to her. Waiting for her to answer. Tears stung her eyes because it was an honor that no one might force Hayden to grant her. He could use her and ride away, and even the church would not be able to force him to wed her. Only affection drew the offer. She did not know if that was love but it was far too tender to ignore. Hayden raised one eyebrow as she hesitated.

"And I'm planning on sharing this room with ye tonight." Hayden didn't lower his tone one bit, there was no shame at all in him—only passion. The maids immediately looked at the bed and Elspeth felt her cheeks burn scarlet.

"I will marry ye but that is all I am promising ye, Hayden Monroe."

Skene clapped his hands together. "Well now, lasses, let's be leaving these two to debate what they will be doing for the next few hours. For myself . . ." His words trailed off as the door shut and Hayden offered her a grin.

"Don't look so cocksure. I said I'd shave ye tonight and that is all I said would be happening this eve."

He held up one finger. "Ye said ye would wed me, sweet lass, so be very sure that I consider it fair to seduce ye."

*Seduce* . . .

Elspeth turned too quickly to look at what the maids had brought and felt her stomach clench. Her hands were trembling from surprise and anticipation, but Hayden didn't chuckle at her even though he must have noticed her nervous reaction to his words. He was a good man, knowing when not to tease her. That was a tenderness many wives lamented their husbands not having. A keen sense of knowing when something meant too much to make light of.

The sharpened blade gleaming in the candlelight made her mouth go dry.

She was keenly aware of the fact that they were alone and that Hayden had done everything necessary to claim her tonight. Everything was moving too quickly. She tried to think but felt as if she were being swept along. She heard him set his sword down and settle himself in a comfortable chair that had a leather back.

Elspeth tightened her nerve. She refused to be defeated by the idea of touching him. She poured the hot water into the bowl and picked up another small bowl that had a cake of soap resting in it. After adding water to it, she reached for the horsehair brush and used it to whip the soap into lather. She had seen her father bare his face, but that had been years ago. She used the brush to spread the lather across his face before setting the bowl aside and picking up the blade.

Her belly was twisting and tightening with excitement. Hayden watched her, remaining still while she pulled the sharp steel across his skin.

"Hold still."

"I am holding steady, lass. 'Tis yer hand that is shaking."

Another chuckle followed his words and Elspeth bit her lower lip, frowning at the small cut she'd just inflicted on her would-be lover. Every muscle in her body was tense as she stared at the bright red blood trickling down from the cut.

"I am no good at this. Ye are a fool to allow me to place a blade against yer skin."

"Nay, lass. I'm merely enjoying having ye come to me."

Shock held her in its grasp. For all her confidence, he was still a very important man, one she should never have gained any attention from. But he watched her with eyes that sparkled like any lad she'd flirted with. The fact that he sought to relax her endeared him to her, awakening a desire to forget the world outside the chamber.

"I still think ye foolish, but 'tis yer skin."

"And it enjoys the touch of yer fingertips a great deal." His tone had become brassy and deep. She suddenly recalled the silk chemise she wore and how sheer it was.

*Would he like it?*

She dipped the small dirk into the basin again. The water glistened in the candlelight when she brought the blade back to his face. Soap bubbles clung to his whiskers and she carefully pulled the sharp edge across his skin again. This time a bundle of whiskers came away, but his skin was left smooth and without any cuts.

"Ye see, lass? My faith in ye is paying off."

"Ye are celebrating too early, Hayden Monroe."

She turned to clean the blade off and moved around him to work on his other cheek.

"What are ye wearing on yer feet?"

He'd straightened up, oblivious to the fact that he had soap covering most of his face.

"Shoes." She couldn't help but tease him now that the chance was at hand. His face turned suspicious and he refused to return to leaning back in the chair.

"What kind of shoes?"

She held his full attention and it awakened something inside her that she hadn't felt before. A boldness that made her want to play with him. Fingering the fabric of her skirt she flipped it back and forth so that he gained only a glimpse of the shoes.

"Heeled shoes. Pherson's sisters claim they are made in the French fashion and that Queen Mary has outlawed them because they are fabled to raise a woman's bottom up." She shrugged. "I never heard of shoes doing such a thing before. I really should finish shaving you now."

Hayden was on his feet in a second. He took the dirk from her hand. He turned to look in a mirror and finished removing his whiskers with efficient strokes that cleared his chin and face down to smooth skin. A quick wipe to ensure the soap was gone, and the dirk was left on the table behind him without a backward glance.

"Show me." His voice was raspy but edged with hunger.

She trembled, excitement leaping to life inside her again. This time it was a full blaze that sent need and desire coursing through her. She rubbed the wool of her skirt before pulling it up to display the fronts of the shoes.

He drew in a stiff breath. But she was equally drawn to his newly shaved face. Her skirt dropped from her grip as she stepped closer to look at him.

Slipping her hands along his jaw, she smiled at the warm feeling of his skin against her own. It was delicious and intoxicating, and she wanted more of their skin to meet. His hands cupped her hips, drawing her against his body. Her attention was centered on his lips and the prospect of another kiss. She craved it, longing for much more than a single one.

Hayden's eyes glittered with anticipation. "Now for that kiss I've been wanting."

His hand cupped the back of her head, tilting her chin up so that his mouth covered hers. It wasn't slow or soft. Hayden took her mouth, demanding a hard kiss that she eagerly met. His tongue pushed against the seam of her lips and she parted them, allowing him to thrust deeply into her mouth. Her body shivered as sensation raced down her back, all the way to her toes.

"Show me the shoes and the stockings."

"I shouldn't."

But she was already opening the first button on her doublet. The hunger glittering in his eyes was too much to resist. She wanted to know what he'd look like if she gave him what he demanded. Boldness had invaded her, urging her to discover if the silk corset and chemise pleased him.

"I shaved for ye, Elspeth, now ye need to give me plenty of smooth skin to kiss."

She gasped, her fingers fumbling the next button. Hidden between the folds of her sex, her clitoris began to throb and her mind filled with the idea of him placing a kiss against it.

She did not fight against the idea. Instead she finished opening her doublet and allowed it to slip down her arms.

"Holy Christ."

The green silk of the corset was visible now. Hayden stared at the abundance of flesh swelling above the edge of the garment.

"I may never allow ye to dress completely again, lass. I suddenly understand why the sultans of the East keep their concubines inside wearing nothing but silk."

He reached out and placed his hands around her waist. He held her still and took another step that closed the space between them. Leaning down, he placed a single kiss against one breast.

Elspeth couldn't contain the soft sound that passed her lips. There was too much pleasure spreading out from that touch of lips to contain it. His jaw was smooth but his skin was not as soft as her own. She enjoyed the hardness, reaching up to run her hands along his arms and the ridges of muscle that lay beneath his clothing. His hands tightened around her waist, telling her how much her touch pleased him.

That bit of knowledge increased her boldness. She found the first button that was still closed on his doublet and pushed it through its hole. Hayden nuzzled her breast before moving to its twin and kissing the eager skin. Elspeth slipped her fingers between the open sides of his doublet, seeking the warm skin hidden from her. She made only the briefest of contacts before he lifted his head.

"Get rid of yer skirts. Let me see ye in nothing but silk."

He began loosening his doublet but his eyes remained focused on her. Nervousness made her fingers slow but heat was rising up inside her, making the idea of being free of her skirts quite appealing.

*Be honest, ye want to be bare so that Hayden can kiss ye . . .*

Her inner voice was correct and it sent another wave of heat over her. This time it settled in her passage, making her aware of how empty she was. She had never noticed such a thing before and her eyes lowered to the front of his kilt, wondering just what he had hidden behind the folds.

A soft growl drew her gaze back up to his face.

"Are ye ready to see me, lass? Most husbands don't allow their brides to look at their cocks until they've taken it for the first time."

"If I were timid, I'd have insisted the maids sleep in here."

Her words drew a harsh look from him, one that hinted at his control being tested.

"Nor would I be brave enough to take me own clothing off knowing that these shoes do push my bottom up."

He sucked in a harsh breath and threw his doublet onto the chair behind him. Elspeth held the sides of her skirt closed, making him wait.

"I'll not be a timid wife, Hayden. Best ye understand that or take yerself away from me."

She wasn't sure why she voiced such a thing. There was no way to enforce her will on him. But flames flickered in his eyes, making them glow with approval.

"Exactly why I will nae be taken from this room by any force save God striking me dead." He pulled on his belt, releasing it, and his kilt began sliding down his thighs. He gathered up the fabric and sent it to lie on top of his doublet. With one more tug he tore his shirt up and over his head to completely bare himself. Her gaze traveled down his powerful chest to where his waist narrowed and his belly lay trim and flat. She swallowed hard at the sight of his cock, standing out, swollen and hard. The head was ruby-colored with a small slit and a thick ridge of flesh running around the head. A sac hung from the base.

"Now drop the skirt."

Hard command filled each word. Her hip roll was already on the floor and opening her fingers allowed her skirts to slump into a heap around her ankles. Lifting one foot and then the other, she stepped out of the garment to face him such as he was doing to her.

The candles flickered, sending orange and yellow flames of light to lick over them.

"I owe Pherson more than I believed."

His gaze roamed over her, touching every inch of her. She suddenly began moving, walking in a large circle so that he could see the effect of the heels on her bottom. Elspeth peeked at him over her shoulder.

"It was his sisters who dressed me."

"I both pity and laugh at the men they will marry someday."

"But you don't envy them?"

She turned to face him again. Hayden returned his attention to her eyes and the hunger blazing there stunned her with how hot it burned.

"Nae, lass, I'm looking at the woman I want to be with." His lips turned up in a cocky grin. "So tonight I'm going to seduce ye and make sure ye marry me tomorrow because of how much ye're looking forward to nights in my bed."

Hayden closed the distance as he spoke, his hands boldly pulling the lace free from the eyelets of the corset. Her breasts hung in their natural shape once he removed the stays. He molded her breasts through the sheer chemise, sending shafts of pleasure through her. He cupped each tender mound, leaning down to suck one hard nipple deep into his mouth. Her skin became acutely aware of every touch, every sharp tug on the sensitive tips, the contact drawing a gasp from her. Never once had she thought her own body might be able to feel such pleasure. It engulfed her while his hands stroked her belly and thighs.

"As much as I adore this silk, I am more interested in the satin of yer skin."

He lifted one of her hands from where it rested on his shoulder and kissed the sensitive skin of her inner wrist before releasing the small hook that held the cuff of her chemise closed.

"I never thought that having someone disrobe me might be so enjoyable."

A soft sound of male amusement shook his chest. He grasped her other hand and unhooked the cuff first before lowering his mouth toward the skin eagerly awaiting its turn to be kissed. Instead he nipped her. A short, delicate bite that sent a jolt of pleasure through her entire arm.

"I am no gentle woman, trained to serve ye with hands soft as whispers," she said as he tugged the sheer chemise up and over her head. "But I promise to make sure not an inch of ye is unattended."

With the last barrier removed, her mouth went dry as excitement continued to twist in her belly. A rustle of unease tried to invade her mind, an uncertainty about whether or not she would enjoy everything he planned to do to her during this seduction. Some women didn't care for the way a man's length felt when lodged inside them. Some whispered of pain.

But others talked about pleasure so intense, they cried out with it.

"Perhaps I shall attend to you." Reaching out, she boldly ran her fingers along the length of his cock. It was smooth and hot to the touch, her fingers sliding easily over its length.

"Sweet Christ . . ." Hayden spoke through clenched teeth. His expression turned harsh but his eyes brightened with enjoyment, giving her confidence.

"Ye may tend to me as much as ye like, lass." Low and harsh, his voice sounded like she felt. Full of excitement and anticipation. Her confidence swelled up, banishing the nagging doubts that had been nibbling on her.

She had only stroked him with her fingertips, but she swiftly changed that, trying to clasp the entire length in her grasp.

"You mean like this, Hayden?"

It was overbold to voice such a question, but Elspeth did not care. She was not meek and he'd been warned about it. But there was something wickedly wonderful about the way his words made her feel, and she wanted to rise up to equal footing with him. There was a quiver of timidness flowing through her and it spurred her into action because standing still was a torment that she discovered she could not endure. Moving her hand on his cock, she stroked it and fingered the slit that sat on top of its head.

"Aye, lass . . ."

He groaned, and although she had never imagined that such a noise would sound enjoyable in that moment, it surely did. Pleasure shone in his expression, a deep enjoyment that she'd also never considered she might give to a man.

"But I can nae be so selfish as to take and not return the pleasure."

His eyes opened and there was a wicked slant to them now. He scooped her up and off her feet in one swift motion. Her weight didn't seem to cost him any effort; he held her cradled against his chest while walking toward the bed. It shook as he lowered her weight onto it. She lost her grasp on his rod and was pressed fully onto her back. Hayden lay down next to her but he remained on his side.

"Now that I have ye in my bed, I plan to feast on ye."

He rolled over her, his larger body pressing her down into the softness of the goosedown bed. The ropes groaned but Hayden made a sound that was more interesting to her. It was deep and harsh but filled with male enjoyment. One of his knees parted her thighs, drawing a gasp from her lips. A kiss smothered it, trapping it between his lips and hers. He didn't rush the kiss but lingered in place while his mouth teased hers. She needed to touch him, her hands smoothing over his sides and toying with the hard muscles of his arms.

But she was growing restless too. Her body was twisting and seeking something that had moved beyond a want, and had become a need. One that chewed on her belly, her clitoris, the center of the longing. Her thighs moved farther apart, the motion in harmony with the need churning in her belly.

"Not yet, lass. First I will prove that there is pleasure in having a husband, not just duty."

He slid down her body, not stopping until his head was centered over her spread sex. She suddenly recalled her thoughts about him kissing her clitoris and the little bud throbbed insistently. His hand delicately pushed open the soft folds covering the entrance into her body, gentle fingers teasing what lay hidden there. Her thighs spread wide as his body lay between them, but it was his fingers that drew a startled gasp from her. That spot that throbbed at the top of her sex was alive with pleasure so intense it made her arch up off the bed. Her hands fisted in the sheets while she twisted in the grasp of intense enjoyment. The urge to push her hips toward that touch was strong and she didn't resist it. She was now at ease with her legs spread, no more shyness or awkwardness distracting her from the pleasure of his touch.

"This little pearl is something I plan to pay a great deal of attention to."

He leaned forward and allowed the tip of his tongue to flick across it once. She gasped, trying to roll away. There was simply too much sensation to remain still.

"Stop."

"Why?" His thumb took over where his tongue had been, pressing against her pearl and rubbing it in a slow circle. A moan crossed her lips before she realized the sound was coming. Pleasure spiked through her but it was mixed with a need so large she feared it might consume her. A soft male chuckle drew her gaze back to Hayden. She hadn't even realized that her head had arched back.

"That's the pleasure that passion entices us morals with. The need that makes ye crave more, even when ye are nae sure what it is ye seek."

He lifted his thumb away and she whimpered. His eyes narrowed.

"Exactly, lass. Ye don't want me to stop. Trust me to show ye pleasure, even if the means is foreign to ye."

He leaned forward and licked her clitoris again. This time her hips lifted to make sure it was pressed against his touch. She needed a harder touch, something just a little bit more than she gained. Her heart was racing and she could hear the blood rushing in her ears as she became consumed by every feeling, every point of contact between them. But most of all she was focused on where he was feasting on her spread sex. His tongue lapped her from the front of her sex to the entrance of her passage. He toyed with that opening, the tip of his tongue circling it in slow motions that drew more whimpers from her. She felt too empty, the need threatening to push her over into madness. But he licked his way back up to her clitoris and sucked the little nub between his lips.

Fire blazed through her. Pleasure and need tearing at her in equal amounts. One finger began toying with her passage and she surged against it, frantic for something she was sure she would die without.

Hayden sent his finger deeply into her body and pleasure burst inside her belly. It was blindingly bright, like lightning splitting the sky open. Intense feeling traveled along her limbs, a pleasure so thick there was no seeing through it. There was nothing but the swirling mass of it. She strained up, trying to press herself even harder against his hand. The storm held her tight in its grasp, time frozen while it surged through her.

"That's the pleasure couples can have when they take the time to love instead of just use one another."

Hayden's voice was sweet and soft but there was a tightly controlled edge that made her lift her eyelids and look at him. Hunger was etched into his face, a muscle twitching along the side of his jaw. When she met his gaze, his shoulders tightened, his large body jerking. He ran his hands along her spread thighs and then slowly took off each heeled shoe before rolling the stockings down her legs. But his cock was still swollen and hard and she realized that she was not completely satisfied, not yet. She wanted that flesh deep inside her.

"Come, Hayden, show me the rest of it."

He rose up, looking powerful and like a legend from Druid lore. Every inch of him was hard and she reached for him, eagerly clasping his shoulders when he covered her. His wider frame completely dwarfed hers, but that too was enjoyable, her softer curves delighting in his weight. The hard touch of his staff against her soft folds drew a gasp from her, but the delicate skin was slick and wet, offering no resistance to him. Her passage didn't receive his girth so well. Pain pinched her, stabbing into the pleasure that still pulsed through her. It became red-hot between her thighs, and her hands curled, the nails biting into the flesh of his shoulders, but he did not withdraw.

Instead he thrust deeper, in a smooth motion that wrung a cry from her lips because her body hurt. She cried out, lacking any other outlet for the agony.

"It gets better, lass."

Elspeth lifted wet eyelashes to find Hayden watching her. Satisfaction glittered in his eyes but she was more interested in the way the pain began to recede. Between her thighs, his flesh was now merely hard and filling, a source of pleasure, instead of stabbing hot with pain. He withdrew but plunged deeply back into her until his cock was fully lodged inside her. A small ripple of enjoyment went through her and she sighed with relief.

"Aye, there's the way, lass. Trust me a wee bit. I'll no leave ye wanting."

"But you already pleasured me." She stumbled over the last few words and Hayden snickered at her.

"There is nothing that says ye may only be pleasured once a night, or that it must be at night, either."

Need began to flicker to life once more; it was deeper, and his hard flesh seemed to satisfy it in a way his mouth hadn't.

She craved friction and the motion of his flesh moving. Her hips lifted to meet his next thrust, ensuring his hard length slid deep inside her.

"Then I will gladly take more of that delight from ye, Hayden."

"A gift I'll gladly give ye, lass."

Her lover increased his speed as he rode her. Control vanished as pleasure attached to their joining and the pursuit of more of it became the only thought her mind could hold. There was so much feeling, so many things she enjoyed, and it all centered on the way his cock filled her, the motion of it plunging deeply into her before leaving and returning.

The pleasure grew, filling her to the point of near madness. She wasn't sure she would recover from it, but willingly allowed it to sweep her into another world where there was nothing but delight and her lover groaning with satisfaction. His seed was hot when it hit her womb, and even that drew another little ripple of delight from her body. Elspeth collapsed back onto the bed, panting, every muscle limp.

Even though her partner caught his weight on his elbows, she could feel his heart beating against her chest. Her entire body was too heavy to move. Satisfaction was like the heat rising off a bed of red hot coals, just as warm as the fire had been but steady instead of flames that danced and flickered.

Hayden moved, disturbing her bliss. He only rolled to the side and hooked his arm under her waist to pull her close. His embrace was warm enough to banish her misgivings. The night felt as if it were created just to shroud them and give them a sanctuary to make love in. For the moment it was all she needed. Her eyes fluttered shut, her body slipping into slumber.

Hayden didn't fall asleep so quickly. As Elspeth slept on, he trailed his fingertips along her shoulder and smiled when she nuzzled against him. Reaching up, he ran a hand along his jaw. The skin was slightly smarting from his lack of shaving but that would vanish if he kept his chin smooth.

He heard something and turned his head. A small figure ran across the room, dressed in a white shift. It headed toward another vision, one that he blinked and still saw. The spirit picked up the small one and he heard his daughter laugh. She turned her head and waved her chubby little fingers at him. The spirit of his wife had her arm looped around a babe that was sucking on a fist while watching him. Hayden felt them both keenly as though all he had to do was rise and join them. But Ruth shook her head slowly and blew a kiss to him before both visions vanished. He felt them leaving more completely than the day that Ruth had died.

Elspeth remained warm against him, her heart beating next to his, and he tightened his embrace around her before allowing himself to sleep.

# Chapter 6

There wasn't a single part of her body that didn't hurt. Elspeth stood in shock the next morning. She'd rolled out of bed and stood up and that was as far as she had gone before every muscle protested. From the bottom of her feet to the top of her head, everything either ached or hurt.

"Aye, that little trip down the river is showing its damage by now."

Hayden groaned but rose from the bed, and Elspeth turned to stare at him in shock. The dim morning light washed over her lover and he didn't seem intimidated by the fact that he was bare. But his face darkened when he looked at her.

Casting her own eyes down, she gasped at the number of bruises marking her skin. There were purple ones and brown ones and a few that were both shades. She suddenly giggled and Hayden lifted one eyebrow in question. Elspeth only raised her hands and shrugged while giggling some more.

Steps outside the hallway drew instant action from Hayden. He moved across the floor and grabbed her chemise, but frowned when the morning light shone through it easily. He reached down and snagged her skirts from where they still lay on the floor and dropped them over her head. The waistband caught on her shoulders allowing the fabric to drape around her like a cloak.

"What are ye doing?"

Hayden didn't get the opportunity to answer. The door opened and Elspeth grabbed the edges of the skirt to keep her bare breasts from being viewed. Skene offered Hayden a tug on his knitted bonnet before clearing the doorway for the two maids who had been there last night. Another woman followed, this one older, and she carried herself in a fashion that spoke of being respected.

"I brought the village midwife along," said Skene. "This is Sara Parkerson."

The woman walked directly to the bed, leaning over it with her eyes aimed at the sheet. Elspeth felt her cheeks warming as Skene and the other maids went to peer at the bedding as well. Sara gave a short nod of her head and turned to study Elspeth. She lifted one hand and flicked her fingers at the skirts.

"Let me see you, girl."

"Skene, take the sheet and go. We'll be down as soon as the midwife is satisfied."

It was one of the maids who pulled the sheet free of the bed. She gave it a snap before folding it with quick efficient motions. Skene took it from her before he quit the room.

"Go on, girl, drop that skirt. Ye have nothing that I have not seen and we needs make sure there is no whispering of ye being marked by a demon."

"Well, I am marked."

There was a soft gasp from one of the maids and a snort from Hayden.

"She's marked by the river that tried to kill us both yesterday." He walked toward her and pulled the skirts away from her in spite of the way her fingers tried to grip the wool. The morning air was cool against her nude frame and Sara walked closer to peer at her.

"Ye're lucky all yer bones are still whole."

The two maids were staring at her in shocked silence, one of them covering her mouth with her hand. But the midwife slowly circled her, missing nothing with her experienced gaze.

"Lift yer arms."

Elspeth did as told but chewed on her lip with frustration. She could not refuse the midwife, or rumors would begin that she had something to hide. The church took such gossip very seriously, often sending their witch hunters to investigate. All brides were inspected, most grooms too. It helped make sure the marriage contracts were solid by having someone attest to the healthiness of both. That made annulment much harder to gain now that divorce was once again becoming impossible to gain.

The midwife reached out and cupped one of her breasts and then the other before she gave another nod of her head.

"The lass is fine and healthy. The sheets prove her innocence and I'll swear to that if asked."

Elspeth hadn't realized she'd been holding her breath. Relief flooded her and she couldn't help but look at the two maids to make sure they had heard the midwife. They both smiled and went to collect her clothing from where it was scattered about the chamber. Sara offered Hayden a quick curtsey before she left the room.

"I've never seen such a shoe."

It was barely a whisper from one of the maids as she held up one of the heeled shoes. Her companion shook out the chemise and stared at the wispy garment in silence as well.

"Daracha Dalry told me they were French."

The older of the two maids raised wide eyes toward her. "Ye've been up to the Dalry fortress? Well, I've heard a few tales of the things that go on there."

She pressed her lips together in a tight line and snapped her fingers at the other girl.

"Pherson Dalry took her with intention to ransom her but she slipped away from him."

The older maid froze. "Well, ye be right lucky to have escaped. There are stories about that man, ones that will fill yer sleep with haunted dreams." She picked up the green silk corset and had to swallow roughly. "I see that some of them are true." She ran her fingers along the silk before recalling what she was doing and placing it around Elspeth.

Elspeth fought the urge to giggle. The garments themselves were nothing more than clothing, but the way that people reacted to them was very interesting indeed.

Especially the way Hayden had responded.

Between the two women, Elspeth was dressed quickly. Hayden finished first though, and was just finishing tying his boots when she turned to see what he was about. She suddenly felt shy, unsure how to face the daylight now that everyone knew they had shared the bed as lovers.

"Come, Elspeth, I'll not rest easy again until we are on my own land."

"But aren't ye taking me back to my brother?"

He frowned at her. "Yer home is no longer there."

"Ye do not even plan to allow me to say farewell?" She wasn't sure why it mattered, but it did. Tears stung her eyes before she found a way to control the emotions churning inside her. Hayden snorted.

"That is nae fare of ye, Elspeth."

"What . . ." she sniffled, "what do ye mean?" It shamed her but she could not banish the emotional tempest.

He shook his head and pulled her into his arms. "Crying. Ye have never shown me tears and I cannot stomach them."

She pushed against his embrace, wiggling free but only because he allowed her to escape. That bit of knowledge only made more tears flood her eyes. She was completely helpless now and dependent on him. She felt off balance, as though she were going to fall off a cliff any second. Everything she knew was gone, and what she felt for Hayden was so new that trusting it felt foreign.

"I am not crying."

She turned her back on him and wiped her eyes. Her fingers came away wet, confirming that she was a liar.

Hayden growled behind her. He wrapped his arms around her once again, his back solid and firm pressed against her.

"Fine, ye are nay crying and I will take ye home to bid farewell to yer kin. But we will nae be staying long, Elspeth. Pherson is not the only man in Scotland who makes his living by stealing it from others. I need ye back at Rams Court to rest easy and secure in the thought that ye are well protected."

He pressed a kiss on her head before releasing her and stomping toward the door. He stopped and turned to look at her.

"We'll get married there, in yer family church. That will be a good use of the trip."

The door shut behind him and tears flowed down her cheeks. Elspeth Leask found herself sobbing like a child and the worst part of it all was that she had no idea why.

\* \* \*

Hayden rode next to Skene.

"How do I talk to her?"

Skene shrugged. "I don't know why ye'd be asking me that."

Hayden snorted. His captain let out a short laugh. "Well, since ye pointed it out, I do have a way with the lasses. But I'm not a bragging man."

"Ye've been in the stocks too many times to count and all on account of the women chasing you."

Hayden felt his frustration growing. His captain smirked, beaming under the praise.

"So tell me how to soothe her."

Skene aimed a look to where Elspeth was riding back far enough to keep her safe should anyone challenge them.

"She looks right content, Laird."

"She wept this morning." And it was eating a hole in him hours later. Hayden had spent most of the day trying to think of the reason behind the tears that had suddenly filled her eyes. "She enjoyed herself last night, so why did she cry?"

Skene chuckled, low and deep.

Hayden wasn't interested in being teased over taking Elspeth to his bed. "Ye know full well what we were doing so stop yer smirking and tell me how to soothe her."

Skene sobered, his eyes taking on a serious cast. "Ah well, yer a good man to see that one has nothing to do with the other." He lifted a single finger into the air. "There's the difference between me and most of these men. The lasses, they need something more than the tickle between the sheets. Not that I'm saying that is nae important, mind ye."

Hayden ground his teeth together but his captain wasn't impressed. Skene pointed at him.

"And there is the root of the matter that makes the lasses flock to me. Patience, Laird, ye need to do things with a gentle hand. The lasses, they tend to get a wee bit shaken if ye just drop things on them without giving them time to adjust. For all that this world tells us men that we run it, that does nae mean that the lasses like being considered property. Ye need to tell her that she rules yer heart."

*Tell her?*

All right, he hadn't done that, at least not in words. Hayden considered his bride and chewed on his thoughts. She'd known what his coming to Leask land was about, but now that Skene's words were floating around in his mind, he could see how she might be fretting over what her place was in his life. The church would tell her she was his wife, his chattel, his property, but a vision of her sitting so proudly on her brother's stallion rose up from his memory. The ideas were in conflict with the proud woman he'd first met. It was that woman who drew his attention, so it stood to reason that she would not be pleased to hear him announce his plans without asking her first.

"Thank ye, Captain. I shall try not to be such an ass tonight."

Skene reached for the corner of his bonnet and gave it a tug but the man returned to smirking too.

They didn't reach the Leask tower until sunset. The horses had been run for two days straight, making it necessary to allow them to walk. Elspeth had never believed that a day could drag on so endlessly. Someone began ringing one of the bells that hung in one of the lookout windows. Another one answered quickly and then a third. Villagers poked their heads around open doors and through windows to see who was arriving. Excited voices began to raise above the horses' hooves.

Dunmore appeared on the lookout balcony. There were scores of men camping around the tower. Elspeth suddenly realized why her brother hadn't come after her; he had been calling in all her clansmen first. She shivered, realizing how much blood might have flowed. Pherson's castle would have been impossible for a land force to take, but she doubted that her kin would have returned home.

"Mistress Elspeth! Mistress Elspeth!"

One woman ran from her home, her voice rising above the others. Her husband followed her, their daughter sitting high on her father's shoulders. The others made way for them and Elspeth pulled up on the reins of her horse.

"Thank ye, ma'am, I can nae thank ye enough for saving my daughter." The man's eyes shone with gratitude and he shifted his attention to Hayden when he rode up beside her. "Laird Monroe, I owe ye too large a debt to ever pay."

"Seeing ye together is payment enough." Hayden reached down and gently cuffed the child on the side of her face. She laughed with the carefreeness of a child.

"May ye be blessed with many children."

Elspeth had to move forward because of the number of men trying to reach the tower. Her horse wanted to seek out its feed too and began to move along with the others. Elspeth didn't think she had ever been so happy to see the courtyard. Dirt or not, it was home.

A pair of hands cupped her waist and she looked down to find Hayden lifting her from the saddle. He had barely placed her feet on the ground when Dunmore swept her up into a hug. He clasped her so tightly she feared her ribs might crack.

"Good God, man, I never thought ye'd bring her back so quickly."

Her brother set her aside and offered Hayden his hand. Elspeth felt the women gathering around her and pulling her toward the tower.

It was much easier to do as they liked, and following them she soon found herself being bathed while they tried not to whisper about the undergarments beneath her wool clothing.

The sun set completely, leaving her seeking out a fire to dry her wet hair. Elspeth sat down in front of the small fireplace in her chamber and began brushing her hair. Wearing only a clean chemise and loose surcoat, she drew her comb through her hair, lifting it up so that the heat might hit it.

"Ye are beautiful, Elspeth."

Hayden wore a small smile that looked very genuine. He cast his gaze around the chamber and frowned. "But that bed is too small."

"It has served me very well."

Hayden offered her a smile that was no longer appreciative but one that looked hungry.

"*We* will not fit in it." He scooped her up and cradled her once more in his arms. "Besides, I have something else to show ye."

He carried her out of the chamber without hesitating even for a moment. She found herself battling tears again, but angrily pushed the impulse aside. It was only a chamber, one that it was coming time to leave. But there was still a tiny part of her that felt the parting keenly. She understood why Lot's wife had turned around in spite of being warned not to look back. She was tempted to cast a longing glance back at the chamber she had spent so many years in.

"I know it is a day late, but I hope ye shall enjoy it."

The chamber Hayden carried her to was sweetly scented with heather. Candles flickered inside it, but not common candles. These were expensive beeswax ones that normally only burned in the church.

Or in wedding chambers.

Elspeth gasped because the chamber was indeed set with all the finery she would have expected to find the night of her wedding. The bedding was turned down and fresh rosemary scattered across it. Heather was lying on the table, and there was even a garland of spring greenery hung from the pole where the bed curtains were attached. It must have taken quite an effort to dress the chamber when there had been so little sunlight left when they arrived. Hayden hadn't had to do it. That idea sent two tears down her cheeks. It was tender and kind beyond anything she had dared to expect. A true sign of affection even if he had not voiced any words. She tried to stifle a sniffle but failed.

Hayden snorted.

"I meant to soothe away yer tears, not induce more."

Frustration edged each word and she cupped his face to keep him from looking away from her.

"Sometimes women cry because they are happy."

He cursed and put her down and aimed a hard look at her.

"The chamber is beautiful, thank you." Elspeth wiped the two tears away and smiled at him.

He crossed his arms over his chest, still not content. Suspicion clouded his face.

"You weren't crying this morning from happiness."

Elspeth propped her hands onto her hips. "Well, ye certainly don't need to yell at me, Hayden Monroe. I know I wasn't crying from joy this morning but I was tonight. And I thanked ye for the kindness, so can we not be content?"

He snorted but looked at her with eyes that were full of a need to understand her. He drew in a deep breath.

"I did nae mean to hurt yer feelings this morning."

"You didn't."

"Then why did ye cry, woman?" He was back to demanding, which made her smile because this was the part of him she was drawn to. He was a man who was used to being obeyed; there was nothing courtly about him. Plain spoken words were his preferred style. Hayden growled when her lips curved up. He pointed a finger at her but a naughty little idea blossomed inside her mind before he figured out what he wanted to say.

"Are ye going to tell me I need a spanking again, Hayden Monroe? Well, I believe we are in the correct setting." Loosening the tie that held her robe closed, she shrugged out of the garment. Only her chemise remained. And she propped her hands on her hips while glaring at Hayden. "Well then. I've little tolerance for a man who cannot follow through with what he says he'll do."

She was pushing him. Something drove her to challenge the man. It wasn't the wisest thing she had ever done; in fact it might be one of the most insane, for he looked frustrated enough to take the chance to work out his ire on her soft bottom. But it was better than returning to the churning confusion that had seen her eyes flooding with tears. How could she explain it when she did not understand it herself?

So she stuck her chin out and challenged him, hoping they would end up between the rosemary-strewn sheets.

One dark eyebrow rose in rakish question. "Is that a fact, lass? No tolerance at all?" He pulled his belt loose and her breath froze in her throat, but he gathered up his kilt and draped it, along with his belt, over a chair.

"Ye don't need to disrobe in order to spank me." But now that the belt was set aside, her mind offered up an image of his bare hand connecting with her bottom. He was already missing his boots, so the only garment left was his shirt, and his cock was standing hard and ready. She could see its shadow cast by the flicker of the candle set on the table.

"Ah, but I do, Elspeth, because there is more than one sort of spanking that a man does with his wife." He rubbed his hands together, his eyes gleaming with mischief.

"Is that so?" Her voice had become husky and heat flickered in his eyes when he heard it. Behind the linen of her chemise, her nipples drew into hard, round beads. Arousal wasn't slow, it was quick and hot. Her body craved another taste of what it had enjoyed so much last night.

"We're still not married, so you cannot spank me."

He chuckled and spread his arms out wide. Her heart rate quickened as she recognized that he was preparing to spring at her.

"I assure ye I can, Elspeth, and that ye will enjoy it."

He jumped toward her before the last word crossed his lips. She turned to run but shrieked when his arms closed around her. It wasn't really a frightened sound, but one borne of the excitement swirling around in her belly. Her passage was heating up, becoming eager for another taste of his hard flesh. She could feel his cock against her lower back, thick and hard. He didn't lift her up but pushed her forward until she was bent over the table. One hand pressed her down and Hayden used his legs to keep her thighs in place against the edge of the table.

But he began to rub her back, using his fingers to work the muscles. A soft moan crossed her lips and then another because it felt so good. He worked her shoulders and then down to her lower back before continuing on to her hips. She lay content on the table, her entire body enjoying the motion of his hands.

"The body can feel so much pleasure. I think we should do our best to experience as much as possible."

"Yer words are so wicked, Hayden. We're nae on yer land ye know. Father Simon Peter might have ye locked in the stocks."

"So long as I am allowed to lie with ye tonight, I will take this punishment."

She turned her head to look at him. "You will not. There is nothing submissive about ye."

His hands gently kneaded her bottom, sending need through her passage that made her mouth dry. She licked across her lower lip and watched his eyes follow the tip of her tongue.

"Yet now that I think upon it, ye were rather submissive when I was handling yer cock."

His lips split into a roguish grin. "Now that's a fact, lass, one I won't quibble with ye over."

Elspeth pushed herself up and off the surface of the table. "We'll see about that, Laird Monroe, for I have noticed arrogance in ye." She turned and her hand closed around his length.

His eyes glittered with hunger, moving to her mouth. He captured the back of her head, his fingers sliding into her unbound hair. He growled softly, pulling his fingers along the strands all the way to the ends before cupping the back of her head once more. His mouth claimed hers a moment later, his lips slipping across hers before pushing her mouth open for the smooth thrust of his tongue. He invaded every one of her senses. It was intoxicating and she allowed it to sweep her away without argument.

The hard flesh in her hand twitched when she began teasing it with soft sliding motions of her hand. Beginning at the base, she pulled her hand up to the crown before releasing it and reaching for the base again. But the memory of what he'd done last night brought a question to her mind. She broke away from his kiss.

"Do women place their lips on a man's cock?"

His eyes widened and flared up with desire so bright it was nearly blinding. She was already dropping to her knees before she thought too much about it, her hands holding his cock still so that she might place a kiss against the head. He jerked and his hands landed on the table with a loud slap.

"It seems to meet with yer approval."

"As much as ye enjoyed my lips sucking on yer pearl, lass."

That poured oil on the flames of her confidence. She wanted to rise up and be his equal when it came to their private moments. Somehow that defined the idea of lovers to her. Lovers shared in pleasuring one another.

She sent the tip of her tongue along the slit that sat on the top of his cock. Her hands wrapped around his girth and her thumb gently stroked the underside of his member. She listened to his breathing, trying to judge what he liked more.

"Open yer mouth and take the head inside it."

His voice was both commanding and needy, the closest she had ever heard to him pleading. She opened her mouth and followed his dictate, enjoying the way he sucked in his breath. It was harsh and rough, and she recalled that sound from those moments when he was riding her and nearing his release. Pulling her head up, she relaxed her jaw before taking his hard flesh between her lips once again. This time more of his length filled her mouth and she experienced the salty taste of his seed. His hips gave a jerk, as though he were fighting to control them and losing the battle. She liked the idea that he had to struggle to maintain his grip on reality just as she did. What she really enjoyed was the fact that her actions were pushing toward that point where he would be surrendering to her actions.

Hayden suddenly stiffened and pulled his member from her mouth.

"Enough, lass, else ye'll unman me."

He reached down and hooked her beneath her arms, lifting her to her feet.

"You didn't stop when you were . . . were . . ."

"Sucking yer pearl?"

He clasped her waist and lifted her up to sit on the table. He stepped forward, parting her thighs with his body. Her cheeks turned hot at the frank way he spoke, but there was no denying that her body liked hearing it. Her clitoris throbbed with anticipation, eagerly waiting the moment when he would act upon his words.

Hayden chuckled and stroked one scarlet cheek. "Yer blush is charming, Elspeth. How can I know what pleases ye if I do not ask ye plainly?"

He pressed her thighs farther apart and the folds of her sex separated. The night air brushed them and the sensitive little nub they had protected. But Hayden only stroked her thighs, rubbing his hands up and down the inside of them, urging them wider apart.

"Shouldn't we go to the bed?"

He smiled but it was not a kind expression. It was full of rakish intention.

"We'll get there later. For the moment, I can think of nothing else that I would like to dine upon than yer sweet flesh."

He gently pushed her back, his hands running up her body until she lay across the table.

"Ah, now that is a sight to behold. Every feast should be so magnificent to look upon."

She felt awkward. The tablecloth was smooth and cold against her bare skin. Never once had she thought that her spread body might be pretty, but Hayden was looking at her, every bit of her, and there was wicked enjoyment in his eyes. That drove away her misgivings.

"There are so many places to enjoy a tumble, Elspeth, and I am going to enjoy making sure ye experience them all many times."

His fingers found her sex, trailing down the center of it and she gasped with pleasure. Sensation spiked into her sharply. He teased the entrance to her body, his finger penetrating her easily, for she was already wet.

"I believe this table is the perfect height."

"For what?"

The head of his cock clarified what he meant. It pressed against her spread body, splitting her open once again. He thrust slowly into her, his hands holding her hips in place while his member burrowed into her passage again. She was sore, her skin protesting with a dull ache as it was stretched wide. But it did not sting with true pain, not as it had the night before. Instead she found herself eager for more of his flesh, the desire to be impaled refusing to be ignored, driving her to lift her hips up to meet his thrust.

But he held her hips steady until his length was completely lodged inside her. On his face she read his impatience, the tic had returned to the side of his jaw.

"I am not fragile, Hayden. Give me what ye did last night, for I crave it."

The hands holding her hips tightened and excitement flared up in his eyes.

"Is that so, lass?"

"It is."

He slid his arm around her body and pulled her up against his while his cock was still deep inside her.

"I want to see ye take it from me." He turned and sat on the table. Her knees hit the solid top as well. His hands cupped each hip and lifted her up until only the head of his cock was still inside her. Then he allowed her own weight to slide her back down his length and lodge it completely inside her passage once again.

"Clasp me with yer thighs and ride me like ye did that stallion the first time I saw ye."

The anticipation in his eyes made her bold. She grasped his neck and lifted herself up. His hands cupped the curves of her hips and began pushing her down when only the head of his cock remained inside her. It was a combination of efforts, but the pleasure that surged through her was reflected in his expression. A soft moan passed her lips as her clitoris slid against his length all the way down, and then she was rising up once more, hungry for more of that delight. The table creaked and the candles wobbled, but she refused to slow down. Hayden reached over and pressed the wick on one to kill the flame. It died in a taper of smoke before he pinched out the others.

It left them in darkness but that only made her bolder. She rose and fell, riding him just like the night they had met. It was hedonistic and Elspeth decided that there was nothing more perfect. She could feel his heart racing so close to her own, hear his breath becoming raspy and harsh. Her own was a string of tiny moans that betrayed how much she wanted release. The tension was balling up in her belly, demanding that she ride him just a bit faster.

"That's it, my lovely, take what ye want."

One of his hands left her hip and landed on one side of her bottom in a sharp slap.

"*Hayden!*"

"Faster, my beauty, yer master says faster."

The sting from that slap somehow added to the growing pleasure inside her.

"I'll show you who is the master. I am the rider." She increased her pace, working her body faster.

Hayden growled at her and she felt his hand leave the cheek of her bottom. Anticipation tightened along that cheek as she waited for his next smack. It landed and she cried out, climax rippling throughout her passage. The pleasure was blinding, stealing the rhythm from her motions. Hayden snarled and turned her back onto the table top, his hips driving his cock into her while the pleasure raced through her. His hands clamped around her hips, holding her in place while he growled and she felt the hot spurt of his seed flooding her. That set off another wave of delight. It was deeper, and it felt as if the walls of her passage were trying to draw every last drop of seed from his cock.

She collapsed back onto the table, her lungs burning as they tried to pull in enough breath to feed her racing heart. Hayden lay over her, the crisp hair on his chest gently teasing the soft skin of her breasts and belly. Her senses were full of him, full of the male scent that trigged something inside her mind that she did not understand but knew she enjoyed. His hands toyed with her hair, smoothing out the curls that framed her face.

When he did move, Hayden picked her up and placed her in the bed that he'd had so carefully prepared for her. The rosemary smelled sweet, but she nuzzled against her lover, more interested in knowing that he was close.

"Tell me what brought tears to yer eyes this morning."

His voice was a mere whisper in the darkness, but there was such tenderness in it that she could not sleep.

"It haunts me, Elspeth, do ye like knowing that? I can nae stop thinking upon it."

"Which makes ye a good man, Hayden Monroe. But as I told ye, I do nae understand it myself."

He turned onto his side and propped his head on his hand. He was studying her in the dark; she felt his keen gaze on her. Reaching out, she touched his face, slipping her hand along his jawline and smiling at the smooth skin there. No hint of whiskers, exactly as she had asked. That was something most women never received—what they asked for. The scent of the rosemary and heather drifted to her nose, reminding her that Hayden did much to please her. Which was why her heart was his. Maybe that was the way of love; only women truly felt it.

He suddenly grinned, her fingertips tracing the curving of his lips.

"Well then, madam, I declare war on ye."

"What?"

He chuckled and smoothed his thumb across her lower lip. Tiny pulses of sensation traveled out from the touch.

"I said war. For I will have yer heart, Elspeth Leask, and make no mistake that I always claim what I set out to win. I refuse to love ye and not have that returned."

"Ye have never spoken of love." She swatted his hand away. "And how could ye claim to love me in so short a time?"

It wasn't really a question, because she feared that he could see straight into her heart and know that she had already surrendered to that insanity known as love.

He scoffed at her and cupped the side of her face.

"We have faced more in that time than most do in an entire season. I almost lost ye twice, once to nature and the other to Pherson. Having the sweet gift of ye being returned to me brought more relief than I had ever thought possible. That is more than lust, Elspeth, more than passion. It is love and I can only hope it will deepen every day that we are blessed to be together."

She let out a whimper and he growled, reaching for her cheek and snarling when he found it wet with tears. Elspeth captured his hand and kissed her own tear where it wet his skin.

"I weep with happiness and love, Hayden."

He drew in a stiff breath. "With love ye say?"

"Aye, with love."

His fingers smoothed over her cheek once more, wiping another tear away. She heard him draw in a sharp breath before lying down on his back and pulling her into his embrace.

"I suppose I shall have to get used to that trait of yers."

Dawn brought the church bells ringing. Hayden grumbled but rose from the bed after shaking her. Elspeth rubbed her eyes and struggled to wake up enough to dress. She dare not miss morning service again. They both dressed and followed the other Leask people toward the church.

Elspeth sighed with relief when the service ended. The morning was bright and the women giggled when they came close to her. Once she was out in the yard she discovered the younger boys that should be training with their wooden swords all staring at the tower instead. She raised her gaze up and gasped when she saw the sheet hanging from a window. It was the one taken from the inn and the stain showed clearly in the morning light.

Hayden looked too smug, but she did not get the chance to reprimand him. Father Simon Peter peered at the sheet before turning his scrutiny on them both.

"Are you married?"

Hayden had the good grace to lose his smug grin before answering the priest. He might be laird of one of the most powerful clans in Scotland, but that only meant that the church expected him to set the proper Christian example for those wearing his colors.

"Nae, Father."

"But they handfasted, I witnessed it myself," Skene spoke up, a grin accompanying his words. "Laird Leask gave his blessing on a handfasting too."

Father Simon Peter narrowed his eyes and looked for Dunmore. Elspeth watched her brother lose a bit of his color.

"Did you give yer blessing on a handfasting between yer sister and Laird Monroe?"

"He did." Hayden spoke up without hesitation. "Under the circumstances, I felt it the best way to preserve my bride-to-be's honor."

Elspeth heard several of the women around her suck in their breath. Obviously whatever priest tended the flock on Monroe land, he was a more mild soul than Father Simon Peter.

The priest tucked his hand up into the wide sleeves of his robe.

"I disagree. You both should have taken the sacrament of marriage before yielding to lust." He raised his voice so that everyone near might hear. "Lust is a sin that will lead all good Christian souls from the path of God."

The priest pulled his right hand out and pointed at her brother. "Two hours in the stocks for agreeing to handfasting." He moved his finger toward Hayden and never hesitated even in the face of the Monroe retainers all glaring at him. "You will join him or I will refuse to marry you."

"Refuse?"

"The sacrament of marriage is only for those with true Christian souls. If you do not respect the priests who serve Mother Church, you shall not have the holy sacrament."

Hayden bristled, his temper flickering brightly, but he nodded in obedience, gaining a soft grunt from the priest.

Father Simon Peter turned toward her. Elspeth lowered herself.

"Did you agree to this handfasting?"

"She did not." Hayden and Dunmore spoke at the same time. "I did."

Hayden shot her a furious glare but she only lifted her chin. She might love the man but that did not mean she would be a meek spouse. Approval flickered in his eyes in spite of his temper.

"Two hours public display on a platform because you might be carrying a child and should not be bent over."

A child. She hadn't thought of that, but the idea brought a smile to her lips and even the stern look on Father Simon Peter's face failed to make her smooth it away.

*Two hours later . . .*

Laird Hayden Monroe and Laird Dunmore Leask stood side by side, their necks and wrists surrounded by wood. When the stocks were in use, a crowd normally gathered, but today everyone seemed too busy to mock the sinners being punished by the church. Father Simon Peter was not pleased. He sent the younger boys who were already training to become priests up the ladders to ring the bells. The villagers who had tried to ignore their laird being shamed had no choice but to stop their work and crowd into the market square. Elspeth stood on the tiny platform that had been hastily built for her public shaming and watched her kin women reach out to tug on the ears of their children when the little ones began to point. The children looked confused, for they were always allowed to point and jeer at those in the stocks, but today their parents pinched them to stop it. They scratched their heads in confusion.

Father Simon Peter was becoming frustrated. His face turned red but the people stood firm in their silence, refusing to mock and berate them.

So the priest began lecturing. His voice filled the market, just as it did in the church every day. He preached against lust and springtime folly. The sun rose slowly, creeping toward the zenith of midday. Sweat was dripping down Elspeth's sides but also glistened on Father Simon Peter's face. He finally shut his mouth, never having reached any real point in his lesson. With a disgusted look, he sent the boys to release them.

Hayden arched his back and her brother snarled while he rotated his neck. Dunmore looked at her.

"Let's get you two married."

"Aye, and quickly, because I need an ale after that."

Father Simon Peter snorted. "You are far too unrepentant, Laird Monroe."

"I agree that I am far from perfect, Father, but I hope that will nae keep ye from helping me to make Elspeth my wife. At least my actions will be considered good in the eyes of the church even if my methods offend ye."

"The most perfect thing a man or woman might do is pledge themselves to the service of the church. Failing that, they should marry and keep themselves from lust."

The priest was facing the people watching him again, and as he moved off toward the church. Hayden curled his hand around Elspeth's waist and drew her into his embrace.

"How about I marry ye and keep all my lust for you, lass?"

"Only if it comes with love."

His eyes darkened. "Oh, it does, sweet Elspeth. I promise ye that I will remind ye of that every day for the rest of our lives."

"I will look forward to each sunrise, my love."

One of his eyebrows rose in roguish display.

"And every moonrise."

Bay had done his duty. When news of his grandmother's illness had arrived, he'd left immediately for Bayard Court, his oceanfront boyhood home. Grace Bayard had raised him, and he owed her everything. She'd been a little bit of a thing, but her tongue and wits were sharp and she'd done her damnedest to set him on the proper path. It was not her fault that he had strayed more than a time or two. She had wanted to see him settled again and a father, and perhaps one day he would be. But at present he had the divine Deborah Fallon waiting for him in his little house in Jane Street, the most exclusive enclave of kept women in London. Deb was the third mistress he'd set up there. The first, Angelique Dubois, had not been much of an angel of any kind or even French despite her name. His last lover, Helena Colbert, had served him well for a year but things had wound down to their natural conclusion. His friend Viscount Marlow was happy to take her off his hands, gushing his gratitude in disgusting fashion at every opportunity.

Bay had been ready for a change, and his choice was the most alluring Deborah Fallon. Those full lips, those fuller breasts, those tip-tilted blue eyes. She looked like a naughty cream-fed kitten. She had some wit, and if she were a bit of a prima donna, it was only because she knew her own worth. Her last protector had to reluctantly marry to further the family line, and nothing he could say would make Deborah part of a triangle. She had her standards—her lovers had to be rich, of course, and completely unattached. Along with several others, Bay pursued Deb for weeks before he persuaded her to move into Jane Street, and he hadn't gotten to warm the sheets even once before he was called away.

He'd stopped at his townhouse to make himself presentable after his long journey, pleased to see that someone had thoughtfully hung a mourning wreath upon the front door. He was truly sad that his grandmother had passed, but she had been nearly ninety-five, a very great age. He was three and thirty—and would be happy indeed to treble that if he remained as shrewd as his grand-mama up till near the end. She had fallen in her garden, tending to her beloved roses. The doctor thought she had had a series of small strokes, and by the time Bay arrived, she was sleeping most of her days away. She had rallied briefly at the sight of him, then went to bed one night and never woke up. Bay had stayed to see to the disposition of her faithful servants and shut up most of the house for the time being. He was a city man now. One day he might try to raise a family again in the stone manor house, but now he meant to raise his spirits in Deborah Fallon's arms.

Perhaps he'd been foolish to ride back to London. Every inch of him hurt, but he was damned if he was going to wait any longer for Deborah. He wondered how she'd amused herself while he was away. He let himself in to the dark house with his own key and climbed the stairs. He could have been blindfolded and still have found Deborah's bedroom. She had changed her perfume to a delicious harmony of orange and lemons and her fresh scent filled his head. He stood by the bed, not wanting to startle her awake, dropping his clothing quietly to the floor. This was not how he pictured his first night with his new mistress, but he was stiff as a poker and could not wait to seduce her over champagne and strawberries.

Angelique's revolting cherubs were still gleaming in the moonlight. Helena had been too superstitious to remove them and had actually acquired several more. Poor Deborah had probably waited for him to return before she made any changes. He fully expected her to make the bedchamber her own, although the rest of the house was exactly to his taste.

Their liaison had not gotten off to a good start. The carters had no sooner delivered Deborah's trunks before he'd left her in tears in the marble hallway. He had sent letters and flowers weekly, of course, and news of his grandmother's death. In a foolish fit of lust he had discovered a ruby necklace in his grandmother's jewel case and sent it to London, with the understanding that Deborah could wear it as long as she was his mistress. He was longing to see it around her white throat—it, and nothing else adorning her luscious body.

Grace Bayard was the rare woman who didn't care much for ostentatious jewelry, so he had never seen his grandmother wear it. He had buried her with the plain gold band his grandfather had given her eighty years ago before he made his fortune. Their marriage had not been an especially happy one. His grandmother had been practically a child when she wed, the fashion of the day. Her husband was older and ambitious, spending much of their married life outside England. Their long separation resulted in just one child, Bay's father.

Grandmama Grace had told him once his grandfather had given her the rubies to atone for some infraction. His grandfather, Bay thought, must have done something spectacularly bad, for the rubies were large and lustrous and very valuable, and the diamonds surrounding them not insignificant either. The collar with its enormous center drop was fit for a princess. Hell, fit for a queen. He hoped it had not been a mistake to gift them to Deborah temporarily. He'd have to tread carefully when he discussed the necklace on the morrow.

He encountered an amusingly virginal night rail, which he made quick work of. She gave a pleased little sigh and wrapped herself around him. Her magnificent hair was in two schoolgirl braids—she certainly had not expected to entertain him this evening, and he was touched at her surprising modesty. And equally touched by her ardent, almost thirsty kisses. She tasted of vanilla and wine and smelled like a Spanish summer. She cupped his balls and brought him to her entrance and he slipped in without any hesitation. She was wet but very tight. Heaven. If she was a schoolgirl, he was as randy as a schoolboy, and didn't last long in her pillowing embrace. He'd spend more time tomorrow morning tending to her needs. He was known as a considerate lover, one of the reasons Deborah had agreed to be his mistress. Even his wife had no complaints while they were married.

Thoroughly spent, he passed a delightful night in his lover's arms. And when the first rays of sun had the audacity to slip through the shutters, he feasted upon her breast as if it were a banquet of cream and honey. She gave a low groan, but he didn't think it was in protest. The faint light showed him his mistress was not quite as young as she appeared to be six weeks ago—there were a few silver strands in her unraveling ink-dark braids. No doubt she resorted to artifice and would have corrected this had she known he was coming.

And speaking of coming, he wanted to seat himself within her again. Last night had been heaven, and now that the empty day was spread before him, the devil in him intended to visit heaven again and again. No, he was not sorry he'd paid the exorbitant price to secure Deborah Fallon's favors. If last night was any indication of what the woman could do when she was half asleep, he would cheerfully beggar himself. He was a lucky man indeed.

He licked her nipple to taut, pale pink perfection, wondering idly if he'd get a child on her someday. He'd been fortunate with his mistresses thus far, but he would do his duty by her if she bore his bastard. He was a gentleman, and that's what gentleman did. Somehow the thought of an infant suckling Deb Fallon's very tempting breast was unbelievably erotic. She would resemble a naughty Madonna, her black hair cascading down her ivory shoulders.

By God, she was making him lose his mind. The touch and taste of her was inebriating, clouding his judgment. One didn't keep a mistress for domesticity. One kept a mistress for sin, the darker the better. And if he knew anything about Deborah Fallon, she would complain loud and long caring for anything that was not her own luscious self. A baby? Proposterous.

As if she heard his thoughts, she stiffened beneath him. And then she screamed.

Ear-piercingly. Perhaps she had not recognized him when she awoke. But honestly, who could she be expecting? She was *his*.

He looked up at her, suspicious. She gave him a look he'd seen only in battle, when the other side was hopelessly outnumbered, pushed beyond recklessness, and there was nothing left to lose. He hoped very much that she was not sleeping with a French bayonet beneath the mattress.

"You! You!" she sputtered.

"Yes, my pet, it is I. I know I gave you no notice, but thank you for your very warm welcome last night. It was worth every minute of the harrowing six weeks we spent apart." He set back to flicking her nipple again with his tongue.

She hit him on the head with a fist. "Get off me! This instant! You are much mistaken, Sir Michael. I am not Deborah."

Try HOT SOUTHERN NIGHTS, the latest from
Dianne Castell, out now from Brava . . .

"Where are you going now?"

"To get my grandmother."

"She's at my place and she's doing just fine. She's probably sleeping by now."

"But she's *my* grandmother." Cal kept walking till Churchill caught up to him and took his arm, the unexpected light touch stopping him faster than any hard punch. She could still do that after so many years. What was it about Churchill that got to him? Auburn hair pulled back in a loose knot and held in place by a pencil? Her slim figure under the simple skirt and blouse? Her long legs? All of it, dammit, all of it. The whole uptight librarian package drove him nuts because he knew somewhere under all that uptightness there was something a little reckless and hot as hell.

"She's fine. I tried to call you about what happened but with all the racket coming out of that heap you call a car the world could have exploded and you wouldn't have heard a thing. Miss Ellie thinks I'm out getting dog food so I better get back in case she wakes up." Church let out a sigh and let go of Cal's arm. "That's not a lie. Seems I always have to get dog food except when he won't eat dog food and I have to fry chicken or scramble an egg or make quiche."

"You cook quiche for a dog?"

"He has separation anxiety. He liked Jersey." She didn't say anything for a moment and stared at him. Her blue eyes suddenly went dark and soft and too damn sensual for a hot summer night in Savannah with no one around but the two of them. "Did you take Dodd's money?"

He had to bring an end to the conversation before her damn questions and her ability to turn him upside down made him say something he'd regret and mess up everything he set in motion. "You want to know why the police hauled me in? One of the guys who worked pit here at the track three years ago wound up dead. They think I had something to do with it. I'm a felon and that means any crime within a fifty mile radius has my name on it. That should answer your question."

"Why would your robbery have anything to do with the dead person?"

"You aren't nearly as smart as people say you are, Ace." She didn't scare off easy, he'd give her that. Bet those Jersey boys had their hands full when Little Miss Know It All showed up wanting her car back. Churchill McKenzie didn't do "I don't know" well.

"Go home." He walked across the track. "Thanks for taking care of Miss Ellie," he added without turning around. He slid through the open window of Mud Monkey and gunned the engine to drown out any other questions or comments Churchill had. She shook her head at him and walked away till Killer ran ahead nearly pulling her off her feet. Who was taking who for a walk? He stifled a laugh making him feel better than he had since . . . since he kissed her. Damn that kiss, why did he do that? Why did she have to be there? Why couldn't she have kept her job in Jersey? Everything was going okay, he had everything under control for a long time now and then Churchill came back to Savannah and talked to Miss Ellie. Cal had a bad feeling things would not end with one talk. He had to keep a clear head and stop her before she got involved.

Trouble was, when it came to Ace McKenzie there was not one thing clear at all. He was attracted to her and shouldn't be for a grocery list of reasons. They were opposites on every front, the librarian and the jailbird. The darling of Savannah—just ask anyone—and the devil—just ask anyone.

Mark your calendars! BEAST BEHAVING BADLY, the newest
Shelly Laurenston book in the Pride series, comes out next
month!

Bo shot through the goal crease and slammed the puck into the net.

"Morning!"

That voice cut through his focus and, without breaking his stride, Bo changed direction and skated over to the rink entrance. He stopped hard, ice spraying out from his skates, and stood in front of the wolfdog.

He stared down at her and she stared up at him. She kept smiling even when he didn't. Finally he asked, "What time did we agree on?"

"Seven," she replied with a cheery note that put his teeth on edge.

"And what time is it?"

"Uh . . ." She dug into her jeans and pulled out a cell phone. The fact that she still had on that damn, useless watch made his head want to explode. How did one function—as an adult anyway—without a goddamn watch?

Grinning so that he could see all those perfectly aligned teeth, she said, "Six-forty-five!"

"And what time did we agree on?"

She blinked and her smile faded. After a moment, "Seven."

"Is it seven?"

"No." When he only continued to stare at her, she softly asked, "Want to meet me at the track at seven?"

He continued to stare at her until she nodded and said, "Okay." She walked out and Bo went back to work.

Fifteen minutes later, Bo walked into the small arena at seven a.m. Blayne, looking comfortable in dark blue leggings, sweatshirt, and skates, turned to face him. He expected her to be mad at him or, even worse, for her to get that wounded look he often got from people when he was blatantly direct. But having to deal with either of those scenarios was a price Bo was always willing to pay to ensure that the people in his life understood how he worked from the beginning. This way, there were no surprises later. It was called "boundaries" and he read about it in a book.

Yet when Blayne saw him, she grinned and held up a Starbucks cup. "Coffee," she said when he got close. "I got you the house brand because I had no idea what you would like. And they had cinnamon twists, so I got you a few of those."

He took the coffee, watching her closely. Where was it? The anger? The resentment? Was she plotting something?

Blayne held the bag of sweets out for him and Bo took them. "Thank you," he said, still suspicious even as he sipped his perfectly brewed coffee.

"You're welcome." And there went that grin again. Big and brighter than the damn sun. "And I get it. Seven means seven. Eight means eight, etc., etc. Got it and I'm on it. It won't happen again." She said all that without a trace of bitterness and annoyance, dazzling Bo with her understanding more than she'd dazzled him with those legs.

"So," she put her hands on her hips, "what do you want me to do first?"

*Marry me? Wait. No, no. Incorrect response. It'll just weird her out and make her run again. Normal. Be normal. You can do this. You're not just a great skater. You're a* normal *great skater.*

When Bo knew he had his shit together, he said, "Let's work on your focus first. And, um, should I ask what happened to your face?" She had a bunch of cuts on her cheeks. Gouges. Like something small had pawed at her.

"Nope!" she chirped, pulling off her sweatshirt. She wore a worn blue T-shirt underneath with B&G PLUMBING scrawled across it. With sweatshirt in hand, Blayne skated over to the bleachers, stopped, shook her head, skated over to another section of bleachers, stopped, looked at the sweatshirt, turned around, and skated over to the railing. "I should leave it here," she explained. "In case I get chilly."

It occurred to Bo he'd just lost two minutes of his life watching her try and figure out where to place a damn sweatshirt. Two minutes that he'd never get back.

"Woo-hoo!" she called out once she hit the track. "Let's go!"

She was skating backward as she urged him to join her with both hands.

He pointed behind her. "Watch the—"

"Ow!"

"—pole."

Christ, what had he gotten himself into?

Christ almighty, what had she gotten herself into?

Twenty minutes in and she wanted to smash the man's head against a wall. She wanted to go back in time and kick the shit out of Genghis Khan before turning on his brothers, Larry and Moe. Okay. That wasn't their names but she could barely remember Genghis's name on a good day, how the hell was she supposed to remember his brothers'. But whatever the Khan kin's names may be, Blayne wanted to hurt them all for cursing her world with this . . . this . . . Visigoth!

Even worse, she knew he didn't even take what she did seriously. He insisted on calling it a chick sport. If he were a sexist pig across the board, Blayne could overlook it as a mere flaw in his upbringing. But, she soon discovered, Novikov had a very high degree of respect for female athletes . . . as long as they were athletes and not just "hot chicks in cute outfits, roughing each other up. All you guys need is some hot oil or mud and you'd have a real moneymaker on your hands."

And yet, even while he didn't respect her sport as a sport, he still worked her like he was getting her ready for the Olympics.

After thirty minutes she wanted nothing more but to lie on her side and pant. She doubted the hybrid would let her get away with that, though.

Shooting around the track, Novikov stopped her in a way that she was finding extremely annoying—by grabbing her head with that big hand of his and holding her in place.

He shoved her back with one good push and Blayne fought not to fall on her ass at that speed. When someone shoved her like that, they were usually pissed. He wasn't.

"I need to see something," he said, still nursing that cup of coffee. He'd finished off the cinnamon twists in less than five minutes while she was warming up. "Come at me as hard as you can."

"Are you sure?" she asked, looking him over. He didn't have any of his protective gear on, somehow managing to change into sweatpants and T-shirt and still make it down to the track exactly at seven. "I don't want to hurt you," she told him honestly.

The laughter that followed, however, made her think she did want to hurt him. She wanted to hurt him a lot. When he realized she wasn't laughing with him—or, in this case, laughing at *herself* since he was obviously laughing *at* her—Novikov blinked and said, "Oh. You're not kidding."

"No. I'm not kidding."

"Oh. Oh! Um . . . I'll be fine. Hit me with your best shot."

"Like Pat Benatar?" she joked but when he only stared at her, she said, "Forget it."

Blayne sized up the behemoth in front of her and decided to move back a few more feet so she could get a really fast start. She got into position and took one more scrutinizing look. It was a skill her father had taught her. To size up weakness. Whether the weakness of a person or a building or whatever. Of course, Blayne often used this skill for good, finding out someone's weakness and then working to help them overcome it. Her father, however, used it to destroy.

Lowering her body, Blayne took a breath, tightened her fists, and took off. She lost some speed on the turn but picked it up as she cut inside. As Blayne approached Novikov, she sized him up one more time as he stood there casually, sipping his coffee and watching her move around the track. Based on that last assessing look, she slightly adjusted her position and slammed into him with everything she had.

And, yeah, she knocked herself out cold, but it was totally worth it when the behemoth went down with her.